The Room-Mating Season

Also by Rona Jaffe
in Large Print:

After the Reunion
Class Reunion

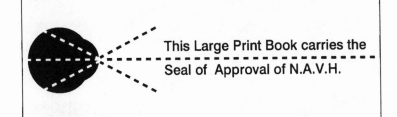

The Room-Mating Season

Rona Jaffe

Thorndike Press • Waterville, Maine

Copyright © Rona Jaffe, 2003

This book is a work of fiction. Names, characters, places, and incidents are either the product of the author's imagination or are used fictitiously, and any resemblance to actual persons, living or dead, business establishments, events, or locales is entirely coincidental.

Published in 2003 by arrangement with Dutton, a member of Penguin Putnam (USA) Inc.

Thorndike Press® Large Print Women's Fiction Series.

The tree indicium is a trademark of Thorndike Press.

The text of this Large Print edition is unabridged.
Other aspects of the book may vary from the original edition.

Set in 16 pt. Plantin by Ramona A. Watson.

Printed in the United States on permanent paper.

Library of Congress Cataloging-in-Publication Data

Jaffe, Rona.
    The room-mating season / Rona Jaffe.
      p. cm.
    ISBN 0-7862-5544-7 (lg. print : hc : alk. paper)
    1. Roommates — Fiction. 2. Young women — Fiction.
3. Female friendship — Fiction. 4. Upper East Side (New York, N.Y.) — Fiction. 5. Large type books. I. Title.
PS3519.A453R66 2003b
  813'.54—dc21
                                      2003048388

I want to thank the following people for their generous help in various ways:

Mark Bregman, Marc Neal Simon, Jill Bugler, Barbara Hunt, Sgt. Steven Marron (New York City Police Department, Retired), Laurie Chittenden, Stephanie Bowe, Anne Sibbald, and Greg Mowery.

As the Founder/CEO of NAVH, the only national health agency solely devoted to those who, although not totally blind, have an eye disease which could lead to serious visual impairment, I am pleased to recognize Thorndike Press as one of the leading publishers in the large print field.

Founded in 1954 in San Francisco to prepare large print textbooks for partially seeing children, NAVH became the pioneer and standard setting agency in the preparation of large type.

Today, those publishers who meet our standards carry the prestigious "Seal of Approval" indicating high quality large print. We are delighted that Thorndike Press is one of the publishers whose titles meet these standards. We are also pleased to recognize the significant contribution Thorndike Press is making in this important and growing field.

Lorraine H. Marchi, L.H.D.
Founder/CEO
NAVH

prologue

Leigh Owen looked back at 1963 as if she were watching other people, almost strangers; not herself and her three room-mates — so far away and different they all seemed. Sometimes it embarrassed her to see those distant girls, with their innocence and their juiciness, their long-limbed breath-less sexuality, and sometimes it made her jealous. They were twenty-three years old, young and pretty and arrogant, excited about being in New York at their first jobs, living together in a nice, but small, apart-ment they could only afford because they all lived together. A town house on the Upper East Side: a brownstone (except that it was gray) with one bedroom for all of them, crammed together in their little single beds, a kitchen you couldn't even sit down in, a bathroom. Since the living room was used to entertain men, they put up with their dormi-tory-style sleeping arrangements: because the purpose of being young and pretty was to meet men, and eventually to marry.

Before they married they planned to live fully, of course. They were filled with wonder and optimism and looking forward to adventures. None of them was a native New Yorker, and to them New York was the magical city. Everything would happen here, whatever everything was.

When she looked at the few photographs she had of the four of them in those days, Leigh was surprised at how soft their faces looked, almost unformed. Almost blank. But there were all kinds of emotions hiding underneath those unrevealing faces: anxiety, doubt (despite the arrogance), and often confusion. At times they felt deeply inadequate. They knew they were naïve, and they wanted to learn.

When those girls looked in the mirror it was to put on their eyeliner, to do their hair. They didn't question the face they saw there, or feel sad at its mortality, its impermanence. Age was a terrible thing, Leigh thought, at sixty now and knowing a great deal more. Age made you invisible. It made you know too much, too late. No one would want that knowledge at twenty-three. So of course, when older people told you what was in store, you thought it would never happen to you. Or, at least, happen so many years later that it was unimaginable.

They had been four young women on the cusp of great social and moral change; the end of the fifties behind them, the rise of the sixties still a few years away. They listened to Beach Boys music, they all wanted to look and dress like Jackie Kennedy, they knew there was civil unrest and that many thousands of people were marching on Washington, and that there was something going on in Vietnam, which was sort of like a war, but not really. The truth was they hardly read the newspapers.

They were Leigh and Cady and Vanessa and Susan. She, Leigh Owen, was the calm at the heart of the whirlwind; the tall, self-possessed blonde who got elected class president. She had always known she had responsibilities, although sometimes a moment of unexpected recklessness surprised her. Cady Fineman was the emotional one. Cady had strong opinions and stronger passions. Cady was the romantic one and, Leigh had to admit, she was a bit of a princess. Vanessa Preet was the gorgeous one, and the one who most needed freedom and adventure. The stewardess who flew high, even when she was on the ground. And Susan Brown? Well, Leigh had finally realized, as much as they knew about her, none of them had ever really known Susan at all.

Sleeping and dreaming side by side, they could not know that the decisions they made in 1963 would be challenged later, not only because they had been young when they made them but because the world itself was going to transform around them. And then, of course, there were the events in their young lives that no one could control . . . the ones that changed everything.

PART ONE

chapter

1

It was late winter of 1963, and Leigh Owen, who was twenty-three and working as an underpaid secretary at the powerful Star Management talent agency, was tired of living in a hovel. Her fifth-floor walkup apartment above a restaurant always smelled of fish and grease. It was one tiny room that looked out on a dismal street below her fire escape, and contained two twin beds only a foot apart — what could she have been thinking of, a guest? — two straight chairs, and a small dresser; a plenitude of furniture that made walking around her apartment an obstacle course that resulted too often in bruises. She had no air conditioner so it was hot and even smellier in summer, and her landlord was stingy with heat so it was cold in winter. No matter how much she cleaned it — and there wasn't much time for a single girl in New York to clean apartments — her studio still looked grimy.

She knew she had to face the fact that

she just couldn't live alone any longer. She needed a better place, and she would need roommates, otherwise she couldn't afford the hundred dollars or more a month that decent living quarters would require.

She was an efficient person, as they often told her at work, and so it didn't take her long to find an apartment she immediately fell in love with. It was a one bedroom with a living room and kitchen in a stately old town house on the Upper East Side located on a quiet tree-lined street of other similar houses. It was only one flight up, which was a relief. There was an air conditioner in the bedroom window, three closets, and the living room looked huge to her, with a bay window overlooking the lovely street, and a nonworking but still picturesque fireplace in one wall.

Leigh had grown up in Weehawken, New Jersey, so close to New York that, from her family's house, she could see the buildings and lights of Manhattan — beckoning, mysterious, and seductive. Sometimes her parents had taken her and her younger brother to Manhattan for dinner or to the theater or to a museum with ice cream afterward. Leigh had always thought these elegant town houses with their lofty windows represented the quintessential New York. Not a high rise. High rises were ugly. In a town house you would listen to music, have a cocktail at dusk, and know fascinating people. You would have walls of books, sit in a chair, and read them. You would have a successful husband who wore a tuxedo.

The town house she had found didn't have a doorman of course, but there was a large apartment building on the corner that did, so it seemed safe. The rent, unfortunately, was two hundred dollars a month. She figured out, regretfully, that she would need three roommates — at fifty dollars each, that would leave her some money for the necessities and pleasures of life, although many of the necessities and pleasures were paid for by her dates. Still, you needed independence. And clothes. And sometimes food.

Recklessly, she put down the deposit, which took almost all her meager savings. Her father, who was a pediatrician, agreed to cosign the lease. Then Leigh called Cady, her friend from college.

Leigh Owen and Cady Fineman had been friends at Pembroke. They had lived in the same dorm, although they went out with different men and had different best friends. But they were both smart English majors, and since Cady lived with her parents in the nearby suburb of Scarsdale and commuted to her job as an English teacher at Dunnewood, a girls' prep school in Manhattan, she and Leigh sometimes met for dinner in the city. Leigh suspected that Cady was tired of commuting. And if she wasn't, Leigh would convince her that she was.

Leigh wondered for a moment if she would mind living in an apartment with Cady. Not that she had the privilege of choice. She had never lived with other people except her family and in the dorm, where she had her own room, but she was now involved in the exigencies of high finance. She had property now. She had responsibility. She hoped Cady didn't snore. She hoped she herself didn't. She had already decided that, as was customary, all the roommates would need to share the bedroom, leaving the living room for their social life.

She thought of Cady's good qualities. Cady was very neat and clean. She was sometimes funny. She had integrity. She had always obviously adored Leigh. They didn't like the same men, therefore no stealing of boyfriends. She was attractive: dark haired, with bright eyes and high color, vibrant, dimpled, quick moving. She liked to go out and have fun.

Her bad qualities were that she was so emotional. Almost hysterical, sometimes, but that behavior usually only involved men. They were both older now, and Leigh was fairly sure that soon Cady would calm down, become more peaceful. They were twenty-three after all, much more mature than they had been at college.

They went to dinner at a local neighborhood coffee shop. "I found the most beautiful apartment," Leigh said. "I want you to be my roommate. We would have a great time together. You must be sick of living with your parents. You can't even stay overnight with a man unless you lie, get out of bed in the cold, to go home and pretend to be a virgin again."

"That's what they'll think I'm doing," Cady said. "Losing my virginity. That's what all the parents fear."

"But you'll have roommates, three of them. Chaperones. Company when you're lonely. Friends who might introduce you to your future husband."

"*Three?*" Cady said doubtfully.

"Think of all the time you'd save not commuting. More sleep in the morning. And the train fare you'll save."

"Oh, you don't have to talk me into it," Cady said. "How much is my share of the rent?"

"Fifty dollars. And I have two beds."

"Can we look at it after dinner?"

"Sure. It's mine now. I move in officially on the first."

"Who are the others?"

"You'll help me pick when they answer my ad."

"I don't think my mother will mind if I move," Cady said. "We've talked about it happening eventually, although, of course she'd rather I don't move out until I get married."

"This isn't the dark ages anymore," Leigh said. "What about your father?"

"When did he ever have an opinion that isn't hers?"

Before they could catch their breath, Cady's mother took them both out shopping for furniture. Cady's mother was only forty-three years old, and seemed more like Cady's older sister than her mother. She was a chain-smoker, chatty, a clucker, a smiler. She was a woman who did not believe in wasted moments. She was also a devoted shopper, and approached the furnishing of their first apartment with as much enthusiasm as if it had been her own. Leigh couldn't decide if she was being a good mother or living vicariously. Her own mother was the opposite of Cady's: she was low-key and pragmatic. Her mother had made no offer to help.

A discount store in the Bronx supplied a couch and a bookcase, and Cady's family's basement yielded a kidney-shaped coffee table, a rug, and some lamps. Leigh's mother finally provided some old dishes and mismatched flatware and glasses she didn't want. And, for the beds the other roommates would bring, some sheets that didn't match either. She said the girls didn't need much; this was temporary after all, and when they found the men they were going to marry they would buy nice things with them.

Leigh hoped that the future roommates would have some furniture of their own, but in the meantime you couldn't ask people to move into an empty apartment. With her own things added it looked really good now, she thought: inviting, pleasant.

She took out an ad in the *Times* that got a lot of replies, and on application day decided to give each girl her own appointment. Although she had been told it was customary to see as many as eight applicants at once, that sounded too scary for her.

The first girl to arrive was Vanessa Preet. She was as beautiful as a beauty contest winner, which made sense because she was a stewardess at Worldwide Airlines, and you had to be young and beautiful to be a stewardess. Somehow her looks weren't intimidating because she seemed warm, and even modest. She had shiny dark hair with red highlights in it, cut regulation short, creamy skin, high cheekbones, classic features, and green eyes. She was wearing a pillbox hat and white gloves, and a Jackie Kennedy–look-alike suit. Her calves and ankles would make anyone jealous. At twenty-four, she was a year older than they were. Her salary, although low, was adequate for what they needed, and best of all, she traveled nearly all the time and would hardly ever be there.

"Do you entertain a lot?" Leigh asked.

"When I'm home I'm usually too busy sleeping."

"Do you have any assets — like a TV set?"

"I have little knives and forks and spoons from the airline. We aren't supposed to take them, but we all do. And I can supply lots of little sample bottles of liquor too. For entertaining your dates." She gave them a dazzling smile. Her teeth were as perfect as her skin.

Cady glanced at Leigh, clearly entranced.

"Do you have any furniture?" Leigh asked.

"No. I don't want to own furniture."

"Well, you'll only have to buy your own bed."

"Sorry," Vanessa said. "I moved into an apartment with another girl who told me I had to buy my own bed. I bought a bed, which cost about seventy dollars, and then I found out I couldn't stand her. I found another apartment, but there was a bed for me, and no room for the bed I had already bought. I had a terrible time getting rid of it. Even the Salvation Army wouldn't take it unless I took it down there myself."

She spoke rapidly, and her voice was breathless, punctuated by a self-deprecating little laugh. "Finally I gave it to someone for five dollars, which I never collected. After I lived with the two other girls for a while I couldn't stand *them* either, so I went back to the first apartment. The girl I couldn't stand there had gotten married and there was a different roommate. And I found I had to buy a bed all over again. Altogether it cost me about a hundred and fifty dollars and a lot of time and trouble, and so that's why I don't want to own furniture — or a bed!"

21

"You've had a bad time with room-mates," Leigh said.

"The worst one was a midget from San Salvador who borrowed my airline uniform and cut it down and wore it for a dress-up suit," Vanessa said. She laughed. "In a dead heat for winner with the older woman who kept wanting to give me massages. I think there was something wrong with *her*."

"We have an extra bed," Cady said. Leigh looked at her, puzzled. "I've been sleeping in it," Cady said, "but I need a very hard mattress for my back, so my mother is going to buy me a new bed. So you can have the one that's here."

You have a bad back? Leigh thought.

"That would be great," Vanessa said. "Am I in then?"

Cady gave Leigh another of those looks. Cady obviously had made up her mind at first sight. She had very firm likes and dislikes, and although sometimes she changed her opinion, her likes were loves and her dislikes were hates. There was no middle ground. And she formed her convictions right away. But, Leigh thought, how could you not like Vanessa?

"You're in," Leigh said. "You get a drawer in the dresser and your own space in the refrigerator and cupboard. You get most of one closet. We'll take turns cleaning. Everyone will shop for her own food."

"Don't worry," Vanessa said. "I don't eat at home."

"She's *perfect!*" Cady said when Vanessa had left.

"And what's wrong with your back?" Leigh asked.

"I didn't want to lose her," Cady said.

"You made that up?"

"My mother will buy me another bed. She'll buy me anything I want."

After Vanessa their luck seemed to vanish. The next applicant was a large, loud, overly made up girl whom they both disliked immediately. Leigh couldn't imagine sleeping next to her every night. The one after her was too mousy, almost furtive. She was like a living apology, and Leigh wondered what she wanted to apologize for. The next girl had a faintly sour aroma and they couldn't wait to get her out.

"Vile!" Cady said, fanning at the air with her hand.

The would-be roommates sat there in their little hats and suits and white gloves like applicants from secretarial school at their first job, nervous, trying to please, thinking if this didn't work out they'd have to go back to their newspapers.

"We'll never find another Vanessa," Leigh said. "We have to lower our standards."

Cady sighed. "Do we really need a fourth?"

"Yes."

The next girl was wearing an engagement ring. "Too temporary," they agreed when they had ushered her to the door.

"Look, if no one works out we can take another ad," Leigh said dispiritedly.

By the time Susan Brown appeared they were both tired. She was the last one. She wasn't wonderful, but on the other hand, there wasn't anything wrong with her either. She was slim with curly light-brown hair, she seemed pleasant if a little dull, and she had a job as the receptionist to an eye doctor. "I have a television set," Susan Brown said.

They could certainly use a TV set. Leigh glanced at Cady, who nodded almost imperceptibly. A TV set was as good a reason as any.

"You're in," Leigh said, and told her the rules of the house. It would be fine, she thought. They would get used to her.

When Susan left, Leigh and Cady opened a bottle of their precious cheap wine. "To us!" they toasted. "To the four musketeers!"

Well, three anyway.

chapter
2

Vanessa Preet was used to being accepted. She was the youngest of three beautiful daughters, born to the owner of a hardware store and a housewife in Minnesota, and she had realized early in life that her appearance made things easier. The kids at school who weren't cute often got picked on or ignored. She knew there was more to her than looks, but people didn't seem to care.

"Beauty is a blessing," her mother told her. "Take care of it." Vanessa tried.

She hated Minnesota's weather — the winters too cold, the summers too hot — and she had always wanted to see other places, so it seemed natural to her to become a stewardess. As soon as she completed the two years of junior college she had attended in order to mark time until she turned twenty and eligible for her intended career, she was accepted at Worldwide Airlines. She had been there four years. At twenty-four, she suspected she was a little older than the other girls in the apartment . . . and she knew she had more experience.

To the outside world, hers seemed a prestigious job: free travel, adventures, being one of the perfectly groomed and glamorous elite that pranced through the cabin like nurturing goddesses. A vending machine on legs, more likely, Vanessa thought. The regulation pumps they made her wear in flight always hurt after a few hours, and she hated the girdle that was also a mandatory part of her uniform. Everyone hated it. But you couldn't get away with leaving it off because the supervisor would run girdle checks, patting the girls to be sure they were suitably firm. Patting her ass, like she was a piece of merchandise! And if you needed falsies, they were suggested. A stewardess had to be perfect.

Hair had to be cut to be one inch above the collar, set in an old-lady hairdo — such a waste because her hair was one of her best features. You were weighed once a month, and if you were over the limit the airline had set for your height, you were suspended without pay, put on a diet, and weighed every week until you were acceptable again. Vanessa had seen more than one girl faint from crash dieting when she got off the scales. Luckily she did not have a weight problem; her mother had trained her well years ago.

Manicures had to be impeccable and were checked before flights. The girls had been taught how to put on neat and natural makeup. Posture had to be erect and poised. The smile had to be friendly and sincere. But what you couldn't fix, what you had to be born with or you wouldn't get the job, was nice legs. The uniforms were of a length to show them off, and one of the things Vanessa had been made to do when she applied to be a stewardess was pull up her skirt to reveal if her legs were acceptable.

We save lives, she thought, annoyed. Does anybody know that? We have to be cool in crises, calm the frightened, minister to the ill, feed the hungry, smilingly slip away from drunken lechers, and for this we are underpaid.

But there were also the perks. Besides travel, there were the men. There was always a man to chat with her while she served him or who made trips to the galley to see her, and who asked if she would have dinner with him when he reached his destination. They were businessmen, rich ones, because she was in first class. Many of them were married and some were twice her age. Sometimes Vanessa had dinner with them anyway.

She loved men. She loved being with them, flirting, knowing they liked her. She had her choice of men, not just on planes but everywhere she went. She wasn't that interested in having women friends, although she had a few. A few were enough. It was men who amused her, made her laugh.

Vanessa did not consider herself promiscuous. She considered herself a healthy young person who enjoyed and needed sexual pleasure often, and what was wrong with that? She had crushes frequently, but she had never been in love. She knew the difference. She felt she was still too young for serious love, too young to settle down, to choose only one man to be her partner for life. She could not even imagine being faithful for very long. And you certainly wouldn't be faithful to a married businessman who lived halfway across the country, no matter what lies he told you.

After three years as a reserve, on an erratic and exhausting flying schedule, she had finally gotten the coveted New York–Los Angeles route. Warm weather, beaches, and movie-star sightings were exactly what she wanted. It was worth all the drudgery of a long flight to be able to spend a day and night in LA, exploring with the other girls or with a man she had met, trying the "in" new restaurant, meeting new people. The pilots and the stewardesses were put in different hotels to avoid hanky panky, which everyone knew was a pathetic protection. Hadn't the airline ever heard of a taxi? Sometimes Vanessa partied with the pilots.

This current apartment, she thought, might work out. She hoped so. She'd had so many disasters. But Leigh Owen seemed like a calm person with her feet on the ground, and Cady Fineman was sophisticated and had terrific clothes, even though she was a bit of a compulsive fuss-budget around the apartment. Everything was labeled. "This peach is mine!" But Cady never cooked and she didn't keep much food around. She would send out to the corner deli every night for a Muenster cheese sandwich. It never occurred to her to buy bread and cheese and make her own sandwiches, even though it would be a lot more economical, and when Leigh suggested it Cady looked at her as if she were crazy. "I don't want to," Cady said.

Their other roommate, Susan Brown, seemed eccentric. In the beginning, when they had all first moved in, she did exercises nude on the living room floor in the mornings before work. But Cady and Leigh made her stop. "There's no privacy here as it is," Leigh explained. "We'd rather not look at that."

"I'm taking an air bath," Susan said, sounding hurt.

"Well, wear a leotard." And then they were all rushing off to work, leaving Vanessa in peace.

Her single bed was comfortable, and the apartment was not too small. She had lived in far worse. Sharing a bathroom with three other girls was the one thing she hadn't ever been able to get used to. She had hated it with her two older sisters and she hated it even more now because they were four. Their bathroom was such a mess you couldn't find anything. Even Cady had given up. Cady's mother had hired a maid to come and clean once a week. The results of that lasted about a day.

Except for making instant coffee with hot tap water, Vanessa never used the kitchen. She ate lunch alone in the coffee shop on the corner, at the counter. Often she had dinner there if she didn't have a date. She would put her expensive Gucci bag with the bamboo handle on the countertop, and order something dietetic and nutritious. Sometimes people looked at her as if wondering what she was doing there all alone, a beautiful, well-dressed girl with a Gucci bag. She liked the solitude. No ringing phones with calls for someone else, no underwear drying over the shower rod, no music that was not her taste, being exhorted to try the food instead of warned: "Hands Off!"

One of the girls almost always had a date. The one who did often wanted the living room to entertain, so the others would have to clear out for the evening. They saw a lot of movies. When Vanessa had a date she let the man entertain *her*. She was not auditioning to be a housewife. Let *him* provide the drinks.

Sometimes the girls all chipped in and Leigh made spaghetti and they drank Chianti and smoked and laughed and talked about men. They were either with men or waiting for them to call or talking about them or getting over one. Vanessa wasn't around very often because of her work schedule, but when she could join the others she enjoyed those evenings. They

31

were so relaxing. Susan didn't quite fit in — she didn't confide about herself, she seemed almost evasive, as if her life was too dull to matter — and perhaps, Vanessa thought, it was. But when Vanessa had drunk enough Chianti she didn't mind Susan or the apartment at all.

There was such impermanence about living with roommates in the city; either you couldn't stand them, or they didn't like you, or else they got married — which was the goal of every girl — and went away. You would find a new one and then one of the others would get engaged. It was like Russian roulette. Vanessa knew there was no way she could live by herself on her miserable salary, so she put up with the transitory nature of her domestic life, knowing she was as much to blame for it as anyone else; she had always moved when she got fed up.

But she really wanted to stay here, and she hoped it would work out.

chapter
3

Cady Fineman had been a little in awe of
Leigh Owen since the first time she set eyes
on her in their dorm at college. Leigh
seemed so sophisticated, so cool, so . . . gen-
tile. Cady hadn't known many WASPs before, or at least not as friends. Cady herself
tried to appear sophisticated, and since she
was from a suburb of New York and wore
the latest fashions, she seemed to be. But she
wasn't really. Sometimes, next to Leigh, she
felt like a child.

When they had graduated and began to
have their occasional suppers together, Cady
was flattered. When Leigh asked her to become her roommate she was thrilled. She
tried not to show her excitement and to be
matter of fact. She pretended to be pru-
dent, cautious, as someone from Leigh's
crowd would probably be. But the evening
Leigh showed her the apartment they were
going to share, Cady was up almost all
night in her little-girl room in Scarsdale,

fantasizing about the fun they would have.

Her mother was a real sport about her decision, as Cady knew she would be. Her mother was her best friend and strongest supporter.

Her father was older than her mother. Her mother had been a teenaged bride. That was customary in her day, and no one thought it was out of place. An older man would take care of you. Cady didn't know why her mother had been attracted to him. All her life he had seemed glum and quiet and depressed, he deferred to her mother in everything domestic, and he seemed addicted to work. He was a lawyer and brought papers home from the office to read at night, alone in the den, planning for the next day. Cady thought he was worried about money. Her mother was cheerfully extravagant, and so was she, and even though her father didn't say they couldn't have something they wanted, he got a pinched look around the eyes.

Sometimes Cady thought that, underneath all the quietness and acquiescence there was anger — that her father was a secretly angry man. This thought made her uncomfortable. Anger was unpredictable; an angry person could hurt you. She tried not to think about it. She was an only child, their joy, who could ever think of hurting her?

The family had moved from the Bronx to Scarsdale when Cady was starting high school. "We did it for you," her mother told her. "So you'll find a better husband." Whenever Cady brought home an unsuitable date her mother would remind her: they were in a higher-class place now, they would have a higher-class life. It was up to her to grasp it.

A town house on the Upper East Side with Leigh and Vanessa was a start on that superior life. Already they had gotten her blind dates, someone Vanessa didn't want for herself (she had so many suitors she could afford to share) or a friend of one of Leigh's men. It was like college all over again, but now she was in Leigh Owen's circle. After a while Cady stopped being self-conscious around the men she met through Leigh; they were just boys after all, just as dopey as a lot of the ones she'd gone out with in college.

The only thing that wasn't good about their apartment, besides the lack of space, was Susan Brown. Cady kept regretting they had let her in. She still didn't know why they had to have four roommates when, with a little more money added by each of them, they could get rid of her. Maybe Leigh and Vanessa had no one to help them the way she did. Her mother would have helped her out. Susan Brown was a nuisance.

The nude exercising was the first sign she was odd. Who wanted to look at her body? What did she think she was showing off? They put a stop to that right away, but then Cady walked into the kitchen one day and caught Susan washing her underpants in the kitchen sink.

Cady was appalled. "We have to wash our dishes there!" she stormed.

Susan just looked at her.

"That's disgusting. It's unsanitary."

"Everybody's in the bathroom."

"Then wait your turn," Cady said.

"What's the difference? It's soap and water."

"Just don't do it."

Susan wrung out her underpants and left the kitchen to hang them up, and Cady scrubbed the kitchen sink with cleanser. She couldn't wait to tell Leigh.

Nothing seemed to bother Leigh. "You told her, so that's okay," she said. "Besides, when do you wash dishes?"

"I have a plate and a glass."

Leigh smiled.

Nobody ever came out and planned it, but they didn't get blind dates for Susan, although she would look at their men with big eyes and try to ingratiate herself. Did he like Dave Brubeck? She would put on Dave Brubeck. Would he like to try some of the chili she made last night? No?

Susan had a series of skinny little guys with short haircuts and big Adam's apples, for whom she cooked bad chili on the nights she threw the roommates out so that she could entertain. While Leigh and Cady were tramping through the snow, or sitting in the corner coffee shop killing time, they thought of Susan in their cozy apartment and even Leigh seemed a little annoyed.

"I hope he gets ptomaine," Cady said.

"We're home at eleven," Leigh said.

"And catch her having sex? That's even more disgusting than ptomaine."

They'd caught Susan in the middle of a love scene once, and now they leaned on the buzzer before they went upstairs to let themselves in with their keys.

"We don't throw *her* out when we have dates," Cady said. "Although we should."

"We don't like any of our dates enough to want to cook for them," Leigh reminded her. "We hardly want to let them in after dinner."

"Where are the ones we want to fall in love with?" Cady sighed.

Dating in the city had been an unexpected disappointment. You felt you had to accept any offer of drinks or preferably dinner, to be fed, and to get out of the apartment, but coming home afterward was usually a great relief. Cady had liked the men at college better. She'd had wild crushes in college. Now the men seemed older, more serious, as if they were sizing her up for a potential wife. In fact, they were strangers. It amazed her that a man who didn't really know her for who she was, a man she'd smiled at and flattered and fooled, and who didn't know or care what her thoughts were, should think she was even considering him. She wondered if these men were nervous because they were thirty. A wife was a definite asset at work. A wife made them look responsible.

She didn't want to be a man's ticket to a promotion; she wanted to be the love of his life. These men were so sensible, so unromantic. One had proposed before he'd even tried to kiss her. And then, of course, there were the ones who grabbed her when she wasn't even expecting it, when she didn't know yet if she wanted it, and who had no good intentions at all. They thought since she had her own apartment they could come up and sleep with her. She always said one or more of her roommates was home, and got rid of those men on the front steps. Where did they get the idea that pouncing on a girl was going to make her excited? They had seen the wrong movies.

She thought it would be relaxing to go out with a man who was just a buddy, a friend, with no agenda. They could laugh and go to the park and confide in each other. But Cady knew herself: That wouldn't be enough. She wanted a man to recite poetry to. She wanted to be swept away.

Unfortunately there was only one male teacher at the Dunnewood School, and he was too old and married besides. Her students, of course, were all girls. They were in high school but they wore uniforms that would have suited a six-year-old: knee socks, short plaid skirts, navy jackets, white blouses, striped ties. Sometimes when the weather was clement, some of the older ones sneaked cigarettes on the street between classes, and from afar they looked like little kids with cigarettes in their mouths. They weren't supposed to be on the street at all, because it was a school rule that you never disgrace the uniform, and who knew what they would do? Smoking was bad enough.

Cady made them stop but she never told the principal. Her students loved her. And she loved some of them. They were so bright, so full of life, so eager. The ones who seemed as if they were destined for great things when they got out were her favorites. She wanted to help be a part of that.

She would probably quit teaching when she got married, she thought, but for now it was so fulfilling and rewarding she was glad she hadn't chosen some other profession like a secretary — like Leigh, who was unappreciated and ordered around by everyone, even though Leigh got to meet famous people in show business and film.

Sometimes Cady wondered if she would be a good mother. She didn't think so. She didn't like babies — they were boring and a big responsibility — and small children annoyed her. She thought she would go insane if she had to stay around the house taking care of little kids. It was only teenagers that Cady liked. She identified with them on some level — partly as a parent, partly as a mentor, and partly because she saw herself in them as she had been at their age, yearning for something but not sure what. She could have a dialogue with a teenager, or at least the ones who weren't sullen or shy. Their ideas were both fresh and silly, things she'd thought herself when she was learning about the world.

Her favorite student this year was Danica Fisher. She was sixteen, like all Cady's girls in Junior English Lit. *Danica,* Cady had found when she looked up her name, was Slavic for morning star. Danica was beautiful, with flawless skin and honey-colored straight hair. She seemed to have missed the awkwardness of puberty entirely. Most of the sixteen-year-olds, Cady felt, were as ugly as they would ever be in their lives. So much for sweet sixteen.

And she wrote good poetry. Cady had to teach writing as well as literature. The school was completely devoted to getting its girls into college, so the board thought it was a waste of time to have a class devoted to only creative writing. No one majored in creative writing at college. You majored in literature.

She had met Danica's parents during coffee hour after the PTA meeting last month. Her father's name was Paul and he was in advertising, and Danica had told her he had created some of the slogans

41

Cady had heard on television. Cady supposed that was where Danica had gotten her flair for words. The mother was kind of a dried-up blonde frump in a sweater suit that was a bad copy of a Chanel. Mrs. Paul Fisher; she didn't have a first name. I could never let that happen to me, Cady thought. But the father was gorgeous. She figured he was about forty, and he had gray in his hair and a beautifully cut suit and elegant tie, and a lean, handsome, intelligent face. He'd smiled at her and her heart surprisingly turned over.

Now that's the kind of man I could fall in love with, Cady thought.

"Your daughter is one of my best students," she said to the parents. They were looking at her attentively. "Actually, I shouldn't say this, but she's my pet."

Danica blushed and the parents looked pleased.

"If she has talent it's from my husband," Mrs. Paul Fisher said.

I could never, never say that, Cady thought. How can anyone just erase herself like that? I bet she's one of those women who says she's "just a housewife."

He didn't try to deny it. Cady was sure he had been hearing that through the entire marriage. "Did you know that my husband writes poetry?" the wife said.

"Really!" Cady said.

"Not poetry, song lyrics," he said. "And only as a hobby."

"They're very good."

Cady felt an unexpected little pang of jealousy that he shared his poetry with his wife, although why wouldn't he? It was a relationship she'd wanted for herself; to read poetry to a man, or have him read it to her. She wished he hadn't shown his lyrics to anyone.

How little I know about marriage, she thought afterward. She felt lonely.

Still, she thought about him sometimes. Danica had his eyes. Cady wondered if he was unhappy with his wife, his life. How would she ever know? Although she would never admit it to anyone, he had become her fantasy. She didn't know if it was his life she wanted, or him. But of course if she had that marriage, it wouldn't be the same. She was so much more interesting than his wife, and so much younger.

She couldn't ask his daughter about him; that would be too strange. So he remained a mystery. And as such, he was much more intriguing and unforgettable.

chapter
4

Leigh's office, Star Management, was on Fifty-Seventh Street, and unless the weather was prohibitive, she liked to walk to work. It was only a mile, a pleasant walk through a nice part of the city, and good exercise. She worked in a large, modern building with big windows and air conditioning, carpets printed to look like animal hides, and many men in identical dark suits making deals. There was only one female executive. Her name was Pansy Pierce, she did casting, and she wore a dark suit, too, but of course with a skirt. Leigh worked for her.

Young men on their way up worked in the mailroom learning the business on the side until they were promoted, while young women were secretaries and usually left before they could get anywhere at all. Leigh didn't even have a cubicle; she sat at a desk in front of her boss's office like a kind of guard. "Cerebus guarding the gates of hell," she thought privately, since Pansy

Pierce, when crossed, could be very mean. Sometimes she could hear Miss Pierce screaming at someone, and Leigh was glad it wasn't her.

Nobody bothered to yell at her; she was very efficient and she wasn't important. She typed, filed, kept the appointment book, answered the phone, placed calls, and lied to unsuccessful actors whom Miss Pierce did not want to see. Sometimes she was invited out for coffee or a drink after work by one of these unsuccessful actors, and she usually went. Famous actors did not ask her out; they didn't want Miss Pierce to make fun of them.

One well-known movie actor had made the mistake of trying to date another of the secretaries, and Miss Pierce never let him hear the end of it. "Can't you do better than that?" she said to him, and laughed. It wasn't as if she were jealous. After all, she had a rich husband she seemed to love. But Miss Pierce believed in the caste system. You did not seek to sleep with underlings. Of course, people did, but they were discreet.

Leigh wondered if show business people were a different breed altogether from the young lawyers and businessmen she dated, since the actors who bought her coffee or a drink always made it clear that they would be happy for her to go directly to their apartments afterward. They were not all her age either. Some were older, but unsuccessful all the same, and the older ones were the worst. They didn't seem to have any time to waste. Or perhaps they were desperate.

Leigh thought casting was interesting and she hoped to do some of it someday. She would have to learn how to make deals too, but nobody was showing her. She eavesdropped on as much of Miss Pierce's business as she could. She went through the casting books on her lunch hour, when Miss Pierce was out at an expensive restaurant on her expense account and Leigh was having a sandwich at her desk, and she soon familiarized herself with every one of their clients, and other people's clients too. It was supposed to be good to steal clients, although she had no idea how to do that either.

She knew Star Management also represented writers and directors, although on her floor there were only actors and actresses. It was a big agency, and it was one of the top agencies in town, with a twin agency in Beverly Hills.

Certainly this was a glamour job, although what she personally did was not very exciting. But it was better than being a secretary somewhere else. It had been sheer chance that she got this job — the employment agency had sent her. It helped her social life as well. Working at Star Management was impressive, but being a secretary was nonthreatening. The men Leigh dated, she had soon discovered, were easily threatened, especially when they were impressed.

I wish I could meet a soul mate, she often thought. A man who loves and accepts me as I am. A man who knows more than I do and can teach me things. One who is confident, knows his way around. A grown-up. She knew she'd never find these qualities in a boy her age. She couldn't imagine one of them taking care of her when they could hardly take care of themselves.

She looked at the agents in her office, listened to their banter, and wished she could get to know them. They seemed like powerful, interesting men. They all had women in their lives — wives or famous actresses they were dating — and she felt invisible to them.

It was so easy to get any boy her age or a little older to pursue her, but the men she really wanted to meet seemed to belong to a different country, with different laws, a different language.

Like all the other girls, Leigh read magazine articles about how to get a man. The articles said you needed to know what kind of man you wanted. Well, she knew, but that didn't seem to help.

It was spring now. The days were getting longer. It was hard to be alone in the spring, it was such a romantic time of year. Twenty-three was still young, but sometimes it felt old. A lot of her friends from high school and college were married already. Some had children. They had gone steady at school and gone directly from that to domestic life. They had missed what she had, and Leigh wondered if they noticed that or even cared. In a way they were sorry for her, even though she was so popular.

"Still beating off the men with sticks?" one or another of these married friends would ask cheerfully, and Leigh knew the concept of a mob of wrong guys pursuing her was pathetic to them, not enviable, or else that these friends thought she was too picky and it was her own fault that she was still single. "It must be exhausting to keep dating," the friends said. "I'm glad I'm out of the rat race." They sounded middle-aged. Their talk was of toilet training, of preschools. When they gave dinner parties, which wasn't often anymore, they had a set of good silverware for that, which they had received as wedding presents, in addition to the set of silver plated they used for everyday.

Leigh had the tiny steel forks, knives, and spoons Vanessa had stolen from the airline. She knew her friends wouldn't think it was amusing, as she did.

Leigh knew what she was: a permanent child. She wanted someone to take her away from all that, to rescue her, although she would never have admitted she wanted a rescuer. She wanted to be a woman who could rescue herself.

There was a restaurant and bar on the ground floor of the building where Star Management was located, and people from the office went there often after work to have a drink. Sometimes Leigh met her blind dates there, because it was convenient to her office and because she could escape more conveniently than if they had met at her apartment. Besides, although Leigh didn't like to admit how much Susan had begun to annoy her, the idea of Susan gazing balefully at her dates was getting hard to take. You couldn't ask her to leave and she didn't take the hint. She just sat there trying to make conversation, looking eager and acting jealous. They were going to have to have a serious talk very soon about that.

Tonight Leigh had a blind date from a friend of a friend of her mother's. No one ever wanted to waste a man who was breathing. She hoped he would be interesting, attractive, and nice, because a part of her never gave up, but the other part of her was already regretting that she had agreed to have dinner with him in order to get a free meal. She sat at the bar to wait for him.

Next to her was one of the agents from the office, waiting for someone too, having a drink. She recognized him immediately as David Graham, one of the partners in the agency. He was one of the older, interesting men she always looked at with such reverence, with his fascinating, sophisticated life that she knew nothing about. He was forty-one, with thick gray hair and a young, animated face, and he looked debonair in his regulation black suit. Some of the other agents looked like mobsters or funeral directors in these dour suits, but on David Graham it seemed a mark of authority. She also knew Pansy Pierce had a crush on him, despite the rich husband she seemed to love, and despite the fact that everyone knew Mr. Graham was also married with children.

Leigh ordered a vodka and tonic. She hoped her blind date would pay for it when he showed up.

"How are you?" David Graham said to her, dipped his head briefly and smiled.

He was speaking to her. She had a moment of shock. "Fine," she said, and smiled back.

"Waiting for a date?"

"Well, yes." She took out a cigarette and he leaned over and lit it for her. "Thank you." She hoped her date wouldn't be a disgrace. What would Mr. Graham think? "A blind date," she added with a helpless little shrug.

"Ah, the dreaded blind date."

"Yes."

"At least we know *he's* lucky."

"Thank you," Leigh said.

"I am waiting for a very fat, very unattractive English playwright with bad teeth," Mr. Graham said. "Don't tell him I said so."

"I won't. I hope at least he's famous."

"Very famous."

"And you're going to make him more so."

"If he does what I tell him to."

"He'd be foolish not to," Leigh said.

"Will you tell him that?"

"Of course."

She realized that she was flirting. But he made it easy, because he seemed to approve of her. What a nice, nice man, Leigh thought.

"I'm David Graham," he said.

"I know. I'm Leigh Owen. I work for Miss Pierce."

"I know that too."

"You do?"

"Believe it or not, I know who everyone in this entire agency is," he said.

"My goodness."

"So what do you want to do with your life, Leigh Owen? Marry the blind date? Become an agent?"

"Become an agent," Leigh said before she'd had a chance to think. Then when she'd said it she realized it was what she wanted. "But it's hard for girls, isn't it. They don't teach us anything. They don't take us seriously."

"No," he said thoughtfully. "They don't take you seriously enough."

"You'd think I'd know something, doing

Miss Pierce's correspondence, overhearing deals, reading the casting book in my spare time. But there's so much more. No one lets me read a script, or meet a client for more than a second, unless it's someone Miss Pierce wants to get rid of, and then I have to do that. They teach the boys in the mailroom, but they think we're just disposable."

"And what if you did meet Mr. Right? After we've trained you?"

"I wouldn't necessarily leave," Leigh said. "The boys get paid more than we do because supposedly they're going to get married and support a wife, but what if I marry a man with no money? I'd have to support him, wouldn't I? And what if I never got married? I should be able to take care of myself."

"Yes, you should."

"Don't tell Miss Pierce I've been complaining," Leigh said. "I'll get in trouble."

"You weren't complaining about her."

"No."

"You don't want to take her job. . . ."

"No. I want my own job. There's room for both of us. I could take the unknowns. She doesn't want to be bothered with them anyway."

"The up-and-coming unknowns?"

"They might be. You need someone young and dedicated for them."

"Young and hungry, as we say. Are you hungry, Leigh?"

She hadn't thought about it. But now, when he asked her, she realized she was. He seemed friendly and understanding. What could he do to her if she said she was ambitious? Fire her? Then she could go elsewhere and be a secretary again. You could always be a secretary.

"I think I am," she said.

"Think?"

"Nobody ever asked me before," Leigh said.

"Think or know? It matters."

"I know," Leigh said. And suddenly, she did know.

"Good," David Graham said.

The fat Englishman came then, and the two men went to sit in a booth because he said he didn't like to sit at a bar. When Leigh's date arrived a few moments later, Leigh discovered David Graham had paid for her drink. She hadn't even been able to thank him.

Her date took her to a table in the back room where they could order drinks and dinner and it would be quieter. He seemed innocuous, with pale hair neatly parted, and pale eyes, and although she thought he was about thirty he already seemed older. Not like Mr. Graham, Leigh couldn't help thinking. Mr. Graham seemed younger. And her date was a banker. She didn't want to talk to a banker. She wanted to talk about her own work. But girls didn't do that on dates.

She glanced around the room, but David Graham was in the front with the playwright and she couldn't see him. She wondered if they were having dinner or just drinks. I wish I were here with him, she thought.

"You're very quiet," her date said.

"I'm a quiet person," she lied.

How soon can I go home? she thought.

The next morning when Leigh had gotten Miss Pierce's coffee and was having some of her own, a mailroom boy in a dark suit arrived and put an envelope on her desk. To her surprise it had her own name on it. Leigh opened it. It contained a movie script and a note.

"Give me a list of ten people for each part," the note said. "Let's see how much imagination you have."

It was signed David Graham.

Leigh could hardly breathe for excitement. She put the script back into the envelope and hid it in her desk. She would take it home tonight. She thought it was probably a good idea she not let Miss Pierce find out.

If they fired her for that, too, she could always go elsewhere and be a secretary.

chapter
5

Vanessa was at a cocktail party in the apartment of a handsome thirty-six-year-old
bachelor, who was the older brother of the
short, overweight accountant she had met at
a different party the week before, and who
had invited her here hoping that she would
become interested in him. She was more interested in the brother. It was a beautiful
spring evening, and the apartment, in a
high-rise with a doorman and an elevator
man, was redolent of money.

She got a glass of red wine from the bar
and went snooping. There were a lot of
pills easily available in the medicine cabinet — he was too trusting. Someone
would be sure to help himself before the
night was over. In the top drawer of the
dresser was some women's makeup; foundation, lipsticks, eye shadow. She wondered if he had a girlfriend, or kept
makeup for girls who stayed over, or if he
wore it himself. She'd heard about men

like that. Now that she thought of it, he seemed a little effeminate, and at thirty-six he should be married by now. No one was so much of a catch that he should stay single forever.

When Vanessa went back into the living room, men surrounded her, as always. The party was crowded and getting noisy. The girls were vivacious, the men were preening, everyone was on the prowl. No matter how many parties she'd been to, the excitement always hit her in these gatherings, the feeling that something unexpected and good would happen. She had never gone to a party without meeting a man, and usually he had some redeeming feature even if he wasn't for her. Even the little accountant had a redeeming feature; he'd invited her here. He had asked her if she would have dinner with him afterward and she'd replied, "Let's see."

He knew what that meant. He was already on a list, and not at the top. He seemed used to it. "I'll be back," he said. He was going to look for a different girl, and Vanessa wished him luck.

She hummed along to "Puff the Magic Dragon" on the hi-fi and sipped her wine, let a man light her cigarette, and flirted. She would have only one glass of wine because she had to fly tomorrow. What an interesting life I have, she thought happily.

There was a darling boyish-looking man smiling at her, and then he walked up to her. He looked like what you'd want for a younger brother; tall, slim but well built, brown hair falling fetchingly over his forehead, smiley blue eyes. "I'm Charlie Rackley," he said.

"Vanessa Preet."

"Do you come here often?"

"Oh, constantly." She laughed.

"What do you do?" They always asked the same things, but when they were cute it didn't matter.

"I'm a stewardess for Worldwide Airlines."

"I'm a graduate student at Columbia," he said. "History and Lit."

How disappointing — he was a mere child. "How old are you?" she asked.

"Twenty-two."

A buddy, a friend, but not a future boyfriend. Oh well. She would never date a twenty-two-year-old who was still in school. He didn't even have a job.

"And what will History and Lit. prepare you for?"

"I don't know," he said.

"You don't know what you want to do?"

"No, I really don't. I might go into business after all that. Take an M.B.A. next."

"It's a luxury to keep going to school. It costs money."

"Yes," Charlie Rackley said, and smiled a sweet smile with no touch of arrogance in it. "My father was in the paper box business. He was very successful. He valued education because he didn't have much of a chance to get one. When he died he left us money specifically for school."

"So you have brothers and sisters?"

"A sister in med school."

"A *sister?*"

"Yes."

"He really did value education." How many girls went to medical school? Vanessa thought they were probably an interesting family.

"And you?" he asked.

"Two boring older sisters. Nobody in my family thinks girls need an education. We just have to be charming."

"And at that you're a success," he said.

"So are you." They smiled at each other.

I'd like to give him hot chocolate, she thought.

"Would you have dinner with me after the party?" he asked.

"We'll see."

"Can I at least have your phone number?"

"Maybe I'll give it to you at dinner."

"You're a difficult woman."

"It's part of my famous charm," Vanessa said.

"I'm going to be following you."

She smiled.

Another man came up to her then to talk, and another, and Charlie Rackley, on the edge of her wave of popularity, looked a little awash and wistful. Vanessa felt sorry for him. He had such a nice face. But she didn't waste her time with younger men. They didn't interest her at all.

Two men asked for her phone number and she gave it to them, and another invited her for dinner. "I have to get up early tomorrow," she said. "I have to fly to California." Then she didn't know why she'd said that, so she gave him her number too. Charlie Rackley was still hovering around looking at her.

Oh, all *right*, Vanessa thought. It's only dinner. Don't cry.

The accountant came back, as she'd thought he would, and Vanessa told him she'd made other plans. He looked crestfallen, and she kissed him lightly on the cheek. "Another time," she said. Her mother had often told her that you never knew when you would be desperate, and you had to keep a backlog. Her mother's unofficial charm-school instructions had been pointed and practical. Unfortunately, some of her advice had stuck, whether Vanessa wanted to believe in it or not.

"I'll call you," he promised, and he looked wistful too.

"Beauty like yours is a burden," Charlie Rackley said when he had a moment with her alone.

"Oh, really? A burden?" She'd always believed it was a wonderful present.

"It gives you too many options."

"When, if not while I'm young?" Vanessa said.

"How will you ever know whom you like?"

"Maybe I like a lot of them."

"Or none."

"None?"

"Paralyzed in the midst of excess," he said.

He was right, of course. She was disconcerted that he was so smart. When you had too many men you always thought a better one was around the corner.

"Oh, let's go to dinner," she said, and was amused to see how his open face lit up.

He took her in a taxi to an expensive

bistro on the Upper East Side. It wasn't far from her apartment, and Vanessa had often passed it and wanted to go there. He was intelligent and educated and sweet, but almost every other thing he said revealed how young and innocent he was. He even still lived with his mother. He will definitely be our house mascot, she thought. I don't want to lose him but I don't know what else to do with him. I'll keep him around until he grows up.

"Would you like to have an after-dinner drink at the Carlyle?" he asked.

Sophisticated, wasn't he, for a child. His father must have left him money for more than school. "I have to fly tomorrow," Vanessa said. "Early night. Another time."

"I'll remember."

She gave him her phone number finally, and he walked her home. He didn't try to kiss her good-night, although he looked as if he wanted to. On an impulse she kissed him, a quick kiss on the mouth. The look on his face was almost heartbreakingly happy. A boy with a crush, she thought, amused.

In California Vanessa had a one-night stand with an attractive pilot she'd had her eye on for a while. She knew he was a ladies' man, so the brief affairette was just for her ego, not for what she thought of as real life. Real life would be the man who came along one day and won her heart. She could not imagine yet who he could be. Real life would be someone she saw at least several times, or for a long time, someone she wanted to know. Luckily she'd met some of those. She made it a point never to leave a man as an enemy, and, if possible, as a friend.

When she came home Charlie called. When she had slept enough, Vanessa called him back. He invited her for dinner, and she told him to pick her up earlier so that they could have a drink. She'd brought a tote bag full of tiny sample liquor bottles with her from the flight and she might as well use them, she thought.

He arrived with a bouquet of roses. They were all there: Leigh, Cady, Susan. As she had expected, everyone liked him, and he liked them. Susan, however, liked him a little too much. It was pathetic, Vanessa thought. Susan would never get any man if she was so desperate.

Not that she wanted to give him away anyway. Sharing did not mean losing. Vanessa had no idea what this feeling meant. How could you want someone you didn't want? She had to admit she wasn't attracted to him. He was too much like a younger brother, someone she'd have to protect, not someone who could protect her. So if she didn't want to sleep with him, and she couldn't fall in love with him, what was he to her anyway?

A friend, she thought. A great date. Those were not bad things either.

The next time she came back from California, Vanessa invited Charlie to one of Leigh's spaghetti dinners. It was the first time they had allowed a man to be there. She didn't feel as if she had to make a big fuss over him, and he seemed pleased to be with them. The girls couldn't talk about men, but they talked about work, and finally they did talk about men and Charlie chimed right in and gave them the man's point of view. It was the best spaghetti and Chianti evening they'd ever had.

And Charlie had brought the Chianti, of course. He had perfect manners.

"How can you not be in love with him?" Susan asked afterward.

"I'm not, that's all."

"I am," Susan said. "I'll take him." She sounded serious.

"He belongs to the house," Vanessa said.

"But if you don't want him . . ."

"If he's anyone's, he's still mine," Vanessa said.

"You're a dog in the manger," Susan said. She looked sulky. "You always used to share the ones you don't want."

"Well, I haven't said I don't want him, have I?"

Susan just didn't get it. Charlie wouldn't choose her in a million years, Vanessa thought. How can she be so unaware? Trying to take one of your roommate's men was the worst thing you could do, far worse than borrowing clothes without permission. It was the cardinal sin, and had caused many breakups of otherwise tolerant roommates. Vanessa always went out of her way to avoid her roommates' men because she didn't want them to like her. It was always the girl who got blamed.

Susan certainly is annoying, Vanessa thought. I wish I could change the location of my bed. I don't even want to sleep next to her. The sight of that curly head on the pillow so close to hers made her feel depressed. Susan was like an irritating, bleating lamb. On the few evenings they were all home together, Leigh would be curled up on the sofa reading one of the scripts she often took home, and Cady would be at the bridge table grading her students' papers, but oblivious, selfish Susan wanted to talk. It was better when she watched TV. At least the television set didn't expect an answer. Vanessa stayed out of the apartment as much as she could.

I'm too old to live like this much longer, she thought unhappily. Why are single women so trapped? It isn't fair. Money is so much more important than it ought to be. Money, or the lack of it, changes everything.

But I can't leave. I've left too many apartments already. I wish she would leave.

Every apartment Vanessa had ever been in, there had been someone she couldn't stand. Someone would get on her nerves, and then because of the forced proximity, it got worse, and finally it became unbearable. She wondered if it were partly her fault, if she was too much of a loner to get along with anyone. But she liked Leigh and Cady. And they liked her. They had become sort of family. They were her type. Susan Brown was not her type.

I'll just have to pretend she isn't here, Vanessa thought. I'll tune her out. I'll make her disappear. It will be an act of will. I can do that — anything is possible.

chapter
6

Cady liked having Charlie Rackley around. She'd never had a brother, or a boy to play with as a child, and he filled her need for a man friend who would never destroy the relationship by becoming more. It was clear that he was smitten with Vanessa, but Vanessa treated him like a pal. Sometimes when Vanessa was away flying he would come around anyway. The girls were always glad to see him. He was one of those men who got along beautifully with women while never appearing either sexual or less than masculine. Cady supposed this was because he had an older sister, close to him in age. She wished she had been his older sister. She would probably know a lot more about how to treat men, who were still a mystery to her.

At the end of the school year, Danica's parents came to school for the year-end summary, which was a critique of the student's marks, capabilities and efforts. Her mother was as dried up as ever, and Paul, as Cady secretly thought of him — not Mr. Fisher, not "her father" — was as sexy and good-looking as she had remembered. He smiled at her once, over his wife's head, and her heart fluttered like a caught bird. She wondered for one wild instant if he were flirting with her. The idea that he might flirt when his wife was right in the room was thrilling, and Cady felt no guilt at all when she smiled back. Danica did not notice.

Now that the school year was over, Cady started to spend weekends at her parents' house in Scarsdale, unless she had a Saturday night date, and sometimes during the week as well, but she was bored at home. She ate her mother's tuna fish salad and drank iced tea, and sat in the sun, and at night she watched television and gossiped with her mother, and she missed New York. In the city even though the other girls were working all day she knew the evenings would bring something interesting. She had outgrown Scarsdale. Her friends were gone. They had moved away, as she had.

During the hot summer days in New York, Cady had a new project. The Fishers lived near her, and it wasn't any trouble to go a little out of her way when out, to pass their building. It gave her the frisson of doing something slightly dangerous. And thus one sunny afternoon in early summer, Cady saw a station wagon at their curb, filled with luggage and bags of groceries, and the doorman helping Mrs. Fisher, Danica, a younger boy who must have been the son, and a fat brown dog into it. Paul was there too, but he stayed at the curb and cheerily waved good-bye. Then he turned and went back into the apartment house.

They're going to the country for the summer, Cady thought excitedly. He's one of the summer bachelors now! This arrangement was quite common, and she knew he would go to the country to be with his family every weekend, but not nights during the week, because he worked long hours and it was probably too far to commute. The city was full of summer bachelors: married men whose wives and children were away, and Cady knew they often cheated. These men were, in fact, notorious for their summer romances with girls in the city, affairs that usually ended in the fall, with a broken heart on the girl's side . . . but of course, if you took it for what it was, you wouldn't get hurt.

Cady wondered if Paul Fisher was a man

who would have a summer romance. She wondered if he had someone lined up already. She wondered if he would ever think about her. She thought how perfect they would be together, and what a thrilling summer she would have if he wanted to take her out. If I concentrate on him enough, she told herself, I can conjure him up. I can put a hex on him. I can make myself sneak into his mind. And then she laughed because it was so ridiculous.

Two days later he called her. "Do you remember me?"

"Of course I do," Cady said.

"I wondered if you might like to have lunch with me," Paul Fisher said.

"I'd love to," Cady said.

They arranged to meet the next day at a French restaurant in midtown, near his office, and after they hung up she just sat there and stared into space for a long time, trying to collect herself. She knew now that he *had* been flirting at school, and that he liked her too. She rushed downtown to Lord & Taylor and bought a new dress, a white, sleeveless sheath that set off her tan, that she had seen in *Harper's Bazaar*. She charged it to her parents.

She didn't tell Leigh about all this. He was married, so it had to be a secret, and besides, she didn't even know what it would turn out to be.

At the French restaurant, sitting next to the object of her desire, Cady was so nervous she dropped her fork to the floor. She was the youngest person in the room. She had never been that close to Paul and she could smell his aftershave; lemony. He ordered a martini, so she did too. After a few sips she felt calmer. They lit cigarettes and adjusted themselves in the booth, side by side, a little closer, not too close. She could feel his warmth. What a beautiful shirt he was wearing. She wondered what it would have been like to watch him dress in the morning, his long, capable fingers on the buttons of that striped shirt. She did not dare think about him taking it off.

He asked her about work, her family, if she had hobbies. She tried to appear grownup and not neurotic. She tried to be cheerful and not complain, to make an apartment full of girls sound like fun, to make her social life with all those wrong men seem interesting. But by the time she had finished her martini she was telling him the truth. And it amused him. He was sympathetic. He told her a funny story about when he was young, a long time ago, sharing his first apartment with some other young men.

"I know it was worse than yours," he said, "because boys are so messy."

"You don't know how messy *we* are," Cady said. She was feeling comfortable with him now.

She looked for hints and portents. A man could mention his wife once or twice in an impersonal, or even a derogatory, way, but a man who talked about his wife all the time in an admiring or an affectionate way, did not cheat, and was sending you a message to that effect. Paul did not say a word about his wife.

He did say how bright Danica was (Cady agreed), and he mentioned that his country home was far away in upper Connecticut. He said he would miss the dog, because you got used to a dog, because it loved you so much and thought you were a hero. Cady decided that it was important that he had mentioned missing the dog and not his family.

"Doesn't your family think you're a hero?" Cady asked.

"Oh, no." He smiled.

Poor Paul.

They picked at their food to pretend it was a normal encounter, and they each had a glass of white wine. Cady was a little high by now, and she wondered if he was too.

The absence of any mention of his wife made her more present than if he had spoken about her. This was so obviously a triangle, right here at the table; and it would always be one, wherever they were. Cady wondered if she would have liked him as much if he were a bachelor. He would probably have scared her to death, she thought. He was much too sophisticated. At least with a wife to feel guilty about he had a disadvantage. It was as if she were doing him a favor going out with him, because he had that accoutrement, that ball and chain, that unavailability that wouldn't appeal to everyone. He has to be nicer because he has a wife, Cady thought.

He took her hand, under the table. She was surprised, and yet not really surprised. Her heart started to pound again. At this rate, if he did anything more I'd probably have a heart attack, Cady thought.

He looked at her. "Do you think it's a bad thing, wanting to kiss my daughter's teacher?" he asked.

I *am* going to have a heart attack, Cady thought. "I'm not her teacher anymore," she said.

"No, you're not her teacher. No more PTA meetings to meet at. . . ."

"No. . . ."

"Then I guess we'll have to plan to see each other elsewhere."

"Yes . . ." Cady breathed.

I don't go to bed with a man on the first date, she thought. She'd had only three lovers in her whole life: one at college and two afterward. She pretended to her friends that she was more worldly-wise than that.

"I want to go to your apartment and kiss you for a long time," Paul said quietly.

She thought that was the sexiest thing anyone had ever said to her. She loved that he kept saying "kiss," as if lovemaking was slow, something to be savored. He would not rush and maul her like those boys who were afraid she would say no, or that they wouldn't be able to do it. But maybe he really meant just kissing. She would love to go to her apartment and neck with this man she'd had a crush on for so long. And what if he wanted to do more? It would be happening very quickly, but after all, why pretend?

"Don't you have to go back to work?" Cady asked.

"Yes. But I won't."

It made her feel powerful, desirable.

"Nobody's home in my apartment," she said.

He told the waiter they didn't want

coffee or dessert and paid the check. They took a taxi to her gray town house. It looked stately and elegant under the leafy trees. The street was hot and still. Nobody was around.

They went upstairs and he stopped her and kissed her in the hall before she fit her key in the lock. His lips were just soft enough and just firm enough; perfect. She felt the kiss shooting through her body. He put his tongue in her mouth and she made an involuntary little sound of joy. They stood there kissing for a moment more and then she pushed the door open.

Susan was lying on the living room floor doing her exercises, naked. Cady screamed.

Susan sat up and tried to cover herself, looking embarrassed and startled at the sight of Cady with a strange man. Paul looked surprised and amused. Cady was surprised and furious.

"What are you doing here?" she yelled at Susan.

"I was . . . I had to leave work . . . I was . . . sick."

"Sick?"

"I think I should go," Paul said, smiling.

"No, I'll go with you," Cady said.

But the moment was over. He kissed her gently and then passionately for a long time in the street in front of her building, but not nearly long enough. "Will you have lunch with me again next week?" he asked. "I have a bachelor friend who has an apartment. He travels a bit, and he'll lend me the keys."

He's used it before of course, she thought, maybe a lot. But she didn't care. Having a place to go was a part of having an affair, and it was competent and capable of him to know where to go and to arrange it. She had never been so attracted to any man before. "Yes," she said. She put her arms around his neck. "I hate my roommate," Cady said.

"So do I," Paul said, and laughed. "I'll call you tomorrow." He kissed her lightly and walked away down the street, looking jaunty and happy.

She stood for a while watching him and then she turned and went back into the apartment. By the time she got upstairs her fists were clenched and her nails were digging into her palms. Susan was dressed, sitting on the sofa.

"Who was that?" Susan asked in her nosy, whiny way.

"Don't ask me who that was! Why are you here and not at work?"

"I had a migraine."

"You were doing your exercises! Why did you leave work?"

"Leave me alone," Susan said sullenly.

"What's going on?"

"Nothing."

"What do you mean, nothing?"

Susan's eyes filled with tears. "I got fired," she said, and started to cry.

"Today?"

"No. Two weeks ago." Susan started to cry harder.

"But you go to work every morning," Cady said, confused.

"No I don't. I go downstairs to the coffee shop and look at the want ads, and then I look for a job, and then after five o'clock I come back here. But today it was so hot that I thought . . . I'd fake being sick, I didn't think you'd come bursting in, I thought I'd have a minute to . . . oh my God."

"Oh my God is right," Cady said. "How are you going to pay the rent?"

Susan was sniffing now, blowing her nose and wiping her eyes. "I have enough money for the month," she said.

"Otherwise you'll have to leave," Cady said slowly. "We need someone with a job."

She'll go away, hurray, hurray, she thought. Good riddance.

"I'll have one. I promise. Don't make me go. I'll get a job next week. I will. They liked me today and said they'd call me back."

"Go to an agency," Cady said. "How hard is it to get work as a receptionist?"

"I will. I'll go to an agency. I just didn't want to pay the commission."

"You get a job next week or else!" Cady couldn't wait to tell Leigh.

"I will. You girls are my friends. I don't want to have to go somewhere else."

Her friends? They couldn't stand her.

And I'm going to have an affair with Paul, Cady thought. For a moment she had forgotten.

The next week Susan started her new job, again as a receptionist, for another eye doctor. Leigh called Susan's office to check up on her, to be sure she really had a job and was there. Cady had lunch with Paul, at a different French restaurant. She didn't tell Leigh or Vanessa yet. It was still her secret. As for Susan, she didn't dare mention the man again and she didn't know who he was.

After lunch Paul took Cady to his bachelor friend's apartment. It was just a studio, overlooking a tiny garden, and when the hide-a-bed was open there was no room to walk around it, but Cady thought this pied-à-terre was the most glamorous and romantic place she'd ever seen. They made love. She had put in her diaphragm before lunch, just in case. He had carefully brought condoms. Since she couldn't get pregnant because it would ruin her life, she decided to use both. Paul was unavailable, after all.

He was so much better than any of her previous lovers, so much more experienced, leisurely, and patient, and he seemed to enjoy her body more than any of them had. His passion matched hers. He introduced her to oral sex. He did it to her, and showed her how to do it to him. The afternoon was perfect. When it was over Cady was in love.

He called her the next day, and every day thereafter, and they began to meet twice a week. Often he took her to dinner at one or another tiny, out-of-the-way place, and then if his friend needed the apartment, he took her to a hotel. She was a little embarrassed about the hotel, even though he'd always gotten the room before they arrived and she didn't have to hide while he registered. But she didn't like worrying that someone she knew might see her. Not that it was likely, but still. . . . She seemed to mind that more than he did.

He wouldn't go to her apartment. Ever after they'd found Susan there, he was nervous about it. Cady assured him that no one would be there, but Paul still said he felt uncomfortable.

She began to depend on his morning phone calls, waiting in the apartment until he had called and she could begin her day. He usually called first thing, but sometimes he had a meeting and then he called her afterward. She would feel insecure if he didn't call, and think he had forgotten her. Sleeping with a man ruined everything, Cady knew, unless you were someone like Vanessa, who took it in stride. But she had gone this far and now she was involved. She didn't let herself think about the end of the summer. Paul told her he was in love with her, and she knew that was true, and she was beginning to be confident that might make him continue to see her even when he wasn't a summer bachelor any longer.

Eventually she told Leigh and Vanessa about the affair, and she told them who he was. They were pleased for her and didn't criticize her, didn't tell her she was a fool or would be hurt, or that she would hurt anyone, since none of them were ever on the wife's side. The wife was from a distant planet, as far as they were concerned.

She didn't bother to tell Susan. Susan was there only because she was a necessary nuisance. Cady never told her anything.

After a while, as the hot, passionate summer wore on, Cady's feelings about Paul's family, even Danica whom she used to dote on, changed. They were all burdens now, obstacles to her happiness. If Paul didn't have his family he would be all hers. She even resented the dog.

"Don't feel that way," Leigh said when Cady told her. "You can't afford to feel that way."

"I can't help it," Cady said. "I want to be in the country with him instead of his wife."

"But then he'd be cheating on *you*," Leigh said.

"I guess you're right."

"That's the trouble with sex," Leigh said. "It makes you want to own him."

"No," Cady said. "That's the trouble with love."

chapter
7

By midsummer David Graham had made Miss Pierce promote Leigh to be her assistant. Leigh had a small office now, while a new girl, good-natured, red-headed Edna, sat at her old desk guarding the gates of hell. Edna also did some secretarial work for Leigh, and brought her coffee. She, it seemed clear, had no wish to be anything but a secretary. At her desk she read *Bride's Magazine* instead of *Daily Variety*. Leigh read all the trades. She never wanted to be a secretary again.

Leigh had also been given a raise: twenty-five dollars a month.

Now that she was no longer an underling, Pansy, as Leigh was now allowed to call Miss Pierce, was nicer to her, and once even invited her to lunch. She acted as if Leigh were a different person. It was interesting what even a little bit of power could do to improve your life.

Leigh could have her own clients now,

albeit beginners; and in search of them she went to Off Broadway and Off-Off Broadway shows and reviews, to screenings where she kept alert for the actors and actresses in tiny parts, and to clubs where comics on the way up performed. Occasionally, if Pansy was busy, or was not interested in going downtown to see someone the agency might sign, or had just signed, she told Leigh to go. Pansy handled people who were already famous. It kept her hands full.

Sometimes on these evenings Leigh took Cady with her, or Vanessa, or sometimes Charlie Rackley, who was good company, and who, because he was a year younger than she was, was not like a date, which was a relief. Sometimes if none of them were available, Leigh went alone. She was no longer afraid to go places by herself, as long as it was business. It made her feel grown-up, a professional.

Leigh knew no one would be jealous if she discovered someone and made that person a success. They were all aware that the chances were that the successful performer would most likely leave her for someone more powerful once Leigh had helped achieve that success — it wasn't fair but it was a fact of life. She was determined to keep her clients, but she knew that even friendship would not inspire enough gratitude to make them stay if someone more prestigious pursued them.

Because she was an optimistic person, she told herself that some might stay anyway. Or she might become well known. You never knew until it happened.

One morning David Graham called her. "Come have a drink with me after work," he said. "Can you? I apologize for not asking you before, but I've been swamped, and then I went to London and Beverly Hills."

"I'd love to," Leigh said.

She had seen him in the halls and in the elevator, and he always said hello and asked her how it was going, but he had never asked her to have a drink and she hadn't expected him to. She was thrilled. They met at the pleasantly air-conditioned bar in the building.

"I see you've signed two new clients already," he said approvingly when they had settled down at their tiny table next to the bar. "Vodka and tonic?"

"Why yes, how did you know?"

"I know everything you do. I have my eye on you."

"Thank you," Leigh said. "I guess."

"Does it flatter you or scare you?"

"Both."

"Actually, I remembered the vodka and tonic from the last time."

"You know everybody's name, you know what they drink, you probably know what they like and dislike. . . ."

"It's the way my mind works," he said. "I have that kind of memory. How was your blind date?"

She laughed. "I've forgotten him."

"I feel sorry for the guy."

"Don't," Leigh said. "New York is full of people who've forgotten each other."

"Don't you think that's sad?"

"It depends on what happened between them before."

"How old are you?"

"Twenty-three."

"A little cynical for twenty-three."

"I hope not cynical."

"Disillusioned?"

"Not at all. Practical maybe."

"I knew you were practical."

"It's possibly my strongest character trait," Leigh said.

She remembered how much she liked being with him. It was like sparring, but in a nice way, and he seemed very interested in everything she had to say. Married men, she thought, know how to deal with women. They have to live with one.

He told her about the clients he'd seen in London and Beverly Hills, all household names, and Leigh was impressed. He'd spent time on a movie set in California, dealing with a temperamental movie star, and that impressed her too. She wondered if he took his wife on these interesting trips, and if he did, did he go to meetings while she sat bored in the hotel room or went endlessly shopping?

She remembered something her mother had told her, one of the few pieces of advice her mother had imparted. "Don't marry a man just because he has an exciting life," her mother had said. "He might not share it with you."

Had her mother married her father because he seemed to have had an exciting life? Had a doctor seemed exciting? A lot of her friends thought so.

Leigh knew she wouldn't be as fascinated with David Graham if he did anything but just what he did. But how could you separate what someone did from what he was? Your job took up so much of your time, you became immersed in it, and if you were successful the success was part of you. She was no longer just Leigh Owen the secretary, she was Leigh Owen the agent . . . well, assistant agent anyway. She was what she did, just as he was.

"I had a dinner date canceled tonight," he said casually. "Do you want to catch a bite with me?"

"Yes, that would be lovely."

Doesn't he have to go home?

"I drove in today," he said. "We can drive down to Chinatown. I love Chinese food. When I was a kid we had it every Sunday night."

"I've never been to Chinatown," Leigh said.

"You are deprived!"

He was driving a little red convertible, which she hadn't expected, and he took the top down. The restaurant was a tiny place on a corner, and she was charmed by the exotic neighborhood and the telephone booths shaped like pagodas. The restaurant's name and the menu were in Chinese, so Leigh let David order for her.

Maybe his wife has something to do tonight with the kids, Leigh thought. Or is he a summer bachelor like Cady's boyfriend? He said he drove in. Does he spend a couple of nights in the city alone? Maybe he and his wife are estranged, and he goes out to dinner in the city very often. Maybe they have an arrangement because of his career. Beware of interesting men. Or maybe they aren't so estranged but he already told her he had a business dinner, so now he can feel free to go on a date. Yes, that's probably it. But how will I ever know, since I can't just ask him these things?

Why do I care? He's not my boyfriend. But is this a date?

She didn't want to get involved with him; she wasn't Cady — Cady was too emotional, too impetuous. She, Leigh, was the rational one. You might get ahead by sleeping with your boss, but it might also get you fired. David Graham was something like eighteen years older than she was, and he was married and had children. Anything between them could only lead to trouble. She knew he was attracted to her youth and her looks, and to the obvious fact that she admired him — and maybe even liked that she was good at her job — and that men eventually made passes at girls, even distinguished men who you would have thought were above all that.

He had said she was cynical. He wasn't so far wrong, if cynical meant knowing how one thing led to another.

She tried to remember if she'd ever heard any scandal about him, if he went out with girls at the office, or if he'd ever had an affair. Pansy would know. Pansy knew everything. She probably even knew they'd had a drink tonight — but not, of course, about dinner.

"You've hardly touched your food," he said. "Don't you like it?"

"I like it a lot," Leigh said.

"Would you like some more wine?"

"Yes, please."

The wine eased her conscience, but it also ignited her attraction to him. He touched her glass gently with his and smiled at her. "In case you're wondering," he said, "I don't fool around at the office."

"Oh, I wasn't wondering!" Leigh blurted, and then she knew she was blushing. She felt like an idiot.

"A lot of people fool around," he said. "Office Roulette. It's not so easy to face someone at the water cooler the next day when you have something to hide."

"And do you fool around outside the office?" she asked.

I can't believe I just said that, she thought; but tit for tat. He started it.

He looked at her for a long moment. "Well, yes I do, sometimes," he said. "I'm not perfect."

"Then your marriage . . . is it perfect?"

"Marriages are very complicated. More than you could ever know. More than even I can understand, and I've been married for fifteen years."

"I just don't know why you'd want to ask me out," she said.

"Then you underestimate yourself. You're interesting, you're bright, you're feisty, and you're pretty to look at. I like your enthusiasm. I'd like to see you become a success."

"Thank you."

"And that's not altruistic," he said. "I don't keep dead wood around me very long."

"Thank you again."

"I'm peaceful with my life," he said. "Or perhaps I should say I've made peace with it. In the end, they're the same thing."

"Then you're happy."

"Happy?"

"Yes."

"I have no idea," he said. "I don't even think about it anymore. You probably think about it every day."

"I probably do," Leigh said.

"Because you're young," he said. "You'll see. You'll get over that — thinking you deserve to be happy."

"Deserve?"

"It is what it is: life, liberty, and the pursuit of happiness. The pursuit. Not the inalienable right. It's not a permanent state of mind."

"It almost is, for me," Leigh said. Now she felt sorry for him.

"And that's the answer to why I wanted to have dinner with you," he said. "I like your happiness."

She wished she could share it with him, as if joy was a piece of cake and you could break off a piece and feed it to someone. "Then have some," she said. "There's enough to go around."

"All right," he said. He patted her hand. "You're a wonderful child."

"I'm not a child."

"Oh, yes you are. Trust me."

He drove her home and stopped briefly outside her building. "Nice house," he said.

"That's why I'm forced to have three roommates."

"And someday, sooner than you expect, you'll be able to afford not to have any. Keep up the good work. And say you'll go out with me again some time."

"I will!"

"Good."

He drove away. Leigh went into her

town house and climbed the stairs. He's so sad, she thought. Restless, unhappy, disillusioned, and he has everything anyone could want: success, excitement, people who admire him, a family, girlfriends, and he's as free as he wants to be. I don't understand him at *all*, she thought.

But she liked him.

chapter
8

It was Cady's twenty-fourth birthday in August, and Leigh and Vanessa decided to give her a small cocktail party on the roof of the building after work. They invited Charlie, and at the last minute they reluctantly invited Susan, because she already knew about it and they didn't want to be rude. She had one of her dreary men coming over for bad chili soon in any case — imagine, chili in this heat — and they hoped she would go back downstairs to cook before too long. After the cocktail party they were going off to dinner in Greenwich Village without her.

It was really just the five of them, as Cady didn't have close friends among the other teachers at the Dunnewood School, and in any case, the teachers were away for their summer vacations. You need only one best friend, Cady thought. Hers had become Leigh. It seemed so long ago that she had wanted to be one of Leigh's friends, watching her from afar, and now they were roommates and buddies. She liked Vanessa too, and this rounded out her circle. It was enough.

They'd chipped in for a bottle of champagne, Leigh brought balloons and crackers and cheese, and Charlie had brought his camera to record the first real party they'd had. There were presents: perfume from Vanessa from the duty-free shop, a scrapbook from Leigh, a teddy bear from Charlie, and a coffee mug full of lollipops from Susan, who had said "I bought this for you last week," just so they'd know she knew about the birthday, and they would feel obligated to include her.

Cady knew that in some dim way Susan was beginning to understand that she wasn't part of their little group, and that, in fact, they didn't want her around. It wasn't that they did anything spiteful. They simply didn't pay attention to her unless they had to. They didn't talk to her except for the obvious, or exchange confidences, or ask her to go places with them, and thus, finally, she had become virtually a stranger.

As Cady's gift from her parents, Cady's mother had paid her outstanding bill from Lord & Taylor, which was a good thing since Cady could never have paid it herself. She'd been more extravagant than usual since she'd been going with Paul. You needed nice clothes for a love affair, even though you couldn't wait to get them off. Her parents still didn't know why she was shopping so much, they just thought she was popular. That was really ironic, because she didn't date anyone but Paul anymore.

Of course Cady wished Paul could have been there, but married men did not go to their girlfriend's birthday parties. That was one of the problems with having an affair with a married man. But he had given Cady a gold bracelet, had taken her to lunch, and then to his friend's apartment to make love, and he had given her a poem he had finally written for her. He could read his dried-up wife his song lyrics, Cady thought triumphantly, but they hadn't been written for his wife. Cady had asked him about that, of course, and he had assured her she was the only one to receive his creativity. In bits and pieces she felt she was winning. But now he was not with her, and she missed him.

The day's heat was still in the tar of the roof, and it was slightly sticky underfoot. Some of the tenants had brought up beach chairs to sit in while tanning, and now the roommates used them for their party.

There was a low edge around the roof, but they didn't sit on it because it was a little creepy to look down. Someone from the building had brought a scraggly tree in a pot, which stood in the corner, but it was halfway dead because it was a city tree. The New York skyline loomed around them, softly tinted in the smoggy haze, and they smiled for the camera, their arms around each other, even around Susan, looking like happy friends.

"You're a Leo, the lioness, the queen of the jungle," Vanessa told her.

"You always have to be the boss," Susan said.

"No I don't!" Cady said, insulted, but she knew it was true. She needed to have her own way more than any of them. Leigh compromised, Vanessa was the free spirit who disappeared, but she was the lioness. Well, so what?

"It's awful to be mundane," Susan said. "You have to try so hard not to be."

"Who did you have in mind?" Cady said.

"Me," Susan said. "It's my fear. I don't want to be like my family. Boring, boring."

"Oh, you're far from mundane," Leigh said kindly, and Cady almost laughed. Weird was more like it. And she *tried* to be this way?

97

"Smile, girls," Charlie said. "One more before I lose the light."

"And one of you," Vanessa said, grabbing the camera and pushing him toward the other girls.

He posed shyly, looking pleased. Poor Charlie, Cady thought. He'd had a few dates, but none of them had worked out for long. He kept comparing them to Vanessa, and that was silly, because Vanessa didn't want him for a boyfriend. Men always wanted what they couldn't have.

"One of me and Charlie," Susan said, smiling at him coyly. She'll probably frame it to feed her fantasy, Cady thought.

"And one of me with Charlie," Vanessa said, handing the camera to Leigh. She was either being nice or staking her claim. That's the one *he'll* probably frame, Cady thought.

They drank the chilled champagne from wineglasses and ate the food. Susan left to prepare for her date. "I'm sorry you gave me so little notice," she said, with an edge of disapproval in her voice. "I wouldn't have made plans." Like we care, Cady thought.

Cady's parents had wanted to drive in to the city to take her to dinner somewhere festive, but she'd refused. She preferred being with her friends. Then they offered to take her friends too, but again she refused, even though she loved being with her mother and didn't want to hurt her feelings. But when you missed your lover, being with your parents on something as important as a birthday made you feel like you'd never get a man. It made you feel like a child again, that you'd always be alone. Her parents could celebrate her unbirthday on Saturday night when she went home for the weekend.

Another thing that was sad about being with a married man, was that you never had weekends with him. She was always so happy when it was Sunday night and she knew Paul was leaving the country. Soon he'd be with her again and not with them: his family.

Getting him away from his wife was as important as getting him to be with her. That was what people meant by a triangle, Cady thought. That tug of war. . . .

She missed him so much. She thought about him all the time. She hadn't thought this would happen. Her dependence on him, her near obsession, surprised her. What was she going to do in the fall when he wasn't a summer bachelor anymore?

There would be no more dinners, that was sure. He would be afraid. And as for her, she would be back at work, with little time to go to lunch, to hotels, to his friend's apartment. What would her teaching schedule be next semester? Would it ruin her life?

One more month, Cady thought, and she felt a pain in her throat.

"Let's go to dinner!" Leigh said, and let the balloons fly up into the red-streaked sky, up over the buildings in which contented families sat around dinner tables and talked about their day. Cady wondered if she could ever have that too. She couldn't bear to think about the future.

"We're off!" she said, pretending to be having fun, and helped them carry down the remains of the party.

They went to a little Spanish restaurant in the Village that Vanessa had recommended, ate spicy food, and drank Sangria. "I feel old," Cady said. "Twenty-four. . . ."

"Old like me," Vanessa said, and laughed.

"I'm still a baby," Leigh said. "And Charlie's the real baby. Oops. Sorry Charlie, I didn't mean it like that."

"You'll see," Charlie said. "Someday

we'll be in our thirties and it won't matter."

"We'll all be married," Leigh said.

"I thought I'd be married at twenty-four," Cady said. "Didn't you think so at college, Leigh?"

"Yes," Leigh said.

"Where does the time go?" Vanessa sighed.

"I'm switching to business school," Charlie announced.

"You are? Why?" they chorused.

"My mother wants me to. She says there is no future in the arts."

"That's not true," Vanessa said.

"Yes it is. Business school will be boring, but I'll be rich."

"Rich is good," Leigh said kindly.

"I'll have a wife and three children and a big house in the suburbs," he said.

None of them could imagine it of course, he was such a child, and they laughed. Cady wondered what would become of them all. They didn't want to decide their lives just yet; it seemed so final. Time stretched and shrunk in such an odd way; you waited by the phone and it was an eternity, you went out with the man you loved and it seemed only moments. Was twenty-four old? She didn't feel very different, but the number took getting used to. When her mother was her age she had been walking her to school.

The waiter came in bearing a birthday cake then, a surprise Leigh had arranged beforehand. "Happy birthday!" the friends and the waiters sang, and told Cady to blow out the candles and make a wish.

Should she wish for Paul? Should she wish that they all stay friends? She felt so warm and cozy this moment with the champagne and the Sangria and the lighted candles on her cake, with the smiling warm faces of her closest friends around her, that Cady closed her eyes, wished for eternal friendship, and blew.

They applauded. "What did you wish for?" Charlie asked.

"You can't ask that, it won't come true," Leigh said.

Cady wondered how anyone could survive without best friends, no matter how much you loved a man. Friends were the warp and woof of your life. They were your safety net. "Then I'll never tell," she said, and beamed at them all.

chapter
9

When you want to make an unhappy person happy, you become more attached to them than you expected. Leigh was too young to understand this, but ever since the evening when David Graham revealed himself to her she felt a certain unanticipated tenderness toward him. When she saw him in the office he seemed human now, vulnerable. She wondered what she could do for him. He was the person in the position of power, but that was only at work. On the playing field of emotions she felt a kind of power of her own.

I like your happiness.

She enjoyed knowing that he was aware of everything she was doing, her little triumphs, her achievements. She was doing it for herself, of course, for her career, but she was also doing it for him, for his approval — not in the way an employee wants the boss to approve, but in the way a woman wants a man to notice and like her. She sensed it, of course. She wondered what was happening to her. She waited to see what would happen next.

He asked her to dinner again on a hot summer night, down to a restaurant in Gramercy Park, with thick white table-cloths, where they sat outdoors. She made him laugh, a wholehearted laugh of pure pleasure. If he hadn't told her that he didn't believe in all the things she took for granted, she would have thought he was just a person you see in many good restaurants, a well-dressed, debonair, sophisticated man enjoying dinner and a slight flirtation with a much younger woman from his office. She would not have known about the melancholy she found so appealing.

It occurred to her that in some way he needed her. As the evening progressed she felt quite sure of this. When he took her home at the end of the evening he kissed her, and she was not surprised. It was a tender and sexual kiss, and that did not surprise her either. Leigh had never felt so much in control of her life and of the unexpected things that were going to come. He had broken the barrier between older man and younger woman, between employer and employee, between near stranger and something much more. She knew everything was different now, although she would never have admitted it to him. The knowledge was just something she owned, a gift.

"I don't fool around at the office," he said again at her doorstep.

"I know."

When she went upstairs she was smiling, humming. It was like a Cary Grant movie. "Of course you don't fool around," the woman would reply, and then there would be more kisses. "This is impossible," they would both say, and then there would be the blackout that implied they were going all the way.

I'm too sensible for this, Leigh warned herself. This will only lead to trouble. But she couldn't stop smiling. She wondered if she was falling in love.

She said nothing to Cady and Vanessa. There really wasn't anything to tell, just a kiss. She made a list of rules for herself in case more happened between them. One: Don't ask questions about his private life. Let him tell you what he wants to, when the time is right. Two: Never discuss love. That will scare him. Three: Do not act as if his wife is the enemy, the way Cady does. Leave his wife out of it and be dignified and independent. You have your own mystery; you're free.

The next day at the office she discovered it was possible to forget about David, to do her work and care about herself the way she always did. But when Vanessa asked her if she wanted to go out on a blind date, Leigh said she was too tired and had to do laundry. Somehow it seemed too much of an effort to make conversation with someone new. Vanessa's blind dates aren't so great anyhow, Leigh told herself. Vanessa isn't discriminating enough; she enjoys the company of all men.

"Then I'll go out with both of them," Vanessa said. She knew Cady wouldn't go. They both felt a little sorry for Cady, because she had given up her future for the present. How could you give up the chance to meet the Right One?

Am I doing that? Leigh asked herself.

"Well, maybe I'll go," she told Vanessa. "I'll do the laundry tomorrow night."

"Good. We're going to Chinatown."

Leigh was a little disconcerted that they were going to Chinatown, because she didn't want to have to compare the evening with the one she'd had with David and find it disappointing. She told herself to stop being silly. The two men were named John and Rick, they were in their late twenties, not bad looking, and Vanessa had met John on a plane. They worked for a shirt company. Rick had a car. When they got downtown they didn't know where they wanted to go.

"I know a place," Leigh found herself saying, and directed them to the restaurant where she'd had dinner with David. "It's good," she said. Suddenly she wanted to go there again, to have the connection. They thought she was sophisticated to have found this no-name hole in the wall, with a menu they couldn't read, and they made a game of ordering things they would be surprised to get. They're good sports, she thought, determined to have a nice time. Still, she wished David were there to order for them. She liked the idea of a man being in control.

"Where did you grow up?" Rick asked her. "Where did you go to school? Do you have brothers and sisters?"

I signed a comic today, Leigh thought, and you've never heard of him but he's going to be big.

Vanessa was telling them about a drunk she'd had trouble with on the plane. John told a joke about a drunk, and a joke about stewardesses. Vanessa laughed delightedly at both.

When Leigh looked at Rick she noticed that he had really ugly spatulate fingers. Did he know? Was he used to it? She felt sorry for herself, not for him. Without expecting or wanting to, she felt David's kiss on her lips again. Is it too much to ask, she thought, to want to go out with someone attractive?

She felt exhausted and wished it were time to go home.

"I'm sorry," Vanessa said when they were safely in the apartment again. "You didn't like him."

"He was all right."

"Well, I tried."

"Thank you for trying."

"Easy come, easy go," Vanessa said cheerfully. "Next time."

I can't see myself going on boring blind dates for the rest of the summer, Leigh thought. Maybe I'll give myself a rest and go out with nobody at all.

A week later David called and asked her to go out with him for dinner again. He never called in advance, and Leigh supposed he thought of her when other plans got canceled. It didn't insult her. After all, he was much busier and more important than she was. She was glad he was seeing her this often, and she was pleased that she was free.

This time he took her to a little Italian restaurant with a tiny garden in back. They sat under the trees and the fire escapes and drank Chianti and smoked. The air was soft and warm. She was wearing a sleeveless dress.

"You've got a tan," he said.

"Last weekend I went to my roommate's house in Scarsdale. And sometimes in the city we sit on the roof in the sun."

"Tar beach," he said. "That's what they call it. I grew up on the Lower East Side. We were poor. My father worked in a cleaning plant. I used to swim in the East River."

"Wasn't it dirty?"

"Filthy. I learned how to swim when someone threw me in. I was lucky; I could have drowned."

"My goodness!" Leigh said. She liked that he was a self-made man. Of course, she told herself, the boys she dated weren't old enough to be self-made.

"And you," he said. "Where did you grow up?" Somehow it didn't annoy her at all that he was asking her the same questions that everyone else did. She was flattered that he was interested and glad to tell him. As she told him about her life growing up, it sounded very protected and comfortable, a lucky girl with no troubles, or perhaps that was how she was presenting it.

Her life had been normal, pleasant, and happy. The kind of life he would have liked for himself.

"I'm getting in trouble," he said. "I find myself thinking about you. I don't do this. Not at the office."

"I know."

"But I like being with you."

"I like being with you, too," Leigh said.

"What's going to become of us?"

She held her breath.

"I'd like to run away with you," David said.

"I'd like to run away with you too."

"Where would we go?"

"Paris," she said.

"Do you speak French?"

"A little. From school."

"Well, I don't. We won't need to speak to anybody anyway."

"When do I get my passport?" she said, and laughed.

They had Sambuca after dinner, with extra coffee beans in the glasses. They were called *moscas,* he told her, "flies." "What do you want out of life?" he asked her again, as he had the first time they had a drink together, but this time she felt it was more personal, about her feelings.

"To learn. To have adventures. To be happy."

"And to be a success?"

"Yes."

"Don't ever forget that part of it," he said. "Don't let the world talk you out of it. You'd be missing too much fun."

"You think we're not alike," she said, "but we are."

"Oh, I know we are," he said.

At her doorstep he kissed her again, this time twice. "What's going to become of us?" he asked again.

"I don't know."

"Will you let me think about it?"

"Yes," she said.

He called her two days later. She was surprised. "Can you meet me for a drink at six?" he asked.

"Yes."

He never took her to the bar in the building where they both worked. Without mentioning it they both knew that people would notice and they might talk. They went to the '21' Club.

She was impressed because she had heard of '21' but had never been there. It was for people who were already successful. There were toy planes and cars hanging from the ceiling, and convivial men lined up at the long bar in the center room. She saw few women. She was glad she was wearing her conservative business suit.

She had a vodka and tonic and he had a martini. He seemed as though he wanted it for courage. He lit her cigarette. "I've thought about you for two days," he said. "It was very disconcerting. This doesn't happen to me."

She said nothing. She didn't know what to say. She waited, feeling hopeful and happy, as if she'd known.

"I live in the suburbs," he said. "Larchmont. I have a company apartment where I stay when I'm in town. It's on Central Park South with an impressive view of the Park. I've never taken a woman there."

"Really?"

"The women I've seen have been older than you, with their own apartments, without roommates. Old enough to understand that what happens between us doesn't matter. But you're not like that. I feel protective toward you. You're very vulnerable."

She didn't say anything. She realized her silence was making him more comfortable, as if he had rehearsed a speech and wanted to get it over with.

"I don't want you to fall in love with me," he said. "But I think I'm in love with you."

In love! She was enormously flattered. But what good will it do? she thought. He's married, so where can it go?

"I've broken one rule of mine already," he said, "becoming involved at the office: with you. If we go to the company apartment, I will have broken another rule. You make me feel reckless. That frightens me."

"It doesn't frighten me," Leigh said.

What could she do — she knew now she was already in love with him, whether he wanted her to be or not. She was young, she had time, he was here and he loved her. How could he possibly ruin her life? She felt that she had some control over that too. Being with him made her feel she was living to the fullest, instead of just going through the motions and being polite as all the other men she'd met made her feel. She felt tender toward him and wanted to make him happy. He would teach her things. It was enough.

"I'd like to see your view of the park at sunset," she said.

"Are you sure?"

"Yes."

They went to his apartment in a taxi. Leigh was relieved to see there was a self-service elevator, and that the concierge tactfully ignored her.

When they got upstairs she was startled to see how big the apartment was: in the living room a wall of stark, modern windows and an impressive view, beige carpeting and soft leather furniture, expensive paintings on the walls, sculpture, bookcases filled with new-looking books. There was even a grand piano with a vase of flowers on it. Someone took very good care of this apartment. She was aware again of how important David Graham was.

Through the open door she could see an enormous king sized bed. He gave her a drink and then he kissed her. After that it was easy.

Her passion with him surprised her, and she realized she wasn't very experienced, or at least the boys hadn't been. This is the beginning of my learning, she thought, and joyfully allowed herself to be carried away. He was skillful and considerate and slow, and she was relieved that he had even supplied himself with condoms. The worst fear, the worst sin, was to become pregnant without a husband. It was even worse than falling in love with someone else's.

Afterward he sent out for Chinese food, not nearly as good as that in Chinatown he said, and they ate it in front of the windows, and gazed at the view of the lights below. He lit candles and opened wine. They kept kissing. A man who is nice afterward, and not just before, is really in love, Leigh thought.

She did not sleep there, of course, because you had to keep up the pretense that nothing was going on. Flowers arrived at her desk the next day, with no card. But she knew. He called her after lunch. "Did you like the flowers?"

"Very much."

"I have a business dinner tonight, but tomorrow . . . could you see me tomorrow after work?"

"Yes."

And thus began their affair. She told Vanessa, who merely smiled knowingly, and Cady, who was thrilled. "Now we have the same life!" Cady said.

The same life? She didn't think so. Hers had a comfort level that Cady's had never achieved. Of course, some of that was due to Cady's volatile nature, but also Cady was worried about the complicated logistics of the future, while Leigh felt safe and secure. David could grow tired of her, he could decide he was bad for her, there could be a scandal. Yes, any of those things could happen, but his life was already set up so he had a good amount of freedom. She didn't have to wonder about the end of the summer, as Cady sometimes did. Her romance would at least last longer than that.

chapter
10

It was a hot August night, one of a series of them that frayed the nerves and caused exhaustion. Cady was stuck in the apartment with Susan. Leigh, she knew, was on a date with David probably making leisurely love in his luxuriously cool company pied-à-terre. Vanessa was in California, perhaps swimming in the ocean, perhaps riding in a convertible with the top down with an attractive man. Cady felt sorry for herself. Susan was in the air-conditioned bedroom writing in the journal she'd started keeping, while she was in the non-air-conditioned living room watching television. Although the windows were open, the room was almost airless. She was miserable, but this way she could pretend she was alone.

She wondered if Susan was pretending to be alone too, but she doubted it when Susan came wandering in and plunked herself in front of the television set. Cady told herself not to be annoyed; after all, it was Susan's set. The others were just using it. But she was annoyed anyway. She hoped Susan wouldn't start to make small talk. Susan did that sometimes, even when someone else was trying to concentrate; it was as if, because they had made her inconsequential, she had made them inconsequential too.

Susan put her bare feet up on the coffee table. "I have these awful warts on the bottom of my feet," she said. "Look."

"I don't want to look," Cady said, and turned her face away, repulsed. Was there not to be a moment of peace in this place?

Susan sighed and began poking gingerly at the soles of her feet. "I went to the doctor, but they won't go away," she said. "They're spreading. Now he's trying something new. I have to put this goop on and sleep in socks."

"Are they catching?" Cady asked, horrified.

"Why would they be catching?"

Why? She had been using the bathtub! Had scrubbing it been enough? Now she could never use the bathtub again. And what about the shower? What if she was infected already? You could probably get them anywhere on your body. She didn't even want to think about that, but the image of warts on her private places jumped into her mind and she felt sick.

"Don't walk around the house barefoot," Cady said.

"It doesn't bother me."

"I meant for us."

"You're not going to catch them."

"How do you know that?"

"The doctor would have told me."

I hate her, Cady thought.

"They don't hurt," Susan said. "They're just ugly. They're all over the bottom of my feet. Who knows where I got them? They're a medical mystery. I can't go to the beach with a date. I don't want him to see them. Not to mention sex — my goodness, I'd have to have sex with my shoes on, wouldn't I? Girls just have to be perfect, don't they? It's such a nuisance."

Cady moved away from her. The picture on the TV was grainy and wavering. The reception was poor in their neighborhood, and she wondered why they had ever thought having a television set was enough of an asset to sway them toward accepting Susan as their roommate. She moved the rabbit ears back and forth but it was no better. Suddenly she had to escape.

"I'm going out for a while," Cady said.

"Bye."

The streets were too warm and humid. She would have to buy a rubber shower mat tomorrow, and keep it under her bed, and use it every day in the shower so she wouldn't get Susan's horrible warts. Wasn't it just typical of her that she'd have something so vile? There was no end to the things Susan did that upset her.

I want to get rid of her, Cady thought in despair. I want her to leave. This is just the last straw.

She found herself walking toward Paul's apartment building. Just looking at it reassured her. There were lights on in his apartment, and she thought he was probably home. What was he doing? He'd told her he was going to bring work from the office, have a meeting before, catch a bite to eat. It wasn't a date night for them, and although she understood she still felt deserted.

He was always home at the end of the evening so his wife could call him before she went to bed, even when he took Cady to dinner. She wished he could take her out every night, but she understood that he had friends and obligations and sometimes even needed to be alone. She knew he had to keep pretending that nothing in his life had changed, or else his wife would suspect something.

Cady stood on the corner for a while looking up jealously at his windows. She felt terribly sorry for herself that Paul and his wife had such a nice apartment, with a clean bathroom and no infected room-mate, while she had to live the way she was living — cramped and miserable, and now in danger. Life was unequal and unfair. Cady turned and went home so that no one would see her, and so she would be sure to be there when he called to say good-night.

The next day she told Leigh about the warts, and that they had to get rid of Susan because she couldn't bear to have her around any longer.

"But what are we going to tell her?" Leigh asked.

"We won't tell her why. Just tell her to go."

"Maybe she'll get cured. You can't throw someone out just because she has warts."

"And what about everything else?"

"Did she say they were catching or not?"

"She didn't really say," Cady said, "and I don't want to find out. I'm scared. We have to protect ourselves. We aren't masochists. We aren't crazy."

"I have to admit I'd love to replace her," Leigh said.

"Then let's do it!"

"Let's see what Vanessa thinks. We'll have a discussion and a vote."

"We don't need a vote. We're two already."

"No, we have to include Vanessa."

A day later Vanessa was back, and after she'd had a good sleep the three of them had a meeting in the coffee shop on the corner. "We can get a better roommate," Cady said. "We'll take an ad like Leigh did when she found you. We'll give her some notice and make her leave. And she can answer an ad and move."

"My other roommates were always leaving or throwing each other out," Vanessa said. "It's probably happened to her before. She had a life before she met us."

"She'll be so upset," Leigh said. "Remember how she cried when we found out she didn't have a job?"

"So what?" Cady said. "I'm upset now! Don't my feelings matter?"

"I don't like her," Vanessa said. "And I'm hardly ever here. She must drive you two crazy. Are we voting?"

"Yes."

"I vote she goes," Vanessa said.

"She goes," Cady said.

"I make it unanimous," Leigh said.

"Hurray!" Cady said. "At last!"

"When should we tell her she has to leave?" Leigh asked.

"The end of the month," Cady said. "That's plenty of time for everybody."

"Labor Day weekend would be good," Vanessa said. "We'll all be away and can avoid an emotional confrontation." Cady and Leigh were going to visit their respective parents, and Vanessa had volunteered to be traveling for work because of the overtime on holiday weekends.

"We'll tell her tonight," Leigh decided. "All of us. By committee."

Susan knew something was odd when the three girls sat down and told her to sit down too. When Leigh, who had been chosen as the leader whether she liked it or not, told her she had to move out by Labor Day, Susan turned pale, then red, and began to cry. They had known she would not take it easily, but still the girls were taken aback, and glanced at each other uncomfortably. Susan sobbed until she was hiccupping. She beat her fists on the arm of the sofa. The other three sat there wishing she would stop. Then, finally, she calmed down. "You never liked me," she said.

They didn't know what to say, because after all, it was true.

"You never tried," she said. "None of you. You didn't act like normal people."

They looked at each other and looked away. They really disliked the way this was turning out.

"I kept telling myself you were my friends," Susan said. "But you never were. I always tried to get along. But you never did." She sniffed back tears. "Why am I always alone?" she demanded. "Walking from school alone when I was a kid, the last to be picked for everything? I'm not ugly, I'm not mean. I'm outgoing; I'm not a drip. I try to be friendly. Why am I cursed?"

Leigh lit a cigarette nervously. "Can I have one?" Cady asked. Leigh gave her one. "And me," Vanessa said. They all lit up.

"Susan?" Leigh said politely, holding out the pack to her.

"Don't think you can be nice to me *now*," Susan snapped, and ran into the bedroom.

That night she slept on the couch, and every night thereafter, despite the heat and lack of air conditioning. After their confrontation they avoided her and she them. The apartment was just a place to change clothes and sleep. They were scrupulously polite. The three girls counted the days

124

until they could have their lives back. Cady had bought a rubber tub mat, which she kept under her bed when not in use so Susan wouldn't use it. But they all felt a guilty awareness, as if it were not just warts Susan had, but something infinitely more dangerous and communicable: the curse of a loser, of someone unpopular and unlikable, someone who would never fit in.

Cady told Paul their decision, and he said she was right; he rubbed her feet and told her he was glad they were so beautiful. Leigh told David, who told her that an executive needed to be able to make difficult decisions like this all the time, and that it was good practice for her. Vanessa told Charlie, who said, "Poor Susan." They didn't tell anyone else because no one else cared. Roommates left all the time. They all agreed that four girls in one bedroom would be difficult for people with the best of intentions.

Susan took her suitcases up from the basement but did not pack them. She asked Charlie to get her a carton and he did. She didn't pack that either, and it sat on the floor in the corner like a burden of guilt. Depressed and crazed she started throwing things away. The girls ignored her even more. It made them too uncomfortable to see her glaring at them. She scribbled in her journal and kept the living room light on long after they had gone to sleep.

They were all relieved when Labor Day weekend came around and they could leave town. "Good-bye," they said, not knowing what else to say to make it sound better.

"Just drop the key into the mailbox," Leigh said.

It would be a long, hot, lonely weekend in the city, and Susan would have time to pack at last. They would leave her alone to her own devices. When they came back after Labor Day she would be gone and they could start again.

In Weehawken, Leigh's parents had a holiday barbecue for neighbors and friends. In Scarsdale, Cady sat in the sun and went shopping for some new fall clothes with her mother. Vanessa, while flying, met a man who invited her to come to visit him at his estate in Hawaii. He showed her a photograph. She said she would think about it.

On Monday night Cady came back first. Susan's suitcases and carton were still on the living room floor, still unpacked. Cady's heart felt as if it had flipped over.

Susan was out, possibly looking at the apartment where she was supposed to move. Or at least Cady hoped so. She didn't even know where Susan was going, since they hadn't spoken. Why hadn't she gone yet? The deadline had passed. Did this mean she would never leave? Would she make excuses, would she play for time? Cady felt rage rising up in her, and her eyes filled with frustrated tears.

"Look!" she shrieked at Leigh when Leigh walked in the door.

"Oh, no, she's not still here . . ."

They thought of packing her things and putting them out in the hall, but that would be too uncivilized. Then Vanessa came in from her New York–Los Angeles flight, and she was appalled.

"I had a roommate like that once," she said. "It took us a month to get her out, and finally I got one of my boyfriends to drive her and her stuff to the next place."

"Oh, no!" Cady said.

"I can't deal with this, I have to get up early to go to work tomorrow," Leigh said.

Cady sighed. She had to start school tomorrow. She didn't even know what the fall was going to bring for her and Paul, and now she had to stew about Susan. They all went to bed, waiting to hear Susan's key in the lock so they could lay down the law, but she didn't come home. They hoped that meant she was trying out her new apartment.

The next morning Leigh and Cady got the phone calls at work. Vanessa had been even less prepared, because two policemen arrived at the apartment, demanding to be let in, while she was barely awake. When Leigh and Cady rushed home there were already yellow tapes roping off the front of their building, and uniformed police were outside.

That morning the superintendent had been putting out the garbage from the holiday weekend when he found Susan's body in the back of the building. It seemed to have been there for a few days.

She had apparently thrown herself off the roof.

chapter
11

How could they deal with this death? They were all in shock. None of them was hysterical or crying, although Vanessa had been badly shaken up when the police came to her door. Now the three girls stood there, confused, upset, frightened, guilty, trying to make some sense of it. Was it their fault? Had they driven Susan to kill herself? Did the police think she had killed herself? If not, who would kill her?

They had never known anyone who committed suicide. In fact, they didn't know anyone who had died except very old grandparents, so it was hard to believe this was really happening. That it *had* happened. . . .

They stood there in their apartment — which had turned from their home to a kind of stage set where outsiders could observe — while the police carefully went through bureau drawers and closets, the medicine chest, the refrigerator and cupboards. The police found Susan's journal and took it. They took her address book. They were looking for clues, a note, drugs, anything it seemed. The girls were relieved there was no note. It would have blamed them, they were sure. It would have said they were bad people.

Then later the detectives came, Lieutenants Breaker and Santangelo, serious men in suits: Santangelo, middle-aged, short, and stocky; Breaker, younger, more attractive, someone Vanessa might have liked under different circumstances. Although the detectives were not in uniform, they were frightening anyway. They were Authority, and they knew things about cases like this. The girls who had scarcely ever seen death looked into their eyes and saw so many deaths there they could not bear to look.

Breaker and Santangelo took the girls off one by one to the bedroom for questioning while the other two waited tensely in the living room. They had to be separated. In case they lied. In case they confessed to something. In case they broke down. The detectives had read Susan's journal.

"She hated you," Santangelo said. "Did you know that?"

"Yes," each had murmured almost inaudibly, caught at last.

Santangelo had a lot of questions: who were her friends, boyfriends, parents, what was her job? Did she get along at work? What was her state of mind? Was she unhappy? Frightened? Was she in love? Did she have enemies? The girls were embarrassed to have known so little about Susan, someone they had ignored and avoided. Her boyfriends had all looked the same to them, nobody they would pay attention to. They didn't know anything about her parents. She hadn't talked about her family, and they hadn't been interested. They tried to be helpful, but there wasn't much to tell, and now it was too late.

"She was terribly upset when we told her she had to leave," Leigh told him.

"She didn't want to go," Cady said.

"Susan was depressed," Vanessa said. "Really depressed."

Breaker had questions for them now. "She wrote, 'I'll show them.' What did she mean by that?" he asked.

The girls were dismayed. They all knew what "I'll show them" meant. Susan had shown them. She had punished them and they would be sorry now. Since she couldn't kill them and she couldn't stay with them, she had killed herself.

Susan had written horrible things about

them; they were unfeeling, mean, cliquish, like high school. *Had* they been mean? She had hated them. Did they hate her too?

When he asked them that they all held back their tears. They had never meant this to happen. Who would even dream of such a thing?

"I couldn't hate someone enough to wish them to die," they each said, each in her own way, each feeling guilty and wretched.

There had been an autopsy already, they were told, and Susan had fallen from the roof while alive. She had died of "blunt trauma." That meant smashed to bits. She was not drunk, although she'd had one beer, and the beer can was still on the roof with her fingerprints on it. She had not been on drugs. She was not pregnant. She did not have any disease.

Apparently she had gone up to the roof on that Saturday night of the long, hot, lonely Labor Day weekend, and had drunk a beer before jumping off.

"It looks like suicide," Breaker and Santangelo said. "We'll get back to you."

When the detectives had left, the girls finally wept. It was partly from relief and partly from guilt and partly because they were mourning Susan, even though they hadn't liked her at all. She had been annoying but harmless, they all agreed. You never hated anyone like that enough to want that person dead.

Harmless. She had been harmless. The word *harmless* made the tears flow. Lambs were harmless, Vanessa thought. Susan's curly hair had reminded her of a lamb. She had been an annoying, bleating lamb. And now whatever Susan had done began to seem less important than it had when she was living with them and driving them crazy. They wished she were still alive.

What would they have done differently? They still would have sent her away. There was no nice, easy way to do it. They couldn't win — they were lost, culpable.

It was even sadder that she had chosen to kill herself on Saturday night, when everyone else was having fun. How alone she must have felt herself to be, and how desperate!

But they hadn't known that. It wasn't their fault. How could they have known? Depressed people who killed themselves were neurotic. Were they responsible for her actions? They were just young girls, and this was so difficult.

They thought they would have been relieved to find that Susan had been thrown off the roof by a lunatic, or by an enemy they didn't know about, and then it wouldn't have been their fault at all.

The detectives were questioning their friends, and hers. Charlie called to commiserate. He said the police had asked him for an alibi, and he'd been with his mother, no place else to go. He seemed afraid to come back to the apartment to visit them. They couldn't blame him.

They didn't like living there with all those mementos and memories of her. They didn't know what to do with her clothes and possessions. Finally, they packed them, and left the suitcases and carton where they were. It would be too heartless to ask the super to take them back to the basement, and her family would want them, they thought, whoever her family might be. Her empty bed was a reproach every time they walked into the bedroom, and so was the sofa where she had slept during her last nights with them. Nothing was untouched, nothing was unchanged by her shrieking absence.

Two days later Detective Santangelo called. "It was suicide," he told Leigh, who had answered the phone, his voice tidy and forgiving. Now it was all wrapped up: just another unhappy girl in the big city. There was a small newspaper item. Career girl in chic Upper East Side town house jumps to her death. Life is lonely and hard for the single, even in fancy town houses.

A week later her parents arrived to collect Susan's things. They had driven from Pennsylvania. They were very ordinary people, made less ordinary by their grief and reproach. But the girls could see why Susan hadn't talked about them much. Her mother looked a little like Susan, wearing a navy-blue suit and a little hat, as if she were still in mourning. The father was a tall, strong-looking, gray-haired man who looked angry. The girls wondered if the police had given the parents Susan's journal, and it made them nervous to think what the parents would think of them now.

"It was a lovely funeral," her mother said.

They wondered if they should have been there. They hadn't even thought of it. Now it was something else to feel guilty about. They hadn't even thought to send flowers. Grown-ups sent flowers, people like their parents and their parents' friends, not girls. They didn't even know where Susan's parents lived, or where the funeral home was. How could you find the Brown family in Pennsylvania? The police had Susan's address book.

But, of course, they had not even tried to find her family. They had been so relieved to be absolved, to be done with it, and so overwhelmed with the materialistic here and now of what Susan had left behind. And they'd had to go back to work right away, of course. There would be no excuses for slacking off because of something like this.

It was a small tragedy. A small scandal. Life goes on.

"I suppose you knew her well," Susan's mother said.

"Not really," Vanessa said apologetically. "Nobody was here much."

"In New York you have separate lives," Leigh said. "But we'll miss her, of course."

Cady pursed her lips and said nothing.

"Why didn't any of you do anything?" her mother cried. "Couldn't you have stopped her?"

"Mother . . ." Mr. Brown said, patting his wife's shoulder comfortingly. The girls avoided each other's eyes. None of them knew anyone who called their spouse "Mother." It made Susan's world seem that much more distant.

"We didn't know," Leigh said. How could they have known? Depressed was not the same as suicidal.

136

"You girls," her mother said. "You lived with her right here. You didn't notice anything?"

They were thinking that she had not read the journal yet. Her mother didn't know they were to blame. But she would read it eventually, and she would know. They wished the parents would leave. Mrs. Brown's eyes filled with tears, and then she began to cry, blowing her nose in a white cotton handkerchief. Her husband put his arm around her.

"She was a happy child," her mother said. "Such a happy child."

"Let's go, Mother," her husband said. He picked up the suitcases. They waited until he had come back for the carton and the television set.

Her mother looked around as if trying to find some answer in the last place her daughter had lived. Then she shook her head.

"Good-bye," she said.

After a while the three girls stopped thinking about Susan's death all the time. There were other things — their loves, their daily routine, pressures of work, new challenges. Paul and David, while concerned, never mentioned it after it happened. It was an unpleasant incident, yes, a tragedy, but it was something that should not haunt them. It was something to be put to rest — the past — so they acted as if they had forgotten.

Charlie didn't mention it either when he started coming around again. Men, the girls thought, had a different way of coping with life's battles.

Time went on, and every once in a while the girls were surprised by the force of their unexpected sadness. They didn't want to be haunted by such a shocking ending to such a young life — after all, they were young too, and they had their lives before them. To deal with these feelings, finally they somehow started blaming *Susan* for making them feel guilty. Why did she have to write such awful things about them in her journal? Why did she have to jump off a roof? Why did she have to be so dramatic, so irrational, that spiteful?

They had placed an ad for a new roommate in the newspapers before Susan died, but now they didn't have the heart to interview any of the responses. Finally they had a meeting and decided it would be better for everyone not to replace Susan at all. They would divide up her share of the rent. Leigh had her raise, Cady's parents would contribute, and Vanessa could economize. It was manageable.

Charlie offered to help the superintendent put Susan's bed into the basement for storage. Vanessa had reminded them how hard it was to get rid of a bed. No one would want to buy it. The Salvation Army made you bring it to them, and that cost money. It was better just to hide it away.

Then the super said he would take it for his family's use. Morbid idea or not, a good fairly-new bed was a good fairly-new bed. They were all glad.

Nothing would ever be quite the same, but the girls were going to try to see that it was.

chapter
12

Paul had planned how he and Cady could continue to see each other when his wife and family came back to the city. Of course there would be no more romantic dinners, because his wife, or one of her friends, might see them. Everyone was back now; the city was filled with spies. Lunches would have to be more infrequent — the places more obscure. He was afraid of hotels now, so his friend's apartment, when available, would be their only recourse for physical contact. However, he would take evening walks after dinner whenever possible, where she would join him. It was more than she had expected, but it still seemed pathetically little after their summer of riches.

Cady tried to reassure him and help him to overcome his nervousness about her apartment full of roommates. Susan was gone, Vanessa was regularly away, and Leigh often had her own plans. Eventually Paul came to her apartment on some of these walks, albeit reluctantly. Of course he couldn't stay long, and the sex seemed hurried.

It was much easier for Leigh, Cady thought, since David's life had not changed with the season and she still spent many evenings with him. Cady was jealous of the freedom of Leigh's relationship. It seemed that David and his wife had some kind of an arrangement, and if not, then he was not as frightened of his wife as Paul was. Paul had told his wife he had become accustomed to exercise over the summer, and that walks helped relieve his tension from work. He was pleased with his successful ruse. But their meetings were furtive and Cady was unhappy. She wanted more. She wanted at least what Leigh had, maybe even more than that.

It was November. The holidays were coming. Cady felt abandoned. At last it had become clear to her that an affair with a married man was less than half a loaf; it was just the crumbs. How could she have been so euphoric to think it was more? She wanted to be with Paul for pivotal events, and for celebrations. She should not just be waiting all the time for the phone to ring, for whispered half sentences, for code.

The next night when he got out and came to her apartment for quick love-making, Cady confronted him. "I want to marry you," she said.

He looked taken aback. "No you don't," he said.

"I do!"

"I can't get a divorce. I have children."

"Danica's going to college next year."

"There's still little Danny."

"You said you loved me."

"I do love you."

"You don't love *her* anymore." They both knew who *her* was.

"No . . . I don't. Not in the same way as I used to years ago. But there is still obligation. Obligation is a very big thing."

"But why can't you be happy? Why can't you make me happy?"

"Cady, where did this come from?"

"I want a real life," she said.

"You have a real life. A wonderful life."

"I don't. I want us to live together."

"Please," he said. He looked very sad. Ordinarily she would have been moved by his expression, but she had made up her mind.

"You're miserable," she said. "I could make you happy."

"You do make me happy."

"Why can't you get divorced and marry me? Don't you love me enough?"

"I do love you," he said. He reached for her but she moved away. "I'll think of something," he said.

"What?"

"Something. You'll see. Trust me."

What did that mean?

She told Leigh. "You're lucky he didn't run," Leigh said. "Married men don't want you to propose to them."

"Married men leave their wives. You hear about it all the time. Paul can't stand her. He's only there because of the children; the little one anyway. Why can't he love me enough?"

Leigh had no answer to that. She was in a similar situation, but she had never made any overtures to David; she just kept drifting along with other things in her life, like work. Leigh loved her work. It excited her. While Cady also cared very much about her work, she could not imagine her career being her whole reason for contentment. It's Leigh's nature to be more reticent, Cady thought. Leigh is so calm, so agreeable. Not me, I have to say what I think. She'll be with him until she's a thousand years old and then he'll dump her and then she won't be able to get anyone

143

else. She'll be alone. Will her career be enough for her then?

After that, despite Leigh's warning, Cady was on a campaign to make Paul change his life. She was tired of her hand-me-down furniture. She wanted nice things, like grown-ups had: chairs, a dining table, matching dishes. She wanted to have dinner with him every night. She wanted to sleep with him all night. She wanted to be Mrs. Fisher. She wanted respect.

"Danica is crazy about me," she said to him. "Danny will love me too. I'm good with kids. I'm a *teacher*, for God's sake!"

"He's too young," Paul said. "A divorce would devastate him. I have to wait."

Wait? This was the first glimmer of hope she had. Not just No, but a mention of the future. "Would you think of doing it when he's older?" Cady asked.

"I might."

He might! She felt she was getting some-where.

"I told you I'd think of something," Paul said, "and I will."

Christmas came. The three girls decorated a Christmas tree with the tiny sample bottles of liquor Vanessa had brought from the air-line, and strung up colored lights. Leigh added a gold star on top. It was Cady's first

Christmas tree. Since her father did not approve of Christmas trees, she did not mention it back in Scarsdale.

Paul was to spend the holidays with his family, skiing, and Cady would go to the suburbs to be with her parents. Before Christmas they exchanged presents. She bought him a tie, which she supposed would engender another lie to his wife, and he bought her gold earrings. "I thought about what I said I was going to think about," he said.

"And?"

He looked pleased with himself. "I want to get you your own studio apartment. I'll pay the rent. Then you can live alone, and I can come over every night when I take my walk, and we can have privacy."

Her own apartment! She had never thought of such a luxury. "Where would it be?"

"In walking distance of mine, of course."

Near here, so she'd still see Leigh and Vanessa whenever she wanted to. "You'd really pay the rent?"

"Yes. Are you excited?"

"I'm in shock."

"I found the perfect place," Paul said. "It's in a new building with a doorman so you'll be perfectly safe. Clean white paint job, everything immaculate. We'll go tomorrow, before I go away, and sign the lease."

"Shouldn't I look at it first?"

"Don't you trust me?"

"Of course."

She was being kept. A kept woman. A mistress. The man always picked out the apartment and put the girl in it. But Cady didn't feel guilty or denigrated at all — she felt like an adult at last. Sophisticated, worldly, more independent than she'd ever been before. She would have a nice apartment and her own things. Of course Paul would have to pay the rent. She could never afford to. But he owed her. He was her boyfriend and he had so far refused to marry her. If they wanted to be together this was a good way to do it. She didn't know any other way. She felt flattered and cherished. Eventually he would marry her, she was sure of it. This was the first step.

"Paul is getting me a studio apartment and paying the rent," she told Leigh and Vanessa. "It's near his. And near you, so nothing much will change, except I'll be with him a lot more."

They were impressed, and as always, not critical at all. It was a coup to have one's own apartment. To have Paul take responsibility, they felt, was very romantic and sophisticated and caring. It gave Cady a relationship. Her status as his girlfriend was being recognized. It was a commitment.

Your father sometimes paid the rent, and Paul was a father figure. He was forty-one.

"Now I'll have to get another roommate," Leigh said glumly.

"Oh, Leigh!" Cady hugged her. "I'll help you interview if you want."

When she went home for the holidays Cady couldn't help telling her mother. She almost always told her mother things; her mother was her real best friend, more than any of her close friends were. She'd mentioned Paul enough so her mother knew something was going on, but now she told her mother everything. She said that Paul and his dreadful wife were estranged, but he needed time to change his life because of the children.

Her mother furrowed her brow for an instant, but then she smiled. Her mother was modern and accepting, far better than any of her friends' mothers, who would not have understood. "Well!"

"Well . . ."

"We won't tell your father," her mother said.

"No, of course not."

"I would love to meet him."

"You will. We'll have lunch." At least Paul was a few years younger than her mother. Cady was sure they would get along.

Her mother went for her pile of decorating magazines. "How do you want to decorate it? Have you given it any thought? I've saved all these magazines. . . ."

The two of them spent the holidays at furniture departments in department stores, and at furniture specialty shops, and antique stores. They decided on modern. They bought formerly expensive dishes at a wholesale outlet, where Cady had to wipe the dust off the plates, and they bought stainless flatware with pretty plastic handles. They bought glasses and wineglasses, and a few pots and pans and a kettle, although Cady did not cook. They chose a double bed, which was a little too big for the space, but that was all right, and pillows and a throw to pretend it was a couch. They bought sheets and towels, a shower curtain and wastebaskets and shelf liner that her mother put on all the shelves. It was as if the two of them were playing house.

It was a fantasy and it was fun, but it was real too.

Cady moved in after the holidays, when

Paul was back. She had left her twin bed for the girls, the symbol of her vanished transient past. Cady liked to throw things out, give things away: clothing, possessions, anything old, no longer useful, and so did her mother. They were both excited about her new apartment.

Paul came to visit her and they christened the double bed. Their lovemaking in it seemed symbolic of her future, a new beginning. Then he went home. She felt lonely and sad, a little frightened even though she was surrounded by all the objects she had coveted. She poured a glass of wine, lit a cigarette, and called Leigh.

"How does it feel?" Leigh asked.

"I don't know yet."

"You'll get used to it. You're lucky."

Leigh and Vanessa had chosen another roommate from the ad Leigh had placed, a quiet, mature-seeming girl, an office manager named Alix. She was very different from Susan Brown. She had just moved in.

"How is Alix working out?" Cady asked.

"She's great. She has a boyfriend, and she spends a lot of time at his apartment. She's neat. She doesn't talk about stupid things, but she's friendly."

"Should I be jealous?"

"No."

"Paul just went home," Cady said. It was first dawning on her that this would be her fate. "He's home with his wife."

"You knew that," Leigh said. "You'll see him more now."

"That's what he said."

Every evening Paul took his walk, and stopped off at Cady's new little apartment. He had his own key, and when she heard it in the lock her heart began to pound. He would run in, snowflakes twinkling on his shoulders, sometimes wearing a ski hat, his face flushed from the cold and his excitement at seeing her. They rushed into each other's arms. It was romantic and tragic and joyous all at once. All day she had saved up everything she wanted to tell him, and it poured out when he came in — all her words, frantically, excitedly, desperately, because soon he would be gone again and she might have forgotten something.

They made love most nights. Sometimes he was tired, and then she massaged his shoulders. When he had gone again she didn't know where to go. It was late, and where could she go alone anyway? She had not dated for a long time, and now she didn't even have her roommates for company. She no longer went with Leigh to a cabaret or a play, because she was so nervous that she always had to leave before it was over, to rush home for Paul. She would never think of going out with her friends the way she had in the past, to a cheap dinner or to a movie, even though Paul didn't mind and told her she was free, that she should keep up with her friends, that he would call her. But she couldn't bear the thought of her phone ringing in her empty apartment, knowing it was he on the other end, missing her. Paul's nightly visit was more important to her than anything else.

Their lunches were fewer and farther between. He had become more circumspect, and when she protested he reminded her that they saw each other every night. He did meet her mother, finally, and her mother liked him and thought he was charming. He *was* charming. He always had been. Cady was hopelessly in love with him. She felt that he was rationing out their time and it was never enough.

He will marry me someday, she told herself. He *must* marry me. He's miserable with her. This is no life for either of us.

When Paul had left every night, Cady called her mother, and they talked for a long time. Cady never said she felt cheated; she didn't want to upset her mother, who had gone along with her plan so wholeheartedly. Her mother was sure that Paul would marry her someday. They reassured each other: Cady plaintively, her mother cheerfully. After all, Paul had agreed to meet her mother. That counted for a lot.

So these were her evenings. After his visit, and her phone call, she prepared for her next day's class, watched television, and went to bed. Sleep became an escape. She had always been tidy, but now she became obsessively so. She'd had dinner alone. She still sent down to the corner deli. When she had finished she washed and dried and put away her plate and her glass, everything in its place, as if no one lived there. She moved her collection of paperweights to be in perfect alignment, wiped off the fingerprints.

This is all mine, she thought, trying to feel proud, but all she felt was scared.

chapter

13

It was late winter of 1964, a year since Leigh had found the apartment and her roommates. It was, and would be, a year of change. The new hot group, The Beatles, was singing their innocent hit, "I Want to Hold Your Hand," shocking the older generation with their long hair. The United States would bomb North Vietnam and escalate their position in the war from "advisors" to participants. Congress would pass the Civil Rights Act. Dr. Martin Luther King, Jr. would receive the Nobel Peace Prize. Cigarette smoking would be linked to cancer, and warnings put on packs and ads. Many housewives who had read *The Feminine Mystique* now felt that they were being cheated by the lifestyle they had coveted and won. Vanessa, Leigh, and Cady were all on the birth control pill.

Leigh and David were circumspect and sly. Neither of them had given up their normal business life, and they attended different events separately as behooved their different responsibilities. They were friends and colleagues in the office, and lovers once a week in the company apartment. They spoke on the phone every day, and face-to-face whenever it would attract no suspicion. They went to dinner, but never where anyone saw them. To the best of their knowledge there was no gossip, although they knew that office gossip could begin from the slightest hint.

It was not that he feared gossip because of his marriage, but rather that he did not want their relationship to hurt Leigh's career. He didn't want to seem to be playing favorites. Leigh was to be respected because of her ability, not her personal connection. David always thought about work.

They were in love. They were best friends, fascinated by each other, passionate and tender with each other, admitting their devotion, and never talking about the future. She tried not to think about it. Leigh didn't know what David thought about it, if he did. She never criticized Cady for becoming such a prisoner to Paul, but she let the situation be cautionary for her: She could never give up her freedom that way. Although she had become so attached to David during the months since they were together that she felt as if he were her blood and her soul, she kept a piece of herself separate, where he could never go.

That unapproachable mysterious place was caused by guilt, a pearl created by an irritant. Ever since Susan had died, Leigh knew she had changed. She would never in her life, especially so early in her life, have thought of the nature of responsibility in its darkest terms, but Susan's suicide had altered all that. No matter how much she blamed Susan for being irrational, the truth was that she and the other girls had not been nice to Susan. They had cut her out, in a way they felt was expedient but was actually unfeeling, and Susan had been deeply hurt. Her journal pointed the finger at them. They were exposed. Since they hadn't the courage to get rid of her, they had pretended she was not there. Maybe it would have been better if they had asked her to leave right away, when they first knew she wouldn't fit in.

Hurting someone else had not been something Leigh thought about before this happened. You went along thinking you were kind. You were polite. You had been taught manners. But you could hurt people, even people you did not know, people who might not know you were hurting them.

As she was hurting David's wife.

She had just turned twenty-four, and girls her age had affairs with older married men and never thought of their wives as actual people with feelings. The wife was traditionally the "old bat," the "hag." The enemy. The obstacle. Her parents had been together all her life, and if her father had ever cheated there was no hint of it, so she had never seen firsthand the pain of a woman whose marriage is being ruined by another woman. In her limited experience Leigh had always assumed whoever the wife was had all the advantages, the upper hand. The wife had the name, the respect, the home, the children, the money, social stature. She could say "my husband."

Leigh still said "Mr. Graham" when she spoke about David to other people. She called him David to his face in the office because she had some professional status now.

David had told her his wife's name was Emma Jean, she was an artist, and painted at home in Larchmont, preferring that to socializing in New York. Occasionally she came in to the city where she saw exhibits of paintings, and then they went to the opening of a Broadway show together before driving back to the suburbs. She never stayed overnight.

He had a framed photograph of his wife and two teenaged children on his desk. All the male executives had such photos, because it made them look settled and therefore more responsible. Sometimes it had little to do with love or fidelity.

A wife could make her husband cut off his affair.

Thus, David's wife had the power to hurt *her*. Leigh had always understood that. It was one more of the pitfalls you had to watch out for, along with his becoming bored or scared or guilty. It was this knowledge that made her hold off enough to become a challenge. David understood that she was afraid of being hurt, and so he was careful to make her feel valued. He also knew there was something more that she was holding back. He just didn't know what it was. When he asked her, she said she didn't know. Their times together were so much of the moment that he always wanted more. If she had been clever or manipulative Leigh could not have done it better.

She was holding back because of her

feelings of guilt about his wife. In truth, she had no idea at all how his wife could possibly feel, but she felt guilty because of what she had done to Susan, and therefore she knew she was capable of causing injury. Once you knew you had mortally wounded someone you could never behave in the cavalier way you once might have toward anyone else.

Every time she went to bed with David and was happy, she thought she was a destructive person. These pangs of conscience stood in the way of her happiness, but she couldn't help it. If she couldn't make it up to Susan, perhaps she could make it up to someone else. She could avoid doing harm again.

She and the other girls hardly ever mentioned Susan, because they all still felt uncomfortable. Now, although Leigh had determined at the beginning not to mention David's wife to him, she found herself mentioning her, out of morbid curiosity more than jealousy. At times, Leigh thought she ought to stop seeing David, because none of this could come to any good.

"Doesn't your wife wonder where you are?" she sometimes asked.

"Not really," he would say. "She's used to my work habits."

"She never caught you with someone else?"

"No."

"Did you ever feel guilty?"

"Why are you asking me all this?"

"I feel guilty about your wife even if you don't," Leigh said.

"But you mustn't."

"But I do."

"What do you want me to do?" He sounded a little stern, ominous, as if he were expecting her to break off with him.

"I don't know," Leigh said. "Maybe our affair is a bad idea."

Just saying it made her want to burst out crying. But she couldn't help saying it anyway. She realized that she was the dangerous one in their relationship, because she had become the one who was more reluctant.

"Do you really think that?"

"Sometimes I do."

And then she would cling to him and the tears would squeeze out of her eyes, and when she looked up at him she saw the same tears shining in his, and she felt much worse for hurting him than for hurting a woman she had never met.

"Don't leave me," he said. "It won't help put together my marriage. I promise you that."

"I'll stay as long as I can," she said, and felt afraid.

"That's fair," he said. She knew he was frightened too.

He respected her opinions and sought them, as she did his. There were clients whose work was to be seen, clients to be calmed down, cheered up. She was skillful with people, as was he. Leigh knew that if they weren't lovers, if they were friends instead, that they would make a good team. She wanted to know him forever. She was learning, maturing. He liked her instincts. Even if she threw him off balance when they discussed their affair, she helped him regain his balance in the rest of daily life. He was happier since he had been with her. She only wanted to make him happy.

But she didn't want to make any other human being miserable, ever again.

"If Susan hadn't jumped off the roof," Leigh said, "I'd be a different person."

"So would she."

"Don't make a joke of it."

"I'm sorry. You don't talk about it."

"Neither do you. You act like you forgot. You never talked about it."

"I didn't realize it still haunted you so much," he said.

"I didn't know it would."

"You mustn't let it ruin your life. She wanted revenge on you. You can't let her win. That isn't justice. It helps nobody. You have to get over it. You have to go on."

"It's just so sad," Leigh said. "I think I'm over it, and then it gets to me again. I didn't like her, you know."

"I know."

"So I think about your wife, who I never met, and your children, who I'd probably like a lot if I did meet them, and I think I don't belong here. I don't want to hurt people."

"You can't hurt people who don't know you."

"What if they find out? I ask myself why I'm doing this."

"Because you love me," David said. "And because I love you."

There had been a time when that would have been enough.

chapter

14

Vanessa was very satisfied with her life these days. For several months she'd had a boyfriend, Bill Cameron, a good looking, tall, well built, athletic, thirty-year-old lawyer with black hair and blue eyes, who was good in bed, and although she wasn't always faithful to him they had never discussed it. She supposed he just assumed she would be faithful because they were seeing so much of each other, and because they had told each other they were in love. When you went to bed with a man and saw him all the time that was what you said. But she liked him more than any other man she knew, and that was enough for now.

She spent all her free New York evenings with him. She had developed a real fondness for him, and while she wasn't starry eyed she was content. Her flings were in Los Angeles, fun but meaningless. She didn't even know why she bothered, but at the time it always seemed like a good idea.

She didn't ask Bill if he were faithful because she didn't want to get into that discussion. She wasn't jealous. She was glad that jealousy had never occurred to him. That was a mark of good character.

Life in the apartment was peaceful with Susan gone. Sometimes Vanessa pretended Susan had simply moved away, in order not to remember why things were better. It was quiet, and there was more room in the bedroom and everywhere else. Their new roommate, Alix, who had replaced Cady, fit in seamlessly.

Vanessa missed Cady, so once in a while in the afternoon she invited herself over to Cady's new studio apartment for a brief visit. Vanessa liked visiting people, she had so little home life since she'd left her family. She and Cady talked about their men, and confided in each other. She thought Cady was fortunate to have the nice apartment, so tastefully done, but she herself would never give up her entire life to wait for some man to come over. Cady's situation was romantic but also a sell out. Vanessa felt sorry for her, but of course she would never say that.

Charlie was at business school and liked it. Now he talked about becoming successful and making money. He would give her a sly look, as if trying to figure out if she would like him better if he were rich. It made her want to pat him, like a puppy. She adored Charlie, but he could never be her love interest — he was her friend.

"Money makes everything easier," Vanessa said. "Believe me, I know."

"When I'm rich I'll take you to Europe," he said. That was a little game he played — the things they would do together when he made his fortune.

"No, you'll take someone else and I'll be jealous," she said.

"You wouldn't, because I'd take *you*."

"You won't, because I'll be married to the prince."

"What prince?"

"The one I'm going to meet someday."

"I don't see you married," Charlie said.

"How smart you are, and how right."

She supposed she would have to be married eventually. Everyone got married. It was one of those things you knew would happen to you, like getting older, something you didn't much like but had to accept. She would have a husband and two children, and live somewhere warm. That was one thing she did know: that she would never live in a cold climate again.

"I'll take you somewhere tropical,"

Charlie offered, remembering what she preferred. "But not too hot. Balmy ocean breezes. Hawaii."

"I've been to Hawaii three times," Vanessa said.

"I'll take you to Spain. We'll dance the tango and stay up all night."

"You do the tango in Argentina."

"We'll see the paintings in the Prado. Eat tapas and drink Sangria."

"That's more like it."

"I'll have to get rid of Bill Cameron," he said.

"And how will you do that?"

"Charm you. Prove I'm a better man."

A man? Charlie was a child! Vanessa tried not to laugh. "We'll see," she said.

"Business school is only two years," Charlie said. "Wait for me."

"I'm not going anywhere." Not with you or anyone else, she thought, and gave him a beautiful smile.

"You think I'm kidding," he said.

"I hope you are."

She felt flattered, not pressured, by these light exchanges. She didn't know how he felt, but she knew he wasn't upset.

She and Bill had settled into a comfortable routine. Sometimes they went out to dinner or a movie, or both, or to a

Broadway play. Occasionally they went to a party, where she had to remind herself not to flirt, and often she went to his apartment where she cooked dinner. She would never have dreamed of cooking anything for herself in her own apartment, but when she was with him it seemed natural. She wasn't a bad cook at all. She hadn't been to the neighborhood coffee shop for a solitary dinner for what seemed like a long time. She didn't miss it; it had been expedient and only that. She knew one thing: she cooked better food than what they served her there.

Since she didn't have girlfriends, except for Leigh and Cady — Alix was too new, she didn't know how she felt about Alix as a friend yet — and she couldn't have men friends, except for Charlie, when Bill was around, Vanessa had found herself relying on Bill for friendship besides sex. It was quite pleasant. She had never had a problem talking to any man, so they had things to talk about. He was intelligent. He was ambitious. She had made his apartment cozy.

Although she used her own apartment mainly as a clothes closet and dressing room, and slept there only when she had come home from flying and needed to be alone, and she had clothing and toiletries and makeup at Bill's apartment, she did not consider herself living with Bill. Whenever there was any hint of that, Vanessa made sure she spent the night back with the roommates. Much as she liked him, somehow the thought of living with a man made her feel claustrophobic.

She was a person who was always surrounded by people, and who was never lonely. When she was alone it was because she wanted to be. But being with others and being attached to one were two very different things. Perhaps Charlie had been right the first night they met when he told her that beauty was a burden. Her looks kept her from being lonely, but did they also keep her from being able to settle for a choice? It was much too easy to be happy without choosing. She always had fun . . . life was fun. Men were fun. She didn't have long miserable moments of self-doubt, or emptiness. There wasn't time.

Or maybe her fear of being trapped was because she had never been truly in love. Did that mean there was something wrong with her? Sometimes Vanessa wondered about that. After all, she was twenty-five now. She'd lived for a quarter of a century. Wasn't that a long time for nothing ever to have cracked within her, for nothing to open, to be totally aware that she had never gone beyond a disposable crush?

People like Cady, who gave her all for love, confused her. Vanessa thought they were weak. When would Cady ever go anywhere, do anything? Even Leigh had settled, in Vanessa's opinion, even though she had an interesting job. Work and love kept both Leigh and Cady happy, with simple goals. For herself, work was not the pathway to success, but only a way to travel to new places, have unexpected adventures, meet interesting people. She didn't want to have to rely on a man to give her those things. And that's what marriage would be. It was clear-cut — she *knew*, she'd heard it all her life. When you were married you were beholden. Most women couldn't get those things for themselves. But she could, and would.

When she missed her period in May, Vanessa felt a cold streak of panic run through her whole body. She counted and recounted, took hot baths hoping to bring it on, and waited. You weren't supposed to have an accident when you were on the pill. Then she remembered that she'd skipped a day in her little disc. But how could you get pregnant from missing only one day on the pill? She'd have to be some kind of super-fertile freak for that to happen, wouldn't she?

Maybe, Vanessa thought, it's nerves, and I'm not really pregnant. But she knew she was. You didn't just miss a period when you were on the pill.

She'd missed the day when she was in California. She'd gotten mixed up, and only realized it when it was too late. Did you get pregnant on the day you missed, or any time during the month? Was the baby Bill's, in New York, or the married pilot's in Los Angeles who she'd enjoyed but already written off?

It didn't matter, because she couldn't have a baby. She would have to find someone who knew where she could have an abortion.

Abortions were illegal, unsafe, and hard to find. No doctor would do it for you, that she knew. She'd heard of people going to Puerto Rico, Mexico, and even Europe. A girl she'd known had gone to New Jersey, but that was some years ago, and the girl, and probably the person who'd done it, were long gone.

Vanessa didn't know whom to ask. She didn't want to lose her job for becoming pregnant, and she couldn't trust any of the other stewardesses not to tell on her. A juicy tidbit like this would travel fast. She told Leigh and Cady in strictest confidence, and asked them to look around. Neither of them had the faintest idea what to do. They seemed numb. In desperation she even asked Alix, who only looked startled and grim. She decided not to tell Charlie.

"Ask Bill if he knows anyone," Leigh suggested. "He has friends; friends of friends. Men go through this more than we do, I bet."

"Ask David," Vanessa said. "Doesn't he have to help out an actress sometimes?"

David didn't know of anyone either. He reminded Leigh that his services for the clients had a limit.

"Marry Bill," Cady said hopefully, as if that were an option. She might as well have suggested that Vanessa ruin her life. But if she didn't get this pregnancy terminated her life would be ruined anyway.

A pregnant stewardess got fired. A married stewardess got fired. An unmarried pregnant woman was a pariah any way you looked at it. Who would take care of the baby if she had one? She couldn't do it alone. She would have to give it up, and that appalled her. She wasn't a baby-making machine for some stranger.

She missed another period. She began to feel and see changes in her body. Her breasts were larger and tender. She felt nauseated in the mornings, and it wasn't airsickness. Soon it would be too late for an abortion even if she could find someone to do it. It would be even more dangerous.

She went to her gynecologist, who told her she was exactly what she feared, and who refused to help her do anything about it. He seemed indignant that she'd had the nerve to ask him, upright responsible citizen that he was. Did she think he was a criminal? He didn't even seem to be sorry for her.

"I could arrange a private adoption," he said. He could ruin her life in another way. She would miss the baby forever.

She knew she would have to tell Bill. She really didn't have any other choice, since it was probably his baby. After all, the pilot had been only a one-night stand. Forget the pilot. It had to be Bill's. Bill was the man she saw all the time.

Maybe Bill could help her. Maybe he would just ditch her. You never knew what a man would do until a crisis happened, even a man you had grown to trust.

"I have bad news," Vanessa told Bill

that night. "I'm pregnant."

He looked nonplussed for a moment, and then he seemed pleased. "Well," he said. "I hadn't expected that."

"Neither did I," Vanessa said. "The pill is supposed to work."

Bill smiled at her reassuringly. "I have news too. Good news, actually. I've been offered a position in a Los Angeles law firm, Voorhiis, Clark, and Stump. I know how much you like Los Angeles. I was thinking I might propose to you and ask you to go with me, and now I think it's a great idea. You and I could get married and go to Los Angeles together."

"What about an abortion?" Vanessa asked. "Don't you know anybody?"

"No, I don't, and I don't want you to die. Aren't you listening to me? I'm asking you to marry me."

She surprised herself by starting to cry. She didn't want to marry him or anyone. She didn't want to be pregnant. Maybe dying wasn't such a bad idea.

Bill put his arms around her comfortingly, touched by her tears. He thought he was rescuing her. Maybe, Vanessa thought, he is.

"We love each other," Bill said. "We would probably have gotten married anyway, and we would certainly want children. I know I do. Don't cry. Everything is going to be fine. We can get married right away."

I guess I want children, Vanessa thought. I always assumed I'd have some.

"They asked me to start next month," Bill said. "Tell Worldwide they can't push you around anymore. And now you can grow your hair."

Her hair, yes, she was always complaining about those bangs an inch above her eyebrows; my God, she looked like Mamie Eisenhower. She could throw away her girdles and have a big belly. They could buy a house with palm trees.

"We'll get a house in Beverly Hills," Bill said. "They have good schools there."

I wanted to travel. I wanted adventures. I wanted to be free, Vanessa thought.

"Our lives will be perfect," Bill said. "We'll have a swimming pool. We'll play tennis. I'll teach you. I'll teach the kid, all our kids. We'll give fancy Beverly Hills birthday parties with donkeys and clowns."

Now I won't be free for years and years, she thought.

"I'm happy," Bill said. He hugged her. "Are you happy?"

Yes, she felt happy . . . and also ambivalent, trapped, relieved, grateful, and disappointed.

"Yes," Vanessa said.

She was going to have a husband. Her life had resolved itself. Sometimes these things happened when you least expected it. Bill was a good man. He was so hopeful. She was lucky he was going to take care of everything. How could she be so petty?

They had a tiny wedding in a suite at the Plaza Hotel. It wasn't a private room, those had to be reserved far in advance. But it was luxurious. There were flowers and Vanessa wore a white silk suit. It was a size larger than what she usually bought. There were only her parents and his; her sisters and their husbands; his brother and his wife; Leigh and Cady, who looked thrilled; and Charlie, who looked disappointed; and Bill's two best male friends. Then there was a wedding lunch, and champagne, and a cake with a bride and groom on top.

Vanessa thought there ought to be a baby on top too, but of course she didn't say so. The baby was a presence anyway, the cause of all of this, a tiny, unthinking, helpless, unformed fetus with more power than anyone in the room. She wished she were happier.

chapter
15

Vanessa was gone now, and Leigh knew there were unavoidable decisions to be made, and quickly. She liked Alix, but she had never let herself get close to her, nor had Alix — who was apparently a veteran of the roommate wars — gotten really close to her either. Now she would be living alone with Alix, whom she hardly knew. The two of them could not afford this expensive rent, and anyway, the apartment seemed too big all of a sudden.

She needed to take out an ad in the *Times* and find a new roommate to join them. It would be another stranger, another person with faults and idiosyncrasies to get used to. The idea made her very depressed.

It had been a year since she had taken this apartment, a year filled with changes and drama. She had known David for almost a year; her mentor and teacher, her best friend, her lover. She felt that she had grown up beyond an apartment with roommates. Her two good friends had gone off to their own lives and it was time for her to do the same. She wanted to live alone again.

Now that she'd made up her mind, Leigh couldn't even conceive of living with another girl or girls anymore.

She thought she could ask Alix if she wanted to take over the lease. The landlord wouldn't mind. He would have an excuse to raise the rent. But Alix would be unhappy, because now she would be responsible for finding two new roommates.

Leigh bought the *Times* to look for apartments and began to search the city. Some of the apartments were as awful as the place she had left for this one, and others were nicer but out of reach. She even looked in Cady's building, but as she had suspected, it was much too expensive.

She didn't want to tell Alix her plans and make her anxious until she found out if she could actually live elsewhere, but time was running out, and she would need to do something soon. Luckily, Alix hadn't said anything yet. She was so busy with her boyfriend that she and Leigh hardly ever saw each other. But surely she must be thinking about her future living arrangements, the next *la ronde,* the next nuisance.

After two frantic weeks Leigh found a decent second-floor studio in a walkup further east. It was a small, clean room with a kitchenette and a bath and an air conditioner in one of the windows. Cheerfully located on the building's front, it overlooked the street and a few trees. If you were honest you would describe the little building as a reconverted tenement, not a brownstone, but the area was safe, and the street lined with similar buildings had the look of a family neighborhood.

She filled out the forms, put down the deposit, signed the lease, and told the landlord she would be there next month. Now she had to tell Alix, who she was afraid might even be angry at this disruption of her life. Roommates left all the time, and quickly. It was one of the hazards of living from moment to moment as they did; they all knew it, but still it was difficult.

She waited for Alix to come in for a change of clothes before rushing off to work, and stopped her. "We need to talk about the apartment," Leigh said.

"I know," Alix said. She looked different today; her stolid face glowing. She looked younger. "My boyfriend proposed last night!"

"Well, congratulations."

"We're going to get married in September. And in the meantime, he wants me to move in with him. We'll save a lot of money, and besides, now that we're engaged, who's going to say anything?"

"So you're leaving," Leigh said. She must have sounded shocked, because Alix looked concerned.

"I'm sorry I couldn't give you any notice, but I told you immediately, and I'm as surprised as you are. I never thought Jerry would propose. I was getting ready to read him the riot act." She smiled. "I guess marriage is in the air, first Vanessa and then me. This must be a lucky apartment."

"Mmm," Leigh said noncommittally. Alix had never known about Susan. None of them would have been crazy enough to tell her the reason for the departure of her predecessor, and Alix hardly ever read the newspapers.

"I'd like to leave at the end of the month if that's not too soon for you," Alix said. "I want to grab him before he changes his mind."

"No, that's fine," Leigh said. "Actually, I was planning to move too. I want to live by myself. It's time."

"Then we're all happy," Alix said. She

held up her left hand, displaying a tiny, shiny diamond. "Look!"

"It's lovely."

"He got down on one knee," Alix said, and blushed. It was the closest and most confiding she had been since she had moved in, and now she was leaving.

As Leigh had thought, the landlord was glad to be rid of them so he could raise the rent. Alix's fiancé, Jerry, a large, blonde, ruddy-faced young man, came to help her move. They laughed and giggled and pushed each other like children. A marriage proposal had completely changed her formerly serious and mature roommate into a new person.

The night Alix left Leigh looked around the apartment and thought how nice it would be to have something like this all to herself, but she knew that was impossible and dismissed it. She would grow to like her new apartment. It would be hers.

In the time remaining she packed and sorted her possessions. Cady's mother sent her favorite thrift shop to spirit away the furniture she had donated when they first moved in. Leigh added her mother's cast-offs and the Worldwide Airlines flatware that Vanessa had left. Leigh had determined that she was going to buy new things for her new studio apartment — things that matched, even if they were few.

If I were someone else, she thought, I would be wishing David would get divorced and marry me so I wouldn't have to do all this. But I'm not someone else, I'm me, and he is who he is, and I deserve to own good things even though I'm single.

She took David to see her new apartment before she moved in. He seemed concerned that she would be living alone and without a doorman, and insisted she get a good lock put in, which he paid for. She gave him a key.

"You don't have to do that," he said.

"I want to."

"I'll never come over without calling."

"I won't be cheating," she said, and smiled.

"I didn't mean that, you do have a life of your own, although you're free to cheat if you want to."

"And do you cheat?"

"When would I have time?"

"Anyone makes time."

"You're joking, aren't you?" he said, sounding upset.

"I am if you are."

She realized her new apartment threatened him a little, the fact that she was moving on independently toward bettering her life without waiting for him. It would never have occurred to her not to. She thought that was one of the reasons he loved her, because she let him feel safe but a little off balance because she was free.

"What do you want for a house gift?" he asked.

"A dining table."

"Where would you put one?"

"It can be small."

"Okay."

"And four chairs if you're feeling extravagant," Leigh said.

"Don't get carried away."

"Don't worry about it," she said. "I'm borrowing some money from my father for furniture."

"I'm not worried about the money, I'm worried about your dinner parties that I'm not invited to," he said lightly.

"They'll be as harmless as the ones I give now — that you're not invited to." Her light tone matched his.

He's jealous, she thought, and was surprised and pleased.

Vanessa called. She was in town for a few days, back from her European honeymoon with her husband. They were staying at the St. Regis.

"People at home think I eloped," she said. "They haven't seen my waistline. They think it's romantic."

"Come say good-bye to our old apartment," Leigh said. "You and Cady and Charlie and me. It's over now, it's going to be gone in two days, our whole old lives."

"Bill has a boring law dinner tomorrow," Vanessa said. "I can come tomorrow. Can we have spaghetti and Chianti?"

"On paper plates," Leigh said. "The old ones are at the thrift shop and the new ones are in my new place. We'll have candlelight so it all looks better."

"How weird," Vanessa said. "A rite of passage."

Cady insisted they have dinner early so she could rush home to see Paul when he took his walk. Charlie brought the Chianti, as always. He was excited at the thought of seeing Vanessa again. Vanessa was showing now, a little bulge under her dress making her look like someone who had eaten a large meal. The apartment was empty, just boxes and cartons waiting for the moving men, with a few essentials left out: lamps, Leigh's bed. She was moving the next day.

"Our last night," she said. "I'm so glad we were able to get together. It's like saying a proper good-bye."

"It's sad," Cady said. "So much I didn't like, so much I complained about, but still, this was our place, where we met and got to know each other. It will always be a happy memory for me, long after the bad things are forgotten."

No one mentioned Susan, but they were all thinking about her.

"I had fun," Vanessa said. "Remember our Christmas tree?"

"And the horrible messy bathroom," Cady said.

"And me, your token man," Charlie said.

"What do you mean?" Leigh said. "You were our token woman." They all shrieked with laughter.

"Your new apartment will be wonderful," Cady said. "You'll have your own things. And maybe when he sees how nice it is, David will leave his wife and marry you."

"Don't be silly," Leigh said. "It won't be that nice, and David isn't getting divorced to marry anybody."

"Men do," Cady said wistfully. Leigh knew she was thinking about Paul, still living every day with hope. Poor Cady, she thought, as she often did, but you couldn't tell her anything, and besides, maybe Paul would surprise everyone but Cady and actually marry her someday. These things were so out of their control, such a mystery. Some men did and some didn't, and none of the girls who waited and hoped and pretended they were already married to these men could figure out why.

"How *is* marriage anyway, Vanessa?" Charlie asked.

"Just like being roommates," Vanessa said. "This is my drawer, this is your drawer, this is my closet, this is your closet. . . ."

"Isn't it magical?" Cady asked.

"Magical? No. But it's cozy and nice. Bill is lovely."

"I envy you," Cady said.

Charlie looked sad for an instant, his eyes clouding over.

Leigh looked around their old apartment, steeped in shadows from the flickering candlelight. She raised her glass. "To old friends," she said. "And new adventures."

"To us!" they all cried.

Of course they would have new adventures, their lives were still before them. One chapter was over and another was beginning. But none of it would ever be gone. Everything in life mattered, everything, even small moments that would never happen again. She couldn't wait to get out of there, the dismantled and discarded apartment already fading out of importance, but she felt sad, too.

Sometimes, afterward, during the long, hot summer, Leigh found herself walking past the old building, looking up at their former apartment with a combination of curiosity and nostalgia. First it had been empty, the windows like staring eyes, and then it had been occupied — curtains, furniture, figures moving through the lighted rooms — four other girls had moved in to start their lives.

chapter
16

Leigh hardly saw Cady that summer. Paul
was a summer bachelor again, and the brief
period of freedom and total happiness Cady
had waited for all year had finally returned.
They could go out in public together. They
dined in restaurants. He even took her to his
apartment once to let her see it, because she
had always been curious. Now she had a
backdrop for her fantasies of the family she
wanted to tear apart, enter, and take over.
She told Leigh she had looked in the closet
at his wife's clothes, and that she was jealous
of the evening gowns. She said she wanted to
own clothes like that, and go to those parties,
with Paul by her side.

Everything in Paul's apartment was expensive. Cady had no interest in the children's rooms, even Danica's. But she
coveted the lush draperies, the massive
sofas, the designer tables. Replacing Paul's
wife would make her an adult at last. She
looked into the mirror at her fresh young

face and wondered why Paul didn't get rid of his wife. Wasn't she pretty enough, interesting enough?

"He couldn't afford you," Leigh said practically.

"Why not?"

"Once he gives her a settlement and alimony and child support how could he buy all those things again? You need to lower your sights. Tell him you don't care. Or at least, don't stop in front of a furniture store and salivate."

"I deserve whatever she has," Cady said. She was becoming impatient, proprietary. The taste of togetherness she had been given this summer only made her hungrier. She proposed to Paul periodically, and he always put her off. He had many good reasons: his children would be devastated, his wife was helpless, and yes, money would be a problem. Someday, he told her. Eventually, in the future. His children would be older and on their own. His wife would finish going to her psychiatrist and become strong. His expenses would be less.

He did not tell her she was too extravagant, and so Cady paid no attention to Leigh.

Vanessa had begun writing letters to Leigh and Cady and Charlie. The time difference between New York and Los Angeles made it hard for her to call them. Besides, she wrote, she had a lot of free time. It was strange to have every day be like the one before, strange not to travel. She and Bill had met new friends, though, through his work, and they had a social life.

Their friends were all couples, like they were. Vanessa didn't much enjoy hanging around with the women. She found them trivial, insecure. But she had to be careful around the men, because some of the husbands had propositioned her already, even in her condition. She said they were depraved. The men had careers, but the women were rich housewives with time on their hands. She couldn't shop for designer clothes with them because she was only going to get bigger, and she couldn't play tennis with them because her doctor had told her not to. Bill was going to give her lessons after the baby came. Maybe when she was a mother herself she would be more interested in her friends' children. Now all she wanted to do was sleep.

"I miss New York," she wrote. "I love the weather in LA and sitting next to movie stars in restaurants, but now that I'm a solid citizen and not a starry-eyed tourist, everybody here, male and female, looks like a dumb blonde. We have to drive too much. No one walks anywhere. Expensive cars are status symbols. So are houses. I am in dread that I will change and be like all of them."

She sent them a picture of her house, and it looked like a mansion.

"Do you think she's happy?" Cady asked Leigh.

"I guess it's hard to settle down in a new place. Especially for Vanessa."

"It should be easier for her," Cady said. "She has *everything*. I bet Vanessa would know how to get Paul to marry her. Every man is in love with her."

"Not every man," Leigh said.

Her life with David had not changed in any way since she had her own apartment, although he seemed to worry more about her well-being. He didn't like her building, especially the fire escapes crawling up the front, which looked to him like a symbol of poverty and danger. He was concerned that she lived alone, that no one would know if anything happened to her. How could he know, since he didn't want to tread on her territory by checking up on her? They still had separate work lives, and often separate social lives. Every morning he called to see if she was at the office, if she had survived the night, although he would never admit his fear. Leigh found his concern endearing.

She was growing more independent, and he was growing to need her more. But Leigh was sure that her bravery was in part due to the confidence she felt that David was on her side, that he wouldn't desert her. She loved him more than she had in the beginning, with a deeper love, and she sensed he felt the same.

"I have nothing to give you," he said sometimes, sounding young and wistful, and she didn't answer, just kissed him. She didn't like it at all when he said he had nothing to give her; there was a lot he had to give and a lot she needed. There were things a man would never understand, even David.

Fall came. Cady was a prisoner again, albeit one of her own making: the princess in the tower. "You're lucky," she said to Leigh.

"Pick a different man," Leigh said. "You can be lucky too."

"You don't understand."

She supposed she didn't.

The holidays came and went, and although Leigh always liked the holidays she was glad they were over. It was on these major holidays, with her family, that she was fully aware she was single and unable to be with the man she loved. Her family was full of married people with children. It made her feel lonely, lonelier perhaps than if she hadn't met someone yet. She told herself you never knew if these relatives, all dressed up surrounded by their spouses and children, were happy — if there weren't estrangements and resentments and unresolved quarrels lurking on the edges of their lives, hidden by their cheerful holiday smiles.

She wondered if David was happy, or at least content, with Emma Jean and his two boys. When he called her on Christmas Day at her parents' house she didn't ask. Cady would have, would have demanded to hear that he was miserable. Why would she ever want David to be miserable?

Although, Leigh thought, it would be nice if he were a little bit unhappy, at least as much as she was.

In January Vanessa had her baby, a nine-pound boy they named Jack. She sent a photo. He was a beautiful baby, with a full head of dark hair, and looked like her. "Look at this bruiser!" she wrote. "No wonder I was such a cow!"

Leigh and Cady and Charlie chipped in to send her a teddy bear that was bigger than the baby. They had immediately agreed among themselves not to send clothes. None of them had any idea how to choose baby clothes, nor cared. Leigh put the baby picture on her desk in a small frame.

"Yours?" visitors sometimes asked, who didn't know anything about her private life.

"Yes," she sometimes said, just to try out the idea. Someday she would want to have a baby, she thought. Someday it would become very important and she would need to think about changing her life. Someday she would want to buy baby clothes.

David took her to dinner at a quiet out of the way restaurant where he asked for a back banquette, away from the other tables. He took a sip of his drink, put it down. "I'm getting a divorce," he said.

Her heart leaped. She didn't know what to say. She was shocked. She remembered she was supposed to feel culpable, evil, but she didn't, she only felt as if a great burden had lifted from her.

"Don't feel guilty," he said. "My wife and I have been estranged for a long time. We waited to separate until after the holidays, for the kids."

What about me, Leigh thought, but she waited and didn't speak.

"We're officially separated now," he said. "We won't fight, so I'll be free in a few months." He paused, looking at her to guess her reaction. "I can't imagine my life without you," he said. "Would you marry me?"

"Oh, yes!" she said, and completely shocked herself, and him, by bursting into tears.

He took her hand. "Is it that dreadful an idea?" he said with a smile.

"I always cry when I'm happy," Leigh said. But it was more than that. She knew now that she had been holding in for so long, keeping sane, molding her feelings around what was practical and wise instead of following the demons that leaped in her soul, that the restraint had choked her. The truth was, she realized now, that she had always wanted him. Always. And had never dared ask for, or even think of, what she was sure she couldn't get.

She had fooled herself so that she could keep him, not scare him away. She didn't have to fool herself anymore. The tears were a relief, an opening up of her deepest feelings. She felt vulnerable and sad and ecstatic all at once, and then warm and calm and released.

"I would like to be a June bride," she said.

He kissed her, and they sat there for a few moments kissing. Now she knew why he'd wanted the booth. She put her head on his shoulder. "I can't keep living in the company apartment," he said. "Not now that I'd be needing it full-time. So I'm going to go look for an apartment, maybe on Fifth Avenue with a view, and I'd like you to come look for it with me, since you'll be living there too."

"Any time," Leigh said.

"Then you can move in soon," he said. "I want to get you out of that death trap."

"It's not a death trap," Leigh said. "But Fifth Avenue is better."

They sipped their drinks, he lit her cigarette. They rememorized each other's faces, as if they were cameras memorializing this moment for the future. She wondered when separated people bought engagement rings. She supposed when the divorce was final. It would be very bad taste to do otherwise.

She looked at her fingers on the tablecloth. A diamond, she thought; something conventional and traditional.

I'm engaged, she told herself. We are engaged. It felt strange, as if they were two different people — stronger because they were together, more vulnerable because they knew now how much they needed each other.

"What are you thinking?" he asked.

"Can I tell people?"

"Of course. Tell anyone you want."

"My mother will be relieved. I'm twenty-five."

"She won't be so relieved when she finds out I'm forty-three."

"You're a lot younger than my father."

"Thank you for that."

"I cannot conceive of being the slightest bit interested in a man my age."

"When you're sixty," David said, "I'll be seventy-eight."

She could not imagine being sixty. Sixty was ancient. "Promise me we'll still be together," Leigh said. "That's all I care about."

"Of course we will," David said.

chapter
17

Vanessa and Bill came to Leigh and David's wedding in June, held in Weehawken, NJ. Apparently David was Jewish, so they had a minister and a rabbi. The fact that their daughter was marrying a Jew, who was divorced, and who was eighteen years older, did not faze Leigh's parents. Vanessa wondered how hers would feel if she hadn't married Bill, her "perfect match." It was 1966, after all, and there were huge changes going on all the time in the world. She thought, though, that her parents were more conservative than Leigh's.

There was a big, festive reception afterward. Leigh wore a beautiful long white dress with a train. There was a flower girl and a little ring bearer — her cousins' children. Leigh had a narrow diamond band to go with the large diamond engagement ring David had bought her, which had always made her slender hand look fragile. It was a storybook wedding, what Leigh had dreamed of, with everything except doves flying out of the cake. Vanessa and Cady were among the bridesmaids.

"I'm so jealous," Cady said. "Not only did Leigh get her unattainable married man, but she got the successful, rich Jewish husband I always wanted. Paul isn't Jewish and he isn't divorced. Leigh always manages to get everything. She's *perfect*."

Cady drank a lot of champagne and danced as often as possible with David's sixteen-year-old older son, who was four inches taller than she was. She teased that maybe she could get a young one to marry her. He looked a little uncomfortable with that, but he thought she was sexy. He taught her to do the Wooly Bully.

It was a good sign, everyone thought, that David's children were there, and that they were not upset. Leigh was lucky. Or maybe David was a man who managed to get his own way. In that case, he was lucky.

Vanessa had lost all the weight she had gained with baby Jack, and she liked the way she looked in her bridesmaid's dress, which was the only bridesmaid's dress she had ever seen that wasn't ugly. She danced with Bill, and Charlie cut in twice. But as the wedding reception wore on she began to be disappointed that no other men ever cut in or asked her to dance. This was a stodgy group. Couples with each other; single people with single people. But she was nonetheless pleased to be with her husband, who was the best-looking man there. She wondered if she looked different since she'd had the baby: older maybe, or matronly, or faded. The thought concerned her.

Marriage had not really changed her. She hardly ever felt settled, and whenever she did, she felt trapped rather than comfortable. There was nothing wrong with Bill that wasn't annoying or silly in any man, and she supposed marriage meant that you got used to being with someone all the time and ignored the bad parts. He was kind to her, he did not get angry, he loved her, and he loved their child. Marriage was compromise. If you wanted peace you would have to forego the fire. Some people she knew had neither.

The best thing about married life was her child. Vanessa was besotted with him. All of her time with him was pleasure, and the boring part was taken care of by their au pair. Jack had a sweet disposition, he was adorable to look at, and he was smart. Vanessa had never realized she could fall in love with any child, even her own, and it came as a pleasant surprise. The truth was she would rather be with Jack than with anyone else. She could play baby games with him for hours, thrilled when he learned something new. She had expected to be bored and she wasn't, although she was realistic enough to know that someone who wasn't his mother might be. She remembered well that before she'd had him, she'd thought her friends' children were totally uninteresting. Actually, she still did. But of course, Jack was better.

Because Vanessa had often mentioned that she missed New York, Bill had given her a present: they were going to New York for the weekend, and then because he had to go back to work he was going to leave her there by herself for three days. He'd gotten tickets for her to two big hits she'd never seen, Barbra Streisand in *Funny Girl* and Carol Channing in *Hello Dolly.* He knew that she wanted to get away from home for a while.

He was an understanding husband. She should be counting her blessings. She couldn't help it if she wasn't capable of loving him more than she already did. She supposed that was her fatal flaw. She would never feel true, deep, passionate, transporting, leap-outside-of-yourself love.

Maybe there wasn't any such thing and everybody lied about how they felt.

Was Cady's passion simply possessiveness, loneliness, and the need to win? Was Leigh's the search for a father figure?

She would never know. All Vanessa was certain of was that she had married for life. What good was it looking for something better than what you had, when you weren't capable of appreciating it anyway? Bill was completely sure of her because he was honorable and trusting. He didn't know that she couldn't really trust herself.

Not that she'd done anything. But how did she know that she wouldn't? She could never be as uncomplicated as he was. If she hadn't been pregnant she would never have married him. And that was that.

When the wedding reception was over, Vanessa and Bill went to New York to their favorite hotel, the St. Regis. Leigh and David were stopping at their Fifth Avenue apartment, and were going to Europe the next day for their honeymoon. Cady had left the reception early, hoping to meet Paul in New York, even though he had made other plans for himself since he had refused to go to the wedding. She could never stay anywhere all evening; she was like a disoriented bird. She'd hired a car and driver to take her back to the city so she wouldn't have to wait for someone to give her a lift. She had made Paul pay for it.

In their luxurious hotel room Vanessa and Bill made love because there was something of a honeymoon feeling about the strangeness of being there. The next day they had brunch and went to the Museum of Modern Art. He had a short list of restaurants where they would have dinner, and they went to one of them.

"Will you feel strange having dinner alone on Wednesday?" he asked. "The whole evening with nothing to do. You should call one of your girlfriends."

What girlfriends? she thought, but only smiled and said, "I'll be fine."

"I guess you'll do a lot of shopping during the day," he said.

"And walking. I want to walk around. Can't do that in LA, you get arrested."

"I'll probably just play with Jack and watch television," Bill said.

"I'll miss him," Vanessa said.

"I'll keep him company."

"You should call *your* friends."

"Oh, you'll be back before I know it."

Three days by myself, Vanessa thought. What a treat.

When Bill had gone to the airport Vanessa called two of the men she had dated when she was single — old boyfriends — one still single and one still married, both still friends of hers. She didn't intend to go to bed with them, she just wanted to see them, to see if they still found her attractive. Thinking of seeing them again made her feel warm and excited, breathless, for no reason, as if she were going on a date.

She made plans to have lunch with Matthew that very day — a lucky cancellation, he said, although she wondered — and a drink with Tom the next day before *Hello Dolly*. Matthew was the single one, and she met him at a restaurant near his office. They kissed hello. After a while he took her hand, and she felt the pressure of his knee under the table.

"What are you doing this afternoon?" he asked.

"Another lucky cancellation?" she said.

"I could clear my calendar for you."

That was all she needed, really, to know he still wanted her, that she was still beautiful. "We're friends now," she said. "I'm a newlywed."

"I envy him," Matthew said.

"Thank you."

Tom, the married one, took her for a drink at the bar in Grand Central, near his commuter train and not far from the theater district. "I don't have to take my train," he whispered, his breath warm in her ear.

"I have to go to the theater," she said. "Maybe another time."

"I'll be waiting," he said. That was a lie, but she liked hearing it. He wasn't waiting for her, but she knew he would be available for a long time.

That left Wednesday for whatever life brought her.

She walked around Manhattan all day, perfectly content, as she had the two previous days, shopping and window-shopping. She bought a little suit and hat for Jack and some makeup for herself, and at the end of the day, pleasantly tired, she went into the bar at her hotel to have a glass of wine. Perhaps she would ask the concierge to make a reservation for her for dinner in the neighborhood, or maybe she would eat at the hotel. She had never minded being alone for a meal, and this was a lot better than her old days at the local coffee shop, although she still had a Gucci bag.

She put her bag on the polished bar by her elbow, the way she had when she was a young stewardess at a cheap counter.

There was a man sitting next to her, and accidentally it brushed his elbow.

"Oh, I'm sorry," Vanessa said, and smiled.

He turned around to see who had spoken, and his eyes widened with appreciation. He was about forty, with thick gray hair, and his eyes were the color of grass. No wedding ring, but that didn't mean anything.

"No harm done," he said, and smiled back. He had an English accent, and was wearing a well-cut suit, probably made for him in London, she thought. She felt her smile go through her whole body.

"You're British," she said.

"I am."

"I'm Vanessa."

"My name is Neville."

"Hello."

"Are you waiting for someone, Vanessa?"

"No. I'm alone; a temporary tourist in the city. And you?"

"A temporary businessman in the city. I'm staying at this hotel."

"So am I."

"It's nice, isn't it? A bit British."

"Yes, it's lovely. I live in California. This is not one bit Californian."

"I think I'm rather glad about that. I like the familiar."

"Surely not in everything?"

"No, not in everything."

And so it went, the way it had hundreds of times before, the way it had on all those plane flights with the eager male passengers: the businessmen who wanted a dinner companion or a lay or just some talk; the ones who were afraid to fly, and thus had imbibed too many drinks, and the ones who were afraid of boredom or loneliness and thus had done the same; the ones who were happy to be away from their wives; the single ones, who thought a glamorous stewardess would be a catch to show off to their friends at home; the shy ones and the pushy ones, the friendly, the familiar, and the jerks.

Neville, she decided, was charming, urbane, and liked her. He was divorced, and had three children at home in London, who lived with his ex-wife. If he had replaced the wife with a serious girlfriend it was not hampering his flirtation here, now, with her.

She told him she had a husband and a young child. She did not say it was an infant. That would make her seem unfeeling — to have deserted a baby for her own pleasure here in the city. She did not say that she had been married for less than a year. He didn't press for details or interrogate her. He was, after all, just making conversation at best, at worst a pickup. But these things remained on her mind the whole time she was bonding with him, while thinking how attractive his green eyes were, and his accent was, and wondering what kind of a woman she was.

What kind of a woman was she, anyway?

Insecure, needing reassurance, wanting excitement. Not wanting to give anything up. Was this a bad woman? She hadn't even done anything yet.

After they had talked for two hours he invited her to go to dinner. She accepted because she was hungry, and he was sexy, and she had nothing else to do. It was only dinner, not infidelity.

They sat next to each other in a banquette in an Italian restaurant. Vanessa was glad that she was adept at acting more knowledgeable than she was, because Neville was interested in politics and current events, and seemed to think she knew a great deal more about England than she did. *I was on the New York–Los Angeles route,* she thought, annoyed. *Not transatlantic.* He was one of the brightest men she had met.

But he didn't seem to mind that she couldn't keep up with him, and she was a good listener. Besides, he was blinded by her looks. They exchanged addresses and telephone numbers. They had brandy with their coffee, and then they walked through the streets, which were now quiet, to their hotel.

He rode with her to her floor. "I want to see you get home safely," he said.

At her door he kissed her good-night. It turned into five minutes of kissing, and then he said in that thick flannel voice that was choked by sexual feeling, which Vanessa knew well, "Won't you invite me in?"

She wanted to. A year ago she wouldn't even have waited this long. But she thought of Bill and Jack and felt chilled. Jack wouldn't care, he was six months old, but Bill would be destroyed. They would never know, of course. But she would know, and then what kind of woman would she be?

She wanted to, though. She was sure Neville would be a very good lover, and she was wet. She pictured him in her room, and in her fantasy they didn't even get as far as the bed, they were undressing and then they were on the floor.

"It's late," she whispered. "I have an early plane to Los Angeles tomorrow."

"It's really no?"

"We'll keep in touch. We'll both be in New York again."

She kissed him a last time, good-bye. She felt a terrible nostalgia. It would be so easy, just say she'd changed her mind. Or say nothing, simply open the door and pull him in. He would understand. He had been ready for her the entire time they had been kissing.

I want you so much, she thought.

"Good-night," she whispered, and went into her room, alone.

She sat on the edge of her bed for a long time until the feeling of yearning went away. Why did she want to have sex with Neville more than she wanted it with Bill? There were tears leaking out of her eyes as if she had lost someone she loved.

Any of this was playing with fire. She had a life, after all. She took his address and phone number out of her purse and tried to tear it up. But she couldn't. She only made a ragged little tear, which she smoothed back into place with her nail. She folded the piece of paper until it was tiny and put it into the flap inside the cover of her address book.

She would never call him but she needed to know it was there.

PART
TWO

chapter

18

Five years had passed since Leigh's wedding. The decade that was to be known as the "Me Decade" had begun and people wanted it all. They still went to discotheques, but the specter of downward mobility was beginning to be seen in their lives. They wanted it all, but perhaps they would not get it. Feminism was rearing its head, confusing Vanessa, annoying Cady, delighting Leigh. There were escalating protests against the military incursions in Laos and Vietnam. Nixon was president; also known as "Tricky Dick," *Time* magazine's Man of the Year. The girls were thirty and thirty-one.

Were they still girls? The feminists said they were women. The culture said thirty was old, or at least that was what they had been told a moment ago in the sixties, but although they had achieved this dreaded milestone they didn't feel old at all. They hardly felt like women, although Leigh and David had a two-year-old daughter now,

Jennie, and Vanessa and Bill had had a second child, a three-year-old daughter named Liberty.

Leigh was a full-fledged agent at the agency, and a good one. She and David had a successful combination of career and home life, they had a lot of money, their large Fifth Avenue apartment was elegant but comfortable, and they were still best friends and in love. Cady admired them and raved about them to anyone who would listen, but also she was jealous.

Jealousy was for inferior people, and she didn't even want to admit to herself that she harbored such resentment. But Leigh had someone she loved to come home to every night, for the whole night, to talk to for as long as she wanted, and could even afford the luxury of silence. She had moments to waste. David wasn't going anywhere. Leigh made a great deal more money than Cady did, and never had to demean herself by asking her mother to come to her rescue and pay her clothing bills. Leigh had a child, not that Cady wanted children, but Leigh had, and so she had gotten what she wanted again. If anyone was an example of someone who Had It All, it was Leigh. David's grown sons even came for dinner frequently, and liked the baby girl who was their sister.

Leigh was Cady's best friend, and also a reproach. Paul was still married, still paying Cady's rent on the side. His wife had finally finished therapy, but now his son was at a therapist, having flunked out of college in his freshman year, with no ambition and no interests. The doctor bills would go on for years it seemed, and the divorce was far away, although Paul was finally assuring her it would happen in two years, maybe three, as soon as he got his life together. This was a proposal of sorts, could even be considered an engagement. Two or three years at least were a time-table.

In order to cement Paul's promise, to make it more real, to feed her optimism, Cady was collecting things for her hope chest. Piece by piece she bought silverware and had it monogrammed. The forks with the long English tines and heavy handles; the knives that looked like weapons; the spoons for soup, for dessert, for coffee. Luckily she and Paul had the same initials, so no one knew this was for when they were married. She kept the silver in its tarnish-proof-lined box and never used it.

Cady Fineman/Cady Fisher. It was her tangible investment in her future. Paul had eventually helped with her project, and this gave Cady a great deal more hope that their marriage would someday be an actuality. Even her mother believed it. Paul had gone halves with her mother on a full place setting last Christmas. Neither Cady nor her mother told her father, because he wouldn't understand.

Cady's mother had also helped her buy two sets of monogrammed sheets for a king sized bed, although the one she slept in now was a double. The sheets were folded in their original box, in her closet next to the silver. Cady Fisher/Cady Fineman. Someday. . . .

It had only been a matter of time before Cady told all her friends about her relationship with Paul. She told the other teachers, and even people she had just met. She volunteered the information to near strangers. Her complicated affair was her credentials. Someone glamorous wanted her. Her life was dramatic, larger than life. Seven years was a long time for a secret affair with a married man. It had become part of the colorful history of her private school, but it was old news by now. Cady thrived on the attention her reputation brought her. Paul wasn't aware, of course, that everyone at Dunnewood knew about him. It was Cady's world, in which she was the queen.

Who could it hurt? Danica had graduated from college and was working at *The Village Voice*, living in Greenwich Village with a bass player; she was a grown-up who probably wouldn't be damaged by rumors. Paul's wife didn't know. And if his son had heard any of this, which perhaps was why he had turned so torpid, he had his therapist to fix him.

Today Cady and Leigh were seeing Vanessa. She had come to New York again, on one of her quick city mini-vacations. She had been doing this for years now, the romantic weekend with her husband to go to the theater and try new restaurants, and then the few days alone to shop. She always called the girls to get together to catch up. They had decided to meet at the bar at the St. Regis, where she was staying as usual. They were pleased that they seemed like three sophisticated New York women having a cocktail together.

Of course Vanessa and Leigh had brought baby pictures, which somewhat dispelled the worldly image. But they were all fashionably dressed, and they looked successful; they belonged.

"Guess who's coming," Vanessa said.

They looked up and were happy to see Charlie.

Getting older had only been to his advantage. He no longer looked like a gangly kid. He was a businessman now, at a company that published men's magazines, and apparently doing well. Better, at least, than he would have had he become a professor. There was not an elbow patch in sight.

He sat in their circle and insisted on paying for the next round. All three of them had kept up with him. He had subtly moved from house mascot to attractive extra man. Cady sometimes had lunch with him. Leigh and David invited him to go out with them, or had him to one of their small dinner parties, which did not often include Cady because they were for business, although an extra man was always welcome.

It annoyed Cady that Leigh didn't invite her to many of these dinner parties. It made her feel that she wasn't good enough, that Leigh, or maybe it was David, didn't respect her. She wasn't important. She was just a schoolteacher. Knowing that Charlie wasn't invited to some of their business dinner parties either didn't make her feel any better. After all, he wasn't supposed to be Leigh's best friend. And he went to more than she did. She knew it was because he was a man, but it hurt anyway.

"To Vanessa," Charlie said, looking into her eyes, holding up his glass of wine. "Welcome back to our city." Whenever they saw him it was clear that he had never gotten over her. They felt sorry for him.

"To my friends," Vanessa said.

"Can I reserve you for a dinner while you're here?" he asked.

"But I'm here now," Vanessa said. She smiled and patted his hand.

"Does that mean no?"

"We'll see."

"She always says, 'We'll see,' doesn't she?" Charlie said. "Ever since I've known her. I don't mind being last minute. Just call me."

"I will," Vanessa said.

"How is California?" Leigh asked.

"A healthy place to bring up kids, but I'm as bored as ever."

"You'd be bored here," Cady said.

"Oh no I wouldn't."

"Life takes over wherever you are," Cady said.

"Not the way my life has been taken over. I'm in a car all the time. I drive to my exercise class, get out and move around, then back in the car again. It seems unnatural somehow."

"At least you go to an exercise class," Cady said. Leigh played tennis with David, but she did nothing.

"I looked up Matthew the other day," Vanessa said. "You remember Matthew? I used to go out with him? Still not married, but he got fat."

"I'll bet he gets women anyway," Leigh said.

"Of course. It's unfair."

"I can't believe you still look up your old boyfriends," Charlie said.

"I'm curious. And loyal."

"She's loyal," Charlie said wistfully.

"You should be glad," Vanessa said. "I'm loyal to you too."

"I like to think I'm more than one of your boyfriends."

"It doesn't matter."

"Our lives were bad timing," Charlie said. "Just a case of bad timing."

"Oh buy me another drink, Charlie, please," Vanessa said. "You're much too attractive to be so lugubrious. It doesn't become you."

They all laughed. Vanessa and Charlie looked good together, Cady thought. Charlie was perfect too, in his own way. It was too bad that they all still saw him as they had in the past, but even if they didn't, they had moved on to their own lives now. She thought about how much they all enjoyed being with him, how he fit in, how comfortable he made them feel. Maybe he was right; it was bad timing that none of them had been interested in him in any other way. Except poor Susan.

Or maybe he had picked the wrong group of women, whose needs he could never have filled. She wondered if that had been accidental.

It was strange about friends. As well as you thought you knew and understood them, there were things you would never know.

chapter
19

Vanessa considered herself faithful. She would not have believed that she could be faithful for six years. Looking up old boyfriends and flirting, the occasional kiss, or perhaps many kisses, did not count. She knew that Liberty was Bill's child, and that he had no reason to be jealous or doubt her fidelity. She had the best of both worlds, didn't she? But a kind of ongoing vague depression followed her everywhere, even when she was supposedly happy. Sometimes her eyes filled with tears and she didn't know why. She was quite aware that it was possible to be lonely with someone who loved you. The only things that comforted her and made her forget were her children.

She spent too much time in front of the mirror, looking for something she would want to eradicate the moment it appeared. All her friends did the same. They had the latest names of where to go, what to do, to remain young and beautiful as long as possible. She was only thirty-one, but she knew it was only a matter of time before she would be undergoing constant repair.

That was what spoiled Hollywood wives did. If it wasn't their idea in the first place, their husbands made them insecure; if not their husbands, their friends, with warnings; if not their friends, the culture. You just had to look around. Anyone, no matter how loving, could be replaced.

Sometimes Vanessa tried to analyze her feelings of not being worth much. It had more to do with something inside her than simply with beauty. Everything had been so easy for her that she'd never thought about it before now. Men had always wanted her. But their attraction had little to do with who she was. She wasn't sure who she was, so how could a stranger know? She even had her husband fooled — he knew none of her secrets.

If she didn't love her husband enough she more than made up for it with her kids. She adored both her children. She had not thought she could love any child as much as she did Jack, but the moment she held tiny Liberty in her arms she knew there was plenty of room in her heart to be obsessed with two.

Liberty, as Jack had been, was an easy

baby: responsive, beautiful, and cheerful. Sometimes Vanessa thought she'd had such good fortune with these two children that she wanted ten more. Then she thought that she'd been so lucky it would be tempting the fates to have even one more. Bill didn't much care either way. The children had probably inherited their equanimity from him. Bill was basically a happy man.

She didn't want to do anything to make him unhappy. He was too good.

But when she was alone in New York it was as if a different persona had taken hold of her. She felt free and searching. She missed a piece of herself and needed to find it. Thus looking up the old boyfriends. Thus the flirting, the pickups, the necking that was as much torment as pleasure. It had been an act of will to remain as faithful as she had.

When she mentioned her New York sexual activities to Leigh and Cady she was lighthearted about it, as if it was normal and didn't matter. If they disapproved they never showed it. This was a time of open marriages, of affairs, of one-night stands that didn't change anything. It was a far different time than the one their parents had lived in, than they had grown up in.

You made up your own rules.

Still, her morality had been forged in the fifties. If you were a woman, faithlessness would hurt you. In some way you would be punished. Nothing was ever so simple as it seemed.

So now it was her last night in New York on this trip, and she had chosen to be alone for dinner. She was sitting at the bar in her hotel, sipping a glass of wine; looking at the people, idly wondering where she might go. She usually left her last night for herself so she could think, try to sort things out. Sometimes this ended up with her having an adventure. She wasn't sure if she planned the adventure or not; she preferred to think not. Already, knowing she was going back to California, Vanessa felt the tension building up in her, the feeling of going back to where she was trapped. She missed her kids, but she would see them tomorrow. Tonight she was single again.

She looked across the room and then saw someone familiar. It was Neville, from years ago, the Englishman. She recognized him in a moment; he didn't look that different. She had never forgotten him, as she had never forgotten any of the men she had said no to. She might as well have said yes for all the good it did her. Every one of them remained in her memory — a symbol of ego and self-restraint and regret.

He was walking with a tall, lovely looking blonde, his arm possessively (or was it protectively) around her shoulders, his thumb absently stroking her bare shoulder. Vanessa suddenly felt so jealous it almost choked her.

You could have had him, she told herself. And now you can't.

As they crossed the room to a table he glanced at her, and a flicker of recognition crossed his face. Then he looked blank again. This hurt more than anything. Neville had no interest in her at all. Nothing.

Maybe that's his new wife, she thought. It's been years and years. Everybody has a life. But it hurt anyway. She had remembered that night. She wondered if he remembered too, and felt guilty now that he was with someone important. No, men didn't care. Men tried to get laid, that was what they did.

When Neville and the blonde sat down Vanessa was glad it was in a far corner of the bar. She didn't want to look at him, nor have him see her still alone, not joined by anyone unless it was a pickup. After a while she felt so uncomfortable that she charged her drink and left.

She went to an "in" Italian restaurant where they knew her and she didn't need a reservation. It was not the same one where she had gone with him. She didn't want him walking in here and seeing her still by herself. She ordered another glass of wine and looked at the menu. She wasn't hungry. She looked in her compact to see if she needed lipstick, and wondered if she looked as inadequate as she felt.

Her favorite waiter, dark-haired little Dominick, came over, smiling and jolly. "The gentleman over there wants to know if you are alone."

She looked at a nearby table where a man was having a glass of wine by himself. The man looked like a somewhat older Neville: handsome, foreign. If not English perhaps Italian.

"Who is he?" she asked.

"Mr. Carlyle. Comes here a lot. Very wealthy; a very nice man. He says if you are alone he would like to send you a drink."

"I am having a drink."

"Mr. Carlyle would like to pay for it."

"In that case I should have ordered a bottle."

"You are not a lady who could drink a whole bottle by yourself," Dominick said with a grin.

"That's true. I suppose he would like to come over here and share one with me."

The man looked at her and smiled and raised his glass.

"He is a very nice man," Dominick said again. He had never seen her with her husband. This restaurant was one of those she went to when she was pretending to be free.

Vanessa lifted her glass to him in return. "He can treat me to this if he wants," she said.

A little while later Mr. Carlyle came over. "I hope you don't mind," he said. "Would you be willing to have dinner with me?"

Vanessa didn't answer, just looked at him, wondering what she thought about this.

He took out his business card and handed it to her. "I'm Charlie Carlyle and I'm quite harmless."

"My best friend is named Charlie."

"Then we know each other already."

She looked at the card. It had expensive raised lettering, small and dignified, a Wall Street address. His real name was Charles.

Up close he was just as good-looking as Neville, and although he wasn't English, he had a kind of prep-school accent that she found pleasant. "I'm Vanessa," she said.

"Someone as beautiful as you should never have dinner alone," he said.

Could he think of anything more banal? But it was only dinner, after all. He could entertain her. "I'm not alone anymore, am I?" she said with a gracious smile, and gestured daintily to the other chair.

The waiter rushed over with his drink.

Charlie Carlyle was interesting, actually, and well informed. As Neville had, he assumed she was as bright as he was, and he was wrong. But Vanessa had never had difficulty making conversation, and as always he was so intent on making a good impression on her that he wouldn't have noticed if she were an idiot.

He had an ex-wife who lived in Vermont in a commune, he said, and two children whose names she had changed a few years ago to Sunshine and Free. Vanessa decided not to tell him her daughter's name was Liberty. Charlie Carlyle seemed a victim of the change in society; a little lost, and lonely. He still ate in fashionable restaurants and carried business cards, and wore a well-cut suit and a tie. She wondered if his wife had run off and broken his heart, and if she were a lot younger than he was and had married him ten years ago for all the reasons she didn't want him now.

She liked his subtle moneyed accent and his soft voice. His eyes were blue, not green like Neville's, but they were sexy.

She picked at her bass and waited while Charlie Carlyle tried to seduce her with charm and kindness. There were worse ways to be seduced. They did have a bottle of wine, and as she drank it her inhibitions melted away. She wasn't lonely or unhappy anymore. She felt beautiful, as he told her again she was. She wondered if her own Charlie, Charlie Rackley, who never seemed to find the right woman, was going to end up in middle age as a man who ate alone in trendy restaurants, trying to pick up women for company. She couldn't imagine her own diffident Charlie picking up anybody, although they had met that way. That was different though, it had been a party.

She wondered if her good-natured Bill would end up eating alone in restaurants if she left him.

She concentrated on this man opposite her. He made her feel young, and she liked that.

After dinner he took her to a bar where they sat at a tiny table very close to one another and listened to a woman in an evening gown singing old songs from the forties and fifties. He said he never went to discos, that he couldn't dance, but that if she wanted to go to one he would take her. Vanessa laughed and put her head on his shoulder. Now she could see why Leigh liked an older man; they had great charm when they were charming. She could see that Charlie Carlyle was well built, and he didn't look old. She might have married a man like him if she hadn't been forced to marry Bill, and she never would have left him to become a hippie.

He put his arm around her and she let him kiss her. She ordinarily would not have been so reckless in public, but it was dark and she didn't see anyone she knew. They explored each other's lips and tongues until she felt the yearning streak down into her groin, and then he said in that changed voice she knew so well, "Let's go somewhere."

Again. She didn't want to do this, and she did; already she was so aroused, she was thinking how easy it would be to go to his apartment or to her hotel. Her plane was not until noon, and he had to go to work early, she was sure. Again. Would she go on like this forever, teasing man after man and herself, through some outmoded notion of morality? Sometimes Vanessa felt like the last holdout. She would probably stop being depressed if she just had a nice, liberating affair.

"Do you want me to take you home?" he asked, and his tone filled in the rest.

Why this man and none of the others? She didn't know. But she was tired of saying good-bye, of losing them, of never being able to forget them. She wanted Charlie Carlyle to hold her, to feel the length of his body against hers, not be cramped at a little table like teenagers. She wanted his arms around her. She wanted him to rub his thumb against her bare shoulder as if she belonged to him. . . .

"Home?" she said.

"To your hotel? Or to my apartment? I live down the street."

She nodded yes.

She paid little attention to his apartment, which was fairly dark and had only a few lamps on as if he had not planned to bring anyone back. In his shadowy bedroom they made love as if in a cave. She was the old Vanessa — no, the young Vanessa, with the future before her. She could have any man in the world, and she might just have all of them. Their time together was everything she had hoped.

She left him at four in the morning because it would have been too complicated to stay all night. He insisted she call him the next time she was coming to New York, because he knew she lived with her husband and he couldn't call her. He said he was afraid she wouldn't call him, and made her promise she would. He stood kissing her good-bye at his front door, dressed in a black bathrobe, looking happy. Vanessa didn't know if she would call him or not. She didn't have to decide right now anyway.

When she got back to Beverly Hills she went into the little office she'd made at the end of her large kitchen. It consisted of a board standing on two small filing cabinets, a phone, and her schedules for their social life and the children's appointments. All the wives she knew had such home offices, to show that what they did at home was serious work.

Bill was still at his office and the children were napping. Vanessa took Charles Carlyle's business card from her purse and brought out from her filing cabinet the plastic-paged business card book she'd bought last year to arrange her clutter. There was Neville's, creased from having been folded, and subsequent ones, pristine. All the cards were from men she had met. She fitted Charles Carlyle's card neatly into an empty slot. It seemed to glow, because he was her first yes.

She still didn't really know why he had been the first one. He was desirable, but no better, no different, than many of the others, to whom she had said no. Maybe it was the times.

Vanessa put the book back into the bottom of the drawer and locked the filing cabinet with her key. She didn't feel depressed anymore, but rather, peaceful and validated. She didn't feel guilty, even though she had always thought she would. She realized there was no reason to feel guilty. No one would ever know.

chapter
20

The three years that Paul had promised would be his cut-off time to get divorced had come and gone, and he was still married. Cady felt impatient and resentful. She had been with him for a decade. She knew people who had not been married that long.

When Paul protested that Danny's therapist had said they should not break up the family at this time, Cady seethed. Danny was a grown-up. When Danica decided to marry her live-in bass player and Paul said that a divorce would cast a shadow over her wedding, Cady was understanding, but angry nonetheless. They were adults too. Did adults remain children forever, tormented by their parents' human failings? If her own parents ever got a divorce she was sure she wouldn't care.

She began to think that Paul's children were too dependent on him, and that it was his fault. He had put his whole life, and hers, on hold for them. But Cady kept her resentment to herself. She didn't want Paul to think she would not be a loving stepmother to his rotten kids.

Paul was like the old joke: the doddering ancient man who tells his girlfriend he can't get a divorce because the grandchildren aren't dead yet. Was this to be her future? Strung along, lied to? Sometimes when she was particularly angry she thought she should break up with him, but then she wondered where she would go and what she would do. She was impaled on her life. She wasn't sure she knew how to start all over again.

And besides, she was in love with him.

Now her retelling of the Paul and Cady romance made it seem more like a tragedy than a luminous love story. They were becoming like an old married couple. More often lately when Paul came to see her on his nightly walk, he fell asleep on the sofa and snored until it was time for him to go home. Sometimes he just watched television. She wouldn't have minded if they had their own apartment, but this made her feel cheated of the precious little time they had together.

"This is normal life," he said when she protested. "This is what marriage is. This is what our life would be."

"Prove it," Cady said.

He saw that she was restless and unhappy and so he insisted she go to cooking school so that when they were married she would be able to cook and to entertain. He said his wife was a gourmet cook. So Cady, who had never cooked a thing in her life, went to the Cordon Bleu New York, where she burned pots and cut her fingers and finally succeeded in making a credible chocolate soufflé and a crème brûlée. She made them for him a few times. But they were hardly a meal, and she hated the precise preparation it took as much as the cleaning up. This gourmet cooking was only another sop from him of course, a gesture toward the future. When Paul left to go to his family she gave the remainders to her doorman, and felt well rid of them.

What good had it done his wife to be a good cook? His wife was virtually a dead issue now, the forgotten woman. His wife was fifty. He said he hadn't touched her in years. So Cady gave up any pretense of cooking, and Paul didn't mention it again except as a sort of joke. He had never asked her to make him a meal to show off. Now Cady knew his sending her to the Cordon Bleu New York had just been another delaying tactic. She didn't give away the expensive pots and utensils however, because when they got married — *if* they got married — they would hire a cook.

She wished she had the courage to date and find another boyfriend. She wondered how she could ever be as free a spirit as Vanessa was.

The big news at the Dunnewood School in the spring semester was the hiring of the new social studies teacher. It was an eligible man, which was a rarity at the school. His name was Steven Irving, and he was only a year or two older than Cady, not that this was so young anymore, and he had recently gotten divorced. He had no children, which made him seem totally free. He had a lean and hungry look, and was quite handsome in a vulpine sort of way; with long hair, for a teacher, and piercing eyes. He had a slight limp as a result of a teenaged automobile accident. The schoolgirls found all these things, including the limp, seductive, and the hormone level at the school leaped up a hundred percent. Some of the more endowed students stopped wearing bras, hoping he would notice.

The person he seemed to notice was Cady.

At the teachers' lunchroom he often sat

with her. After a few communal lunches he asked her if she would like to have lunch with him at a restaurant, somewhere away from the school, where they could have some privacy to talk about themselves. Cady agreed, feeling flattered. They went to the local upscale coffee shop because there wasn't that much time before his class.

"I've just gotten divorced," Steven said. "And you, have you been married?"

She was surprised he hadn't heard. She told him the Paul Fisher story in great detail, trying to make it sound sophisticated and romantic. It must be old gossip indeed, Cady thought, if no one told him about us. But instead of being impressed he seemed surprised and upset.

"Ten years!" he said. "How could you throw away your life like that?"

"I didn't throw it away."

"It's your whole adult life! You were a child when you met him."

"I was," Cady agreed.

"You need to be rescued," Steven said, narrowing his eyes.

"And how do you intend to do that?" Cady asked, smiling.

"I'll think of a way. Are you allowed out?"

"I can do anything I want."

"Does he take you to the movies?"

"In the summertime."

"And in the wintertime?"

"No."

Steven sighed. "I would go into withdrawal if I couldn't go to the movies."

"I love them too," Cady said.

"You need to go for a long, romantic walk somewhere not in your neighborhood. You need to hold hands in public."

"Ha," Cady said.

"Will you go to a movie with me?"

She thought for a moment. What would she tell Paul? That she was going to a movie with a colleague. He had told her to have a life and he had no right to protest, even if the colleague was a male. If Paul got jealous . . . good. Maybe then he might get a divorce at last.

"All right," Cady said.

"Have you seen *Cries and Whispers*?"

"No, but I'd like to."

"Then what about tomorrow night? It's Friday, we can stay up late."

Suddenly putting an actual night on it scared her. Tomorrow night. . . . She would have to tell Paul not to come over. And Saturday night, he had told her several times, he had plans with his wife. Could she not see him for two nights? She had never done this. She might miss him terribly, like a homesick child. Should she suggest Saturday night to Steven instead of Friday? Would that give their plans too much importance?

"No? Yes?" he asked.

She sighed. "Is this a date?"

"Sure sounds like it."

"Teachers at Dunnewood aren't supposed to date each other," she said.

"Where did you hear that nonsense? Teachers at Dunnewood can even marry each other."

"No chance of that in this case," Cady said.

"Don't be so sure."

She looked at him. He seemed perfectly serious.

"Oh?"

"I might have to marry you just to pry you away from him," Steven said. "We're both single. He's not. Who has the better chance?"

"You're a big flirt," she said.

"We'll see."

He took her hand. No one but Paul had held her hand in years. It felt strange. His hand felt cool and solid and comforting and good.

"Pick me up at seven," she said, and gave him her address.

When Paul called, Cady told him she was going to the movies with another teacher. "Who?" he asked, since he knew the names of all of them. She told him everything about school on his visits, whether he was interested or not.

"Steven Irving," she said, and waited for him to protest.

"That's good," Paul said. "You should have friends." Suddenly she was not nervous anymore but only annoyed that he wasn't jealous.

"He's a recent bachelor and he's not gay," she reminded him with a little giggle.

"I don't see you with a penniless schoolteacher," Paul said.

As if you give me so much, Cady thought, but did not say it.

"Isn't he the cripple?" Paul said. Now he was really being nasty.

"He's *not* crippled. He has a little limp. You can't even notice it."

"Should I be jealous?"

At last. "No," Cady said.

"Saturday night you know my wife and I have that black-tie dinner," Paul said. "So I won't be over. But maybe I can arrange to come over Sunday afternoon."

"I remember about the dinner," she said sulkily.

It served him right. If he was going to continue escorting his wife — who he said meant nothing to him — to parties where they appeared to be together, then she could have a date to go to the movies with an eligible man, no matter how much Paul put him down. But was she sure she could bear not to see Paul for two nights? And why didn't he care more? Maybe they were getting estranged and he needed a shock. She intended to supply him with one. Cady hated that he had such a capacity to hurt her, over the smallest thing. Sometimes she hated love too.

Steven took her to see *Cries and Whispers*, where he bought a giant bag of popcorn, which they shared. Again he held her hand, which again she found very comforting, and this time even sexy. She didn't feel guilty about that, only a little pleased, as if she had been given a secret present. The movie was about a woman dying, and was very symbolic and esoteric. Cady thought about her own life. Her arrangement with Paul had seemed unconventional and glamorous at first, but now it seemed as if she had turned into a dreary kept woman with little future, as conventional as a character in a bad novel.

After the movie Steven took her to a tavern he liked, where they had beer. It made her feel young again, drinking beer in a tavern, like her old college days. They talked about their childhoods and what it had been like when they first came to live in New York — he was from New Haven, Connecticut — and Cady told him how perfect Leigh and Vanessa were, and finally even told him about Susan. She was feeling friendly and close to him.

"I blamed myself about Susan," she said.

"You shouldn't. People who commit suicide are on their way for a long time."

"But she blamed us."

"So?"

"I like that you make everything so simple."

"I was in therapy for five years," he said. "Every time someone did something that upset me I asked myself why, I asked the therapist why, and endlessly we figured out what their problems were, their motivations, their craziness. Then I had an epiphany. It doesn't matter why someone does something destructive. They're bad, that's all. Things happen. It is not for us to understand or forgive, just to survive, to forget them and move on. They're negative energy.

"Susan was neurotic and lost. That was her business. It was not your job to save her. Paul is selfish. You can't change that. It is not your job to get blood from a stone. You are a nice girl who is deluded. You deserve a better life, with someone who can be there for you all the time. When you finally understand that you will move on."

"Maybe you'll help me," Cady said.

"I'll be glad to help you."

He smiled at her. How nice he is, Cady thought. I want him on my side. I want him to be my friend. I want him in my life.

When he took her to her door Steven held her for a little while in a gentle hug. His body felt young and taut. He was younger now than Paul had been when she first met him, when she thought he was the sun and the moon. She compared Steven's body to Paul's, which had grown stockier with age, and thought about all the things she was missing. She wondered what it would be like to go to bed with Steven. Then he kissed her on each cheek in the European way, which he probably considered nonthreatening and which Cady found disappointing.

"Thank you," she said. "It was fun."

"We'll do it again."

Alone in her bed she thought about

Steven. He seemed like a genuinely good person, someone who wanted other people to be happy. How many people were there like that in the world? She began to resent Paul more than ever, out with his wife tomorrow night, pretending to everyone that Cady didn't exist. Paul definitely had negative energy.

As she drifted off Cady thought about Steven, as she had thought about boys she liked when she was sixteen, as she had relived her first teenaged kiss, and she fell asleep smiling.

On Saturday night when she was alone she wished Steven would call her, but, of course, he did not. She watched stupid TV alone, angry, and sweaty. On Sunday when Paul arrived with cookies and coffee, she felt a barrier between them that had not been there before. His offerings used to touch her heart with gratitude, melt her with the sweetness of his gesture, but now he seemed a creature of habit who wanted a snack.

"How was your date?" he asked.

"Fine."

"And the movie?"

"Fine."

"Do you want to take a walk in the park?" Paul asked.

This was unusual. Now she knew he was worried. "Sure," Cady said.

The day was clear and cold. Cady wondered what Steven was doing and felt no guilt at all for thinking about him. They walked to the Bethesda Fountain among the Sunday families with their children, and among the happy Sunday lovers who had slept together Saturday night. Paul stayed at a dignified distance from her. *You should have someone who holds your hand in public,* Steven had said, and Cady felt alone and rejected.

They sat on a bench. "How was your party last night?" Cady asked.

"Boring," Paul said.

"Then why do you go to them?"

"Responsibilities," he said.

"Your life is just full of responsibilities," Cady said.

"You're my responsibility too," Paul said mildly. "I take care of you. I would never desert you. You should be glad I'm the way I am."

At least he tried to make her feel safe. But she couldn't help thinking that what he had said was self-serving. She felt like only another one of his properties, something he had set in place and kept for his comfort level. Her gloved hand inched toward his on the bench but then she kept it there. She didn't want him to pull away and give her a warning or a lecture. A while ago she would have thought their Sunday outing to the park was romantic, but now she felt nothing.

"If you met someone you knew while we were sitting here, would you introduce me or not?" Cady asked.

"Who would I know?"

"Someone might come along."

He didn't answer.

"That means no, doesn't it."

"Cady, are you trying to pick a fight with me?"

"Maybe I am," she said, and hunched into her coat, holding her arms around herself.

"Let's walk," he said, sounding annoyed.

When they got back to her apartment Paul looked at his watch and then said he had to leave. They hadn't had sex and she didn't care. They didn't make love very often anymore, but of course Paul said that was the way it was when people had been married for a long time. Cady felt she had all the bad things about marriage without any of the good ones; except, perhaps, for the rent being paid.

On Monday when she saw Steven in the

hall at school Cady felt relieved and glad. They smiled at each other almost conspiratorially. "Lunch?" he asked.

"Out?" she asked.

"You bet."

In the coffee shop they laughed and chattered as if they had been separated for a long time. He touched her arm, and even, once, her cheek. He told her he had watched football on television all weekend, with his brother, and Cady found it interesting to hear what he had been doing. He asked her if he could take her to dinner on Saturday night. "A real date," he said. "You're not going to be with him, are you?"

"No," she said, without offering details. She had a right to be taken to dinner on Saturday night, on a real date, with someone who wanted to be seen with her. Would they be two of the Sunday people in the park, the Saturday night lovers who'd slept over? It didn't seem impossible, and she felt happy, as if suddenly her whole life was really ahead of her at last.

She didn't tell Paul she would be unavailable until he came over on Wednesday. She didn't want him to know it was important. Now, instead of wanting to make him jealous, she was afraid he would be. She knew just what that meant, that he had reason. The power balance had shifted, and she liked it.

chapter
21

Cady went to Bonwit Teller and bought a sweater for Saturday night, a poorboy that made her look slim, in a soft apricot cashmere that made her look fresh and glowing. Or perhaps it was the anticipation of her date that made her seem that way. She finally told her mother that she was interested in a new man.

"It's about time," her mother said. She too was tired of Paul's behavior. "Who is he? Where did you meet him?"

"He's the new teacher at Dunnewood I told you about."

"That's nice," her mother said. "Maybe something will come of it." Although she had always hoped for money for her daughter's future, she did not say that Steven was too poor to be a viable suitor. Obviously at this point in Cady's life anyone who was at all eligible was to be applauded.

Her mother also did not ask if Steven

was Jewish, as by now that didn't matter either. He was, but he wasn't much of a Jew. Cady didn't bother to volunteer any information. She and Steven had both agreed that their religious education had been woefully lacking, but that they were spiritual anyway. Everybody was these days. Spirituality was much more important than any specific organized religion. It was good to embrace the whole world.

Steven came upstairs to Cady's apartment when he picked her up. It was the first time she'd had a man there, and almost the only time she'd had anyone at all there except for Paul. She had bought apricot-colored roses that matched her sweater, and had lit scented candles. The tiny apartment looked warm and inviting. You see, she thought, I'd be a good catch for someone.

"You're like a princess in her tower," Steven said, and kissed her hello, again on the cheek. He looked around. "So this is it."

"My love nest and my prison."

"I told you I'm going to rescue you."

He looked at the photographs of Paul she had everywhere, in their silver frames. "So this is him."

"Yes."

He didn't comment. But what could he say, after all?

They each had a glass of wine while Cady played one of her old Sinatra albums. She hoped Paul wouldn't call, and he didn't. He probably thought she was already out. Looking at herself through Steven's eyes she felt tragic, complicated, and interesting. Definitely someone in need of rescuing.

"I've reserved at the Russian Tea Room at eight," he told her.

How nice to be out on Saturday night with a man who was splurging, really extending himself, who was glad to be seen with her, was even showing her off. The Russian Tea Room was opulent, glittering, and bright, and he had managed to get a booth so they sat side by side. He chose a bottle of wine, lit her cigarette. He himself didn't smoke. I'm going to stop smoking, Cady suddenly thought. It makes one more independent.

She was too excited to be hungry and picked at her food. He was easy to talk to; he talked just enough and listened just enough. Again she felt the gift of time. This is what normal life is like, Cady thought. Not what Paul says, being bored and boring. It's having fun and feeling the future is going to be different than the present. This is what other people must feel. She thought she must have been more isolated than she had even realized.

"I've decided I want to marry you," Steven said.

"Oh, really?"

"I'm not kidding. I mean it. I want to take you away from him, and what can I offer you that he can't? A real life, love, a home, children."

"Children?" Cady said doubtfully.

"You don't like children?"

"I don't know."

"We could have the first one and see."

She laughed. "You want to marry me and you haven't even kissed me yet."

"I'll make up for that later."

She felt electric tingling go through her at the thought. A real date with an attractive, attentive man, followed by sex, lovemaking if you will, not an evening that ended, but one that might go on all night. She wondered what it would be like to marry him after all. They would have friends, they would go out with other people, entertain. They would spend every holiday together. They would make plans that they kept.

If he made her have a baby she could always get a nanny for it. Her mother would help pay. Her mother might also baby-sit.

"We hardly know each other," Cady said.

"We know each other very well."

"My parents didn't really know each other when they got married," Cady mused. "My mother was too young to know much of anything."

"And they're still together."

"I don't think they're very happy."

"We'll be happy. You know a lot about what you want. You just haven't been able to get it — yet."

"You can't expect me to cook," Cady said.

"I cook."

"Oh, you must cook for me."

"I will. This weekend."

She wondered if someone else would feel trapped by all this attention, but she didn't. She felt grateful, even thrilled. Maybe their conversation was a fantasy, a game, but she was perfectly willing to go along with it. She couldn't think of anything more delightful than having fantasies come true at last.

They had coffee but no dessert. After he paid the check Steven said, "I want you to see my apartment. I've cleaned it thoroughly in honor of your visit."

"Well, that's good."

He lived on the West Side, on the second floor of a brownstone that had been converted into small apartments. He had a living room with a fireplace and tall, filled bookcases, a kitchen, a bathroom, and down a long narrow hall, a bedroom with a queen sized bed next to windows that overlooked the garden. There were books piled on the floor next to the bed. The apartment had an exposed brick wall and much leather and dark tweed. It was prototypical bachelor and Cady found it sexy.

"Does that fireplace work?" she asked.

"But of course."

He took her coat and lit the fire. He poured a brandy for her, put on some kind of classical music very softly, and they sat for a few moments looking into the flames. "Do you think you could live here?" he asked.

"Maybe."

"I love you, tragic princess."

"I love you too," Cady said. At the moment it seemed true.

He took the brandy glass out of her hand then and enveloped her. She'd had no idea he could kiss so well, and when soon they proceeded to the bed, she was surprised and delighted at the passion of his love-making. His lean body was as she had suspected from his hug, and she liked the way his skin smelled. He wasn't in a hurry. Cady was relieved that there was nothing that could possibly disappoint her about the way the two of them blended in sex. He was better than Paul, or perhaps he was just newer, but whatever it was she was insatiable and smitten.

"Do you still want to marry me?" she asked afterward.

"Yes."

"Good, because there's no way you're going to get away."

She spent the night, and they made love again. She wondered if Paul was telephoning her, and felt both guilty and pleased that he probably was. He would be wondering why she wasn't home. She would say she had been asleep. He could lie and so could she.

In the morning Steven made her very good coffee and scrambled eggs. She had brought her birth control pills and her toothbrush just in case, and of course her makeup, but in the morning she felt so relaxed with him that she didn't bother to put on any makeup after all. She wore one of his shirts and they watched the news on television. She had no interest in going home and thought she could probably stay there forever.

However, at four o'clock, after making love again, she felt guilty about the lateness of the hour and Steven had papers to grade, so she left.

"We'll have lunch tomorrow," he said.

"Does that mean we won't have dinner?"

"Don't you have to wait for him?"

"I suppose so. He's going to be angry."

"He'll be angrier when you tell him you're leaving him," Steven said.

Leaving Paul? It was so soon.

"I can understand if you're afraid," Steven said. "But you'll have to make your choice eventually."

"Give me some time," Cady said. "I have to think. This is a big decision."

"How much time?"

"Does it matter?"

"Of course it matters. I want to be with you."

"Well, I want to be with you," Cady said, "but this is going to kill him."

"Serves him right."

"Give me two weeks," Cady said. That seemed reasonable.

"All right. Maybe he'll suspect and then it will be easier."

"It won't ever be easy," Cady said. "It's taken him ten years and he still hasn't broken off his marriage."

"You're not married," Steven said.

That was certainly true.

"Are you sure you love me?" Cady asked.

"I'm sure. Are you?"

"Yes."

She didn't know whom to call first, her mother or Leigh.

She called Leigh. She was home, and Cady imagined her reading the remains of the *New York Times*, or perhaps a script, or spending time with her daughter, Jennie. What would David be doing? Watching a sports event on TV, or working, or he might be bonding with their daughter too. Whatever it was, they would be having a family Sunday afternoon. Maybe they had been to a restaurant for brunch, or they had all come home from a walk or a movie. Soon they would think about what to do about supper. Someday these things would be hers too. Now she knew it. Only the cast of characters had changed.

"I have big news," Cady said.

"What?"

"I've been seeing a man. He's a new teacher at the school, Steven Irving.

We're in love. We're engaged."

"You're *what?*"

"Isn't it exciting?" Cady said. "We started to date and he proposed to me. I'm going to have to tell Paul it's over."

"But this happened so fast," Leigh said.

"I know. It was right."

"I think you should break up with Paul and have a life," Leigh said. She sounded worried. "But this man . . . does he know about Paul?"

"He knows everything."

"And you're sleeping with him."

"Naturally."

"Did he propose before or after you slept with him?"

"Before, of course," Cady said. "It would take a lot for me to cheat on Paul. I never have before."

"I'm happy for you," Leigh said dubiously, "but I'm concerned too."

"Oh, you're always so guarded; the woman in armor. I'm not like you."

"I know that. Cady, dearest, this guy may be the nicest man in the world, but most men are self-serving and they'll say anything to get a woman into bed. Not that Steven Irving is like that, but you have to be careful."

"No man would propose to get sex,"

Cady said. "That's too extreme."

"Your situation with Paul is extreme. It's a whole lifestyle. Now you're going to live with Steven?"

"As soon as I tell Paul."

"I wish you luck," Leigh said. She still sounded like she didn't believe a word of what Cady had told her.

"Don't you think a nice man would want to marry me?" Cady asked, insulted. "Steven and I have everything in common. We're soul mates. He's *perfect*."

Leigh sighed.

"What?"

"I don't know why you're surrounded by so many perfect people and none of the rest of us are."

"What is that supposed to mean?"

"You fall in love with everyone immediately. With men, women, everybody. Or you hate them. I'm not saying this new man isn't the one for you. But I just don't want you to be hurt."

"Any more than you're hurting me now by doubting me?"

"All right," Leigh said. "I don't know anything about it. Forget what I said."

"I intend to."

"I'm sorry," Leigh said.

"You're forgiven."

But when they hung up Cady was still annoyed. Smug, perfect Leigh, with her adored husband and happy home life; her great career; her money; her pretty, intelligent child. She just couldn't believe Cady could have happiness too. As she had sometimes before, Cady felt that Leigh looked down on her. Although she loved and even worshiped Leigh, sometimes she wished something bad would happen to Leigh — not too bad, not a tragedy, but something — to make her like the rest of them.

She telephoned her mother.

"You know the man I told you about?" Cady told her. "Well, we're in love, and we're going to get married."

"Married!" her mother cried, delighted. "When did this happen? You little devil! I can't wait to tell Dad."

"I'm going to have to tell Paul."

"Of course. Serves him right. He never appreciated you enough. When do we meet the new man? When do I start planning the wedding?"

"Soon," Cady said.

"Bring him home to dinner," her mother said. "No, let's do something glamorous in the city. Let's go out to dinner at the Four Seasons. Next Friday or Saturday night?"

"I'll ask him," Cady said. As always, her mother had accepted her life. She hadn't said the new development was too sudden, or asked questions meant to deflate her euphoria. She was lucky to have a mother who was good-natured and young at heart.

When Cady hung up with her mother she called Steven. It was a wonderful feeling to be able to call the man she loved any time she wanted to. "My parents want you to come to dinner with us at the Four Seasons next Friday or Saturday night," Cady said.

"Whichever one you prefer," he said, and her heart sang. He was totally free, for her.

Now that left Paul, and the frightening confrontation. She was going to tear up his whole life. For the first time, without understanding why, Cady felt a little sorry for him. She had loved him so much. And he, she knew, had loved her too.

But not enough.

She began to pace the room. Paul would be calling her soon. She hoped he didn't just decide to come over. She dreaded the familiar sound of his key in the lock. He had been so sure of her, so confident that she was his property. And she had been so grateful for whatever attention he could give her. He had no idea that was over now. When the phone rang she jumped.

"Where have you been all weekend?" Paul asked. He sounded worried and a little angry.

I should tell him he'll find out when he comes here tonight, she thought, but she couldn't say it. "You must have just missed me every time you called," Cady said.

"Should I come over?"

I can't, she thought. It's too much emotion for one weekend. I need to stay happy for a few hours more at least. Besides, she suddenly realized she was very tired. No wonder, she hadn't had much sleep.

"I feel like I'm coming down with a bug," she said. "I feel really rotten. Why don't you come over tomorrow night and tonight I'll just go to bed."

"All right," he said. "Take care of yourself. I'll see you tomorrow." He hung up.

She was glad he was at home making a sneaky call with his wife in the next room, talking briefly as if she were business, so they hadn't had to discuss anything in detail. She would tell him tomorrow. Or if she wanted to, she could wait. She had told Steven she needed two weeks. It was all up to her now. She was in control . . . of both of them.

She looked at Paul's framed photographs. Most of them had been taken early in their relationship, when she was greedy for souvenirs, when he had, she now realized, looked much younger. Paul would want to have sex, she supposed, if only because she had disappeared and he wanted to reinstate his claim. But she could put him off. Cady caressed the photographs lightly and sighed. She knew one thing. She never wanted Paul to touch her again.

chapter
22

Leigh was worried about Cady. She supposed that if this Steven were the catalyst, then he would be as good as anything else to propel Cady to get rid of Paul. But she was surely letting herself in for future disappointment. It had happened too quickly, and he was not at all the kind of man Cady was drawn to. Cady would have said if he were glamorous, so he wasn't. He was an underpaid schoolteacher. If there were family money Cady would have mentioned it. Perhaps he was terribly handsome, but that was something Cady would never have omitted raving about.

Did they both know like a flash of lightning they were meant for each other? Leigh wondered if Cady had been right about her, if she was the woman in armor, someone who couldn't be impetuous or believe in fantasies coming true. Or was Cady doomed to mistake after mistake, a victim of too much romanticism?

No . . . she decided she was a different person now and Cady was wrong about her. She was still levelheaded and realistic, but these years of security and happiness had softened her. She was able to trust in good fortune and stability. Her own fantasies had certainly come true. The only thing that frightened her was the thought that her family could be taken away from her, that her child could get sick or her husband could die. The world was full of accidents. She had perhaps been too lucky. She wondered if other happy people felt the same way about their lives.

And now she was pregnant again. It was so soon that she hadn't told anyone but David. Was she being cautious, superstitious, or sensible? Whatever, it was her nature. She and Cady were opposites, and always had been.

She dialed Vanessa in California. The Cady situation was a good excuse to connect with Vanessa again, since they were both busy and didn't keep in touch as much as either of them would have liked. But luckily their friendship was so comfortable that whenever they did see each other, on Vanessa's New York visits, it was as if no time had passed at all.

"I have news," Leigh said. "Cady is in

love with a new man and says she's engaged. She's going to break up with Paul and marry the new one."

"When did this happen?" Vanessa asked, surprised.

"That's the trouble, they just met."

"Well, maybe he wants to save her. And she wants to save herself."

"Do you believe in love at first sight?" Leigh asked. Vanessa, of all people, with her history, should know.

"I don't believe in love at all," Vanessa said.

How sad! Leigh was shocked. "But don't you love Bill?"

"I love my children," Vanessa said.

There was a moment of silence.

"Are you . . . having problems with your marriage?" Leigh asked.

"Not at all."

"Am I missing something here?"

"No. Lots of couples go along contentedly without any great passion. We're good friends. We're used to each other. We're kind to each other. I have friends whose marriages are far worse."

Vanessa sounded like a middle-aged person. Leigh remembered how carefree Vanessa had been when they were living together, and thought how little they all really knew about each other even though they were longtime friends. Vanessa had seemed so happy whenever they met in New York. But she'd been on vacation, and she always saw her friends without Bill. She had her little flings when she was free in New York, and apparently that was all she needed. Keeping her hand in, she sometimes called it.

Leigh wondered why she thought Vanessa's married life was so poignant. If anyone was, Vanessa was a creature of her times. The barriers had tumbled in the late sixties, and people behaved even more freely and openly now in the seventies. Bill probably cheated too. Leigh and Cady hadn't been shocked to find that Vanessa picked up strange men when she was in New York. There was something about Vanessa's attitude, that she could always take care of herself, that had reassured them. But it had never occurred to Leigh or Cady that Vanessa hadn't loved her husband on some level. Now she seemed like someone who had given up, and she probably had from the beginning.

Vanessa should never have married the wrong man, but what choice did she have? Maybe her mistake had been in staying with him. If there was something atypical about

Vanessa in the spirit of the times it was that she was holding her marriage together. People didn't bother to anymore. Women left their husbands to "find themselves." They went away to seek independence. Vanessa found hers in her own way. Perhaps the new breed of women would think her too dependent on men and would not approve.

"Don't worry about Cady," Vanessa said.

"No?"

"No. She's always been crazy. This is probably her stroke of luck at last."

"Maybe you're right. I'll keep you appraised."

"Do."

When she hung up Leigh went into the den. David, who was old enough to be Jennie's grandfather, had introduced his precocious five-year-old daughter to his childhood hobby, which was stamp collecting. To Leigh it was a sweet, old-fashioned boy thing, but Jennie was adaptable and wanted to humor him, and besides he told wonderful stories about the stamps. Each one reminded him of something, and Leigh supposed it was much the same as reading to her. She was always pleasantly surprised at his inexhaustible wealth of knowledge and his flights of imagination. Different countries, exotic places, historical figures, all sent him off on another tale.

The two of them were sitting together under the lamp, their heads bent over the large scrapbook. Leigh wished she had a camera and could take a photograph of it. These moments didn't occur all the time, but when they did they represented such an idealized picture of family life that it made her catch her breath.

And she was going to have another child. She would have the two-child family she had always wanted.

"What do you say I send out for Chinese food?" Leigh asked. They both looked up, pleased. In a happy family, how little it took to make people happier.

Maybe she was being too harsh on Cady. Maybe Cady could have all this too. Cady deserved a second chance. Everyone did, no matter how foolish they were, no matter how long it took.

chapter
23

After an unexpectedly restless night Cady decided the best thing would be to tell Paul right away. Now that her future seemed so close to being resolved after all the years of not knowing, she wanted to be done with it. She felt a little sad, a little nostalgic. Paul would be furious that she was rejecting him for another man, and he probably would never want to see her again.

It occurred to her then that he might be so taken aback to find she was her own person that he might actually leave his wife at last. But she doubted it. And the truth was, she wanted the new life she could have with Steven. She felt young again. The past was over. There was no reason to try to patch things up. Besides, how could she trust Paul? He might promise anything to keep her. Cady was beginning to like him less and less, and this of course made it easier to tell him the news she knew would devastate him.

She washed her hair, dressed to look sexy, and applied her makeup carefully. She wanted Paul to remember her at her best. She ran over her script in her mind, but kept changing it. She should tell him the truth about how much he hurt her. No, she should be gracious. No, she should be as nasty as she wanted to be. It served him right. Paul seemed like a stranger, a victim, a withholding father, but saddest of all, a figure who was already receding into the past: a tiresome lover. Poor Paul.

No, poor me, she thought. I'm the real victim here. Paul wasted the best years of my life. I'm lucky I found Steven, and I wouldn't have if he hadn't been right under my nose.

When she heard Paul's key in the lock she broke into a cold sweat.

"Hi, sweetie," Paul said, and kissed her lightly. He took off his jacket and loosened his tie. She couldn't tell these days if he were preparing to have sex with her or just getting ready to relax. She remembered when he used to rush into her arms, and it seemed a lifetime ago.

"Hi," she said. She looked at him, thinking that after tonight she would never again see him in shirtsleeves or naked either. She didn't care about the naked part.

She remembered him at his best and his worst, and could bring either one up at will. Now she brought up the worst. It gave her courage.

"We need to talk," she said.

"All right." He sat in her armchair. He looked impassive, obviously thinking she was going to complain again that she didn't have enough of him.

"I've met another man," Cady said.

Suddenly there was some expression on his face. He looked alarmed.

"We're in love with each other," she said.

"Who is the man?" Paul asked. He sounded stern, but his voice was shaking. He was trying to hold himself in, but she could see he was terribly shocked.

"The one I told you about. Steven Irving. The teacher I went out with, remember?"

"You're in love with *him?*"

"Yes."

"How could that happen?"

"The way these things always happen," Cady said.

"This is . . . ridiculous."

"Only you would think so."

Paul's look of shock faded a little. "Did you go to bed with him?"

"I suppose I owe you the truth. Yes."

He looked very pained. "I can't believe you did that."

"Well, I did."

The silence seemed long. "A fling," he said, finally. "All right, you were angry at me and you cheated. You wanted to hurt me. I am hurt, but I understand. But you must promise me you will never do such a destructive and childish thing again."

"I'm going to marry him," Cady said. "He asked me to, and I said yes."

"Marry him? But you just met!"

"We met two months ago."

"Two months?"

"So what?"

"I don't understand. When did you sneak off and have sex with him?"

"I have more than enough free time," Cady said sharply, "as I've told you very often, but you never listened to me."

"How could you do this to me?" Paul asked.

"To you? It's all about you, isn't it? What about me? I'm sick and tired of being your property. I'm tired of waiting for you. I'm tired of having no life. I want to get married. Maybe I even want to have a baby. Why should you have everything I want and I can't have it too?"

"I've been promising . . ." he began.

She was furious now. "Promises!" she snapped. "That's all I ever get. You live with your wife. You don't live with me. How do I know you ignore her as much as you say you do? You still take her places. For all I know you still sleep with her. I can't listen to anything you say to me anymore. I'll be old one day and then you'll get bored with me and dump me, and I'll have nothing at all. I don't have an apartment. I don't have a home. I have nothing."

"You have this apartment," Paul protested.

"It's just a place where you stow me away. I wanted to live with you but you wouldn't. I'm tired of being your summer wife. I want to be someone's only wife. I'm marrying Steven."

His face was pale now. "You don't know what you want, Cady. You're being emotional."

"I've always been emotional. Haven't you ever noticed?"

"Oh yes, I've noticed. So I guess this is it?"

"Yes. I'm going to move in with Steven," she said.

"When did you plan to do that?"

"Right away. I needed to tell you and

274

then I'm getting on with my life."

"Do you think I can get rid of this lease so quickly?" Paul asked. "I have to talk to the landlord."

"Then talk to him."

"You throw this bombshell on me. . . ."

"Are you more concerned about the apartment or me?" Cady asked bitterly.

"You. But you have no sense of practicality, of finances, of business. . . ."

"You think I'll stay on and change my mind?"

"I'm beginning to wonder if you even have a mind."

"I hoped maybe someday you and I could be friends," Cady said. Then she wondered why she'd said it. She didn't love him anymore; she didn't even like him. He had almost ruined her life.

"Friends are considerate," he said.

"I'm sure the landlord will be very happy to take back this apartment and raise the rent," Cady said.

"What about me?"

"What about you?"

"Don't you think I'll miss you?"

"I missed you every night for the last ten years," she said. "Whenever you left I missed you. When I went to sleep alone I missed you. When I couldn't share things

I missed you. When I couldn't call you I missed you. I don't know what possessed me to put up with you and that stingy pathetic little existence you doled out to me."

"I thought you loved me," Paul said.

"I did," Cady said. "More than life."

Yes, that was true. "More than life" was a saying, but it told very clearly what had happened to her.

"I have to go now," Paul said. He stood up and tightened his tie.

I have to go now, his favorite words, Cady thought. How many thousands of times I have heard that, and every time my heart ached.

"When are you moving out?" he asked.

"By the end of the month," Cady said. "I need to pack."

"You'll change your mind when you move into his hovel, and I won't take you back."

"It's not a hovel," Cady said. "And I won't want you to take me back." Go, she thought. Just go.

Paul went to the door, and then turned and looked at her, his hand on the knob. "I thought you and I would grow old together," he said plaintively.

What a bid for sympathy, Cady thought. Their eyes met. Now that her anger had come out at last, after all these years, she couldn't resist offering her parting shot.

"How could we?" she said. "You've already grown old with your wife."

When he left he slammed the door so hard the walls rattled. It frightened her a little. If you loved someone who broke your heart that person could become your enemy. So be it. Let him hate her.

It wasn't till a few moments later that Cady realized she hadn't asked him to give back her key.

It wasn't important. He could leave it with the doorman. He wouldn't be coming back again, and she wasn't going to be staying long.

That night she had dinner with Steven. "I told Paul," she said.

"Good. What did he say?"

"He tried to keep me, of course. But he couldn't."

"Was he angry? Did he threaten you?"

"What could he possibly threaten me with?"

"Then now you're free," Steven said.

"Yes," Cady said. "Free."

When they made love she felt cleansed. She was all his now. And he was all hers.

That very night she began leaving things in Steven's apartment, preparatory to moving in altogether. Now she could stay overnight and they would be able to spend entire weekends together. The next day Cady spent an hour on the phone with her mother, deciding what things she would weed out because she didn't need them anymore.

The bed, of course, needed to go. Cady didn't want those memories, and besides, Steven's was bigger. The armchair where she had spent so many lonely evenings would go to Goodwill. She and Steven could use an extra television set. She would get rid of the monogrammed king sized sheets. They were too intimate and reminded her of her fantasies of playing house. But after a brief discussion with her mother Cady decided that the expensive monogrammed silverware would come to Steven's apartment with her. They had her initials on them after all, and an "I" would take up very little room when she had them remonogrammed before she and Steven were married.

The next day when she came back to her apartment she discovered that Paul had been there. It was clear; it could be nobody else. He had taken every one of his pictures out of their frames. The empty frames stood there blankly, as if he had never existed. Cady felt her face grow hot.

Her first reaction was anger because he had encroached on her territory. Then the anger turned into resentment. Since she was through with him, Paul didn't want anyone else to know that he had ever been in her life. He was destroying the evidence. How easy it was. . . .

Cady rushed to the closet to see if her precious silverware was still there in its box. It was. Paul didn't want it. It didn't incriminate him the way his photographs would.

She would never understand him, she thought. Or perhaps she understood him too well. Whichever, she couldn't wait to get away and start to live.

chapter
24

Cady moved in with Steven and replaced Paul's missing photographs in their silver frames with pictures of herself. She and Steven were both neat people, luckily, so they got along. They ate at home most nights and he did the cooking, she did the washing up. They never argued. It was still such a new relationship that they went out of their way to be kind to each other, and she hoped it would stay that way forever. She was very happy. It was good to be able to have great sex whenever she wanted it, to talk, to be silent, to have all the time in the world.

He bought her an ugly ring. Cady was shocked when she saw it, but Steven seemed so pleased with his choice that she didn't dare complain. She had assumed that he would give her a traditionally-set diamond, and that she would go with him to choose it, but instead he appeared with the box. He said a friend of his in Greenwich Village, who was an artisan, had designed and made the ring. It looked like a lump of dark-yellow gold, which perhaps could be a gnarled tree branch. There was an oddly shaped, dark gray-blue pearl set in it. She didn't even want to wear the thing, but she didn't see how she could refuse without hurting his feelings.

It was clear that there were things she did not know yet about his taste. The engagement ring was probably cheap, as well as something for a hippie, but she didn't want to fault him for not having money. That would make Paul win. Still, Cady couldn't help being jealous of the ring David had given Leigh. As always, Leigh had what she wanted.

"Don't worry," Cady's mother said cheerfully when Cady told her. "People aren't wearing traditional diamonds anymore; they're old-fashioned. They aren't buying engagement rings at all. You're marrying a young man, get with the times."

Yes, she thought, David is old. Leigh's life isn't *that* perfect. She concentrated on looking at wedding rings she would like, and determined that she would pick this one out herself.

They hadn't set a date. When Cady

mentioned that she would like to know if Steven wanted to get married in the summer so they could take a trip, he said he didn't know yet. He suggested they get to know each other better first, since marriage was difficult at best, even for dreamers.

"Ours will be different from your first one," Cady said.

"That certainly is what I had in mind."

"If you want a big wedding," her mother said, "it will take me a long time to plan it."

"I want a small wedding," Cady said. "I just want a wedding, to tell you the truth."

Leigh and Vanessa were pleased for her. Leigh had no more criticisms, or, if she did, she kept them to herself.

Cady never heard from Paul. She thought about him from time to time, as how could she not after he had been so important to her for so long, and wondered if he was as lonely as he deserved to be, but she didn't miss him. She had what she wanted now.

At Christmas the four future in-laws had dinner together at Cady's parents' house in Scarsdale, with Steven and Cady and Steven's younger brother, Josh, with his latest girlfriend. They had met before, of course, and they all still got along. Cady enjoyed feeling like part of a family instead of the outcast she had always felt herself to be at family occasions.

Then on New Year's Eve she had her first New Year's Eve date in a decade, with Steven. She felt a part of the world. And on Valentine's Day he remembered to bring her flowers.

But spring was coming, and Steven still refused to talk about a wedding date. "Aren't we happy?" he asked.

"Yes. So?"

"Maybe we could go to Europe in the summer," he said.

"What about Europe for a honeymoon?"

"Why are you bugging me?"

"I'm not," Cady said. "It's normal for engaged people to talk about when they'll get married."

"We're not ready yet," he said.

That made her a little nervous. What was there about her that made men keep putting her off? Did she seem like bad marriage material?

"I'm thirty-four," she said to him. "Soon I'll be too old to have a baby."

"You said you didn't want a baby."

"I did not!"

"Yes you did."

"Well, if I ever said it, I changed my mind. Don't you want one?"

"I don't know," Steven said. "This is a bad world to bring up a baby in."

"It will always be a bad world," Cady said. "People keep having children anyway."

He sulked in front of the television set. What was wrong with him? Was he another man she didn't know, would never know? Or did she not know anything about any man?

They hadn't talked about their live-in relationship at school, but Cady couldn't resist telling just one friend, and then a second, and by then the word was out all over Dunnewood. A romantic and happy story had replaced a romantic and tragic one. The loser who had been involved in an ill-fated love affair with a married man was now the winner who had snagged an eligible bachelor. The two most attractive teachers at the school had found love with each other. The little girls, who had crushes on Steven, were both disappointed and excited.

Still, Cady thought, they should set the date. She wanted to nail him down.

She brought home copies of bridal magazines and tore out pictures of wedding gowns. From *Vogue* and *Harper's Bazaar* she cut out photos of cocktail dresses. Steven was polite but noncommittal. He would rather choose a movie for them to see, a restaurant to go to. He had stopped talking about their trip to Europe.

Vanessa was in town again, and Cady, Leigh, and Charlie met her at the St. Regis for drinks. Vanessa never appeared to be any older, and Cady wondered if she'd had something done. Not that they were old, but they weren't twenty-three anymore either, and living left its traces. Leigh's pregnancy was showing and she looked serene. Was it possible that Charlie was losing his hair already? Their little Charlie? What did *she* look like to *them?* She hadn't wondered about that before, but now she did.

Cady had brought along Steven to introduce him to Vanessa and show him off. The friends toasted the future bride and groom with champagne. "When are you getting married?" Vanessa asked.

"I don't know yet," Cady said.

"We don't know," Steven said, almost in unison.

"That's okay," Vanessa said. "Take your time. That's always wise."

"So now there's you, Charlie," Leigh said. "You're the last of the group, and it's supposed to be easier for a man to find a mate than a woman."

"I almost proposed to someone last month," Charlie said. "But then I had second thoughts, so here I am, still free, available, and charming."

"Life is too easy for you," Leigh said.

"He's scared," Vanessa laughed.

"I can't blame him for that," Steven said.

Cady stiffened. She was beginning to think Charlie was not a good influence to have around Steven. "Are you scared?" she asked Steven.

"What man isn't?" Steven said. He and Charlie smiled meaningfully at each other; two men sharing the secrets of relationships.

She didn't like this at all. Cady hated the two of them ganging up against her. She felt so hurt she could hardly pay attention to the rest of the conversation.

The next day when she could be by herself Cady called Leigh at the office. "What's wrong with Steven?" she hissed.

"It's normal to be frightened," Leigh said calmly. "Don't pressure him. Leave him alone."

"That's what he says."

"Then listen to him."

"But I can't go through this again,"

Cady said. "All those years with Paul, all his promises . . ."

"Do you think he's Paul?"

"No."

"It's still early," Leigh said. "You two need to get to know each other. That's what an engagement is for."

"Do you think there's something about him I don't know?"

"I'm sure there are lots of things."

"I don't want any surprises," Cady said. "I just want a peaceful, happy life." Like yours, she thought, but she didn't say it.

"You're living with him," Leigh reminded her. "What's wrong with that?"

"Easy for you to say. You're married."

"The person I'm worried about is Charlie," Leigh said. "No one ever lasts with him."

"He's spoiled," Cady said. "Men have all those choices."

"No, there's something rather sad and unfulfilled about Charlie," Leigh said thoughtfully. "There's a piece missing."

"Do you think there's a piece missing from Steven?"

"That's for you to ascertain."

"I thought you could tell me," Cady said. "You're the smartest person I know."

"I hope I'm not," Leigh said cheerfully.

Cady decided that, as her new strategy, she would not mention setting a wedding date again, but that didn't mean it wasn't on her mind all the time.

The following weekend she decided to straighten out their closets. It was a daunting task. Like most New Yorkers they were two people trying to squeeze themselves into a space meant for one.

"You have too many clothes," Steven told her. "Why do you need so many clothes?"

"To please you," she lied.

"You had them before I met you."

"We need an apartment with more closets," she said.

"I like this apartment."

First we'll get married, and then we'll look for a larger apartment, she thought.

"What is that look on your face?" he asked.

"Nothing."

"I thought you liked my apartment too."

"I do. And it's our apartment now."

"It's always been too small for two," he said.

"You never told me that."

"I didn't realize until there were two people in it."

"Then we should get another," Cady

said. "I mean, come on, it's only an apartment. People move all the time."

"Why do you keep trying to change my life?"

"I thought that was what I'm here for," Cady said.

"To change my life?"

"Yes. To make it better."

He didn't answer.

"Don't I?" Cady asked. "Don't I make your life better?"

There was a long pause. "Yes," he said, finally.

What was wrong with him?

"I'm going out to get the newspaper," he said, and left.

Was that their first fight? She hadn't even known it was a fight.

Bridegroom's nerves, Cady told herself, but she didn't understand what was happening at all. She finished the closets as quickly as possible, virtually abandoning them, so he wouldn't have to look at the mess.

When Steven came back, after quite a long time, with his newspaper, he was lovely again. Cady supposed he had just needed some time away from her.

The weeks went by and Steven had gotten no closer to discussing a wedding date than he had ever been. Now even her mother had mentioned it. Cady didn't want to start trouble. She could see that marriages were falling apart all around them. Marriage was hard, especially nowadays when people didn't really try. He'd been married. He knew what it was like. But she had not, and he had promised marriage to her. Cady only wanted what was her due. She thought they should have met when she had just graduated from college, when all her friends were getting married, before he'd met the girl who was to become his wife. Then they would have gotten married, just like everybody else, and they would still be together to this day. Fate, she thought, was unfair.

Now that summer was coming Cady began bringing home travel brochures. Steven wouldn't commit himself to anything. Europe, he said, was too crowded with tourists in the summertime. But he had no better suggestions. They were not the kind of people who could take a group house in the Hamptons. It was as if he had turned to stone. She had the uneasy feeling they would end up spending the summer in the hot city, with occasional weekends at her parents' in Scarsdale, and she didn't like that at all.

Leigh had her baby: another girl, whom they named Sophie. Cady and Steven went to see her, bearing gifts, and when he seemed taken with the baby she felt a little encouraged. Leigh's children were beautiful and responsive. David seemed like a man who had everything anyone could ever want. Cady hoped his happiness would influence Steven in some way, make him think that being married was better than being single.

But Leigh's apartment was so big that both of her children had their own rooms. As for her walk-in closets, it made Cady sad to look at them. What couldn't she do with such wonderful closets! And Leigh had a nanny. She would have to reconcile herself to the fact that she would not have these things. She would have day care and an occasional baby-sitter. Maybe Steven understood what she didn't. Would their baby — if they ever even had one — sleep in the living room?

People lived like that and so could she. He hadn't ever complained about money, so perhaps money wasn't the issue. Perhaps it was something deeper, more complicated. He seemed unable to think about the future, as if it would take care of itself.

She felt as if her life had stopped, and she didn't understand.

chapter
25

Cady decided not to have her silverware engraved with Steven's last initial. It seemed to be tempting fate. She had tempted fate often enough in the past, and now she needed to be cautious. She was a person who never gave up trying to get what she wanted, and yet she seemed to be doomed to failure.

When school was out for the summer Steven bought a stack of new books to read. He seemed to be settled into their apartment for the duration, with no traveling, no adventures, no vacation, not to mention a honeymoon. He took her to Jones Beach one Saturday, where the water was black, there were far too many people, and she got a painful sunburn because they stayed too long. Often he didn't want to go to Scarsdale with her on these hot summer weekends, and she couldn't very well go alone and leave him, so she stayed in the apartment with him and felt depressed, especially on Sundays.

She remembered how much she had disliked Sundays when she was a child because they were so boring. At the time she had sometimes thought these boring Sundays were her parents' way of making her appreciate school more the next morning, since ordinarily she would have been reluctant to go. In a way she wished their summer hiatus were over. Was Steven taking her for granted, or did he want to show her what marriage to him would be like?

But she knew that was what marriage would be like. She was a romantic, but she wasn't stupid. Steven was the way he was. It didn't matter. She didn't want to be alone or lonely. She was in love. She could bear to be serene, as Leigh was. There was always an old movie on television.

She hadn't proposed to him for two weeks. She would leave him alone. It wasn't as hard as it used to be.

He started looking at her travel brochures again. She didn't say anything. Then one day, out of the blue, he said, "I want to go somewhere by myself for a week or two."

"By yourself?" she cried, horrified.

"Yes," he said. "I need it."

"But why? How can you? What's wrong?"

"I need to think," he said.

"Think about what?"

"About us."

Cady felt her skin crawl. "What about us?"

"I think maybe we made a mistake," Steven said.

Living together was a mistake? Falling in love was a mistake? She had left Paul for him!

"I've been thinking about this for a while," he said.

"But why?"

"It's just not what I thought," he said sadly. "I'm bored."

"You're *bored!*" She had never been so hurt and insulted in her life. "You're the one who won't ever do anything."

"It's not that," Steven said. "Doing things isn't the issue. It's just how I feel. I don't know if we're not meant for each other, or if it's me. It's not you. It's us."

"But why? How could that happen?" She felt her throat close and she began to cry. "You said you wanted to rescue me."

"I rescued you," Steven said. "You're free. You're rid of him."

"But you were going to . . . take me away." And then she realized that was what he had done. He had taken her from Paul.

She had thought the ride on the white horse with her knight would last forever, while he had simply thought he would carry her away from the tower.

"Why don't you want me anymore?" Cady asked. He handed her a box of tissues.

"I don't know," Steven said.

"Am I different from the person you fell in love with? Did I change?"

"I didn't know you then," he said.

"But you made all those promises! How could you make them to someone you say you didn't know?"

"You were hurt," he said. "I wanted to save you."

"And now you're hurting me."

"I'm sorry," he said.

He had been won over by the idea of a romantic adventure. He was even worse than she was. Or perhaps not: Perhaps he was a boldfaced liar. She could hardly bear to think that he had manipulated her entire life for his own selfish fling.

"I don't want to wait for you to come back from a vacation and tell me if you've decided to dump me," Cady said, angry. "I'm not on trial here. You're as bad as Paul."

"Maybe you have bad taste in men."

"You picked *me!"*

"You're so beautiful," he said. "I couldn't help it."

"And now I'm ugly?"

"I'm going to Puerto Rico next week," Steven said.

Next week! He had been planning this for longer than she'd realized. "With a girl, I suppose," she said.

"No, by myself."

"And if you meet someone?"

"Well," he said, "that could happen. I have no idea."

"So you're not going away to think about us. You're going there to be a bachelor."

"Yes," he said reluctantly.

She felt as if he had hit her in the heart. She could hardly breathe. "If you go away I won't be here when you come back," she said.

He looked at her and sighed. He didn't tell her not to leave.

This was Steven ditching her. This was good-bye.

She ran into the bedroom and slammed the door and sobbed until she was drained. When she came back out he had gone. He hadn't even tried to comfort her. He obviously couldn't face emotions, at least not hers.

She didn't know what to do so she paced up and down and then drank a glass of vodka. She smoked several cigarettes even though she had been trying to stop. She was afraid to call her mother or Leigh. She didn't know what to do. She couldn't tell them yet that he had broken up with her because maybe he hadn't meant it.

He would have to come back some time.

He came back at eleven o'clock. She'd had two more drinks and was high. He was carrying a brown paper sack, which contained Chinese food. "I thought you might be hungry," he said.

"How did you know I'd be here?"

"I didn't. But I thought if you were."

Why was he being considerate when he was breaking her heart? "Are you still going to Puerto Rico?"

"Well, yes. That hasn't changed."

He ate heartily, watching her, but she couldn't eat a bite. He put some food on a plate for her but she ignored it.

"So you're leaving me," he said finally.

"No, you're leaving me."

"I guess it's for the best," he said.

"You guess?"

"No. I'm sure."

"You really want me to go?"

"One of us has to," he said. "It's not

happening for us anymore. Hasn't for a while."

She had no more tears left or she would have cried again. The alcohol blurred the shock a little. "Tell me," she asked, "when did you know?"

He sighed.

"When did you know it was over?" she demanded.

"I can't tell you exactly," he said. "It just crept up on me."

"There was no event?"

"No."

"Is it because I kept wanting to get married?"

"No."

"There's no reason?"

He shook his head. "I need to be free," he said.

"Didn't you know that about yourself before you got involved with me?"

"I mean free of . . . all this," he said.

He could not possibly have made her feel any worse. She felt like an anchor in the worst meaning of the word — a person who stood in the way of someone else's happiness. She felt deceived. How could she have loved him? And yet, she still did. Or was it what she thought he was offering her that she loved? Was there a difference?

He had changed so much, in less than a year. Men changed. She knew that now. Cady wondered if she could ever believe in any man again.

That night they slept restlessly in the same bed, far apart. Neither of them seemed able to separate completely, even though they had decided their love affair was over. In the morning Cady took off the ugly ring and dropped it into her jewelry box. Steven made coffee as he always did. There seemed no place in this small apartment to make a private phone call, but finally she took the phone into the bathroom on its long cord and called her mother. When she heard her mother's voice she started to cry again.

Her mother came into the city to help her pack. Before she arrived Cady had called Leigh, even though she was embarrassed because Leigh would have been proven right.

"I'm so sorry," Leigh said. She didn't say "I told you so," but also she didn't act surprised. Cady got off the phone as quickly as she could.

Steven said he was going to a movie so he wouldn't bother her, and she was relieved to see him out of the apartment. She and her mother sorted and packed her things as if they were straightening up after a loved one had died.

"What a nerve," her mother said. "What a nerve. Your father is going to have a fit. In the old days a father would shoot a man for doing a thing like this."

Cady couldn't picture her father shooting anyone, not even in the old days. She thought of Steven being shot, falling, and she didn't feel satisfied; she felt bereaved.

Steven came back in time to help her load her mother's car. Cady had so many things that you could hardly see out of the windows. He stood awkwardly on the sidewalk while her mother glared at him, grim-lipped, and Cady, trying not to cry, felt as if her insides had been ripped apart.

"I'll call you," he said, but she didn't know if he would, and if he did, she didn't know what there was to say.

She didn't even know where to go, so she would have to go to her parents' house. She could stay there at least for the rest of the summer, since there was no school. She was numb, devastated. It was as if all her grown-up life had disappeared and she was back where she had started: alone and single, but this time she was not looking forward to the future but was afraid of it.

PART THREE

chapter
26

Five years had passed: It was 1980. Business was booming, women were entering the workforce in unprecedented numbers, and the huge baby boom generation had begun earning and spending a lot of money. It was a time of opulence, of splendor, of showing off. Leigh, as a successful career woman, was no longer an anomaly; perhaps not even a role model anymore since many other women were successfully juggling work and home. The TV series *Dallas*, depicting a very rich Texas family, was a huge hit. That year Ronald Reagan would be president. John Lennon would be assassinated. Smallpox, against which most people had been vaccinated as babies, would be considered eradicated.

Leigh was about to be forty. Cady already was. Vanessa was forty-one.

The world called them and everyone like them middle-aged. None of the three friends liked starting their fifth decade.

They felt they were at an unwelcome milestone in their lives and it was almost unimaginable. They didn't feel wiser. Worse, they were finally at an age that people wouldn't admit.

Leigh and Cady had met the men they loved when they were twenty-three and the men were in their forties. At the time it had seemed sophisticated to be so old. Now the men seemed to have been young, but they felt it was different for themselves.

The three women still met for drinks at the St. Regis when Vanessa came in to New York, and as always Charlie joined them. He was only thirty-nine, and they were jealous. It was easier for men anyway. A forty-year-old man was still considered in his prime.

Leigh had begun to think of him as a permanent bachelor. Occasionally she teased him about it, but she liked having him as an available single man at her business parties. There weren't so many good ones out there. He was straight, successful, attractive, and he had a kind heart. Everybody needs a Charlie Rackley, she sometimes thought warmly, and she thought what a shame it was that Vanessa had never liked him as a boyfriend, because then her life might have turned out quite differently. He obviously had a special place for Vanessa in his affections, and Leigh thought he might even be still in love with her.

As for herself, she felt blessed with her life, so much so that she was always a little frightened that everything she had would vanish. She cherished her work and treasured her family, everyone was healthy, her husband was faithful, her two daughters liked school and loved their parents, they had friends, and gave her no trouble. All she wanted for them was to be independent, happy people, but that, she knew, was hard come by. David said the children had her good and sensible nature. She said they had his. Sometimes Leigh thought that no matter what you did, with the best of intentions, your children grew up to be what they would be.

Take Vanessa, for example. She was a devoted mother: her children were her life. In casual Vanessa fashion she didn't mind that her teenaged son, Jack, was not a scholar, since she had never been one. But she was haunted by the discovery that her twelve-year-old daughter, Liberty, was anorexic. She blamed Beverly Hills, the California lifestyle, and their warped values. Vanessa felt that Hollywood had reached out and poisoned her child. Or perhaps it was what was happening to the whole country. She had a twelve-year-old daughter who weighed sixty-five pounds, who had to be taken to the doctor every week to have her electrolytes checked, who worried about being fat. People cared too much about how they looked. But she knew that she was the same. The furrow that had appeared between her brows from worry was smoothed out regularly by her dermatologist's injections, but her eyes showed her fear. If she couldn't save her baby, what good was she?

Sometimes, in this past year, Leigh almost couldn't look at Vanessa because her anxiety was so sad. The little self-deprecating laugh that had captivated them when they first met her years ago had deeper meaning now. A part of Vanessa, Leigh knew, felt she was a failure, and didn't know what to do.

How could she help her? What kind of advice could she give? It seemed that her own lucky life was just as much a product of chance as Vanessa's unlucky one. Vanessa still had her little dates, her little flings. She kept up with some men for years, even after they had become platonic. She found new ones, who were not.

Vanessa's behavior no longer seemed to Leigh like an amusing part of society's new permissiveness, the attendance at the national party, but a need for validation; and that was sad too. It was hard for Leigh to imagine that someone as beautiful and nice as Vanessa needed such constant proof that she was wanted.

And then there was stubborn Cady. That summer she had retreated to her parents' house in Scarsdale, rejected and defeated and deeply depressed, which was natural. But she had, without waiting very long, called Paul again. And he, to Leigh's surprise, without even waiting as long as Leigh would have expected, had taken her back.

They had met for lunch in New York, and made up. Of course Paul had been furious that she had left him for another man, but Cady had reminded him that she had also left him for a normal future, and it was not her fault that the man had turned out to be deceitful.

Paul had missed her when she was away, so much so that he had not found a replacement. And so, in the fall, he had rented another small apartment for her, and put her in it, and their lives resumed as before, with one change: He said he would marry her after a year. The year of waiting was her penance, to prove she wouldn't cheat on him again.

But five years had passed, and Paul was a grandfather, and Cady was forty, and Paul had still not married her.

Now, at last, Leigh thought she understood. Cady wanted the romance, the breathless waiting. So did Paul. He really loved her. He had come back after she had hurt his heart and his pride, and he had stayed. No matter what either of them said, neither of them really wanted marriage and normalcy. Both of them wanted the fantasy. All those years Leigh had thought Paul did not really love Cady, that he was using her, but now she realized he did love her a great deal, and Cady was using him too.

Cady always said that Leigh's life was perfect, but Leigh knew that Cady had lived through quiet moments of her own and had never appreciated them. Cady had eventually become bored. She had never understood that boredom was as much a part of the normal life she said she wanted as excitement was. It was not fun to do homework with children, or at least it had not been for Leigh. It was not fun to watch your husband perfectly happily watching sports on television if you didn't like sports, as she did not. No matter what Cady fantasized, not everyone at business parties was interesting to talk to, and sometimes none of them were. Sometimes Leigh would have much rather gone home to bed.

In the long run Cady didn't have to think or worry about anyone but herself, even though she obsessed about Paul. The bite of loneliness was her trade-off. Hadn't she learned from her ill-fated affair with Steven that you could be just as lonely when you were living with someone else? Apparently not.

So now the friends were meeting again at Vanessa's hotel bar. It was a cold fall evening, and Vanessa looked glamorous in a fluffy fur she only wore in New York. Her husband had done well and was very good to her, and that was part of her own trade-off — living in a place that had enriched her family, but a place whose values she despised. She didn't seem to understand there were anorexic schoolgirls living in New York too.

Cady and Vanessa — each one thought her problem was uniquely her own: Vanessa's ill daughter, Cady's long romance with a married man. Oh, of course it happened to other people too, but that thought did not serve for solace or caution.

I will not ask her about Liberty, Leigh thought. And she will not ask Cady about Paul. And everyone will have fun.

They kissed hello and ordered white wine. Cady was flushed and pretty from the chill air outside, wearing a fashionable new black coat. Charlie was the last to arrive, all smiles, ruefully squeezing his long legs under the tiny table. He had brought Vanessa a rose.

"Charlie, that is so sweet," Vanessa said.

"I took it off the other table," he said, and winked. They laughed.

"What a sport," Cady said.

He looked around at them appreciatively. "Remember how poor we were when we met?" he said. "And look at us now."

"Those wonderful spaghetti and Chianti suppers!" Vanessa said.

"We aren't so old now, are we?" Cady asked.

"Oh, yes we are," Vanessa said.

"Old enough to worry about spaghetti," Charlie said cheerfully, and patted his lean stomach.

"Can you believe we slept four in that little room?" Leigh said. "It boggles the imagination."

"Good thing I was hardly ever there," Vanessa said with her little laugh.

"How popular we were," Leigh said. "All those boys."

"Men," Vanessa said.

"Speak for your own," Leigh said.

Cady looked off into the middle distance. "Do you realize that if Susan Brown were still alive she would be forty years old?"

They fell silent. Charlie looked uncomfortable and cracked his knuckles. Vanessa toyed with her rings. "Yes," Leigh said finally, "that's strange but true."

"I'm sorry I brought it up," Cady said.

"No, she's part of our past too," Vanessa said.

Leigh raised her glass. "To Susan," she said. "I wish she were still here." They all raised their glasses too, solemnly, and it occurred to her that they were much nicer to Susan's memory now than they had been to her person when she was alive.

"I bet she would be married to one of her skinny little guys," Cady said. "Still making bad chili for him and their kids."

"But I think of her as twenty-three," Leigh said.

"Because she is," Vanessa said.

Charlie sighed quietly. "A wasted life," he

said, and his voice was almost a whisper.

If things had been different they probably wouldn't have remembered her, Leigh thought. Now they would never forget her.

"Well, let's drink to us now," Vanessa said. "Let's not be miserable another minute. I don't come to New York every day, you know, and I don't see my friends nearly enough, so let's be happy we're together."

"And what are your plans while you're here?" Cady asked her.

"Shopping, a museum or two, and then you never know."

"Don't ask her," Leigh said with a smile.

"I always find a way to entertain myself," Vanessa said, smiling back.

"Or be entertained *by* someone," Charlie said.

"Maybe I'm not so old, right?" Vanessa said, and patted his hand.

"Certainly not to me," he said. "Next time I'll get you roses from a real shop."

"It's the thought that counts," Vanessa said.

Now that I'm an adult I wish I could take back all the hard words that were ever spoken, all the thoughtless childish acts, Leigh thought. We had no idea, really, when we were young, how we affected other people. But what else could we have done but what we did? Now that I look back I can't even remember what Susan Brown did that was so unbearable, just that she annoyed us so much we didn't want her around and eventually couldn't live with her.

Would things have ended differently if we had been kinder to her? Would *she* have been different, better, more bearable? Would she have gone on to find the man of her dreams and leave us in peace? Would she be making someone happy today, a husband perhaps, a child, someone who needed her?

Or would she have had an unfulfilling and miserable life, still sometimes wishing she was dead, perhaps even killing herself later?

How can we even try to know, Leigh thought. She looked at her friends, their bright eyes, their smiles, the disappointments they hid or had perhaps briefly forgotten, and for the first time since she had turned forty she didn't feel "middle-aged" anymore. She felt young, with all the promise of life still ahead of her. And so were they.

chapter
27

Vanessa had never made real women friends in California. The women she knew thought they were her friends, but she knew they were more acquaintances. A friend was someone you confided your secrets to. She had always been a lone wolf, and besides, her secrets were dangerous. It was her two ex-roommates, Leigh and Cady, from long ago, who lived far away, that she considered her real women friends. By the same token, in some way she had never felt her life in California was her real life. It was as if she were in a dream, waiting for something to happen. The days here were too sunny, too alike.

It was only her daughter's self-starvation that kept her anchored to the here and now, and afraid of the future. Liberty was going to a therapist at last, and Vanessa could just hope for the best. Anorexics could die. Or they could start to eat for some reason, and recover. It depended on how sick they were. She didn't know which her daughter would be.

In the mornings when she had dropped the children off at school and Bill was at his office, she would take her coffee to the large picture window that looked out over her gardens and swimming pool and the tall buildings of the city in the distance, and she would feel lonely. No one really needed her at home; she had a housekeeper who cooked and ran errands, a cleaning woman, and a gardener. There were people working in those tall buildings, seeing other people, worrying about their daily career problems, and she had never been one of them. Sometimes Vanessa thought she ought to get a job.

But what was she good for? She couldn't be a flight attendant anymore and didn't want to be, and she didn't know how to be a secretary. She didn't much want to sell things in a boutique. She thought it would be boring to be a receptionist, and besides she was probably too old. Some of the wives she knew had gone to school and gotten real estate licenses, or were calling themselves interior decorators, but she was not interested in other people's homes. She was hardly interested in her own.

Her few charitable endeavors threw her in with the same women she knew socially, the ones she also lunched with, played tennis with, and shopped with. These were not the contacts she imagined in those far-away office buildings that gleamed pastel in the bright blue air. She fantasized herself making deals, selling scripts or buying them, having something to do with the movie world; but she knew she wasn't good at the arts either. Was she good at *nothing?*

Or was she just lazy? Was she selfish? And was self-absorbed so terrible a thing to be, when the world didn't need her anyway?

Her family needed her. Perhaps. Her husband and son took her for granted and her daughter had a life Vanessa couldn't help her with.

Now, what would she do today?

She swam forty minutes of laps in the pool and washed her hair. After school Jack would stay to play football and Liberty would be in the school gym, working out far too long. Vanessa didn't even have to get them until time for supper. She had offered to take Liberty shopping to get her out of the gym, but Liberty had refused. She probably didn't want her mother to see how skinny she'd gotten, but her mother had noticed.

All I want is a *touch* of anorexia, a piece

of hers, Vanessa thought, and decided to forego lunch.

When her friend Pamela called and asked her if she wanted to go with her to look at some houses, Vanessa was bored enough to say yes. Pamela was her age, an attractive blonde who had married a rich man she treated as if he were even richer, and she had lived in three houses already and remodeled the one she was in now. She wanted a larger one. Vanessa tagged along.

While Pamela chatted with the realtor Vanessa thought how unattractive most of these huge homes were. The furniture was too big, and so were the rooms. Some of the paintings were hideous. Some of the décor was still from the fifties and sixties. The houses had been scrupulously neatened for showing, but in one Vanessa noticed that the family cat had diligently scratched the sofa arm to shreds, and no one had seemed to care enough to get a scratching post. She tried to picture the lives of the people who lived in these rooms and wondered how many people there were in each house. She was sure most of it was wasted space.

"Look at this house!" Pamela whispered. "She got it in the divorce! I could live here."

"So could a football team, and here's their field with a bar in it."

The photos of family and friends interested her the most. The divorced woman was apparently a former trophy wife. She appeared in almost every picture: in an evening gown, skiing, on a beach, with groups at a dinner, and with celebrities in limbo. In the bedroom, framed photos were lined up on the dresser. There was one picture, though, that wasn't framed. It was just stuck into the edge of the frame as if it were new, or perhaps temporary. Vanessa looked at it, curious.

It was a photograph of her own husband, Bill, smiling.

What was her husband's photo doing in the bedroom of a woman she had never even heard of? Vanessa felt a jolt of shock and realization. It couldn't be possible . . . and yet, it was the only explanation she could think of. Her nice, easygoing husband, whom she had trusted, was having an affair.

She felt both pained and perplexed. She had always assumed they had a happy marriage. She knew Bill took her for granted, as she did him, but she had never considered that he would cheat on her. But why not? She had been cheating on him for years. What had made her so confident, so blind, as to think he could never want an adventure of his own?

But he couldn't have one on her home turf. That was going too far. That could hurt her and the children. This assignation was too regular and would have to stop.

She didn't want Pamela to know — certainly until she had decided what to do about this threatening situation. The worst thing would be gossip. Vanessa quickly pulled the photograph of Bill out of the corner of the frame and tucked it into her handbag. If the woman wondered, fine. She would have more to worry about soon.

"Whose house is this?" Vanessa asked Pamela innocently when Pamela had finished going through the woman's closets.

"Her name is Jean . . . uh, Wildruff. Her ex-husband is the big movie attorney."

Uh-huh. And does she think she has another attorney lined up, Vanessa thought. Not for long.

They still had another house to see. Vanessa was sorry she and Pamela had come in the same car because she wanted nothing more than to rush home where she could be alone and think, and now she had to pretend to be composed. Her mind was full of questions. The viewing of the next house passed in a blur. When she drove home, in her own car at last, Vanessa narrowly averted an accident, and when she got there she had to take a tranquilizer, which she seldom did, in order to be calm enough to pick up the kids later.

While she waited for the pill to work she looked at the photo of Bill again. It was no mistake. She even recognized the tie that she'd given him last Christmas. The idea of her husband wearing the tie she had given him, while he was romancing another woman, infuriated her. He probably didn't even remember where he'd gotten it, or maybe he didn't care. Maybe he was thinking of leaving.

She thought about their sex life together. It wasn't very frequent these days, but it wasn't infrequent enough to make her worry. They'd have a drink, a little togetherness, sex; the reminder that they had a bond. She didn't really want more with him.

How stupid I am, Vanessa thought, to think something like this could never happen to me. It had happened to so many couples, and she heard the stories from the angry and aggrieved wives. Couples who had been happy together for many years were the exception. Leigh and David, of course, and, until now, she had thought herself and Bill. She had not counted her transgressions in the mix. She and Bill had been contented enough to pass for people with a good marriage.

Now she realized he had always been a stranger. If she had really known him, wouldn't it have occurred to her that he could have a yearning she wasn't a part of? Wouldn't she have thought he was capable of wanting more than he had, or something different than what he had: something new and exciting, something that was his alone?

Bill was an attractive man. Why didn't she think other women would be after him, and that he could say yes? It wasn't respect, she realized now, it was lack of respect.

Vanessa wondered if she wanted him to leave. No, of course she didn't, even though she felt like making him suffer. She was in pain so why shouldn't he be? But the children needed him. She couldn't let him break up their family, when their daughter was so fragile.

She couldn't let him continue this affair right under her nose either. If he'd strayed while on a business trip it would be one thing, but not this — lying to her and sneaking around. She had her faults and foibles, but she had never done anything at home.

Was her need for him to stay merely for the sake of the children, or was it for herself too? Vanessa wondered what it would be like to be single again. She knew she would have no difficulty finding men. But would they be kind men, marriage material? She'd been out of the mainstream for a long time. She didn't want to start again, to disregard different faults than the ones she'd already gotten used to, to try to fall in love. And to be realistic, there weren't as many available men around as there had been the first time. She saw how desperately attractive women connived and scrounged for partners.

Her marriage to Bill, while not exciting, was a part of her life, and she had assumed it would go on for many years. She hadn't thought much about a lonely future because that would be so far away: when they were old, when he was dead.

She should have thought about it.

The family had supper together and Vanessa managed to act normal. But as soon as the children were safely in their rooms doing homework she took Bill by the wrist, led him to the bedroom, shut the door, and hissed at him. "Sit down. I want you to tell me all about you and Jean Wildruff."

He looked stunned for a moment and then Vanessa could see the silky mask slide over his face as he began to think how to dissemble. "Who?" he asked.

"Your girlfriend."

"What did you hear?"

"Enough."

"People tell lies," he said.

"And photos tell the truth," Vanessa said. She took his photo out of her handbag and showed it to him. She could see the mask begin to slip a little. "Why was this in her bedroom?"

"What were you doing in her bedroom?" Bill asked.

"What were *you* doing there?"

"I don't know what that was doing in her bedroom."

"Please, don't insult my intelligence."

He was silent.

"Are you in love with her?" Vanessa asked.

"No," he said. "You don't understand."

"Then explain to me."

"She's just someone I know."

"Wrong," Vanessa said. "Try again."

"Why were you in her house?" he asked, trying to sound stern.

"It's a small world. I'm still waiting for an explanation."

"I don't know what you want me to say," he said. He looked upset and vulnerable and caught.

"How long have you been seeing her?"

He shrugged.

"I don't go through your things but maybe *you* have a picture of *her* too," Vanessa said.

"I'm sorry," he said. "I don't know what to say."

"Start with the truth."

"You don't want the truth."

"Yes I do," Vanessa said.

"It's just my middle-aged crisis," Bill said. "A man gets to a certain age, he gets crazy. It has nothing to do with you."

"But I was obviously not enough."

"It has nothing to do with how I feel about you."

"But I was not enough," Vanessa said.

What am I doing, she thought. He hasn't been enough for me either. How hypocritical could she get?

"It's not like that," he said.

It occurred to her then that he didn't really know why he was having an affair, that he hadn't thought about it, that he couldn't express his motivations even if he had some idea. She was not sure she could explain why she picked up men in New York. I need the reassurance, she thought, but how would you tell your husband he wasn't able to reassure you? Just as she wasn't able to push away his fears of being older, of being mortal, of missing out on something.

"Are you planning to leave me?" Vanessa asked.

"Of course not! Are you going to leave me now?"

"Not if you stop seeing her."

"I'll stop."

"You'd better," Vanessa said. "I have my ways of finding out." This was not true, but he believed her.

"It's the only affair I ever had," he said.

"I don't care. As long as it's the last."

"It will be."

She wondered if he would really stop. He would be careful, though, and he would be afraid of her. He might break up with this woman and start up with another. Now Vanessa didn't know anything anymore. This was her marriage, and it was flawed. They would stumble along, but something was broken. She had preferred thinking she was the bad one. She was more disillusioned today than she had ever dreamed she could be yesterday, but they would keep up their pretense and they would make their marriage whole — as whole as was possible for a union based on lies and insecurity and the need for a peaceful home.

chapter
28

Cady was basically a forgiving person. Although her love affair with Steven Irving had ended so badly, it had been a long time ago, so now they had been friends again for several years. After all, she had to see him at school every day, and acrimony would only make her uncomfortable. Time healed all wounds, it was said. They had lunch together frequently, with the other teachers, or alone if no one was available, but not alone in the coffee shop outside of school. That would be too friendly.

He told her about his new girlfriends. He had a few live-in affairs, but they ended badly. He had never married again, and she was not too surprised. Sometimes she gave him advice. He never gave her advice, since she was still with Paul, and Steven's interference with that relationship was the only thing they would never mention. There were wounds even time would not heal.

Cady thought of him as a sort of cousin. She could never think of him as a brother, but cousin was close enough. She wasn't attracted to him anymore, although she could still appreciate that he was attractive. She felt she was mature to be handling this friendship so well. She could even tell Paul, who didn't mind. He trusted her at last.

No one at school cared either way. She and Steven were old news, just as she and Paul were, although eventually the new girls were always told the Paul and Cady story, and the Cady and Steven story (what they knew of it), and they looked at her with interest. She was a forty-year-old teacher with a past, and even better, with a present.

She liked being a legend. After all, what else did she have? Every year Paul had a new excuse why he couldn't marry her yet, and every year Cady accepted it. She hardly ever proposed to him anymore. Since he felt guilty, he was the one who mentioned it more often. Everything at home was drama that demanded his attention. His wife and Danny were long finished with their analysts. Danica had two children, and the younger one, a daughter, had been born with a hole in her heart.

That was high drama indeed, demanding that Paul remain in the family, and then when there was a successful heart operation Paul felt that everyone was still emotionally fragile and could not bear any bad news from him.

What an ego he had, Cady thought, but put up with it. What about the hole in *my* heart, she thought, but kept quiet. Sometimes she looked at other men but thought it wasn't worth the trouble. She was beyond the age of attracting every man she met. She knew someone could still come along, but she wasn't interested. Paul was her investment, a part of her life. She just wanted to close the deal.

They spent another summer together. By now Cady was convinced that he and his wife were so estranged they might as well be legally separated, except that they lived together some of the time. She was sure his wife knew. She had to know. And she obviously didn't care. It seemed odd for someone to be in such deep denial, although Paul said his wife didn't know.

I would know, Cady thought. I've seen the games he plays.

When fall came and they had to play their own games again she was depressed, as she was every fall, even though she had been dealing with this for sixteen years. When it rained or snowed he didn't come by. Cady thought of his wife snug and warm in their apartment, with him there, and felt jealous and sad. Then she told herself he probably wasn't even speaking to his wife. She knew firsthand how lonely you could be in the same room with someone else who didn't want to be with you — even someone who did — and she appreciated these separations because they made her long to be with him again. She knew he felt the same.

"I can't go on like this," Cady told him that fall, although she said it more out of habit than emotion. He would only make up some other excuse. But they had just made love and she thought it might have made him vulnerable. After all, who else did he have to make love with? Now he was satisfied, drowsy, and comfortable. He wasn't dressed yet, although he was pretty quick at dressing, and therefore he couldn't get away until she had her say. "I can't," she said. "You have to decide. It's her or me."

"It's not just her," he said. He slid his leg into his trousers.

"But it's me," Cady said. "You have to make up your mind if you want me or not."

"Of course I want you."

"Not enough to be with me all the time."

Paul looked at her blankly. She had never seen just that look before. And Cady suddenly realized that he had run out of excuses. She waited.

He finished dressing and then sat down heavily on the edge of the bed as if he were exhausted. He sighed. "You deserve more than I've been giving you," he said.

"That's correct. A-plus."

"I don't know why you put up with me."

"Neither do I."

"I love you," he said.

"I love you."

"We've been through a lot together, you and I," he said. She thought he looked older. But then, of course, he *was* older. He had been getting older all the time, as she had, as everyone had. What adventure could the two of them have that they hadn't? Travel, vacations, normal time, and marriage, of course. This was something she had neglected to remind him, but now she felt it loud and clear.

It was time for them to get married. They needed the change.

It was not just that she needed something different from her years of waiting, but that there was an excitement missing, at last. You couldn't keep tension going forever. They'd had their ups and downs, but things had subtly shifted during all these years, as she supposed was true during a long marriage. But people in a marriage didn't expect what she and Paul had engineered during their long affair. The way their affair had been structured there was supposed to be an edge. She didn't dare explain this to him, but she knew it was true. Things needed to be better.

"I haven't been fair to you," Paul said.

"No, you haven't."

"Do you really want to marry me?"

"Of course I do."

"I'm going to leave her," he said.

Oh sure, that was what he always said. She almost yawned. Don't tell me what you always do, she thought. I'm too tired.

"I'll tell her tonight," Paul said mildly.

He would *what?* At first she couldn't believe he had actually said it.

"You'll tell her you're leaving?" Cady cried.

"Yes."

She threw her arms around him and hugged him as if he had come home after a long journey.

"Yes! Tonight, yes!" she cried joyfully.

"Even if she has a headache, even if she has a gun in her hand, you'll tell her! Do you promise?"

"Yes."

"And if she's asleep?"

"She's never asleep when I come home."

"Will you tell her about me?"

"No, I don't think so. Why upset her more than I will anyway? She'll figure it out soon enough. I'll call my lawyer in the morning, and of course she'll call hers." He looked at her carefully. "You know, Cady, she'll get a lot."

"I don't care." She knew that even with the division of property and money, she would be better off with Paul than she was now. She had thought about it often enough. She would have what she had wanted for so long: him, the life he led, and all the things that made life comfortable. Cady Fisher. Mrs. Paul Fisher. The prophesy of the monograms would come true at last. She would have silver-framed photographs of the grandchildren on the living room tables.

When he left he looked anxious. Cady kissed him. "Don't be afraid," she told him. "We deserve this. It's our long overdue happiness."

She was up most of the night by the phone: anticipating, worrying, wringing her hands, sighing, giggling nervously, hopeful. When she wasn't staring at the phone willing it to ring she was pacing the floor. Finally he called her, at two o'clock, whispering, sounding as if he were hiding.

"It's done," he said.

"Thank God," Cady said.

"She took it badly."

"But it's done."

"Yes."

"I love you," she said.

"I too. I'll call you tomorrow morning."

"We'll make plans," Cady said.

"Yes," he said guardedly. "Good-night."

She went to bed hugging herself, and fell into a deep and dreamless sleep, the winner of the battle.

The next morning Paul called her from the office before she had left for school. "I didn't have much sleep," he said. "I'm going to have to move out. I'll go to a hotel. You'll live with me there until everything's sorted out, all right? So many things to be divided. . . . Eventually we'll find an apartment. When I'm single again we'll get married. I think for now the best thing would be a residential hotel, with a small kitchen. Something near my office."

"A hotel will be fine."

"That's what I thought. I was up all

night thinking and planning."

Planning for us, she thought happily. "I'll give up my apartment," she said. "Why should you pay two rents?"

"Yes, you should. Could you leave by the end of the month?"

He was always so practical. "I could leave tomorrow," Cady said.

"Have lunch with me and we'll start to look."

When she hung up she called Leigh at her office. Leigh was a partner now at the company, and she was always there very early. Cady had never been sure if Leigh's promotion had been partly nepotism because of David, but it was true that Leigh was very capable and a hard worker. Two more women had been hired at the company too. It was a sign of the times.

"You won't believe this," Cady shrieked. "Paul told his wife last night that he wants a divorce. He's actually leaving her. We're going to live together in a hotel while he gets his divorce. Then we're going to get married. Married, Leigh, married!"

"I'm amazed," Leigh said. "And thrilled for you."

"I waited and patience paid off," Cady said.

"Yes, it did."

"I'm still kind of in shock," Cady said.

"You've wanted this for so long."

"It just . . . happened," Cady said. "It was the right time."

"That's when those things do happen," Leigh said. "When it's the right time. That's what happened with David and me."

"So we'll both have our happy ending," Cady said.

She remembered how surprised and overjoyed Leigh had been when David left his wife for her. And now it was her own turn to have a future. One woman's happy ending is another woman's disaster, she thought, but she couldn't make herself care. His wife had never been a person, she had been a mountain. The mountain had been moved.

She and Paul found a respectable residential hotel in walking distance of his office. The suite was rather fusty and old, with ugly brown-velour furniture in the living room. And the kitchen hadn't seen work since the hotel was built, but Cady didn't care. When Paul's elegant suits were hanging in the closet it looked much better. Her clothes joined them. For the moment her furniture was put into storage. Who knew how much or little

Paul would keep after the divorce?

Her mother, as always, was indispensable in the move, helping with advice and coordination. Although one would think her mother would be suspicious by now of all this moving around, or at least annoyed at the work involved, her mother was pleased and optimistic. Cady thought, as she always did, how lucky she was to have a mother who was always on her side.

Her father was pleased too. "He finally did the right thing," her father said. He just wanted to see Cady's life settled. Eventually, through the years, Cady's mother had told him everything. He had been shocked at first, and then finally resigned, although he had never really sanctioned Cady's behavior. But time, and the things that were happening in the morals and mores of the society around them, had softened him. What his daughter had done was not something you could take lightly, but she was his daughter, and he wasn't old-fashioned enough to throw her out into a snowstorm. Besides, she wasn't living at home and he wasn't paying her rent, so he couldn't throw her anywhere. He was sad perhaps, and bewildered, and wondered where he and her mother had gone wrong; but now everything would be all right.

It had not occurred to Cady before how happy she would be to be conventional at last and have the approval of her parents and the world. It was a bonus she had not dared to let herself think about. She had only thought about love.

chapter
29

Cady did her best to make their hotel rooms homey. She put fresh flowers in a crystal vase on the coffee table, and she bought colorful scarves and draped them over the itchy, brown sofa and armchairs. Her dishes and silverware were in the small kitchen. What a life her monogrammed flatware had led! It had been as peripatetic as hers — rejected, and accepted, and rejected, and accepted, and so much waiting — it seemed now that the only thing to do was use it and stop saving it for "good." If you saved things for "good," good never came.

She was happy now, her face radiant. She looked well. There were shortcomings to their new living arrangement, of course: the hotel apartment still didn't look pretty or elegant, there wasn't much sunlight, and it had that odd hotel smell, a combination of anonymous use and detergent. It felt strange to make love in stiff hotel sheets, as if their joining were illicit. She didn't find the experience erotic, but distancing. The last few years her little apartment had been like a romantic cocoon, and now she appreciated it. But Paul seemed not to mind the hotel. Still, Cady thought she should have brought more things from home — her silky sheets and fluffy towels for certain — although the linen and maid service came with the rooms so it would have been impractical.

Since they had moved in together Paul had continued to live his life in much the same way he would have if she weren't there. He worked late at the office, had early evening meetings, and after the first two weeks, which they treated as sort of a honeymoon, he began going to dinner with clients more frequently than she would have liked. She realized she hadn't really thought about the reality of their life together, although he had warned her often enough in their later years.

"Why can't I come too?" she demanded.

"They wouldn't understand. This isn't a date thing. I never brought my wife."

"I'm not your wife."

"Then it would be even more inappropriate to bring you along when I'm trying to make a deal."

"I should think the presence of a woman

would cheer things up," she said.

"Some of the clients are women," he said.

"Oh."

Who were these women? Masculine, unattractive career women, Cady thought, and then she remembered Leigh. Leigh was beautiful, fashionable, and feminine, and she had business dinners with difficult men, weaving her spell to get what she wanted.

She knew that on some of those evenings when Paul was living with his wife he went out to restaurants with clients. She remembered that occasionally he had arrived in her apartment looking frazzled and smelling of secondhand smoke, and she had known he had come from a restaurant, even before he had told her. But he had only stayed for a few minutes on those nights, because it had been late.

Now he was going out with clients more than he used to. She supposed he was going through a busy period. And he needed the money. He would have to make more now that his wife was taking half of what he had. He was doing it for her too, and at least she had him all night, even if he went right to sleep.

She was auditioning to be his next wife,

and she couldn't complain. She was going to show him how much better his life would be with her.

He told her the divorce negotiations were turning out to be unpleasant, but he got upset when Cady pressed him for details, so she let him tell her when he wanted to. She knew getting a divorce was always difficult. He said Danica was shocked and disapproving. Danica told him he was too old to change his life and owed more than that to her mother. Cady wondered how she could have been so in love with Danica all those years ago when Danica was a fresh-faced schoolgirl who worshiped her and in turn could do no wrong. Now Danica was just a judgmental housewife, still the impediment she'd been for years.

Cady made breakfast but no other meals. She and Paul had dinner in the hotel dining room, or sometimes at a restaurant, and sometimes he just sent for room service if he was tired. She liked the table wheeled in, the silver covered dishes, and the single rose. It reminded her of travel. "Where should we go for our honeymoon?" she asked him.

"It depends on the season."

"Paris? Venice?"

"Those would be good."

She had never been anywhere, and he hadn't for years. If he had taken his wife to Paris or Venice she knew she wouldn't have been able to put up with it. The only thing that had made the years with his wife bearable had been the knowledge that neither of them was having a good time. Now she felt a certain sympathy for him. Poor Paul, he had put his life on hold just as she had. But they would live now.

One night when Paul had a business dinner Cady called Charlie Rackley to see if he was free. He was, and happy to hear from her, so they met at a little French bistro halfway between his office and her hotel. There was a shiny copper bar with bowls of oysters in ice on it, and they ate some, and drank white wine.

"Now that my life is settled you're the only one left in our group who's single," Cady said.

"Don't rub it in," he said. "Besides, you aren't married yet."

"But I will be."

"And someday I'll find the right woman," he said.

"That's an old excuse."

"But it's true."

"You're such a catch," Cady said.

"The more reason for me to be discriminating," Charlie said, and laughed.

"I don't know what's wrong with men these days that they don't want to get married," Cady said. "My friend Steven Irving is just as bad as you are."

"I don't know why you consider him your friend," Charlie said.

"Oh, I'm tolerant. And he's an idiot. Deficient. He can't help the way he is. But it's better to be his friend than an enemy, considering that I have to look at him at school every day."

"I can't imagine anyone doing what he did to you," Charlie said.

"That's because you're a good person."

"It's hard to be one," Charlie said. "I try. I don't want to hurt anyone, lead anyone on. I do the best I can. I never want to harm another human being."

"Then how can you possibly date?" Cady said with a smile.

He smiled back. "I do date. But very, very carefully."

"Obviously too carefully."

"No, I don't think so. I've had my share of lunatics. Sometimes you don't know until it's too late."

"Someday you're going to sit down and tell me all about your love life," Cady said.

"There's nothing interesting to tell."

"*That's* tragic."

"So, have you set a date yet?"

"No. Paul has to get divorced first. That takes time. We may just elope when he's free, and have a party. We're adult, sophisticated people."

"That sounds good."

"I'd like to have a dress I can wear again. It's going to be expensive. Or maybe a suit. A Chanel suit would be fabulous. A white one. Especially if we elope."

"Of course," Charlie said.

"I have so few close friends," Cady said. "It should be a small wedding in any case. But then there are the relatives, and I have the feeling my mother is going to want to invite all of them to prove I finally got married after all. I have cousins I wouldn't recognize if I fell over them. I'd rather have a party for my friends. No one will be insulted that way."

"And you can send out the announcement later," Charlie said.

"You're the only man I know who I can talk to about things like my wedding," Cady said.

"You can talk to me about anything."

"Do you know how unusual that is?"

"Yes," he said.

"I hope you can talk to me about anything too," Cady said.

"I can." But for an instant, just a flash, almost imperceptibly really, he looked guarded. Cady noticed, and then the look was gone.

"You really can," she said.

"I know."

There's a part of Charlie Rackley none of us will ever get to, Cady thought. We never have, either. But he's so sweet and good and docile that we think we own him. Strange, isn't it? You just assume some people are less complicated than they are because they're nice.

He picked up the check after dinner and put her into a cab. Before he opened the door he leaned over to say good-night and kissed her on the cheek. "Christian Dior," he said.

"Or Givenchy," Cady said. They smiled at each other, old friends who could speak shorthand, who understood and cared.

She got home before Paul. She was in her robe watching television when he got in. "How was your evening?" she asked.

"Boring," he said.

He undressed and she heard him washing up in the bathroom. He was always a bit grumpy after his business dinners lately and she thought he might be working too hard. He had too much on his mind.

"Is there a problem at work?" she asked.
"No."

It must be the money, she thought. I won't bother him. When he kissed her good-night perfunctorily and turned over to go to sleep with his back to her she understood. They would be together for years and he would have his moods. He had warned her that marriage was sometimes difficult and she was ready for whatever would come.

Dior, Cady thought. Or Givenchy. Or Chanel. The color should be ivory.

The next evening he was late, and while Cady was waiting for him his office called. She was a little flattered that his secretary was calling him at the hotel, as if it were his home and she his wife, but she wondered where he was. "Your office called," she said when he showed up.

"Okay. Too late to call them back; it'll have to wait."

"Where were you?"

"I stopped to see if I could buy a suit," he said.

"And did you?"

"No, I just looked."

This was the stuff of everyday life, the things she hadn't known about, which would all be part of hers now. Still, she thought it would have been nice if he had asked her to go with him. She liked to shop. Didn't wives help their husbands pick their clothes?

The next night he was late again. This was becoming a pattern, and for the first time she wondered, oddly, if he was becoming bored with her, if he would always be late, if he wouldn't come bounding in anymore the way he had when their time together was limited. Did she want too much? Were her desires fantasies, the stuff of teenaged girls' imaginings? Why did men get bored with her when they moved in together? Was she boring? Unlucky? Was this just the way men were, needing to be independent, to have free time even if it was just to do something unimportant? Was she too needy, too dependent?

"Where were you?" Cady asked, trying not to sound accusatory.

"I had a meeting."

"Where?"

"A client's office."

They ordered dinner from room service. He wanted to watch television while they were eating. Then he wanted to go to sleep right after dinner, saying he was exhausted. The weekend is coming, Cady thought. It will be all right. I will not turn into a harridan. I will not turn into a wife.

chapter
30

"Cady's been complaining about Paul," Leigh told David. They were at dinner in one of their favorite restaurants, a small informal neighborhood bistro, and it was a date. From time to time they sneaked away for an evening of their own, away from work, from the kids, from everything. She thought how it was one of those clichés you read about in women's magazines, the old-married-couple date, but it worked for them. Leigh had a friend who had been married as long as they had and who occasionally went to a hotel with her husband, where they watched rented pornographic movies on the TV and had sex, but she and David were pleased they didn't need that. They were such good companions and lovers that they just needed some time alone to make things fresh and new.

"She says he's ignoring her again," she said.

"She doesn't understand, does she?" David said.

"You mean the cycles of marriage."

"Yes."

"No, and that's why she stayed with a man she couldn't marry, but poor thing, she never could see that the cycles happen anyway."

"Except the changes of that villain Steven, of course."

"Oh, him," Leigh said. "That was doomed."

They thought about it for a moment, remembering.

"You and I are blessed," David said.

"We always were." She smiled at him and he took her hand, playing with her rings.

"How could I be so lucky to get you?" he said. "You were too young to know any better."

"I knew," Leigh said.

But she realized it had been chance. She could have fallen in love with a different man when she was naïve and new to New York, but David had come along and that was that.

They shared a bottle of wine and had brandy with their coffee. Then they decided to take a walk home in the chilly air. They held hands and stopped to look in the Madison Avenue store windows, some covered with heavy protective gratings now, the jewelry store windows empty except for photographs of what had been removed for the night because of potential burglars. New York was not the same city it had been when they met, but they had adapted and hardly thought of it. A lone cruising taxi came by, driving slowly along in the empty streets. Leigh didn't think she would like to live here. Their neighborhood was friendlier somehow, more domestic; the watchful doormen looked solid.

A man came out of one of the little Madison Avenue apartment buildings and shouted "Hey!" and waved at the taxi. It stopped and he walked briskly toward it. He looked familiar. Leigh wouldn't even have paid attention except that there was something frantic about him, and something almost furtive. Then she recognized him.

"That's Paul Fisher," she said. "Isn't it?"

"Yes," David said.

"I thought he was a robber," she said. "What do you think he was doing there?"

"Visiting someone? A meeting?"

"A meeting at someone's apartment?"

"It's possible."

"Paul has a bad history with people's apartments," Leigh said.

"Do you think he has a girlfriend?" David asked.

"Oh, I hope not. I'm not going to say anything to Cady."

"No, you shouldn't."

But she thought about it afterward, and wondered. He had not noticed them.

It was hard to run into people in Manhattan — you could disappear there if you wanted to. All you had to do was change your habits. But Paul had changed his habits, and he had run into them. Ordinarily Leigh never saw him. And then, a week later, she saw him again.

She was having an early business dinner with a difficult client, Lucille White, a nervous older woman whose acting career had suddenly taken off after a decade, and who had instantly begun making demands. They were on Madison Avenue once more because Lucille wanted to have dinner at a café there that featured a Tarot card reader. While Lucille was having her reading Leigh looked around, bored, at the shadowy, candlelit room, the tables for two, the whispering diners, and there was Paul with a woman.

The woman was young — perhaps late twenties — and pretty, slim, with short, spiky red hair and pouting lips. He was leaning closer to her than he had any right to. She ran her fingers through her dramatic little hairdo and then Paul took her hand and kissed her fingers. Leigh felt her heart turn over, and then felt revulsion, because the moment had been as intimate as if she had caught them having sex in bed.

Let him tell Cady this was a client, Leigh thought. That would be a lie. She wondered if this same woman lived in the apartment she had seen Paul leaving a week before. If he had not changed his habits to avoid Cady he would not have accidentally put himself right into trouble with Cady's friend.

Leigh knew he hadn't seen her, he had been too occupied. She turned her back, wanting to leave. She listened distractedly as Lucille raved to her about the accuracy of the reading she'd just had. When Lucille tried to persuade her to have one too, Leigh demurred, saying she had to go home to her children. What she really needed to do was go home and think.

As soon as the kids were settled down for the night she told David what she had seen. "What should I do?" she asked him. "This time I *know*."

"Let it play itself out," he said. He hated gossip, even when it was completely justified.

"But she's planning to marry him."

"Let that play itself out too."

"You don't think he will?"

"I have no idea."

"But you're a man!" Leigh protested, as if that meant he could understand Paul far better than she could. David smiled.

"I'm sure Cady is the one he loves," he said. "This might be a fling."

"He has no right to have a fling," Leigh said.

"Premarital jitters," David said.

"He's like a child. He's impossible. He left his wife, then immediately turned Cady into the wife, and now he's found another girlfriend. He's a man who will always need two women."

"How do you know that?"

"I know it."

"Maybe he always had another girlfriend," David said. "One or another. How would Cady find out? He said he was with his wife, but Cady was never allowed to call him there."

"You're so diabolical."

"I've listened to the stories of a lot of men," David said.

Leigh pondered that. "I need to tell her," she said.

"If you tell her she'll hate you."

"Do you think so?"

"Yes. It's the way people are."

"But if I don't, I'll hate myself."

"Then tell her."

"It's not as if they were already married," she said. "Then I'd leave well enough alone. But she can still escape so much heartbreak." She sighed. "I wish I'd never seen him tonight."

"I'm sure he'll wish that too."

"I just can't believe it," she said. "That hole. If I hadn't been with Lucille I would never have gone to a place like that — the sort of place you take your secret lover because no one you know would ever go there."

"Maybe it's fate," David said. "He was meant to be caught."

"Do you think she can make him stop?"

"I don't know."

"Vanessa made Bill stop. She says he never cheated again."

"He didn't have Paul's pattern."

"Maybe Cady will have to leave him."

"You knew that was a possibility."

"Poor Cady," Leigh said. "If she leaves him I'll feel so guilty."

"Then don't tell her."

"I have to. Maybe she won't leave him. If she stays with him it will be informed consent, and people do that, don't they, close their eyes, and go on? At least she'll have a chance to decide."

"Just tell her," David said. She knew he wanted to end the discussion, so she dropped the subject.

The next evening she called Cady at the hotel. "I have to call you back, Paul just came in," Cady said, rushed, frantic. Leigh recognized her tone from the old days, when there was never enough time.

"I only wanted to make a drinks date with you," Leigh said.

"Oh. Well, the day after tomorrow. I have my mother tomorrow."

"Six o'clock, the bar in my office building. Okay?"

"Okay." They hung up. Soon, she had the feeling, one way or the other, Cady would have more than enough time.

chapter
31

Once in a while Cady had a date with her mother in New York. Her mother drove in from Scarsdale to enjoy some city attractions: a museum or perhaps a matinee or a drink with an old friend, and then she and Cady went shopping and had a meal together, gossiping and catching up, even though they spoke on the phone every day.

Of all her friends — and Cady included her mother as one of her friends — Cady's mother was the most like her. It was not as if Cady had turned into her mother, because she hadn't. Her mother was much more practical than she was. Her mother was a born housewife, or, as they were called now, a homemaker. She cooked and baked. She lined shelves and tacked on edging. She had a garden. She enjoyed decorating. She sorted her husband's clothes in his closet according to fabric weight and color, with all the hangers facing the same way. Her own clothes were neatly arranged in long, dust-protecting moiré bags. She wrapped presents beautifully. She would not dream of having a pet.

Although Cady had inherited her mother's neatness, compulsiveness and fear of germs, she could do none of the housewifely things, nor did she want to, but she admired that her mother could, and that she liked doing them.

Now that Cady was living with Paul, her mother was playing house again, albeit vicariously. She had helped Cady choose the scarves that covered the dreary furniture. And this time when she drove into New York she brought a care package of small diet dinners she had made and frozen, for Cady to thaw so he could have a home-cooked meal. There was an oven in their little hotel kitchen, and her mother advised her that the aroma of good food cooking would cheer him up.

"You have to make those rooms a home," her mother said. "Otherwise he'll take your life too casually and keep going out. Men like permanence."

"He certainly did, didn't he," Cady said. "With that wife."

"You should get a nice case of wine. You should have candles."

"You know I can't afford any wine that I would like."

"Then I'll treat you to it."

"Puligny Montrachet," Cady said, as long as her mother was treating.

"You need to start thinking of things you want for your real home," her mother went on. "You'll be moving before long. It's time we bought new sheets and towels."

Now Cady was sorry she'd given away the monogrammed sheets when she went to live with Steven. She felt like a nomad, carrying her few possessions on her back. But did a nomad ever give so many possessions away? How many *things* it took to create a pleasant life!

She wondered if other people felt the same desperate need she did to have all the accoutrements — from her clothes to her apartment — of a perfect environment. She felt unfinished, somehow, without them. She had always striven for that perfection and it had always eluded her. There were so many things she wanted that she couldn't have. She felt she should have been born very rich, or married a very rich man, but instead she had depended on the kindness of her parents for treats during her entire life, as if she were still a child.

After all, though, Cady thought, I *am*

their child, and the only one they've got. It gives my mother pleasure to take care of me. If I had a daughter I'd be the same way.

"We'll go to the Lower East Side," her mother said. There was a linen store there that had all the things the expensive uptown boutiques carried but at a fraction of the price. If there was anything her mother liked more than shopping it was finding a bargain. It was a given that her parents would pay for these things for their engaged forty-year-old daughter. She should not be penalized for coming to her good luck so late in life. "They even monogram," her mother said.

"Where will I keep them?"

"I'll keep them at my house until you get an apartment. How's that?"

"Mom, you're so sweet."

It was a crisp night in late fall, store windows showing Halloween ornaments that hadn't been taken down, along with Thanksgiving ornaments it was too early to think about. This year I'll have Thanksgiving dinner with Paul, Cady thought. We'll go to my parents. He can't go to his vile children and grandchildren, can he?

She worried about that. What was the protocol? They would have to discuss it.

They'd discussed so little lately, he seemed so busy, and now she began to worry about Thanksgiving even though it was almost a month away. Married people, she thought, knew where their loved ones were going to be, but Paul had told her he didn't want to think about Thanksgiving yet, that he would like to take a Valium and sleep right through it.

"Oh, Mom, do you think Paul is going to want to spend Thanksgiving with his kids?"

"Didn't you ask him?"

"He won't say."

"With the divorce in the works I'm sure it will be unpleasant," her mother said. "Dad and I can come into the city and we can all go to a very lovely restaurant, early, and then if he wants to see his family he can go after dinner. That way everyone will be satisfied."

"Maybe he'll do that. It sounds sensible. I'll suggest it."

Cady had already looked at a few potential apartments, but Paul said he needed to find out what his financial status would be before they could choose one. They had discussed renting versus buying, cooperatives versus condominiums. They had at least decided that they would stay on the Upper East

Side, and that it should be an apartment building, which they were both used to, not a town house. His wife was going to keep their apartment, even though Paul said it was too big for one person alone. But she was attached to it; she had spent a lifetime there.

Now my life will start, Cady thought. She complained to Leigh and to her mother about Paul's absences from home, but she thought her mother was probably right: that once she and Paul had a real home he would enjoy spending more time there. If I had a business meeting, Cady thought, I'd be glad to get out of that hotel too. She was looking forward to her drink with Leigh tomorrow.

She and her mother took the subway down to the Lower East Side, bought vast amounts of linens, took them in a taxi to the garage where her mother had parked her car, and then went to dinner in a restaurant, where they each had a glass of white wine, a salad, and a piece of dry, broiled fish. They sent the bread away so they wouldn't eat it. Her mother, who was trim, was always on a diet and thought everyone else should be, no matter what they looked like. But now that Cady was (let's face it) middle-aged, she was always on a diet too. She remembered fondly the thick cheese sandwiches she'd ordered every night when she was rooming with the girls, and knew those days were gone forever.

She resolved to take good care of Paul. He was seventeen years older than she was, and she wanted him to live a long, healthy life. She would scour her new neighborhood to find take-out places that specialized in good, nutritious, fat-free, low-salt food, and if they couldn't afford a cook that was what she would give him. She would see that their new apartment was even more tasteful than the one he had given up for her. And she would start to do these things now, the candlelight, and the expensive wine: the little touches. Paul had sacrificed a lot. She wanted to make him happy. He had so much on his mind.

When she met Leigh for a drink the next day, Cady looked around the bar at the avidly conversing people and realized how vibrant and interesting Paul's business life probably was, compared to coming home to relax. Even if he had problems, as he complained he did, it was still exciting to have a meeting; to try to win. This was Leigh's life too. Cady felt the familiar little pang of envy mixed with admiration she always did when she thought about Leigh. Leigh was wearing a beautiful new outfit. Although she complained she never had time to buy clothes, she managed to have them.

They ordered white wine. People were hardly smoking anymore, even Leigh had given it up. "Where's Paul tonight?" Leigh asked.

"Oh, working late. I told him I was going out for a drink with you."

Leigh smiled.

"I bought the most amazing linens with my mother yesterday," Cady said. "I have a regular hope chest by now. All we need is the apartment to put this stuff in."

"How's that coming along?"

"Slowly."

Leigh took a deep breath and tapped her fingernails nervously on her glass. Then she realized she was doing it and stopped. "I have something to tell you," she said.

"What?"

"I was in a little out-of-the-way restaurant the other night and I saw Paul having dinner with a woman, and it didn't look like business."

Cady felt a cold streak of pain. "What do you mean?" she cried.

"They were . . . well, they were, or at least he was . . . affectionate."

"What do you mean 'affectionate'?" Cady demanded. She was furious with Leigh and felt betrayed by Paul, but also unbelieving.

"I know it doesn't sound like much, but he kissed her hand."

"Her hand? How old was she?"

"Young. And attractive."

"Paul doesn't kiss hands."

"Well, he did."

"That's out of Jane Austen. Maybe he was kidding."

"His whole demeanor was inappropriate," Leigh said gently. "I could see it was a date. I needed to warn you."

"Where were they?" Cady demanded. Under Cady's questioning Leigh willingly told her everything: the name, the address, why she was there, how it was that she had discovered Paul. It certainly sounded like a place a man would sneak off to if he wanted to cheat with another woman. Cady had never heard of that restaurant, but now she would never forget it.

"What did she look like?" Cady asked. "What kind of eyes? What kind of mouth? What kind of nose? What kind of hair? What kind of body? What was she wearing?" Leigh told her all that too, in as much detail as she could remember. The woman sounded like trouble.

"He told me he was having a business dinner," Cady said. But she knew she was trying to convince herself as much as Leigh.

"With who?"

"Brewster Knowles. That's somebody from a client's office. I don't know who it is. Maybe that woman's name is Brewster. He wouldn't have told me her name if he was having an affair with her."

"I think he's having an affair," Leigh said.

Cady thought of all the nights Paul had been late, of the times he had been uncommunicative, tired, and distant, and she felt a lump in her throat. Everything was falling into place. Prickles of anxiety sped up and down her body and she found it hard to breathe. "I'll ask him," she said. "But I don't believe it's anything. He'll just laugh at me. He has a lot of meetings. Everyone in business has meetings. You should know that. If David didn't trust you . . ."

"I saw Paul coming out of an apartment too," Leigh said.

"When?"

"A week before that. It was at night. I don't know if it was a meeting or a rendez-vous."

"Why didn't you tell me?"

"Because I didn't know what it was."

"Where was the apartment?"

Leigh told her, but Cady didn't know anyone who lived in that neighborhood, and she had no idea if Paul did.

"I'm sure it was nothing," Cady said. Was it true that Paul had been in that woman's apartment? Obviously Leigh thought so.

He didn't even give me any time to feel safe, she thought.

"I'm sorry," Leigh said. "I didn't want to tell you and hurt you this way, but it would have been dishonest of me not to warn you."

I'm sure she's gloating, Cady thought bitterly, even as she knew she was being unfair. She took a sip of her wine. Leigh with her storybook happy marriage, she thought. Leigh has always had everything and I've had nothing. She drank the rest of her wine quickly, and the image of all her soft, new linens, neatly folded, waiting for her in her parents' house, sprang to her mind and she tried not to cry. While I was innocently making plans he was wrecking them, she thought. She was grateful to Leigh for the truth but she also hated her for ruining her happiness.

"I have to go now," Cady said. "Have you finished everything you had to tell me?"

"Yes," Leigh said gently. She looked regretful.

Cady stood up. "Good-bye. I'll call you. Maybe he has a very good reason."

"Maybe he does," Leigh said, but she sounded unconvinced.

Cady ran out of the restaurant, blinded by tears, and hailed a cab. She had left Leigh with the check, which served her right. Leigh had done the inviting, and besides, she had an expense account. How totally unjust that fortunate, contented Leigh had to be the one to drive this knife into her heart! As the cab crept through traffic Cady looked around through the window as if she were going to find Paul on the street with his arm around a woman. She was sure she would be home before he was, but she was too anxious not to be. She needed to hear what he had to say.

chapter
32

Paul came home shortly after Cady did. By then she'd had a glass of wine, frantically pacing the floor, wondering what was going to become of her. She was too upset to worry about dinner. They could just order room service. She had no appetite anyway. Maybe he would have an appropriate, believable excuse for the other night, but she couldn't imagine what that would be. Paul was not affectionate in public places. He must be getting reckless, and Cady wondered why this was.

As soon as he walked in he noticed that she was distraught, and his usual look of wary tolerance was replaced by one of concern. He gave her a brief kiss on the cheek and she sniffed at him, as if to find the scent of sex, or lust, or perfume, or perhaps only guilt.

"Where were you?" she asked.

"I told you I was going to a meeting. Didn't you have a drink with Leigh?"

"Who is Brewster Knowles?"

She felt the brief pause. He looked almost too innocent. "She works for a client," he said.

"She?"

"Yes? . . ."

"I thought it was a man."

"I never told you she was a man," Paul said.

No, he hadn't. Cady had simply assumed it. Those WASP women often had male first names, their family names. She pictured the spiky red hair, the pouting lips. "Were you with her tonight?"

There was another very brief pause. "Among other people."

In order to lie well, Cady thought, you tell a partial truth. The more truth to a lie the better. She didn't remember where she had heard that.

"Where did you go?"

"To '21'."

That's the part that is the lie, Cady thought, he wouldn't go there if he were alone with her. But maybe he wasn't alone with her, and maybe he *was* at '21'. She felt left out.

"People are talking," she said. "They say you and Brewster Knowles are having an affair."

He looked at her innocently again. "What people?"

"Never mind. I want to know if it's true."

"Of course it isn't true," Paul said.

"Can you prove it?"

"I wouldn't cheat on you," he said. "I left my wife for you."

"So your life with me is no longer dramatic," Cady said. "You must miss sneaking around."

"How do you invent such utter nonsense?"

"Someone was in" — she named the little restaurant with disdain — "the other night, and saw you kissing her hand."

"Oh," Paul said, sounding relieved. "Well, Brewster Knowles is a big, ugly, truck driver of a woman and I would never kiss her ham of a hand, so just back off. You're wrong. Completely wrong."

"Then whose hand were you kissing in the restaurant the other night?" Cady demanded.

"I wasn't kissing anybody's hand. I don't do that. Does that sound like me?"

"I don't know anymore what you're capable of," Cady said.

"Somebody is just making trouble," he said. "Come on, Cady, don't be silly."

"That same person saw you coming out of someone's apartment" — she told him the address, watching for his reaction — "at night when you said you were at a meeting," Cady said. "Whose apartment was it?"

"Nobody's. Did this person speak to me?"

"No."

"Then it wasn't me. You'll hear all kinds of drivel now that we're together. People are jealous."

"Why would they be jealous?"

"Because we're happy."

"Who says we're happy?" Cady blurted out. "You hardly ever act happy. You act tired and harassed and sick of me."

"Now, Cady." He took hold of her shoulders and looked into her face with an expression of sincerity and regret. "How could you think something like that?"

"Because you do!"

"It's true that I'm tired. I work very hard. And yes, I'm harassed. This divorce is taking a lot out of me. But I am certainly not sick of you, and it's very unfair of you to think that."

"Well, I just don't know what to believe," Cady murmured, backing down.

"Believe that I love you," Paul said. "Because I do."

She wondered if it was possible for him to love two people.

"What do you want to do about dinner?" he asked.

"I don't care," she said.

"What about room service?" he asked with an appeasing lilt in his voice that said room service was nice, instead of ordinary, something that should appeal to her. It made her sad that he was trying to please her, because she had doubted him, and because she probably should.

"Fine."

She couldn't swallow more than a few bites, and he solicitously tried to make her eat. He was being very nice, and she couldn't decide why, which made her even sadder.

When they got into bed he kissed her good-night and held her comfortingly for a while before he turned over and went to sleep. He made no overture to have sex with her, and Cady didn't try to initiate it because she didn't want to be rejected and humiliated. Had Paul already had sex? She sniffed at him again to see if he had showered at that woman's apartment, or perhaps not showered at all afterward, but his smell was ambiguous. She remembered he had gone directly home to his wife from her bed in the old days, but he had kept a distance from his wife . . . that, at least, she was sure of.

But what about the woman of tonight? Had they done it? That would have been enough for him. Cady was certain a man his age couldn't make love to two women so quickly one after the other . . . although maybe that would have excited him. Maybe that was what a man his age needed to function when he was bored with only one woman. She didn't know what to think. She couldn't sleep.

After a while, when Paul was sleeping soundly, she got up and went into the living room. His attaché case was still on the floor where he had put it when he came in. She opened the closet door for a little light and searched through his attaché case. She had no idea what she expected to find. He didn't keep old credit card bills around because he had to file them for his expenses. But there was nothing for tonight. If he had indeed been with a group someone else might have picked up the check. Or maybe Brewster had. Or maybe he had been at her apartment, and the drinks, if they had even bothered to have any, had been free.

Cady went back to bed and tossed and

turned all night in a nervous sweat. Paul, however, slept the deep sleep of the just — or perhaps of a man who has depleted his seed and needs a rest. Her mind was churning. She was going to have to find out more tomorrow.

The next day Leigh did not call, and Cady didn't call her either. Leigh was being tactful, or perhaps she was just busy. As for Cady, she was still annoyed. Paul said he had a meeting with his lawyer but would be home early. He told her to eat and not wait for him; he'd catch a bite with the lawyer. That was all she needed to hear. She took a cab to the apartment building where Leigh had seen him. There was no doorman. The names of the occupants were on cards beside their buzzers. Cady inspected them. There was a B. Knowles.

So now I know who it is, I just don't know what he did, she thought. Truck driver indeed! If he had been visiting the truck driver he would have admitted it. Innocent people didn't get themselves tangled up in nets of invention.

She waited around for a while in case Paul showed up, but he didn't, so she took another cab to the restaurant that had the Tarot card reader, where Leigh had seen him with the mystery woman. He wasn't there, so she sat by herself at a small table in the back and had a drink. When the Tarot reader came over Cady declined. She was too depressed to ask about her future, and besides, she didn't believe in those things.

She waited, nursing her wine, until the restaurant filled up and the waiter had asked her twice if she wanted to order. If Paul were going to eat out it wouldn't be here tonight. She tried to figure out where else he would be.

With no other clues, Cady took a cab to one of the places where Paul had wined and dined her in their halcyon days. He might well return to being a creature of habit now that his recent hideaway had been discovered. The headwaiter recognized her and asked her if Paul was joining her. "No," she said, thinking that probably this was the wrong place. "I'll just have a drink at the bar."

If he thought that was odd he didn't show it. Cady had white wine and waited. The restaurant was full. Paul wasn't coming here. She paid the check and left.

She was high now from the wine, and she figured only one more place would do it for tonight, at least for her. She went to another of their old favorites. From the restaurant's foyer she could survey the entire room. He wasn't there either, so therefore it would be a waste of time to hover around. "Oops, wrong place," she said cheerfully to the headwaiter. "Unless . . . did Mr. Fisher make our reservation here?"

He looked at the reservation book. "No. Not tonight."

But another night? Cady wondered. She was getting closer. She looked at her watch and decided to try one more place. She felt like a person in a nightmare: chasing someone she loved, looking lost, afraid, miserable. She'd had those nightmares as a child. But back then the people she had been chasing were her parents. How relieved she'd been to wake up and find they were safe at home, loving and protecting her.

She tried the last restaurant, but looked around the crowded room from the front door. Paul wasn't there either. She began to feel stupid. She would never know where he'd been tonight. But she had a new question to hammer at him: about the apartment.

When Paul came back to the hotel Cady realized she had forgotten to eat. "Where did you have dinner?" she asked.

He mentioned a place where, to her knowledge, he'd never been before. Now maybe she would have to chase around every restaurant in New York City to accommodate his new tastes, unless he hadn't really been there.

"Brewster Knowles lives at that address where you claim you haven't been," Cady said. "Isn't that a coincidence?"

"Yes it is," he said.

"But why would she live where Leigh saw you? Leigh didn't get that address out of the air."

"So Leigh's your spy," Paul said. "I was never there."

"I don't believe you."

"Believe what you want," he said. "You trust me or you don't."

"I don't."

"I have never given you any reason not to trust me."

"Yes, you have."

"What?"

"Well, Leigh has," Cady said.

"So you believe her? She's jealous or crazy."

"She's neither."

"What kind of friend would put these ideas into your head?"

"A real friend," Cady said.

"I have never been at that address."

"But Leigh saw you there."

"No, she didn't."

"What about the restaurant with the woman?"

"Who could it have been?"

"I'm asking you."

He thought for a while. "Last week?"

"Surely you can remember."

He pretended to be racking his brains. She knew he couldn't claim he hadn't been there at all. Leigh had seen him for a long time, not just a fleeting glimpse on a dark street. "Oh," he said, finally.

"Oh who?"

"A girl who wanted a job, a friend of my lawyer's. I gave her an interview."

"And kissed her hand," Cady said.

"No hand kissing. Just dinner. She has no money. You can't be jealous of a meal."

"Are you going to hire her?"

"No. I don't need her."

"Then why did you see her in the first place?"

"As a favor to my lawyer."

"Is she *his* girlfriend?"

"She's nobody's girlfriend. She's married, and so is my lawyer."

"And so are you."

"Are you going to attack me for that now too?" Paul asked. "I can't continue this ridiculous discussion."

"I want to know if you've been seeing a

woman," Cady said. "It's only fair of you to tell me. I won't leave you. I need to know."

"None of the many women I meet in the course of my work mean anything to me," Paul said. "They're just work people. I love you and I don't want you to break up with me. I'm so much older than you are, and I won't have much money when this divorce is finished, and I worry that you'll find someone younger and better than I am. I would never jeopardize what we have by cheating on you."

"But you'd want to," Cady said.

"Most men have fantasies," Paul said with a little smile. "But I can honestly say I don't. I'm happy with what we have."

"Then why are you away so much?"

"I'm trying to be able to take care of you," Paul said. "You're not in business. You have no idea what it's like."

Cady sighed. She was exhausted. She didn't know what else to ask him to wear him down. She would try to believe him, but she would keep on following him. Somewhere there had to be an answer.

After that Cady and Paul fell into an uncomfortable routine. He went out alone and stayed out late a few times a week, and she went to places where he might be, to catch him. When he returned home she interrogated him relentlessly, to such a degree that she began to wonder why he didn't leave her for being such a shrew. She no longer felt his passivity was a sign of innocence. Rather, it was an indication of his determination to keep her. But if he really wanted to keep her, she thought, he would give up his girlfriend.

The trouble with Paul, Cady realized, was that when he became involved he was insatiable. Even if he wasn't having sex every time, although why wouldn't he since this affair was new, he wanted to *be with* the woman. He could have seen the woman only once a week and Cady knew she would never have suspected him. But that wouldn't have been enough for him. She didn't know if he was in love, all she knew was that he had to have what he wanted.

She had been back to B. Knowles's apartment, and waited outside in the cold, but she had never seen him entering or leaving. But there were friends from whom he could borrow an apartment, so she wasn't fooled. There were even hotels. She knew all the old tricks.

She thought that if she actually saw him going into that apartment with the woman, she would not be able to bear it. Cady was sure that one day she would trap him somewhere, but at the apartment would be too painful. She hoped it would be at a restaurant.

She had called Leigh eventually, and told her everything. From being the messenger Cady had wanted to kill, Leigh had become once again the wise and sympathetic friend. "Maybe you should hire a detective," Leigh suggested.

"I'd be too embarrassed," Cady said.

"Well," Leigh said, "they do say that when you get to the point where you hire a detective you already know he's guilty."

Cady was tired and looking drawn these days. The emotion of her spying was taking its toll. But she couldn't just drop it. Nor could she leave him until she really knew. She had begun to understand that breaking up was inevitable. If Paul needed two women then she couldn't be one of them.

Maybe, she thought, he'll stop seeing the woman and never go out with another one, and then we can live happily ever after.

Her mother, of course, was furious. "He's just like that Steven," her mother said.

"No, not exactly."

"Why do you meet such bad men?"

"Only two," Cady said sadly.

"So many divorces these days," her mother said. In her mind Cady was already married, and this was going to be her divorce. After all these years, Cady thought, her mother might be right.

The strained Thanksgiving dinner with her family, followed by Paul's visit to his own family, was over, and now Christmas was coming. There were too many holidays in the fall and winter where you were supposed to be happy. It made being alone even worse. Cady looked through Paul's attaché case for credit card slips or store receipts to see if he had bought his girlfriend a present. If there was a receipt, which of the two of them would it be for?

Then a few days before Christmas, when Paul was supposed to be at someone's office party, Cady went dispiritedly but still determinedly to one of their old haunts, feeling like a fool, and there, behind the swags of fir and little colored lights, was Paul, sitting at a table with the pretty redheaded woman. Cady recognized her instantly with a jolt, even though she had never seen her. He should have picked someone ordinary. Her skin was perfect, her lipstick was perfect, and everything about her was elastic and youthful and pliable. She was sexy and animated. Their heads were too close together, his face was too besotted, and his hand was under the table, apparently holding hers, or worse, resting on her leg. Cady's heart turned over and she thought for a moment that she might throw up.

She walked directly over to the table with her coat still on.

"Hello," Cady said coldly.

He looked guilty and surprised. The woman looked confused.

"Cady," he said.

Cady just looked at him. It felt like a long silence.

"This is Cady Fineman," he said. "This is . . ." He almost choked and fell silent.

"Brewster Knowles?" Cady said.

The woman smiled and nodded, but she still looked surprised, as if she and Cady were supposed to know each other. He never mentioned me, Cady thought. He must have said he was hiding from his wife. He didn't have to mention me and complicate things, and make her know what a sleaze he is.

"Merry Christmas," Cady said, and walked out of the restaurant.

Paul caught up to her on the sidewalk as

she was trying to hail a cab. "Don't," he said.

"Don't what?"

"It isn't what you think."

"You make me sick. It's over. I can't live with a two-timing liar."

"Cady, go home and wait for me and I'll explain."

That was the most ridiculous thing she'd ever heard. It suddenly occurred to her that she couldn't go back to that hotel at all, not like a prisoner, not to listen to his excuses, not to look at the wreck of her life, a life that hadn't even started yet. She felt frozen and lost. She looked at him. For the first time she realized that he looked old. And through the lump in her throat and the threat of tears she pulled herself together to say one last thing.

"You were right," she said. "Brewster Knowles is ugly." She got into the cab.

As the cab drove away she was shaking, a fierce trembling that wouldn't stop. She didn't know where to go. "Just drive," she said, and then, finally, she gave the driver Leigh's address.

She didn't even know if Leigh would be home, but the children would, and Cady could wait for her. But when she got to the building the doorman said the Grahams were there, and Cady let him announce her and went up.

Leigh opened the door. She didn't have to ask any questions. She took one look at Cady's stricken face and she knew. Cady fell into her arms, sobbing.

chapter
33

Vanessa was always surprised that the department stores sold clothing in adult sizes small enough for her daughter Liberty to wear. Her skinny little jeans and tiny tank sweaters belonged in the children's department. Thus it was clear, anorexia was an accepted part of fashion. It enraged Vanessa. If Liberty had been unable to find clothing that fit she would have noticed that she was different. But she belonged to a group: models, genetic freaks, and the self-starved. When she shopped she made her mother drop her off at the mall, and pick her up, but not accompany her. She claimed she wanted her independence. Maybe she did.

Vanessa couldn't go on pretending to ignore the situation forever, even though she didn't want to be a nag. It was hard to find a chance to talk at any length to her very own daughter, and truthfully, Vanessa wasn't sure how she would begin. Liberty's therapist had reassured her parents that

Liberty's anorexia was not their fault. She didn't hate her parents. She thought she needed to lose weight because she didn't know what she really looked like, and when she was thin enough for her taste she really thought that a single bite of forbidden calories would change everything instantly. Thus when she ate half a green salad with no dressing as her entire meal, Vanessa didn't want to pressure her to have more because she knew if Liberty was made to eat she would only throw it up.

"One and a half cups of raw spinach has forty calories," Liberty said once. "Cooked it becomes half a cup, the same forty calories. Isn't all that frightening?"

"What's frightening about it?"

"It should be zero. It's just a vegetable."

As such, the portion of spinach became the meal. As often as possible Liberty avoided having dinner with the family at the table, and when she did, she was finished almost immediately and had to go somewhere or do something to get away from them. The therapist had said not to force her to eat, not to make an issue of it, or have a fight. Too much attention to food, she said, caused children to become obsessed with it. But wasn't Liberty already obsessed?

Even difficult children were not forced

to eat these days or punished for refusing. Child rearing had changed. When she had been a child Vanessa had thought kids who refused to eat were normal. It was the parents, with their rules, who were the bad ones. Why should parents care if you ate or not? You would eat eventually. She'd never known a child who died from refusing to finish her dinner, although she knew some who had been made to sit there for hours and look at it.

But today children died from refusing to eat, and her daughter might be one of them.

She thought how her mother had gone from a parent who tried to persuade her to clean her plate to one who put her on a diet when she got older. First it was all about health, and then it was all about looks. Vanessa wondered if, despite what Liberty's therapist said, it hadn't been partially her fault that Liberty had her problem. Was she too mindful about thinness? Had this affected her child?

Sometimes Vanessa and Liberty took a long walk together, since a chance for physical activity was one thing Liberty wouldn't refuse. They went up and down the hills of their quiet, tree-lined neighborhood, where there were security gates with barking dogs behind them, and Bentleys in the driveways, and swimming pools you couldn't see in the back. Vanessa always missed New York, where you walked to get somewhere, not just to exercise, and you had somewhere to go. She wondered if Liberty, now that she was older, resented her mother's solitary trips to New York and thought she should have been invited to come along.

I can't take her, because then I wouldn't be able to have my own life; so maybe I am a bad mother, Vanessa thought. Or maybe she's a little like me, because we both have our self-destructive and secret ways of surviving.

She had decided to talk to Liberty today, during their walk, about anorexia. She had thought for a long time about how to do it, and finally she felt she knew a way. Maybe a perplexing tragedy of her past would have some use after all.

"When I was young and single and lived in New York with Leigh and Cady," Vanessa said, "we had another roommate too, named Susan Brown."

"You didn't tell me that," Liberty said.

"We hardly ever mention her. It was a long time ago and it's still a painful subject. She killed herself."

"No!"

"She jumped off the roof of our apartment building."

"That's awful," Liberty said. "Why did she do it?"

"We never really knew. She was depressed and angry with us. She didn't like us and we didn't like her. We had told her she had to move out."

"That's why?"

"I guess it was enough for her."

"Did you blame yourselves?"

"Sort of, yes. Then after a while we sort of blamed her. But even though we never liked her, and had very little to do with her, we never got over her dying. We never forgot her. We don't talk about her much, but she's there."

Liberty looked subdued, mulling this over. She had never known anyone who committed suicide.

"I don't think she knew what she was doing," Vanessa said. "When you're young you think you're immortal. You think you can get into danger and take it back. You really don't know what death is, and you think it can't happen to you. If she had really known that it would be the end forever I wonder if she would ever have jumped off that roof."

Liberty didn't say anything.

"People have no idea how much they're going to be missed," Vanessa said. "You, for instance, have no idea. Your family loves you so much. If you died it would end our lives as we know them. You can't imagine what a terrible heartbreak it would be."

"Why would I die?" Liberty said.

"That's just it. You think you're immortal but you're not. You're in great danger."

"Me?"

"Anorexia is a life-threatening disease," Vanessa said. "You could kill yourself by not eating."

Liberty bristled. "I eat. You see me eat."

"Not enough. You know that. That's why you have a therapist and a doctor."

"They know I can't help it."

"You can."

"I can't."

"You're more important than you know," Vanessa said. "I just wanted to tell you that. I don't think I tell you enough how much I love you."

"You do tell me," Liberty said.

"I don't want you to die," Vanessa said. "It's as simple as that." She looked at her daughter. Her arms were like sticks, the bone at the top of her spine like a knob where her fragile neck began.

Liberty didn't answer.

"Try to see what you can do for me."

"For you?"

"Yes, for me. If not for yourself, then for me."

Eat the bite of carrot for Mommy, Vanessa remembered from her childhood. How different it was now. Life had become so much more sinister. She wondered if any of this conversation had had any impact at all. She didn't know what else to say. She felt inadequate, as usual, in every way, but most of all by not being able to help her child.

They went back to the house, and then it was dinnertime again. Liberty ate a portion of vegetable and went to her room to do homework. Jack ate heartily and fast, then went to his room too. Vanessa was left with Bill. She wondered briefly if he had ever cheated again, but thought it unlikely. He was afraid of her. He wanted to preserve the status quo as much as she did. He probably dreamed about an affair, and he played tennis for hours to get lust out of his mind. In his attempt to be a good husband he was getting to be a very good tennis player.

She thought, as she sometimes did,

that they were a family living on the edge of disaster. Except for happy, healthy Jack — how had he been spared — the rest of them narrowly skirted danger. Was this what a normal family did? Was this life? Were other people happier, without those doubts, temptations, and fears? Without the magical charms her family used to keep disaster at bay? She knew other families who were not very happy — knew about their adventures, their lies. All she had to do was look around her, listen to their complaints, read between the lines. She knew she wasn't alone. It didn't make her feel any better.

chapter
34

Like an earthquake victim who has lost everything, including, perhaps, her sanity, Cady
was living with Leigh and David and their
two daughters, and no one knew for how
long. After she had caught Paul with his girlfriend, Cady had moved out, implacable, furious, and disillusioned. Since she knew it
was true anyway, he admitted he had been
having an affair, and after that nothing he
said could persuade her to stay. Moving in
with Leigh was a form of triage. Cady could
not survive being alone right now.

Paul had returned to his wife. This surprised no one. It was clear that if he was
going to cheat on someone it would be
easier for him to cheat on his long-suffering
wife. Although now that Cady had left
him, it was Cady he wanted, and Leigh
suspected Brewster's days were numbered.

Again Cady's mother had helped her
move. "It's that poor woman's other job:
mover," David said to Leigh.

Cady was sleeping in the second maid's room (the first was occupied by the au pair), and she hid in her little cell as if it were the bedroom of her infancy. There was no room for all her clothes in the one closet, but her mother had bought her a storage box, which slid under her single bed. The Dunnewood School was closed for Christmas vacation, which was just as well, since Cady was in no condition to teach.

She slept a great deal, and she showed up for meals. She complained about noise, about music. She sipped a lot of vodka. She demanded certain foods: thin-sliced bread, fresh every day; dietetic cottage cheese of a particular brand, until she changed her mind and required a different brand; special cereal which she ate only once; skinless chicken breasts, no salt. She wanted only white towels, only new cakes of soap. She criticized the toilet paper. She left piles of laundry to be washed. She threw her used sheets into the hall every day so the housekeeper could give her new ones. She tossed out the bathmat too. She had turned into Lady Macbeth.

Leigh gave her whatever she wanted because she seemed so perishable. They were in a difficult position because Cady was putting a strain on everyone. She acted as if everything they did for her was her due. She needed to get on her feet emotionally and financially, but they were not her family after all. They had not expected to have a grumpy adult child inflicted on them. She had not paid her own rent since she had lived with Leigh so many years ago, nor had she ever been totally alone, and eventually she would have to learn to do these things. She complained that she was poor, that they had everything while she had nothing. Sometimes there was an edge to her voice — angry and jealous — when she said this. She was not making it easy to succor her. Much of the time, although she was sorry for Cady, Leigh was on a slow simmer.

David's way of coping with Cady was to kill her with kindness. He was good to her and he was charming. He pretended he didn't think she was crazy. The girls avoided her because it was clear she didn't like children. Leigh was the person who had to mother her. She didn't know how long she could.

The family had planned to spend Christmas in New York and then go to the Caribbean, where they had taken a house for a week over New Year's. David offered to take Cady with them, since they didn't know what to do with a person in her distraught condition, but she refused to go. She went to her parents', and the family was relieved to be away from her. They wished she would stay in Scarsdale. Then they came back and so did she.

Paul called her every day and she refused to speak to him.

After New Year's Cady took Paul's phone call for the first time. "We're not enemies," she said to Leigh. "We have too much history."

He told her he had spent a miserable holiday with his family and that everyone hated him for leaving and did not thank him for returning. Cady said she was glad. She didn't mention Brewster Knowles. Brewster didn't matter. She was interchangeable with any other attractive, sexy younger woman who might catch his imagination. The main thing was that he had destroyed Cady. "When you've been murdered who cares what the poison was," Cady said to Leigh.

Leigh remembered some of the reasons she had liked Cady: She was funny, she expressed herself well, and she was intelligent. But after not having lived with her for so many years she realized that it was only their long years of friendship that was keeping them friends now. If she had just met such a neurotic woman she would have avoided her.

Charlie Rackley came to visit Cady as if he were calling on the ill, and in a way he was. He sat in the living room and drank with her, tried to cheer her up, listened as she berated Paul. After a while when she became drunk and began repeating herself he just nodded sympathetically, but he didn't rush away.

"Men are pigs," he agreed.

"But not David," Cady said.

"No, not David."

"You're so lucky, Leigh," Cady said. "Why couldn't I have met David?"

He wouldn't have been able to stand you, Leigh thought.

Her daughters knew when Cady had had too much to drink and took it in stride, but still Leigh didn't like her doing it around the kids. Life was unpleasant enough and she wanted to protect them a little longer. She'd explained to them that Cady's boyfriend had dumped her and they understood that. To them Cady was someone interesting who was to be avoided. Kids today are so much more sophisticated than we were, Leigh thought. But her own parents had thought that about her.

She wondered how long this mourning period would go on, and for how long she would have to take responsibility for something that was not her doing. Of course, she had told Cady that Paul was cheating. So, in a way, perhaps it was partly her fault that she had ended up with a grieving and angry Cady living in her apartment. And she *had* invited her. She had offered Cady a room during a crisis, but now Cady was part of the household, and that had never been Leigh's plan.

"Thank you, thank you," Cady would say on a good day and embrace her and weep. "What would I do without you? You're my best friend. You saved my life. Where would I go? What would I do? A friend is truly a precious thing. I'm so grateful. I love you."

Love-hate, Leigh thought. She was all too aware that Cady resented her, resented her hospitality and her material things and her happiness with her family, that Cady despised her own dependency on these self-sufficient people.

"I don't want to live this way," Cady would say. "I'm like a child, I'm dependent, it's embarrassing. I shouldn't be living in your maid's room."

"Then maybe you should start to look for your own apartment."

"I have no money."

"You do. Paul paid your rent for years. Didn't you save?"

"Who can save anything on a school-teacher's salary? I had to buy clothes, have my hair done, eat. . . ."

"So do other people."

"I can't live like other people," Cady said.

"Obviously not."

"Why should I?" Cady snapped. "You don't. Why should I have a terrible life? What did I do? I work hard. I'm a good person."

"You don't have a terrible life," Leigh said. "Read the newspapers and you'll see what a terrible life is."

"I'm old," Cady would say. "My best years are over. He took my best years."

"You're not old."

"Look at me. Should I have a face lift?"

"You're much too young for that," Leigh would say. But grief and anger pulled people's faces down. Sometimes Cady looked truly forbidding. It was her expression: the pursed lips, the blazing eyes. It had not occurred to Leigh before that Cady had so little inside. It was as if her friend, whom she'd known for so many years, had disappeared and she hadn't even noticed until afterward.

When Paul called and Cady spoke to him she looked a little like her old self, at least for a while. "It's just a friendship," she said. "He's an old friend."

"Then you don't hate him anymore?"

"I'm used to him," Cady said. "I'm sorry for him. He ruined his own life too. What will he have now? He's where he started, but he doesn't have me."

"Are you going to take him back?"

"No. He's never going to change."

There were times when Leigh wished Cady would take him back if only so she could move out.

Cady was back at school now, but it made no difference to the household because she was always there at night, and no one else was there in the daytime. David and Leigh were at work and the girls were in school and had after-school activities. Cady insisted on using the dining room table to grade her students' papers. She could have used Leigh's office, but Leigh didn't want her there, messing up her things, taking the last bastion of freedom she had in the house.

Water-packed tuna, Cady would write on

the shopping list in the kitchen. *Nonfat mayonnaise. Shredded wheat.* The shredded wheat she had wanted two months ago was still there in the cabinet.

Vodka. The vodka was not.

The sight of Cady's precise little handwriting made Leigh seethe.

"What are we going to do?" she asked David.

"Tell her to go."

"Go where?"

"Find her an apartment. Preferably rent controlled."

"I don't have time to go apartment hunting," Leigh said.

"Well, she won't if you don't."

Leigh began looking with a realtor in the few free moments she had from the office, and found that rent-controlled apartments were scarce. There were long waiting lists. Cady would have to downgrade her tastes and accept something small, on the verge of shabby, not in her favorite neighborhood, not like the places Paul had provided for her. Leigh thought that if she did find anything practical and suitable that Cady would refuse to take it.

Cady went out to lunch with Paul, on a Saturday. It was the first time they had met since she had left him. But they did not reconcile at that lunch. They had a pleasant hour, though, she reported. There was not too much to talk about. Since he wouldn't talk about his affair, or affairs if there were other women now, and since that was what Cady really wanted to know about, that left little else. She didn't know if she was still in love with him. She knew, though, that he was still a part of her life. He didn't ask her to come back, but she said she knew he would be glad if she offered to. But that was over, she said. After she returned from their lunch she was calmer than she had been for the entire time she had been staying with Leigh and David.

Maybe they'll become friends, Leigh thought. That would be a sensible solution, since none other had worked.

Leigh took Cady to look at an apartment she had found and Cady burst into tears and ran out. "I hate it!" she cried.

That evening Cady sulked and sniffled and felt sorry for herself. "We can't change your sheets every day anymore," Leigh told her, adding insult to injury. "It's too much work for Mary. Once a week like everybody else."

"But she's here anyway," Cady said.

"She has other work," Leigh said.

"I'd go if I had a place to go to," Cady said. "There's nothing in New York."

"There is."

"My life with Paul was so nice," Cady said.

"Then go back to him."

"No, the apartment was nice, that's all. I can't start with him again, ever. I know too much now."

"You need to start looking for an apartment," Leigh said.

"I will."

But Cady didn't.

Finally a client of David's was leaving New York to live in California, and Leigh took Cady to look at the small, clean, one-bedroom apartment. Cady actually liked it. David pulled a few strings, including a bribe, and Cady obtained the sublet. It was for two years with an option to renew. Two years was a long time, Leigh thought. By then Cady would have her own life, whatever it would be.

Cady's mother came to New York to help her move. Leigh had a funny mental picture: her entire family standing on the curb eagerly helping Cady's mother; David with a bottle of vodka, the girls holding the smaller suitcases, everyone beaming with relief, and the thought made her smile. She was so pleased by the departure that she bought Cady an orchid plant, so she would have a touch of the elegance she always wanted and felt she deserved.

"You're so sweet," Cady said, hugging her. "Thank you for everything."

Neither of them said how thankful Leigh must be to be rid of her. But they both knew. They were too mature to live together anymore, too solidified in their ways, too different. They had been friends for too long not to know that separating like this was the only thing that could save their friendship. It was already almost terminally strained.

PART
FOUR

chapter
35

It was 1990 and the economy was still booming. George Bush was president. Clothing was grunge, preppie, and hip-hop, with oversized jeans, tattoos, and body piercings for the young. The three women saw the clothes they had worn when they were in their early twenties now on television in old movies. Their clothes seemed to be amusing artifacts. They laughed, sometimes in derision, sometimes ruefully. They remembered panty girdles, waist cinchers, and how tiny their bodies had been. Ninety-nine percent of all American households had televisions, and people were watching *Cheers*, *Seinfeld*, and *60 Minutes*, and bringing their families to New York to see *Cats* on Broadway.

The new decade brought in a significant period for all three of the women, because no matter how old they had thought they were at thirty and forty, now they were fifty and fifty-one. Time had to be respected. Not that they were willing to respect it. All three of them — Vanessa first, of course — the bellwether, the *fashionista,* had had plastic surgery, and they all colored their hair and kept trim. None of them had any desire to grow old gracefully, and they knew few people who did. They looked younger than their ages.

Only Leigh had celebrated her fiftieth birthday, albeit quietly but elegantly with her family at the Four Seasons. The other two had ignored theirs. Vanessa had been lying about her age for several years, so how could she have a fiftieth birthday party? She made Bill buy her an expensive piece of jewelry instead. Cady said it was unfair that men had a huge bash for their half-century birthdays, usually given by their doting wives, while women had to pretend theirs hadn't happened. Turning fifty made her bitter. She had been on the verge of bitterness for quite a while, but this did it for her. She worried that her life as she had known it was over. She thought it was because she was single.

However young they claimed they were, and seemed, Vanessa and Leigh were concerned with menopause. It was the unavoidable sign that their lives were changing. While they were glad to be rid of the monthly nuisance they were concerned now about estrogen replacement and osteoporosis, hot flashes, night sweats, and mood swings. The next child to be born in their families would be a grandchild.

Vanessa's son Jack was twenty-four and married. Sometimes it seemed that the years had rushed past in an instant. He and his wife were in no hurry to have children, which at times suited Vanessa just fine, and at other times disappointed her because she thought it would be lovely to have a baby around. She could say she was a young grandmother. Actually, she would have been.

Her daughter Liberty was twenty-two. At seventeen, for no reason any of them could pinpoint, she had begun to eat again. At first she ate like a normal person and Vanessa was ecstatic, but then she began to overeat compulsively and became overweight. She still exercised diligently, so she was firm and heavy. She moved gracefully, like a boxer. Her waist was the same size as her father's. Vanessa didn't dare say anything to her because she didn't want Liberty to starve herself again. She was just glad that her daughter was alive and well. If she was doomed to have a fat daughter then so be it. Liberty didn't mind at all and was almost militant about her appearance: a big strong woman, a presence in the world. She thought of the years when she had dwindled away as a foolish and terrible part of her past. No one talked about that time, as though they might curse her again by even the mention of it, but they all remembered.

She had a serious boyfriend now, and he thought she was sexy.

Leigh's eldest daughter, Jennie, was in college at her mother's alma mater. But Pembroke no longer existed, now it was Brown. The all-girls adjunct to a men's university had been eaten up and had disappeared, as many of them had. After college Jennie planned to go into her parents' business, as an agent for Star Management. Her younger sister, Sophie, wanted to be an actress and told Jennie she expected to be a client. Leigh and David had somehow hoped their daughters would be doctors or lawyers instead, but it was all right. You couldn't run your children's lives, and it was a compliment that they wanted to follow their parents into show business.

The main event of the years that had just passed was that Charlie Rackley, to the three friends' surprise, relief, and a little disappointment, had finally gotten married. The bride, Kimberly, was an attractive blonde stockbroker, not so different from any of the other women he had dated. It was probably simply time for him to settle down.

All three women went to his wedding. They liked Kimberly, although they secretly resented her a little too for taking their Charlie away from them. But the marriage lasted only two years, and then his wife left him.

Charlie told them afterward that she had claimed she never knew him, couldn't get to him, found pieces of him hidden. They could understand that. They had always known parts of Charlie were private, but it hadn't bothered them. A wife would want more than they did. They were satisfied with him just the way he was. They happily welcomed him back into their lives as an available bachelor.

Cady was still living in the apartment Leigh had found for her. She had long since taken over the lease, and it was rent controlled. She complained it was too small, but after all these years there were fewer rent-controlled apartments in the city than ever, and she liked her neighborhood. She claimed she intended to stay in the apartment forever, and as proof of her permanence she had put expensive fabric on the walls. "Why should I be deprived just because I don't own it?" she asked, as a subtle dig at Leigh and David, who owned theirs.

"Why should I have to wait forever just because I'm single?" she would say when she bought the luxurious carpeting, an expensive oil painting she loved, or her new bathroom tiles. As always, her mother helped her pay for these things.

"What will you do when I'm gone?" her mother said. "I worry."

"You and Dad will leave me your money, won't you?"

"Of course we will," her mother said. "But you just don't know how to economize, and you never save. You need a husband."

"Well, give up," Cady said. "Because it's too late for that."

Paul had never really left Cady's life, although the relationship had changed. On the surface it seemed simpler. Underneath, it was more complicated. Cady met Paul almost every week for lunch, and they talked about pleasant, impersonal things, gently, preserving the odd tenor of their friendship. They were still so tied to each other that it was possible for them to hurt

416

one another. They tried not to do this. She didn't hate him at all anymore. In fact, in many ways she loved him as he loved her, but she didn't want to marry him. He was too old, and he cheated.

"I'm not going to take care of him in his old age," she would say, although her heart always beat more quickly whenever he phoned. She could phone him too, and did, at the office. She was harmless now, or at least he thought she was.

She knew he was unhappy, but that he would never leave his wife. His wife suited his needs, and apparently he suited hers too. He had told Cady he was seeing a new woman, but that he didn't love her. Cady chose not to tell him what she was doing. It made her feel powerful to keep a part of her life away from him. She knew he would have liked to ask her but he didn't dare. For the first time Paul treated her with respect, and that, Cady felt, was as it should be, at last.

Occasionally he came to her apartment. He sat there, exhaustedly, as if he had come home to a safe haven. She would give him a drink and they would talk about innocuous things, as they did in restaurants. Once or twice he fell asleep briefly on the couch, waking suddenly, looking alarmed.

Where did he think he was going to be when he woke up? Or did he think falling asleep had made him too vulnerable? She remembered when he had felt free to doze, no matter how much it had disappointed her.

In the summertime when his wife was away he occasionally took Cady to the movies, and sometimes to dinner. They were affectionate but there was no sex. That was reserved for his current paramour. She and Paul were like a venerable married couple, beyond so much but still attached. Somehow there was the chance that they might reignite, but she doubted it and would make sure that it didn't happen. He wasn't to be trusted, and yes, he was too old for her, for the new Cady who wanted to enjoy herself before it was too late.

She liked only younger men now. She felt she had wasted her best years waiting for Paul, and now she wanted to recapture them. "I hate old men," she would say with a vengeance. However, it was not so easy to find these young men. She didn't go to bars, she wouldn't take a personal ad, and she was not invited to many parties with eligible young men at them. She had several disastrous blind dates, arranged by friends at the school, and several from Leigh and Charlie, and there were even a few divorced or widowed men her mother's friends knew. . . . But none of them were young enough. She flirted with the handsome tile man who did her bathroom, and occasionally with the young waiters at restaurants, and was sorry that her hairdresser was gay. Although she had a few drunken one-night stands with contemporaries, which she regretted immediately, her fantasies were livelier than her existence. Her fantasies were the waiters and the tile man.

"Old men are set in their ways," she would claim to Leigh.

"You're more set in your ways than anyone," Leigh would laugh.

"Old men can't deal with an independent woman," Cady would complain.

"You're less independent than you imagine," Leigh would reply.

"Old men aren't sexy," Cady would say, but she was furious when a man said that about women. Life, she felt, was hard.

The one thing that made her feel worthwhile and happy was her relationships with her young female students, whom she loved and felt very protective and loyal toward. She knew she was a good teacher, and she found respect in that. The older she got, the more Cady appreciated her career. Every year there was a new girl student for her to "fall in love" with — as a mother figure and mentor, to someone who reminded her of her lost youth, and these quasi love affairs verged on obsession, but not sexually. But she always had to be in love with somebody, so every year another sixteen-year-old girl became the "perfect" one, the recipient of her attention and encouragement and devotion. For a year she would rave about this perfect girl, and then when the girl moved on to her senior year she would be replaced by someone Cady loved as much or more.

Sometimes Leigh thought Cady should have had a daughter after all, but when Leigh mentioned it, Cady became annoyed.

As time went by Cady was becoming rather irritated with Leigh. She still loved Leigh, but her resentment toward Leigh was getting harder to control. It seemed unfair that all the things she wanted were dangling right in front of her, as the possessions of someone else. And Leigh was so critical! She acted as though having had a happy life gave her the right to critique someone else's unhappiness.

From time to time, because of her extravagance trying to dress well in the latest designer clothes, with bill collectors breathing down her neck, with her mother temporarily turning stubborn, Cady had been obliged to borrow money from Leigh, and this made them both resentful. It was a small loan to Leigh, but not to Cady. They both knew it was unlikely that she would pay it back. Not unless she found a rich husband. The rich husband had become a sort of running joke. Cady had decided she didn't want to have any husband at all, rich or not, and as for the money, Leigh could more than afford it.

Finally Leigh told Cady there would be no more loans from her. "Ask your mother," Leigh said.

"My mother's not made of money," Cady snapped.

"Neither am I."

"More than I am," Cady said.

They glared at each other. It had popped out again.

"Why do you always think you're entitled?" Leigh said.

"I am! Why should I have a rotten life?"

"You *don't* have a rotten life!"

"If I had your money," Cady said, "I'd know what to do with it."

"You seem to know what to do with it already."

Then Cady didn't talk to her for a few weeks, until she missed their friendship, whatever it had turned into. They had been friends for so long that it would be silly to break up over an argument. Cady felt that her long-suffering loyal ways were unappreciated. Look how she had forgiven everyone: Paul, Steven Irving, and even holier-than-thou Leigh. She didn't know why Leigh was so often impatient with her. She seemed to anger Leigh, although Cady couldn't understand why. She felt sometimes that she had to watch her step not to irritate her. Maybe it was just Leigh's menopause. It was probably worse to have the symptoms when there was a man in the house who would notice. Cady felt at these times that she was lucky she lived by herself.

She was lonely, though. All those years so long ago when she had been lonely waiting for Paul's brief visits were not so different from now when she could go out, do whatever she wanted, and was still alone. She knew she watched too much television. It was an escape. Unless she had plans, weekends were endless and unbearable. Everyone who had an attachment was with someone on the weekend. Sundays were the worst.

At least I don't have to worry about AIDS if I have no sex life, Cady thought. There had always been something to be afraid of: getting pregnant when you were young and single, and now, death. She knew people her age who didn't worry because they thought only young people got AIDS, but she knew better. All kinds of bad things waited for you when you got involved with someone, and other bad things waited when you were alone. At times she became very depressed.

Lately, since his divorce, Cady found herself thinking about Charlie Rackley. He had improved through the years until he was pretty nearly the perfect man. He had been too young for them when they were all in their twenties, and so they had gotten into the habit of not taking him seriously, but now the age difference had fallen away, and she felt he was a hidden treasure. He was worldly and kind and generous. He liked to have fun. He could talk to a woman. He was good looking. She liked that he was just a little younger than she was. There was something boyish about him, but he was also mature.

His wife had been a fool to leave him. That he was slightly private, slightly secretive, gave him dignity. It was not a flaw to keep something of your own. I would never mind it, Cady thought. We all have private places in our souls. The only people about whom you know everything are actually shallow. Paul had had secret places too. It had been part of his allure.

Then the thought hit Cady like a thunderbolt: *I could see myself married to Charlie.* Why not? She had known him forever. They were the best of friends. She could imagine going to bed with him. The idea, in fact, was intriguing. He was probably a good lover: sensitive and caring. Those long fingers. . . . He had nice lips, and a sexy smile, which she had never noticed before. His calmness was a good foil for her passions, he had seen her at her worst, and he had always been there for her. Both of them had been through disappointment and heartbreak. He was over Vanessa; his marriage had proven that. He seemed ideal husband material for someone who knew how to catch him. Wouldn't everyone just faint if she and Charlie got together after all this time?

Very quickly Cady made up her mind. The major decisions of her life had always come fast. Why had she never noticed Charlie before, when he was right there for the taking? What a fool I've been, she thought, not to see what was under my nose. It was like the old fairy tales she'd read as a child. Home was the best. The jewels were hidden under the straw in your very own barn.

She called him. He was glad to hear from her, as always, and immediately asked when they could get together. Did she want to see a movie?

"Why don't you and I have dinner together at my apartment Saturday night?" Cady said. "Saturday is a good time to stay home."

"All right." He seemed pleased. "Should I bring Chinese food?"

"Steamed. I don't like salty."

"I know that."

"And I'll supply the champagne," Cady said.

"Champagne and Chinese food! What a good idea."

"I'm full of ideas," Cady said.

He should only know.

chapter
36

Cady was excited preparing for Saturday night. She bought and chilled two bottles of expensive champagne, chose the proper music — Sinatra because he was timeless — and arranged fresh flowers in her crystal vase. She changed her sheets, just in case. She bought three of the newest, expensive scented candles, one for the living room, one for beside the bed, and one for the side of the tub. Since she had a cleaning woman every week, and she herself was extremely neat, the apartment looked immaculate, although that was for her own sake, not for Charlie's; she knew he didn't care. She decided on the proper seductive lighting for the occasion. She wished she had a fireplace like Leigh did, since firelight was so romantic, but as usual she had to make do with what she had. She'd had her hair done, and decided on a black-velvet lounging suit because she would be at home. It made her look slim, and soft fabrics, she'd read, were sexy. She spent extra time on her makeup.

Charlie rang her bell at precisely eight o'clock, and kissed her hello on the cheek. She took his coat and the two paper bags he proffered, and suddenly she felt unexpectedly sentimental that he had brought their dinner. Love for him swelled in her heart.

"How pretty you look," he said appreciatively. He sniffed the air. "Smells good too."

"I was going to buy essence of meatloaf," she said, "but why fake it? We know I can't cook. Patchouli is better."

He smiled.

She took the food into the kitchen. She planned to drink for a long time, and if the food got cold she would nuke it. She'd put out a few little silver bowls of nuts in case Charlie got hungry, but not enough so he'd stay sober. She wanted to get down to the real Charlie, the man instead of the pal. Liquor always worked. It did for her.

Music was playing softly. He opened the champagne with the pop that always made her think of celebrations, and Cady held out two of her Baccarat flutes. "To us," he said.

"To us."

She led the way to the couch.

He cheerfully told her what he'd been

doing since she saw him last, that the office was a pain, that he'd seen two good movies, that he was forcing himself to work out regularly at the gym. "And are you seeing Paul?"

"The usual," Cady said. "He's just a bad habit. I feel sorry for him."

"Old attachments . . ." Charlie began. Then he smiled at her and got up and walked around the apartment looking at everything. "You are the neatest person I know."

"I think now I need a little chaos in my life," Cady said.

"Haven't you had enough?"

"The good kind."

"Oh, the good kind." He sat down on the couch again. She refilled their glasses.

"You should buy a little animal," he said. "A puppy, or a nice little cat."

"Heavens no!"

"I forgot, they shed."

"If I'm going to take care of anything it's going to be a lover," Cady said. "He'll have all my attention."

"We like that."

We? He was flirting with her. Good. "Or even a husband someday," Cady said. "You never know, I could change my mind about staying single."

"It's never too late," Charlie said.

"Exactly. Do you think you'll ever marry again?"

"If a diehard like you could change your mind, why couldn't I?"

"You see, we have all the choices," Cady said. "The future is ours."

"You're mellow tonight."

"I've decided to be a nicer person."

"Don't get too nice," Charlie said.

"Oh, really?" She tapped his arm playfully. "Do you think I'm not sweet?"

"You're sweet to me."

"You deserve it."

They smiled at each other. "Here," he said, "have some more champagne. You haven't said a cynical word all evening."

"It's the new me." She almost blurted out: I'm going to try to seduce you! but she restrained herself. She felt a little light-headed and fuzzy-tongued. She moved closer to Charlie on the couch.

"When did you want to eat?" he asked.

"Oh, in a while. I'm not hungry yet, are you?"

"Not really."

She held out the nuts and he took some. "You are one of my favorite people in the world," Cady said.

"And you're one of mine. It was a good

idea you had to spend Saturday night at home. I hate restaurants on Saturday. This is so much more civilized."

"In our cozy lair," Cady said.

"Who could ask for more?"

It occurred to her that she had not the faintest idea of how to seduce a man. The men she'd been seriously involved with had been just as eager as she, and the casual affairs had been mutual too, even if they wanted nothing more than a one-night stand. Here was Charlie, one of her oldest friends in the world, and she had to move the atmosphere from affection to lust. Other women seduced men all the time, didn't they? How did they do it?

She had fantasized about him until the attachment was real for her, but he knew nothing about what she was feeling. He sat there, innocent and friendly and pleasant, and she didn't want to frighten him. Maybe they should eat. A hungry man wasn't thinking about sex.

"How about dinner now?" she asked brightly.

He helped her reheat the food in the microwave, and she put it on her nice plates. She put out the chopsticks instead of her monogrammed silverware, because why bring up past failures? They sat at the tiny table in her dining corner, the second bottle of champagne between them. So as not to conflict with the smell of food, plain unscented candles burned on the table between them. Everything was comfortable and elegant. They leaned forward toward each other in the softly flickering light.

How did you change friendship to love?

She picked at the food, too nervous to eat. Another glass of champagne calmed her down. "Dear Charlie," she said. "None of us ever appreciated you enough. Now that I'm older and wiser I realize you are a very sexy man."

"*I* am?" He looked pleased.

"Yes. Do you think I'm sexy?"

He paused. "Of course you are. You always have been."

She smiled. "Shall we dance?"

They stood and she moved into his arms. This was where she wanted to be. It was perfect. She felt safe and titillated. He was just the right height for her. She had never been this close to him for so long, feeling the warmth of his body. He led her in a slow fox-trot. She could tell he wasn't aroused at all, but that was all right, he wasn't a teenaged boy anymore. A man of nearly fifty needed a little help. She moved even closer to him.

"You're a very good dancer," she said.

"So are you."

They danced till the end of the song and then he led her back to the table. "What about some tea?" he asked.

"I'd rather stay with the champagne, wouldn't you?"

"All right. But I'm a little drunk."

"Well, so am I," Cady said. "That's what it's for." She tapped his glass playfully. "To drunken confessions."

"I don't have any of those."

"Well, I might," she said.

"Really?"

"You never know."

"I'd like to hear them," Charlie said.

"All right. Let's repair to the couch."

He stood and began to take the dishes into the kitchen.

"Oh, leave them," Cady said.

"Are you sure?"

She tugged him over to the couch, the champagne bottle in her hand. He followed with the two glasses. They sat side by side. She was so close that she could kiss him if she wanted to. She almost did; her lips were tingling. His mouth that was so familiar was also unfamiliar, a challenge that was right before her. Would kissing him be the right thing to do? Would that explain everything

432

to him, since so far words hadn't even gotten close? One instant would change everything. She wanted him, and she wanted him to desire her too, to become her lover. She wanted him in her bed, on her clean sheets, making her feel that her life would begin again. There, in her bed, or even here on her couch, she would be skillful and passionate, but now, before she had made her move, she felt only ineffectual and clumsy. She was sure he would never kiss her. He thought they were friends, and he would be afraid to. Good, timid, decent Charlie.

"Do you want to hear my drunken confession?" she asked.

"Sure."

"I love you," she said.

"Well, I love you too. What's the confession?"

"That was it."

He looked at her.

She couldn't resist, she was drunk, impatient, and inflamed, and she flopped on him like a fish. She kissed him on the lips. How warm and firm his lips were! She felt him moving, and then she realized he was trying to get away from her. He pulled away from her weight and sat straight up on the other end of the couch.

"Cady. . . ."

She was speechless and embarrassed, but also she wanted to kiss him again. But even in her condition she knew that would be the wrong thing to do. He put his hands up as if he were trying to fend her off.

"We're friends," he said.

"I know that."

"I hope you didn't think I meant I was in love with you," he said desperately. "I love you as a pal. You're like my sister."

"Kissin' kin," she said, and forced herself to laugh lightly.

"I didn't mean to lead you on," he said.

"You didn't. I was trying to lead you on. I've thought about this, Charlie, and I think you and I would be a wonderful team. We don't have to be just friends forever. We could be more."

He shook his head and looked sad.

"Don't you want to have an affair with me?" she asked. She sounded pathetic and as soon as she had said it she wished she could take it back.

"It would be totally incestuous," he said, with a little smile.

"No it wouldn't."

He patted her shoulder and stood up. He cleared the table and put the dishes into the dishwasher. She just sat there and watched him through the open kitchen door, and she thought how nice it would be if they lived together and he was helping around the house because he was so sweet, and then they could go to bed. But he would be gone in a few moments, and the realization hurt. He didn't want her.

He was done. "Thank you for a wonderful dinner," he said. "Thanks for saving me from a lonely and boring Saturday night."

What a lie, Cady thought. Charlie's Saturday night would not have been lonely and boring if she hadn't rescued him. He knew other women. He had friends. He was in demand as an extra man.

"I apologize for jumping on you," Cady said.

"Oh. . . ." he said. "It was very flattering. You go to bed now and get some sleep. And be sure to blow out those candles. You don't want to burn down your apartment."

He was pretending she was that drunk. She let it stay.

"Walk me to the door," he said. She did, and he put his arm around her. "Friends?" he said.

"Of course."

He kissed her lightly on the cheek and was gone.

I hate all men, Cady thought; I hate them. But no one could have been kinder than Charlie had been. He could have rushed out of her apartment in revulsion. He had escaped, but first he had tried to make sure she wasn't hurt and rejected. He was too nice. It wasn't fair. She felt humiliated no matter how tactful he had been. She didn't know if she could ever face him again.

He would probably forget eventually, and accept her again as his old friend. He would accept invitations from her — safe ones outside of her apartment, in public places. He would still be her escort. Or maybe not. Maybe she had ruined everything. Maybe when he was safe at home he would have second thoughts and decide she was a horny, disgraceful, middle-aged woman and it would be too embarrassing to have to see her.

Cady wondered what Charlie would have done if Vanessa had been the one to make the pass at him instead of her. Would he have wanted Vanessa? She felt like a complete failure. My life is nothing but losses, she thought, but she felt that despite tonight's fiasco she still deserved Charlie. The fact that she could never get him didn't change anything.

She didn't know if she would tell Leigh or not. She didn't want to admit she'd been a fool, but Leigh might say that nothing ventured nothing gained. She wouldn't tell Vanessa. Vanessa might laugh at her.

Cady felt her old bitterness coming back, the bile that had been gone for that brief time when she had thought she could get somewhere with Charlie. She knew she depended on men too much, that they were too important in her life, but there was nothing she could do about it. She liked to tell herself that she was independent, that she didn't care, but in the end it always came down to the same thing: she felt incomplete and lonely when she was alone. Was that such a crime? After all, maybe it was just the human condition.

chapter
37

Vanessa knew her children were resigned to Mom's little trips away by herself. She and Bill had taken them to New York City once when they were young, to the usual tourist attractions: the Museum of Natural History, the Planetarium, FAO Schwarz, Radio City Music Hall, the ice skating at Rockefeller Center, Broadway, and Times Square. They had liked New York, but thought it was too busy. Vanessa had made it her business to give them too much to do, and to drag them through throngs of people, so they would be glad to get home. She didn't want them to ask to come with her all the time.

Although they might have enjoyed another family holiday in New York, Jack and Liberty had gone on to their own lives now. Eventually they had understood that, once in a while, Mom needed to be alone and away from them. They didn't take it personally. They thought she was shopping and going to museums, seeing her old friends. They considered her trips harmless. So did Bill. After a number of years Bill had stopped coming with her. He was busy at the office, and he didn't want to miss his tennis.

The family didn't think that wanting to be rid of them for a few days was such a bad thing. They knew Vanessa had never really acclimated to her role of a privileged housewife in Beverly Hills, and that sometimes she became restless. But she didn't sit around drinking, she didn't take pills, and she didn't flirt with men. She didn't complain about her husband and children to a psychiatrist. If brief vacations alone in New York were all it took to keep her satisfied, then they felt they were really lucky. She was a good mother. Bill was a good father. Vanessa and Bill had taken the children skiing and to Hawaii. They had taken them to London and to Paris. They gave them their share of time.

Vanessa's trips to New York had always been the same. She did what her family thought she was doing, and also she saw a few of her old boyfriends, and, most importantly, she found a new one. Finding the new one was the exciting part. But then the years went by and the magic touch left her, and one day there was no new one to be found.

The first time she sat at a bar and had no one to talk to but the bartender she thought maybe it was the kind of crowd that was there. But the second time it happened she went into the ladies' room and scrutinized her face carefully in the mirror. Was it the lighting? It wasn't too harsh, was it? She didn't look like a woman in her fifties, did she? Was there a look in the eyes, an expression of having seen too much, of knowing too much, that gave her away? She knew her nubility was totally gone, but was her ripe maturity gone too, leaving only an attractive older woman, a husk, whose attempts at seduction were perceived as merely friendly conversation?

Had she already turned into the kind of woman about whom people said: *I bet she was a knockout once?*

Women in their fifties could not pick up men in bars. She had finally reached the age of dignity, whether she wanted to or not. The flip side was making a fool of yourself.

She had known for a long time that she wouldn't be able to enchant strange men indefinitely. What happened to other women would happen to her too. Plastic surgery would continue to delay the inevitable, but she would never look thirty again. She might be more sexual now than she had been when she was youthful, but men didn't notice, or care. When she had been in her twenties having her cheap dinner at the neighborhood coffee shop, people had stared, and she hadn't paid much attention. Then, after her marriage, she had dined alone as a successful predator, never alone for long. And now, for the first time in her life, Vanessa had begun to eat dinner in restaurants alone unnoticed . . . invisible.

Her former New York lover, Charlie Carlyle, was her platonic friend now. At least she had kept him on that level. He liked to see her, and bought her a drink and told her what had been happening in his life, but he didn't want to go to bed with her. He always left after the one drink, with somewhere else to go. There were no more expensive dinners. He was an older man who liked younger women, and she was no longer young enough.

Matthew and Tom, the men she had been seeing in New York for years, sometimes saw her for lunch when they were free, but when they did see her it was as longtime friends, and not to make passes, even lighthearted ones they knew would be rebuffed.

Some of her other men through the years had been one-night stands. Others had stayed in her life until she had tired of them and stopped calling. None had been difficult to get rid of. They had not cared any more than she had. They were all gone now, erased by her need to find someone new.

But for the last few trips there had been no one new.

Vanessa knew the last door that had not closed yet was the one that led to a relationship. Women in their fifties and older — eighty even — met the right man, fell in love. When that happened everyone was delighted. They liked to tell the story. You see, they said, it isn't over. You can fall in love at any age. Aren't those two old people cute, they can't take their hands off each other! But that was a person looking at a person, two people looking for late-blooming romance and companionship, not a horny man on a business trip looking for a sexy ego-building evening. Unfortunately she didn't want another husband. She had never looked for love.

Once again she was sitting at the bar in the St. Regis, and she was drinking a glass of wine alone, a tourist who had been out all day, taking a rest. The men next to her were talking business to each other. She remembered when such conversations had been halted by the fact of her presence. The men who were alone at the bar were deep in thought, their gazes far away. She remembered when they had looked at her and tried to meet her. She thought of all those business cards so carefully saved in her secret scrapbook at home, and knew her collection was becoming an artifact. Men had pressed their business cards on her — had wanted her to have them, to have her remember their owners. But that scrapbook was only nostalgia, like a book of old vacation photos displaying the faces of temporary friends, now strangers, unrecognized.

Where were those men who had been so eager? What were they doing now? Did they remember her? Did it matter? They wouldn't want her.

Vanessa had tried to prepare herself for this part of her life, and she felt she was handling it pretty well. She was disappointed and depressed, but that was understandable. Without her flirtations and her conquests New York wasn't the wonderland it had been. There was no more special excitement. She wondered which was worse: to have been a goddess with all those men vying for her and to have lost it, or to have been an ordinary, rather plain woman who was satisfied with what she could get because she knew there was nothing else. Ordinary, plain women wanted validation too. But Vanessa had never understood why she needed it so badly. Now it was gone, and she still didn't know why. It would have been so much better to have known.

Maybe she should have been going to that psychiatrist, talking about herself not her family.

She had another glass of wine while deciding where she would eat her lonely dinner. She would go where she was recognized and they were cordial to her, and she would eat slowly, pretending this meal was an event. Or perhaps she wouldn't go anywhere at all. A sandwich from room service in front of the TV would be more disappointing than relaxing, but at least she wouldn't have to put on a happy face.

She wondered if it were time to stop taking her private trips to New York. She could tell Bill this city held no more charm for her. She could say that it had changed, become less gentle and more brutal. She could decide to never come back again.

But then she wouldn't see Leigh and Cady and Charlie, and then her past would have vanished. There was no way Vanessa could ever say good-bye to her past with those people. They were joined forever. They were her friends. Even knowing she would see the three of them tomorrow evening for dinner made her feel young again, when not much did anymore.

There had been a period when she would have had time to meet them for only a drink, but now she was grateful they would take up an entire evening.

They met at a new midtown restaurant Leigh had discovered on one of her expense-account lunches. During the day it was crowded, trendy, and noisy, but in the evening it was appealing and peaceful. They had all come to the point in their lives where they liked to hear and be heard in a restaurant. They could say that to each other with a smile, acknowledging their maturity and appreciating it.

Charlie arrived first. "I have you alone," he said happily, and sat next to her. "How lovely you look."

"Thank you." Charlie always made her feel better.

Leigh was next, and Cady last. Vanessa had noticed that the last few times she had seen Cady, Cady was a little too frantic, pressed too hard. She seemed uncomfortable. Vanessa had no idea why. When Cady looked at Charlie her eyes widened as if she wanted to devour him, and then they slid away as if she couldn't bear the sight of him. Leigh was her usual calm, well-groomed self. Vanessa thought how difficult it must be for Leigh to put away the stresses of her high-pressure day and greet them all with so much relaxed pleasure.

"Jack's wife is pregnant," Vanessa announced.

"Hurray," Leigh said. "Our first grandchild."

"Ours?" Cady said.

"Of course."

"I can't wait," Vanessa said.

"Neither can I," Charlie said. "I need a grandchild."

"And Vanessa is still having adventures," Cady said. She sounded both envious and bitter.

"Oh no I'm not," Vanessa said lightly. There, it was out. She had admitted it.

"No?" Charlie asked. He seemed pleased.

"No. I have reached the age of sanity."

"That's what happens eventually," Leigh said.

"Yes, it does. I am brand-new and pure."

If I act like it's nothing then no one will care, Vanessa thought. She smiled in a lighthearted way and shook her hair. Even now it was a gesture that worked well.

They laughed and drank and shared the news, and ordered the dishes Leigh recommended from her lunches there. Vanessa looked at Charlie and thought for the first time, now that she had retired involuntarily from the competition, that it was a shame she had overlooked him all these years, too bad he had become only a member of the family when he really was an attractive and eligible man. She had missed an opportunity. He had always made it clear that he had a crush on her and she had made light of it. But he didn't flirt with her anymore. He was just very nice, very kind.

I've probably missed many other chances, she thought. They might have been better than the ones I chose. My life is a blur of mistakes and ignored possibilities. That's what happens when you have too much.

"David is talking about retiring," Leigh said.

"But why?" Vanessa asked.

"Why indeed? He would be bored to death. The company needs him. Retiring is just one of those things men his age threaten when they think it would be more fun to do something else. I told him, I'm

447

not retiring. I'm not going to travel around the world with you. I'm going to work till I die."

"I suppose I am too," Cady said.

"I don't want to think about it," Charlie said. "I don't want to die in *this* job."

"I wished I worked," Vanessa said.

"You can," Leigh said.

"No, I'm too lazy."

"At least you know it," Cady said.

"David is almost seventy," Leigh said.

"I can't believe it!" they all cried.

"Well, he doesn't look it, or act it," Leigh said. "But these days people keep working if they like their job. It's not like our grandparents when they retired at sixty-five and died a year or so later from old age."

"No, we stay young," Charlie said.

"You *are* young," Leigh said.

"I'm fifty this year."

"Young to us," Leigh said.

"Susan Brown would be fifty-one," Cady said.

They looked at each other in silence. It seemed almost impossible to imagine. As they always did, they wondered what her life would have been like, and wished they had been able to keep her from taking it. They always came back to her somehow, no matter how many years had passed.

They had had lucky lives, nothing really shocking or dreadful had happened to them, except for that. They had been spared life-threatening diseases and tragic deaths. Even Cady's romantic disappointments had been survivable. Vanessa's marriage, while not happy, was bearable. Charlie was easygoing and Leigh's life was charmed. They were more fortunate than most people, when you looked around at other people's lives.

They hadn't thought so years ago but now they did.

Susan had become a kind of caution to them; the person who had given up hope, who didn't believe it was worth it to wait around to see if things got better. *Never let that be you.* Again they thought, as they always did, how in her absence she was so much more important than she had been in her presence.

I would love to be young though, Vanessa thought. I would like to still have my sexuality and my power. I'm glad I have all the good things I do, but I miss those. I will never stop missing them. Someday I suppose I will be resigned, but I wonder if I will ever be content.

chapter
38

Vanessa had determined that if she were going to continue going to New York then she would make plans in advance for her trips and not spend any more ego-destroying evenings alone in bars. To that end, six months later when she was ready to go to New York again, she called Charlie Rackley and invited him to the theater. He wanted to see *Dancing at Lughnasa*, which had been very well received, so she got the tickets from her broker. Charlie said that he would take her for an early dinner before the show, and a drink afterward. For herself, she bought tickets for two musicals since they were more to her taste. And with an evening with the group planned too, she thought, she was protected against disappointment.

She did not bother to call any of her former men. They wouldn't know she was there if she didn't call them. Let's see if I can get along without them, she thought. After all, what did they give her anyway these days?

She felt floating and free. She decided she would never again spend time with people who didn't much want to be with her. She was impatient with their excuses, their back and forth, their emotional stinginess. She supposed when she was old she would just have to end up with her husband, trying to figure out reasons why they had stayed together all these years.

To her surprise she found herself looking forward to her date with Charlie. She knew that whatever else, he would be good to her.

Even though he was alone too, as she was, his life wasn't so bad. He was busy. Hostesses begged him to complete the number at their dinner tables. He was everybody's favorite extra man. Vanessa couldn't imagine anyone inviting her to a dinner party as an extra woman. The thought made her laugh. At twenty-five it had been different, but even then she hadn't really been an extra woman, because someone already had his eye on her, which is why she had been invited. The early phases of her adventurous life had gone by relatively unnoticed, as merely her due, and now that they were gone she was sorry she hadn't appreciated them even more than she had. Sometimes she couldn't help feeling nostalgic about her lost days. But she had used them. She certainly had.

It was mild enough to walk through the city, and she did her usual shopping for things she didn't really need. This was her homage to her vacation. Then the evening she was to meet Charlie for the play, she lay down and rested for a while before it was time to get ready for dinner. Feet up, sipping from a bottle of mineral water, then a bubble bath, but not such a long one that she would get tired again. There had been a time when she had not needed to rest. But you adjusted to your different needs, and she wanted to have fun and feel refreshed.

Charlie picked her up in the hotel lobby and hugged her hello. "You look beautiful as always," he said.

"Thank you. I need to hear that these days."

"Why?"

"Do you think anyone compliments me at home?" she said, but that wasn't what she meant.

"Well, they should."

He took her to a restaurant in the theater district, which he said was new and special. She had two appetizers and a glass of wine.

"Is that all you want?"

"Yes, I'm fine."

"I have a car meeting us afterward," he said, "and we can have a drink and something else to eat wherever you like."

He was her past, the good past, all the men who had tried to make her happy, to impress her, to be sure she had a nice time.

It was so pleasant sitting next to him in the theater, watching the people come in and reading the Playbill. And when, every so often she noticed he was looking at her, he would smile at her.

"Why did I never take you to a play before?" Vanessa asked.

"I don't know why. I would have gone."

"I was such a lone wolf in the past," Vanessa said.

"And now?"

"Not so much. There's not much point in being a lone wolf if you're not going hunting."

"Their loss is my gain," Charlie said.

He has no idea that no one wants me anymore, Vanessa thought, and beamed at him before she went back to her Playbill.

At first she found the play boring. It was too arty for her: unhappy people with dead-end lives in a dreary place. She knew she was supposed to like it, it was, after all, the best play of the year, but she had never liked what she was supposed to. And then when she had about given up and was thinking of sneaking a little nap, the women onstage began an unexpected, spirited dance, whirling and tossing their skirts, their faces glowing with joy. Vanessa wished they would keep on doing it, but they stopped and went right back to their monotonous little world. Just for a moment they had revealed what their lives had been like at some point in their youth and the joy that they were still capable of, the ecstasy that lies at the bone, gone but not forgotten.

That's me, Vanessa thought, and even though she didn't really understand the play or even like it, she began to cry.

She saw Charlie glance at her. He thought she was touched by the work. She'd let him think so. It was always good to get some points for intelligence.

When the show was over their car was waiting. He had a list of places to offer her, or she could suggest something else. She picked the bar at the Rainbow Room, high in the sky. When she sat there she knew she had made the right choice. She loved New York and here it was at its best: glittering, exciting, mysterious. The city she had left too soon and had been tantalized by forever after. The lights of

Hollywood, glittering as they were, had never meant anything to her. You had to be too young and beautiful in Hollywood.

And here too.

They had champagne. She felt very comfortable with him beside her, and remembered how carelessly she had treated him when they were young. In any event, all that was over now. She felt as if she owed him an apology.

"This is the first time the two of us have been alone together since we were in our twenties," he said.

"Is that true?"

"You know it is. I always tried. . . . Then I gave up."

"I guess I wasn't very nice to you in the past," Vanessa said.

"I understood."

"No, I remember how disappointed you looked when I wouldn't take you seriously."

"I didn't think you noticed," he said.

"I tried not to."

"You always were an extraordinary woman," Charlie said. "I'm lucky I got to know you and that we've been friends for so many years."

"So I guess I can't disappoint you anymore," Vanessa said lightly.

"Do you want to?"

"No. No, I don't."

"That's good. You were terribly talented at it."

"Empathy was never my strong suit," she said.

"But you had your life. I did understand."

They looked at each other, each of them looking back at the past. "I've changed though," Vanessa said. "Have you?"

"In some ways. I'm not that gawky, yearning, pathetic boy anymore."

"You were never pathetic," she said.

He laughed. His eyes are so kind, she thought. And his face is so vulnerable. He's someone I would never want to hurt now that I know exactly how to.

"And in some ways I haven't changed and I guess I never will," Charlie said.

"In what ways?"

"You can't guess?"

"No, I can't guess. Tell me."

"I've always been very much in love with you," he said.

The words hung there. She knew he meant it. He had always loved her, and he had never stopped. She hadn't realized it. After all, he'd gotten married. And quickly divorced.

"I'm so glad," Vanessa said. She took his hand. Then she leaned over and kissed him on the lips. It was their first kiss, and they were both aware of it. He was tentative and she was curious. Then she liked it and kissed him again. We are going to be one of those disgusting couples that neck in bars, she thought. But she didn't care.

They pulled back after a while and looked at each other. This could be serious, Vanessa thought. She felt as attracted to him as she had been to any of her old conquests, and while it wasn't as appealingly strange, this was more satisfying because he knew her. She wanted to see what he was like in bed. She didn't think the idea would shock him. It had probably been his life's fantasy. She found this enormously flattering.

"Would you like to come to my hotel?" she asked very softly.

"Yes."

How convenient that she had chosen drinks at a place that was in near walking distance. They went to her hotel right away, since there was nothing more that could safely be said at this moment. He did look a little stunned.

But when they were safely in her room he didn't look stunned anymore. They undressed each other and to her surprise he took his time making love, as if he wanted to enjoy it and remember it. This turned her on. It was her favorite kind of sex, and rare. All her past disappointments disappeared and she felt enormously happy. She and Charlie Rackley were eminently suited, and who would ever have known?

He held her in his arms all night. Charlie, who had always said "bad timing," could believe in good timing now, she thought. It was definitely timing. What did it matter if she had begun this evening thinking of him as a kind of last resort? Now she was thrilled she had discovered him. She didn't know if he would feel guilty in the morning and try to get out of what he might think of as a destructive affair because she was married, but she knew she wouldn't let him go.

In the morning they made love again and she ordered breakfast from room service. "I have to go to work," Charlie said.

"Say you're sick and we'll stay in bed all day," Vanessa said.

He made a call. She couldn't believe she had so much power over him.

It was like a honeymoon. They couldn't stay away from each other. Eventually she ordered more food.

"We have Leigh and Cady tonight and we have to decide if we're going to tell them," Vanessa said.

"I'll do what you want."

"I vote for full disclosure," Vanessa said. "I tell them everything else."

"Cady might be a little upset," he said.

"Why?"

"Well, for about five minutes she liked me."

"Cady?"

He shrugged.

"But you didn't like her that way?"

"No. It was always you."

How lucky and young and desirable she felt. It was as if no matter what happened to erode her beauty Charlie would never notice.

"Would you ever leave Bill?" he asked her.

She shook her head. "Even though I'm not in love with him, we have too much of a history together to throw it away. That's what our marriage has become. We're two horses in harness, and we have no idea what we're pulling, but we just do it. In his way he needs me, and I guess in my way I need him."

"Did you ever love him?"

"No. You know my story: I'm a victim of

my times. I got married because I was pregnant, because there was no abortion, then I stayed married because we had kids, and eventually I had affairs to save my sanity. I married the wrong man, but who's to know if someone else might have been just as wrong?"

"All right," he said.

"You're okay with that?"

"I just want to love you," Charlie said. "And be your last affair. And see you whenever we can without jeopardizing your marriage."

"That can be arranged," Vanessa said. "That's easy."

Her life had started again. She was perfectly happy for him to be her last affair. It was the best proposal she had ever had. Charlie Rackley! A day ago she'd had no idea.

chapter
39

At dinner Cady and Leigh noticed right away that Vanessa and Charlie were radiant. They were unable to hide it. Before too many minutes had passed they sneaked their hands together under the table. Cady felt an unpleasant sinking feeling in the pit of her stomach. Vanessa and Charlie! To see a man who hadn't wanted her wanting someone else was almost unbearable. Finally, when it had become perfectly obvious, they announced shyly that they were an item now. Leigh looked pleased and Cady tried to.

Leigh glanced at Cady with a look of sympathy, since Cady had admitted to her two years ago about her ill-advised evening with Charlie. At the time Leigh had told her she hoped she wouldn't ruin the friendship by carrying a grudge. Cady had assured her she would not, but the truth was she had never been able to feel exactly the same way about Charlie as she had before she humiliated herself. Sometimes she still wanted him because she couldn't have him, and sometimes she almost hated him for having brought out the worst in her.

"Congratulations," Cady said. She tried to make her voice warm. She told herself this pairing was inevitable, since Charlie had always been in love with Vanessa, and Vanessa had probably run through every other man in the world before settling on the one who at least cared for her. Friends know the truth, she thought.

Neither Cady nor Leigh asked about the future, if Vanessa would get divorced to be with Charlie, or if this was just a fling. It was probably so new that they didn't know, or at least they hadn't volunteered. The only thing that was clear was that this trip for Vanessa was different from all the others.

After the dinner was over, and Vanessa and Charlie seemed very eager to be on their way, Cady and Leigh shared a cab. "I'm so surprised," Leigh said. "Who would think, after all these years?"

"Do you suppose it will last?"

"I hope so. I've never seen her look so content."

"Because he's probably good in bed," Cady said bitterly.

"You're over him, aren't you?"

"There was nothing to get over. I had an idea and it didn't work."

"She lives in California. He'll be just as available to be your favorite escort."

"That's all I want. Wouldn't it be ironic if she finally left Bill?"

"For Charlie. . . . Yes, it would be ironic." They sat there for a moment in silence, thinking about how all their lives had turned out.

"I want to come back in my next life as Vanessa," Cady said.

"No, you don't. She has too many issues."

"I was just kidding." And she was. In her next life the only person Cady wanted to come back as was Leigh.

They hugged good-bye in the cab in front of Leigh's apartment and, as always, Leigh pressed the entire cab fare into Cady's hand. Then Cady went home. When she let herself into her silent, empty apartment, she thought how unfair it was that, of all of them, it was only she who was alone tonight.

She wondered idly where Paul was. They were due for a meal together. She would call him tomorrow. He had become her stability, and she knew how close she was to falling in love with him again, if only because they were linked in their crazy way. She had tried to leave him, she *had* left him, and now they were whatever they were. They had been together for almost thirty years. She knew too much about him to try to make it work, and yet, because she was beyond being hurt by him, she felt a fondness for him that would never go away. Perhaps that was good. She didn't think a long marriage could be more complex than the things she and Paul had been through together. A marriage of thirty years was given plaudits, but what would you say about an affair that long? You didn't get credit for it, and yet such a relationship was much rarer than marriage.

The next morning before Cady was able to call him, Paul called her. "I was just thinking about you," she said.

"Obviously I was thinking about you too."

"So how are you? When will I see you? I want to hear all the news."

"You act as if my life is exciting," he said.

"It is. You just won't admit it. Your life would kill a lesser man."

"What about dinner tomorrow?"

"Dinner! It's not summer. Where are your wife and your girlfriend?"

"My girlfriend doesn't deserve me and my wife has plans."

"Then you and I have plans." Suddenly she had an inspiration. "Come to my place and I'll send out for a gourmet meal," Cady said.

"I'd better come early with my credit card."

"You'd better," she said, "or you're getting neighborhood Chinese."

How relaxed they had become together after all they'd been through. They could tease each other. They knew each other so well that they had the capacity to hurt each other, but their good-natured jibes didn't sting. I could do worse than Paul, Cady thought. Too bad he's such a bastard.

It was the first dinner at home with a man she'd had since the disastrous evening with Charlie. This would wash it away. Thinking about Paul still made her feel warm with feeling and a little excited, as if they were still dating. But she was no longer his victim. Not waiting for him, trapped in her apartment, had changed everything. Paying her own rent, dating other men when she could, had changed things too. She wasn't his little girl anymore.

He showed up at her apartment at six,

with his credit card and a tiny azalea plant. His face showed strain. He took off his jacket and tie and Cady gave him a drink. "Next your pipe and slippers, sir," she said.

"I always feel so comfortable here," he said.

"Then you must come more often."

"Then I'll feel uncomfortable."

"Of course you will."

"Why is it that you know me better than anyone else in the world?" he asked.

"Better than your wife?"

"The poor woman doesn't know me at all."

"Better than your children?"

"They're just my children. I'm their bad betrayer."

"Better than your girlfriend?"

"How well did you know me when you were my girlfriend?"

"Point taken," Cady said.

She had lit the perfumed candles she liked, and put on soft music. She had put her collection of take-out menus on the coffee table, and when he had unwound they would choose what they wanted to eat. She sipped her white wine. Paul had changed from wine to vodka recently because he said he found wine acidic. He was sitting on the couch and she was next to him, the little azalea plant on the coffee table in front of them. Tomorrow I'll take off that hideous foil and buy a nice basket for it, Cady thought.

"My family has been through a really bad week," Paul said. "My wife was diagnosed with cancer."

"No!" What a terrible thing. She felt shock, fear, and compassion. She didn't dare think how glad that news would have made her twenty years ago, but of course she did think it anyway. "What kind?"

"Breast. I know there's often a good survival rate, particularly if you're not that young, and she's sixty-nine. But she's been going for all sorts of tests, and the doctors are talking about surgery and chemotherapy. It's going to be rough."

"I'm so sorry," Cady said.

"It was a shock," he said.

"Of course."

"I never thought there was even the faintest possibility of her dying before I did," Paul said.

"Do they think she'll die?"

"Anyone could die."

"But what exactly did the doctors say?"

"They don't know. They're being encouraging."

"Then allow yourself to be encouraged."

"Illness scares me," he said. "Especially cancer."

"It scares everybody."

"I tried to leave her for years, and now I might lose her."

"No," Cady said, "you tried *not* to leave her."

He sighed. "You do say it the way it is," he said.

"Now I suppose you realize you always loved her," Cady said gently.

He shook his head. "No. We had a bond and we have it still, but this just made me sad and afraid and terribly guilty. Do I love her? I don't even want to talk about that, or think about it, when she might die. There's something I suppose that goes beyond love. Do you understand what I'm trying to say?"

"Yes."

They sat there in silence for a few moments and then he put his face in his hands and Cady saw his shoulders trembling. He made a quiet, strangled sound, and she realized he was weeping. She put her arms around him and held him that way, close to her: mother, friend, ally, lover, accidental bystander. She had never seen Paul cry before. He had been the stronger one, the catalyst. Now he seemed as if he couldn't take care of anyone. He must be feeling that way too.

She was his former girlfriend, who had wished for years that his wife would disappear, and now she wished his wife were well and safe. She wanted to comfort him, to make him safe too. All she could do was hold him, and continue to hold him, the least likely consoler, and yet, because she realized she loved him, an appropriate one.

After a while he calmed down, and then he went into the bathroom. When he emerged he was washed and combed, with an enigmatic face. Cady wondered if he hated her because men weren't supposed to cry in front of women.

"How about a refill?" he asked, picking up his glass.

She filled it up again. "Are you hungry?"

"Not really, but it will take some time to come."

They chose their food and she phoned in the order. They listened to the music, and he put his arm around her. "Nice album," he said. "I like Sinatra."

"I know."

"I feel peaceful here."

"Good."

Don't hate me, she told him in her mind.

She could still feel him in her arms. She nestled against him, letting him be the strong one. She wasn't sure if the silent moment was awkward, or so comfortable that they were beyond small talk. I should know him well enough after thirty years that I know he doesn't want to talk all the time, she thought. She was certain the moment that had just passed when he showed his grief and vulnerability would not happen again soon, if ever. She felt privileged that it had happened to her.

I thought I knew everything about him, she thought, but he can still surprise me. Somehow that made him even more interesting.

"I will be there for you," Cady said.

"I know you will."

Perhaps that was what he needed. It was what she needed.

chapter
40

That night, after the sex, Vanessa and Charlie talked for a long time. It had been easy to know what those other men had wanted from her, and to keep her distance, but she didn't know what he would want.

"Can't you come to New York more than twice a year?" he asked.

"I might be able to come three times. I'll think of something."

"It's still so little."

"It's every four months." He was right, it wasn't much. But if she changed her routine too much everyone would know something had happened.

"I could come to California," Charlie said.

She shook her head. "I can't cheat when I'm on Bill's territory. You may find it hard to believe, but I've never cheated in California, only in New York. It's not that I couldn't keep it a secret, but I don't want to be like those other wives. I don't want to

471

be banal. And I feel it's disrespectful."

"May I call you?"

"Of course," Vanessa said. "There are long hours during the afternoon when I'm all alone. If *you* call *me* it won't show up on our phone bill. I hope you do call, and often."

"I'll call every day."

"No," she said, "don't call every day. I'll start to wait for your call and get obsessed. You can call me twice a week."

"Twice a week!"

"At first. We'll see."

"Ever since I've known you you've been saying 'we'll see' to dust me off."

"Ah, Charlie . . ." She kissed him and ruffled his hair. There was a small bald spot at the back of his head like a baby's. She found it touching; it made him more vulnerable. "I'm not getting rid of you, I'm saving our relationship."

"Which one, the friendship or the affair?"

"Both."

"I want to give you something you need," Charlie said.

"You are." That sounded cold. She didn't want him to think she wanted him only for sex. But the truth was she hadn't really thought about it much. Everything had happened so fast. Was it so terrible to want someone only for sex, even though you valued your friendship with that person too? It was confusing. Vanessa thought she might never understand how she really felt about sex, that she had been brought up one way and lived another. "Making love with you is different," she said. "You mean so much to me."

"I love you," he said.

"I know."

"You don't have to love me," he said. "I'm not sure I'm someone anyone should be in love with. I have a lot of faults."

"Who doesn't, at our age?" Vanessa said. She laughed.

"I cherish your laugh," Charlie said.

"Thank you."

"I thought my marriage lasted such a short time because I was still in love with you," he said, "but afterward I thought about it a great deal, as one does about failures, and I realized there's a part of me that doesn't want to belong to anyone."

"That's all right," Vanessa said.

"Let's face it, what man would put up with an affair with a woman he sees only three times a year?"

"Many have settled for less," she said with a smile.

"I don't mean those guys. I mean someone who's involved."

"I don't want you to get too involved," Vanessa said. "I don't want to hurt you."

"You hurt me every time I had to say good-bye to you, for thirty years."

"Oh, Charlie!"

"But I can handle this. I can."

"It's going to be difficult for me too, you know," she said. She would probably think of the sex with longing. It was the best she had ever had.

"Why won't you leave Bill?" Charlie asked. "Then we could see each other so much more often. You hate Los Angeles. You could move to New York. Or you could take long trips here; stay as long as you liked. I would visit you all the time in LA. We'd have a bicoastal relationship. I wouldn't try to make you marry me."

She wondered why she was so adamant about not leaving Bill. He was a good man, and they had a history together, such as it was, and he was family. But if she left him he would survive. Surely her life without him would be better. She could keep Charlie forever; she knew that. When you were involved with a man, didn't you want to be with him? Was Bill her protection against really falling in love, against being hurt? She was just as neurotic as Charlie was.

"I don't want to marry again," Vanessa said. "I didn't want to get married the first time."

"I won't propose."

"But I told you I won't leave Bill," she said, "and you're already trying to make me do it. What's next?"

"If you left him then we could at least work out a way to live in the same state."

"Airplanes are fast."

"We're going to be old, we're going to die. . . ."

"I feel now as if I could live forever," she said. She kissed him. "Let's keep the excitement and the yearning. Let's keep the romance. Let's keep the lust."

"We will."

She had never felt prettier. He was her second chance . . . no, her last chance. Just when she had thought it was all over, Charlie had appeared in a way she had never seen him before. "You and I are so lucky," Vanessa said.

"I suppose so, in the scheme of things. People don't always get what they want without a penalty. Although the penalty is that I won't see you enough."

"Let's enjoy what we have."

"Oh, I do," he said. "I do."

She wondered if he would be hard to handle, but she didn't think so. Charlie had always been one of the most accommodating men in the world.

After that they kept to their routine and their promises. He called her in California twice a week. Sometimes, for a special occasion, or when she felt particularly lonely, she let him call her more often than that. He talked about how much he missed her, how much he loved her. Vanessa found this immensely reassuring, particularly because he was thousands of miles away.

She found herself being a little nicer to Bill, although she had always been nice to him. She had lived with the secret of her double life through most of her marriage, but now the secret was with her all the time. Telling Charlie he couldn't telephone her didn't make her not want to speak to him. She looked forward to her next trip to New York.

Bill was not suspicious that she was going to New York sooner than usual. He knew she was restless. He wanted to keep her happy so she wouldn't do anything silly like have an affair with the pool man, or turn into a disagreeable nag, or ask him to come with her. The two of them had grown very much apart. Yet, they were content on some level. He loved to show her off. He was proud of her. Vanessa was always available for sex with her husband, although she no longer initiated it. There wasn't that much sex anyway, since nothing about their marriage was new. The sex was comforting; it was part of their claim on each other.

She managed to compartmentalize very well. She did not, for example, think of Charlie while she was doing her wifely duty with Bill, even though the mental substitution might have aroused her. Most of the time she faked rapture to be polite. In her personal system of morality, fantasizing about your lover when you were having sex with your husband was only a different form of cheating. She felt Bill had little enough of her without taking away more.

She was trying to be an ethical person.

On her trips to New York she and Charlie were voracious for each other. She still went to the theater, because she enjoyed it and because Bill would ask her about the plays or musicals she had supposedly seen, but now when she got a ticket Charlie got one too, and they sat next to each other. They went out to dinner. They saw Leigh and Cady. Paul's wife was very ill, Cady reported, and the four of them discussed the ramifications of that, how it made her feel, how unpredictable and tenuous life was. Vanessa tried not to be impatient in her own. She tried to be calm. This was her life, and that was someone else's. Someone else's mortal disease was not a warning to seize the day and mess up the protections you had set up.

Vanessa knew that when Charlie was alone he went to dinner parties and the theater and movies and sometimes on dates with available women. Women invited him to things and he accepted. She tried not to be jealous. "You can cheat if you want," she told him, "as long as I don't have to know."

"But what will you imagine?"

"I sleep with my husband. You are a free, healthy, mature man. Do what you want, as long as you don't tell me and don't fall in love with any of them."

Poor women, she thought. But Charlie was no worse than any of the other men they dated. Everyone their age had baggage. Most women wouldn't find his situation an impediment. A man who was having an affair with a middle-aged married woman who lived across the country and only came to see him three times a year? How could that even be taken seriously? She doubted Charlie would mention it on a date. She was sure he was having sex with other women from time to time, but that made it easier for her to stick to her rules.

Sometimes she thought her rules were crazy, that she should toss away her hypocritical life and start anew with him. But whenever she did, she felt the viselike pressure of what she knew to be panic, that made it difficult to breathe. She needed both of them, Charlie and Bill, to keep each other at bay. She needed a portion and a portion. She wasn't ready yet for the whole.

chapter
41

Paul's wife's illness was going badly. The mastectomy and subsequent chemotherapy had seemed to be a success, but now three years later the cancer had metastasized and her prognosis was not good. The doctors gave her more chemo. She worsened anyway. There was a shunt in her chest for the drugs because the veins in her hands had become useless. To Cady, this woman who had seemed simply an impediment to her happiness, was now more than real: She was present. In these days of crisis she knew more about his vulnerable wife than she ever had during her long affair with Paul when his wife was the mysterious powerful presence.

Cady listened with great interest to every one of Paul's reports on the progress of the disease, every detail he was willing to tell her, not because she was waiting for the woman to die, but because she felt so sorry for her, and suddenly close, as if they were sisters. This could happen to any of them. There was also some guilt. She had not wished this on his wife, and she wondered if her subconscious had cursed the woman with childish, violent, selfish retribution just for existing. She had to remind herself she was not so powerful. She could never have dreamed this would happen, and she never could have wanted it for anyone.

Paul said there were attendants at home now, that his wife looked terrible, like a skinny, ninety-year-old, bald man. Cady remembered so many years ago when she had first met Paul's wife she had thought of her as a dried-up blonde. The woman she had met at the Dunnewood parent-teacher meeting had been much younger than she was now. How young and arrogant she had been!

He spent many evenings at home, trying to give what comfort and companionship he could. He also continued to sneak out to see his girlfriend, who probably thought she was next in line to be his wife. Cady's relationship to him had changed into best friend. He told her he could only feel free, feel like himself, with her. He was in his early seventies now, with a dying wife, a hopeful girlfriend, and a best friend who had been so many things to him over the years that they were almost each other's family. He assured Cady that he would never marry his girlfriend, that he didn't intend to marry anybody when the day came that he was single, but certainly not his girlfriend who he said was superficial and demanding. Why then did he continue with her when she was so bad, Cady wondered, but she didn't want to upset him.

The girlfriend wouldn't last forever. Cady had seen his girlfriends come and go. Brewster was long in the past.

Someday his wife will die, and then he'll find a forty-year-old who doesn't mind that he's so much older than she is, and who wants a baby, and they'll get married, Cady thought, and he'll start the whole cycle of hurting people all over again. She had seen those couples. The husband hadn't wanted the baby but the wife had insisted. He had said he was old enough to be the baby's great-grandfather, and that he didn't want to be bothered with child rearing at this late date. So while the wife was home with the small child he was out with other people, acting single.

It seemed so unfair that a man could always find a younger woman, could even have a child, could ignore the wife and child, could have a new life on his own terms, could have all these choices, when she herself had become invisible. If it were not for Vanessa right in front of her having a torrid affair with Charlie Rackley, Cady would have thought her own life with men was over for good.

And maybe it was. She had never been as carefree as Vanessa, and never as beautiful.

People said finding a man was attitude, that you had to be ready. They told stories about unattractive aged widows who met their next husbands at their own husband's funerals. It was said you had to believe in yourself to be sexy. Cady didn't believe in herself very much anymore. And they said you had to be needy. She had gone beyond being needy.

Although the magazines for older women promised that one's best years were after fifty, she felt that was about other women, not her. She was fifty-five. That wasn't old. She read about women her age who ran marathons, got married, lived with much younger men. They were obviously so unusual that they deserved an article. The only time she ran was for a cab. She wanted to be old and interesting, like Chanel or Colette, but they had had lovers too, and besides, they were French.

The fathers of the girls she taught looked young to her now. None of them seemed interested in her as Paul had been so many years ago. That had been a *coup de foudre,* an aberration, just a circumstance: destiny putting its teeth in her throat. Paul looked elderly to her these days, but still handsome. There was an advantage to having a much older man in your life — it made you feel young, particularly if he was conscious of the difference. Sometimes Cady thought he was all she needed, even in the limited way she had him now, because he made her feel content.

She wondered how many women there were in the city who, like her, no longer young, slept every night alone and really didn't mind. But she had slept alone when she was young too. For that she could thank Paul . . . and herself.

"Paul and I are an old married couple," Cady told Leigh. "We don't even have sex anymore."

Leigh just smiled, and Cady realized with a stab of jealousy that Leigh and David still had sex together. Maybe not so often, but they still did. They still wanted each other. She thought the thrill of newness and cheating kept Paul functioning with his younger women. Was that why he always had more than one woman, to keep him going? She didn't know the answer and she didn't want to ask.

Paul told her she knew him better than anyone else in the world, and Cady thought if this was true then no one really knew him.

On a hot summer night Paul called to tell her his wife had died. For one reckless, sentimental moment Cady wanted to go to the funeral, for his sake and for the woman she had never known, and then she realized that his children disliked and resented her even after all these years, that his friends would whisper that she was the one he had once left his wife for, and that she had no business being there. She could comfort him later when he came to see her. She was one of the most important parts of his life and yet she was not a part of his life at all.

She imagined friends and family grieving and thought it was perverse that she felt so close to a dead woman for whom, for so many years, she had felt nothing but ill will. Cady thought perhaps it was age, or the pain she had been through herself, or her new, relaxed relationship with Paul, that had brought her to this state of empathy. She knew his girlfriend didn't feel the way she did. His girlfriend would think good riddance. His girlfriend would nail him in a minute, if she could. His girlfriend was much younger than any of them.

After the funeral, when the friends and family had gone from his apartment, Paul came to see Cady. He looked tired and drawn. He lay on her bed, in his clothes, and she put her arms around him. For a while he slept. She kept a vigil over him, thinking how strange this was, how they had been through many strange things, and yet they were still together. When he woke up she gave him water.

"What are you going to do now?" she asked him.

"I don't know."

She didn't ask him how his children were faring, because after all, his children didn't like her. She waited to see what he would say or do. After a while he put his arms around her in a hug and kissed her goodnight. "I'll call you tomorrow," he said, and left.

After he was gone Cady sat there for a long time thinking. She realized that she could tell herself she was only his friend, but she felt more for him. She couldn't help it. The love was still there. For better or worse, through all the things they had done to each other, she still loved him. Now he was single, and the best or the worst was yet to come.

chapter
42

That summer, after Paul's wife had died, Leigh's father, who was eighty-five, had a heart attack and died too. *It's starting,* Leigh thought. For the three friends, this was the first death in their immediate families. Like it or not, it put her into the next generation. You always thought of that when a parent died: that now you would probably be next, that you were no longer young and immortal as you had believed when your parents were there. At least she still had her mother. But if nothing else had made her accept the fact that she was an aging adult, the death of her father did.

Leigh knew how fortunate she had been to have so far avoided any other disasters in her life. This death was a normal part of the cycle. Her father's death made her remember scenes from her childhood: following his sturdy legs on the walk to the beach, being taught how to ride a two-wheel bike, waiting for her parents to come home from a party and finally hearing his voice in the hall talking to her mother, saying the mysterious things adults did in conversation. When she had been a small child her father had seemed the only man in the world, or at least the only one who counted. She remembered wishing he was home more, despite knowing men worked, and that they wanted children to be quiet. Now she felt sad and a little bit numb, and wished she had known him better.

She resolved to spend more time with her mother, whom she had basically ignored for years except for holidays. She had ignored them both. She had left home so young, and then so quickly had her own life, her husband and work and then her children. She had just assumed her parents had each other. So far her mother was handling her loss with grace. She had attentive friends and she was busy. But Leigh felt guilty. And she was thinking of the inevitability of her mother's death in the not-so-distant future, although she was eighty and healthy.

Cady and Vanessa came to the funeral in Weehawken. For Vanessa it was an excuse to come to New York too to see Charlie. The family was glad she was there of course, as it was a grand gesture to fly in from California. They assumed she had done it for Leigh. Cady, somber-faced, dressed in black, was there in a kind of panic, partly left over from Paul's wife's funeral, which she had not been able to attend, and partly because her father was in his eighties too.

"You're lucky he wasn't sick, and not in a home, and had all his faculties," Cady told Leigh. Her own father was crotchety and complained and drove her mother crazy. Her youthful mother, who liked to have fun, had turned into a caretaker, an unwilling homebody in a bathrobe, albeit a chic one. "You can't win," Cady said. "It's one thing or another."

"Sometimes I think I should change my life," Vanessa said. "I worry about time." They were at Leigh's parents' house after the burial, drinking and eating sandwiches. Vanessa glanced at Charlie. "None of us are getting any younger."

"That's what I tell you," Charlie said. "You need to be with me."

How nice, Leigh thought, to have a boyfriend who didn't make you feel getting older was a reason for you to worry about losing him, but a reason to be with him more. It made her think about David, of course.

David was in his early seventies. He was younger than her mother. He didn't look old. He was still handsome and healthy. He wasn't the oldest man in the room, but he was up there right along with her uncles' and mother's generation: a little creaky. Men his age got sick, needed surgery, developed problems. David had already lost friends.

Mortality was on your mind when you reached seventy, and more so when someone died. For the first time in her life Leigh read the obituaries, and when someone in his seventies died she always asked herself: Why so young? And they usually told you the reason. In your eighties and older they didn't always bother to print the cause of death, since it seemed natural to die near that age, but David's age was just on the edge of borrowed time. She couldn't help being frightened about that. Elderly, they would call him. A senior citizen. In his golden years.

Despite all of my luck, Leigh thought, despite my contentment, despite what was in so many ways a charmed existence, there is one thing I can be sure of, and that is mortality. She knew Cady had always been jealous of her happiness, thought her life was too perfect, too self-contained. If I were a lonely widow, Leigh thought meanly, Cady would be relieved because she'd have me to play with again. It was not a nice thought, but she knew it was true.

She couldn't imagine living without David. She didn't want to think about it. Maybe he would live to be a hundred. He was healthy and took good care of himself. She took good care of him too. But now as they grew older, especially because he was eighteen years older than she was, Leigh thought about David's eventual death more often, and knew it was the thing she couldn't control. It was the one big shadow over her life. It spread its wings and stayed there, vulturelike, even when she thought it was gone.

She looked at her beautiful daughters and knew they didn't think about it. They had their careers, their busy lives, and their love affairs. They were innocently carefree, as she had been when she was their age. She had thought her father was old because he was her father, not because he actually was so old. But David was not young, not even middle-aged.

Off in a corner Cady took out her cell phone and called Paul. Now that he was officially alone they were in communication more than before. She hunched over her phone, whispering, and then she asked Leigh for the number of a taxi service. She was going to go back to New York to meet him. It was the same as it had been years ago, when she had left social events to be with him, but this time it was more in her control, and she didn't wait all alone for him to show up.

Although Leigh might have thought a few days ago that Cady was still ruining her life, now Leigh thought Cady's choice made sense. Paul wasn't so young either anymore. You might as well enjoy what you had. Cady knew he saw other women. He made no secret of it. Sometimes she seethed and sometimes she was philosophical. He was newly free, and men like that went crazy it was said. He was a catch. Women pursued him and he wouldn't resist their advances. Should he grieve forever and give up his life? He and Cady had been together for more than thirty years. Cady was sure nothing about Paul could surprise her anymore. She knew only one thing to do: hold on.

Friends and relatives surrounded Leigh's mother. She and they were trying to be sure everyone was taken care of, and Leigh knew she would be fine. She remembered that she had never thought her mother's marriage was a love affair. Her mother, who years ago had told her not to marry a man because you wanted his life, had been disappointed, although she had never talked about it. In Leigh's childhood home people didn't discuss their disappointments, they just went on and survived them. Leigh had acquired her calmness, and it had stood her in good stead, and yet . . .

Nothing had prepared her for bliss. It had lulled her, softened her instincts. Cady's life had been one hysterical moment after another, and Vanessa's had been danger and compromise, but her own had been solid and good. Leigh wondered now if that had not been the worst. How could you stand to lose that?

She went over to David and took his hand. "Live to be a hundred," she told him.

"I intend to," he said.

As always, she didn't have to explain. He understood.

chapter
43

Cady knew Leigh didn't understand the true nature of her relationship with Paul. She could hardly understand it herself. But ever since he became a widower she had, despite her better instincts, decided she had a chance with him again. This was absurd on the surface, since his freedom enabled him to be a popular bachelor, and therefore she had to compete. She couldn't understand why a man in his seventies would be considered such a catch, but he was, and women of all ages went after him — at work, socially, at gatherings, not to mention the women he found for himself, a skill he had always been good at.

Married, he had been no one's property; not his wife's and not hers. But single, Cady felt she had a claim on him. Why not? He had said himself that she knew him better than anyone else. They had a history together. And she loved him. So what if she was in her late fifties? She was a lot younger than he was. It would be inappropriate for him to run off with a bimbo and it could only make him miserable. She determined to get him, to be seductive, to change his mind about her. She knew only one way to seduce a man, the candlelight, alcohol, and music route, even though it hadn't worked with Charlie, but Charlie had been a lost cause from the start. His heart had belonged to Vanessa. Paul's heart, if it belonged to anyone, belonged to her.

Cady was certain that Paul had never stopped loving her, at least in his way. In the old days, at the height of their emotion-charged miserable affair, he had said he loved her but he had not told her his feelings. Now, mature, settled, comfortable, he told her his feelings but did not act romantic. That was something she would have to remedy.

To that end, the next time he called she invited him to her apartment for dinner. She had a dreadful sense of déjà vu as she prepared her love nest. How often had she done this over the years? The perfumed candles, the ambience, the clean sheets, the carefully chosen seduction outfit, the hair professionally done, the makeup. Even the idea alone of makeup, when you thought how many times she had applied it in her life, was tiring. She brought in his favorite foods from an expensive gourmet shop. She chilled the champagne. He would get the point and it would be up to him to act on it. She was terrified that he would say no.

When she let him in he looked surprised and then appreciative. "I didn't think you cared," he said lightly.

"You deserve it," Cady said.

"It's been a long time."

"Yes."

They drank, side by side on the couch. "This is so pleasant," Paul said.

"I didn't want you to forget that we always had fun together," she said. That wasn't exactly what she meant, but she couldn't think of a better way that wouldn't scare him off. After a glass of champagne she felt more confident. If he didn't want to have sex with her, then fine, at least they would have a special evening. He would know not to take her for granted.

"You know, Cady," he said, "through all these years, through everything, you were always my little girl. And now I realize you've grown up. I used to take care of you. Now sometimes I feel there's nothing I can do for you."

"I still want you to take care of me," Cady said. "That's the way I am. Even though I've learned how to take care of myself, there are things I can't get from anyone but you."

"That's flattering."

"It's true."

"I like you better this way, independent," Paul said, sounding surprised. "It was worth the wait."

"It wasn't easy."

"No, I'm sure it wasn't."

They smiled at each other. He was here because he wanted to be, not because he had been forced, and he could leave when he liked. They had another glass of champagne and she was careful not to get drunk, and not to make him so drunk that he wouldn't be able to do anything later. Then she served the food, and they ate it sitting across from each other at her little dining table in the corner near the kitchen, with the same monogrammed silverware — her albatross, the memory cutlery — and the beautiful plates. The napkins were hem-stitched linen. She could do everything for him that his wife had, and he would not be deprived but only made happier, because he would be with her. Cady hoped he noticed that.

"I don't know why I see all those women," Paul said.

"That's easy. Because you can."

"But they don't mean anything to me. I feel as though I missed something all those years, but I'm not finding it now."

"Maybe you've grown up too."

"Maybe they're the wrong women."

She felt a chill. Don't keep looking for the right one anywhere else, she thought. Know how much I could do for you. Choose me, oh, choose me. "Maybe they're all the wrong women," she said.

"Maybe they are," Paul said.

They paid attention to their food. It was getting a little too close. After a while she cleared the table and brought out some chocolate-covered strawberries for dessert, which they ate with the rest of the champagne.

"They do this too, you know," Paul said.

"Do what?"

"Cosset me. Treat me like a king."

"That's not why I did it!" Cady blurted out, angry that anyone else had been so nice to him, and then not surprised because, of course, they would be trying to get him, just as she was. She felt her face flush with humiliation and rage. Ungrateful, hateful wretch.

"But it's not the same," he said.

"Oh?"

"Do you know how manipulated some of those women make me feel?" he asked. "How desperate they are?"

"I'm sure," Cady said.

"There are the ex-wives, who only know how to do the same thing they always did, and the ones who are auditioning to be wives, and the ones who pretend they're trying to cheer me up. Those are the worst. I certainly don't want a mother."

"And a daughter?"

"No," he said. "The young ones don't impress me. Nor do they try to. They think their youth makes up for everything, and to many men I'm sure it does. Skin texture goes a long way toward hiding vapidity. But lately I just feel silly lusting after women young enough to be my children."

"Well, that's new," Cady said spitefully. She was still annoyed. Why are you telling me about those other women, she wondered.

"Are you angry that I'm telling you all this?"

"Yes. I mean, no. Both."

"Don't be jealous, Cady. I'm telling you how unfulfilling my bachelor life is."

"Oh."

"I thought you'd understand."

"I do. But I don't want to be lumped in with all those women. I'm different. What we have, and always had, is different."

"I know that," he said mildly.

She got up and went to the couch, turning her back on him. Suddenly she had the unexpected feeling that she was going to cry. Champagne usually made her happy. It wasn't the champagne that was upsetting her, it was he. She didn't bother to ask him if he wanted coffee. He seldom drank it after dinner anyway.

He followed her to the couch and sat next to her. He took her hand. "Cady," he said, "don't be angry."

She didn't answer. What could she say?

"Do you think there's another chance for us?" he asked.

Her heart leaped. "Yes."

"But I don't want to treat you the way I did for so many years. I feel guilty. You always had to wait for me, so patiently. Now I'm making you compete again and it isn't fair. It's monstrous. I love you too much to do that to you."

Love! Why did he put it in a context that made it sound like a rejection, when he apparently thought it was a compliment? She hated men, and Paul the most. He had given her one second of excitement with his talk of a second chance, and now he was taking it away.

"I can't even ask you to wait for me," he said.

"Why not?"

"That's humiliating."

And where would I go anyway, Cady thought. To the suitors who are beating on my door? She remained silent and couldn't look at him.

"I am who I am," Paul said, "and that isn't much. I'm too dependent on anticipation. I love the chase. I used to love the convolutions and problems of my life, the things I pretended I didn't like. I made two good women unhappy: you and my wife. Neither of you deserved that. I don't know why either of you bothered to stay with me. Now that I'm free and I can make a clear-cut choice between the monogamy you deserve and the philandering I'm drawn to, I can't. I have to get to know myself at this advanced age, that or wait until I'm so old that I don't want anything anymore. And then who would want me?"

That's honest, she thought. She looked at him finally, and love flooded her again. She was addicted to him. He was her fate, her punishment. She had been tied to him almost her whole life. And he was a bad man.

"I would be lost without you," he said. "I'm sure you don't believe that."

"I want to believe it."

"It's true. What are we going to do?"

She had no idea. "Make love," she said.

He touched her, tentatively. It had been such a long time that there was something almost poignant about the idea of holding each other again, of throwing off their inhibitions. There was a sweetness in his eyes that made her sad. He kissed her.

Then it was as if they had been together only a while ago. She took him into the bedroom, and they made love as they had in the old days when it had been mindless. She knew what he liked and she was good at it, and he knew what she liked and he was good at it too. Some of it took longer and some took less time, but they were still suited for each other. They held each other afterward and Cady remembered that he didn't have to go anywhere unless he wanted to.

I can get him, she thought. I can. There was a depth of feeling between them that she was sure he couldn't find in any of those exciting strangers. This is where you belong, she thought.

Finally he got up. "I have to go home to sleep," he said. "What I've discovered is that I can't sleep unless I'm alone."

"Why?" she said.

"When my wife was sick I slept in the den," he said. "I got used to it."

"And before, when you did sleep with her?"

"I tossed and turned. I thought it was my personal life keeping me awake. Now I see I'm just an old dog who needs his own blanket at the foot of the bed."

"I like to sleep alone too," she said.

He called her the next day, and then they began to see each other at least twice a week. She knew she was an important part of his life but not all of it. She was willing to accept that because he was so genuinely fond of her.

They had sex sometimes, not every time, but as often as befitted an old married couple. Cady thought of polygamy, of tribes with many wives, and decided she was the number one wife in his tribe. She and Paul were free to date each other and they were comfortable with each other. It was another phase of her life. She decided that, despite his random women, she and he were seeing each other again. Eventually she told Leigh.

Leigh kept her own council about the new development and did not criticize. At this point, who was being harmed? Cady had actually convinced herself that she didn't want to marry anybody, didn't want to live with a man, preferred to sleep peacefully in solitude. Cady was a little jealous of Paul's women but she could deal with it.

The following summer Paul rented a small house on the eastern shore of Long Island and invited Cady to spend every weekend there. Sometimes he had a roving eye at cocktail parties, but by and large he also treated her as if she was the number one wife, and as such, was deserving of affection and respect. Paul's grown children still resented Cady, and Cady supposed they always would. Danica, Danny, and their families each spent a separate weekend there while Cady stayed in New York. They didn't know that Cady was there on a regular basis. Maybe they thought their father had all kinds of different women visiting him. His children thought of him as the bachelor he had always wanted to be. Cady thought that Paul did too. She let him think it. She didn't ask for more. She waited for whatever time would bring.

PART
FIVE

chapter
44

The millennium was here. Like many others, Leigh and Cady and Vanessa had thought about it as children, and then through the years, thinking how old they would be when it came — sixty and sixty-one. Imagine — their lives lived, their adventures over! Like almost everyone, they invested the approaching year 2000 with some kind of magical powers. They would all now be a part of history, witness to a new century, straddling both eras.

As the year 2000 approached, people were anxious, expecting the end of the world, the breakdown of society, of computers, of everything safe and familiar. Many people stockpiled food and water and medicines and even guns. Everyone who could hoarded cash for when the cash machines would refuse to work. Some left the cities, some prepared shelters for their families.

People had made reservations at expensive places years in advance, but a lot of others spent New Year's Eve at home instead, watching the millennium arrive around the world on television. Times Square was mobbed. And when the millennium did come, it was anticlimactic. After all the anticipation and excitement and worry, nothing really happened, and people felt strangely sad. But at least it was clear to Leigh and Cady and Vanessa that, despite what they had anticipated, their lives had not yet been completely lived and their adventures were not yet over — that the ages they had achieved were somehow not so old after all.

Vanessa and Leigh were finally grandmothers. Vanessa's son, Jack, who was a partner in a vineyard and lived in Napa, had two lively boys. Liberty, who had married an Internet entrepreneur and lived in Seattle, had given birth to twin daughters. Vanessa was a grandmother of four. In New York Leigh's older daughter, Jennie, had married an entertainment lawyer and also had a daughter, whom she named Sonia. Leigh's younger daughter, Sophie, who was an aspiring actress still, had married a fellow actor, but was postponing having children for the time being. David's sons from his first marriage had grown children, as did Paul's two children. So the new generation was fully represented.

Only Cady and Charlie, of the group of old friends, had no children. Neither of them had regrets, or if they did, they didn't think about it. Cady was still with Paul and Charlie was still with Vanessa, both according to the rules of their game. They had both chosen alternate lives because of love, and that seemed to be enough.

Cady's mother was a sprightly eighty. She'd had a face lift right after Cady did. She looked more like Cady's young aunt than her mother, especially since she'd recently had a second one. She and Cady's father had finally sold their large house in Scarsdale and moved to a small apartment in New York City, with a terrace overlooking the East River. Somehow looking so youthful and living in New York so close to entertainment and culture reenergized her, and she decided not to spend her remaining years in a bathrobe looking after her husband. Other people could be hired to do that. So now she played bridge with her friends, who had also moved to New York, and went to concerts, art galleries, and matinees with them. Cady's father was becoming even more crotchety and forgetful every year, so he didn't go to these things with his wife. And when he was alone, their reliable housekeeper stayed with him to be sure he didn't do something foolish.

Leigh's widowed mother also lived contentedly in a world of women. She came into the city from time to time to see her great-granddaughter Sonia. She referred to herself lightly as "the matriarch." David was seventy-eight, and when his sons' children had children of their own, possibly in the next few years, Leigh thought she would be calling herself a "matriarch" too. Sometimes the past seemed close, and sometimes far away: Time stretched like a rubber band with so many people to think about. There was always a gift to be bought, an occasion to go to. Her life was busy and full. She still worked, of course.

These days, of all of them it was only Vanessa who felt shortchanged. The millennium had made her think about what was important. During the long, arid spells when she was in California with Bill, away from Charlie but always thinking about him, she had begun to wonder where her life was going. She was sixty-one. She visited her children and grandchildren, but they didn't live nearby and they didn't need her. She wasn't sure if Bill needed her anymore either. She went through the motions like a mechanical doll. Did he too? Surely there had to be more to a marriage than that. She and Bill hadn't had sex with each other for over two years. Neither of them ever mentioned it. She didn't miss sex with Bill, in fact, she was relieved. Was he?

She wondered whether her affair with Charlie was so passionate because they were so often deprived of each other, yearning and needy. Then she told herself that she would be happy with Charlie even if she left Bill and moved to New York and could see Charlie all the time.

She had chosen Bill because she had no choice, but she had chosen Charlie because she wanted him. Of course, she was also aware that she had picked Charlie because there had been no one else. But that had been so long ago. Now it didn't matter why, only that they were joined in a way that seemed both new and permanent. Charlie made her feel alive.

From time to time he still asked Vanessa to leave Bill, and more and more often she thought about doing it. It was merely hubris to think that Bill couldn't survive without her. He had his habits, his hobbies, and he would not find it hard to meet another woman to take her place. Maybe there even was one already. How would she know, since she didn't care and therefore didn't look for signs? She had told him not to cheat again and he had said he wouldn't, but he wouldn't be the first married man to lie and she wouldn't be the first married woman to believe him. Vanessa rather hoped Bill had found someone else. It would make everything easier for both of them.

She didn't want to spend the rest of her life like this. It just wasn't enough anymore. New York would be a wonderful place to live. Her two closest women friends were there, she had always loved the life, and she would get used to the cold weather. She would buy a big fur coat with a hood. She knew she would never marry again, but she could think of no real reason to object to living with Charlie. Or if that seemed impulsive then perhaps having her own little apartment in his building so they could see each other whenever they wanted and have privacy when they needed it. Wasn't that living arrangement perfect for older people who didn't want to adjust to anything new? If she changed her mind somewhere down the road she could sell the little apartment and move in with him.

She would be so glad not to live with Bill. He was not a real companion even though he was there, because she felt lonely with him. Did he feel lonely with her?

Now Vanessa wondered why she had so adamantly refused to consider divorcing Bill for so long. It seemed sentimental, nothing more. Her grown children wouldn't be too upset. They had their own lives, and children of their own. Whatever their parents did at this point would merely seem eccentric. She would see them just as often living in New York as she had while living in California.

If Bill sold the house she wouldn't care. She had never felt an affinity for the house. She was a person who had never been attached to a living space in her life, and even this house where she had dwelled for so many years, was just a house. It was too large and lonely. Her life was boring. She knew many women who were passionately attached to their homes and their things, but Vanessa had thought of that as a form of vapidity. She would take some of her furniture to furnish the small apartment she would buy in New York, but that was a practical matter not an emotional one. The furniture was there already, and paid for. It was nice enough.

She remembered the single bed she had bought and sold and bought and sold when she was a young stewardess living with those different roommates in New York years ago, and she smiled. She hadn't really changed.

That night she told Bill she wanted a divorce. He didn't seem to react at all. "All right," he said. "I know you aren't happy."

"It's not your fault," Vanessa said.

"I know. It's just one of those things. We won't be the first couple we know to split up. Let's do it amicably."

"Of course," Vanessa said.

"No fights about money," Bill said.

"Fifty-fifty," Vanessa said matter of factly. "It's the law."

"We might have to sell the house," he said. "I don't have enough cash to give you half."

"The house is too big for either of us alone," she said. "It's too big for both of us now as it is."

"That's true, and it's appreciated a lot since we bought it. We'll make a good profit. I think I'd like to live in the Marina. Maybe buy a boat."

"A lot of divorced people live in the Marina," Vanessa said.

"And where do you think you'd like to live?"

"Maybe New York."

"Yes, you've always been a New York sort of gal."

I hate men who say "gal," she thought.

"We'll get lawyers tomorrow," he said. "Would you mind sleeping in the den?"

"Not at all," he said pleasantly.

The conversation was over and he went into the den to watch television. Vanessa brought him sheets and blankets and pillows and then she went into the kitchen and danced around by herself for sheer joy.

The next day when Charlie called her, Vanessa told him. He was as happy and excited as she had known he would be. "Now our lives can begin," he said.

They spent an hour on the phone making plans.

It had all been too quick, too easy, and too friendly with Bill. He had seemed almost relieved to be rid of her. She was sure he had another woman waiting for him, if not more than one. And why not? She had a man waiting for her.

chapter
45

Although Cady was independent now, she sometimes wondered what would become of her. She still had not a penny in savings. She was sixty. Her extravagant habits had not abated, and whenever her mother bailed her out these days, as she sometimes had to do, Cady felt a little sorry for herself. But to whom else could she turn? She never wanted to have to ask Paul.

When she was very old and her parents had died, which was a sad thought she usually avoided having, she would inherit their money. That would keep her from going to the poorhouse after she retired, although her beloved mother was so young for a mother that she might live for years and years. In that case, her mother would keep on coming to her rescue. She imagined herself with her mother, hand in hand, registering themselves at the old folks' home. Paul, of course, would be dead.

The more these disturbing thoughts came to her, the more Cady felt she wanted to have a good life. Thus she celebrated whatever and whenever she could, and denied herself little. Paul was amused at her extravagance and liked her spirit. He said she kept him young.

She was helping him to redecorate his apartment now. She spent time there with him since he was alone and free and no one could complain, and the first thing she had discovered was that it had the shabby air of an ill-kept museum. It was the place where his children had grown and his wife had become ill and died, and there were still artifacts everywhere. It was a repository. Cady told him this would depress him, if it didn't already, and asked her mother to find a good decorator.

This was the mysterious apartment of which she had been so envious in her youth. She had stood on the street and looked up at its mysterious windows and fantasized. Of course everything had been new then, and fashionable, while now it was just pathetic, except for the antiques. Everything else had to go. The place was much too big for him, of course, but he said he would never move. It was a valuable piece of real estate and there was no reason that he had to downsize when he was so fond of it.

Her new fantasy was that she would one day be asked to live there with him, but Cady didn't give it much hope. Still, she and the decorator turned Paul's apartment into something she herself would like. It was fun to be able to spend so much money, and he only complained weakly when Cady found something he "simply had to have." Sometimes it was something she herself simply had to have. This was part of the fantasy, like playing house.

She knew she had been playing house for years, and she supposed she always would. It was all she had.

Still, she wasn't unhappy. She and Paul were probably a couple, even though he cheated. She was more than a legend at the Dunnewood School; now she was a fixture. She knew she had left many decades of young women with her imprimatur, and had in some small way changed their lives for the better. Some of them even sent her Christmas cards, thanking her. She liked the look of admiration on her young students' faces, since she was clearly the most elegant of their teachers, most of whom didn't much care about such things. While she could never, and would never, make peace with her desire to be Leigh, Cady had made a kind of peace with the reality of who she was. When she looked around she saw women with lives that were far worse than hers.

Paul was seventy-seven now and in good health. He was semiretired, just keeping his hand in so he wouldn't get bored. He had his meetings, his lunches, his drink dates. He could take the afternoon off whenever he wanted. He avoided stress and delegated enough duties so he could enjoy the ones he had. He was a partner at the agency, so barring some pernicious coup, no one could think of asking him to step down.

Cady remembered when she had met him and had thought a man in his early forties was old and sophisticated. She supposed some of them were, although now to her they seemed young.

It was spring. Paul's apartment was nearly done. Sometimes Cady slept over at his apartment in the guest room, because he liked to sleep alone in his own bed, as did she. She kept some clothes at his apartment now, in the guest room closet. She wondered if he had women there who saw her clothes and were resentful and curious about her the way she had been about his wife years ago. Or did he have sex only at their apartments? There were a few things she did not discuss with him. They kept their façade of normalcy.

Thanks to the decorator, the two children's rooms were now a luxurious guest room and an elegant den, which converted easily to another room for guests, not that he ever had any. Plus he had his original den, which was now a television room and home office. Sometimes when she slept over, Cady imagined that she was indeed Leigh, and that this was her home with a devoted Paul, that she and Leigh were equals at last. Her own apartment, much as she liked it, was her reminder that she was still alone, and probably always would be.

"Come to my place for dinner tonight," Paul said. "I'll have Henrietta cook something and leave it." They did that sometimes, a nice domestic evening. But this time when she arrived Cady noticed with surprise that he had a bottle of Dom Perignon chilling in a cooler, and that he had bought flowers.

"Well, what is this in honor of?" she asked.

"Us."

"How nice."

He opened the champagne and poured it. "I'm going to change my life," he said.

"You're retiring?"

"No."

"Another job?"

"It isn't about work."

She shrugged and held up her glass in a toast. "To whatever it is. You'd better tell me."

"I will." They sipped. "Do you remember a while ago that I told you there would come a day when I would be different?"

"Yes?"

"Well, after considerable thought I realize that day is here."

"And how are you different?"

"I'm ready to be faithful."

She didn't know whether she should laugh or be serious. It was hard to believe. He saw her look of skepticism.

"No, I mean it," Paul said. "It's better to settle down while I'm still relatively young enough to enjoy my life. Before it's too late. Look, I know I'm no prize. I've put you through a lot. I hope you want me, although I'm not sure I know why you would."

"But what does that mean?" Cady asked.

"Marriage. I want you to marry me. You've earned me."

Marry him! She had dreamed of this and then told herself she didn't care, and now she was stunned. "Oh my God," she murmured, at a loss for words.

"I hope you'll tell me yes," Paul said. "You know I love you. I want to spend the rest of my life with you. Nothing will change that you don't want changed, but it really will be different. There will be no more women. I promise. I don't even think I can handle them, to tell you the truth. I just want peace and happiness. We'll travel. You'll be well off and won't have to worry about anything. I'll take care of you. We'll live here together. You've already fixed up the apartment the way you want it." He took a little black velvet box out of his pocket. "I've even bought you a ring. I'd get down on one knee, but I don't think I'd be able to get up."

Cady opened the box. Inside was a large, glittering, blue-white square diamond with a long baguette on either side, in a yellow-gold setting, just what she liked. She put it on and it fit. This was the first time he had actually bought her an engagement ring. Before, everything had fallen apart before there had been time. But now he must really mean it. The number one wife would be the only wife.

"I'd love to marry you, sweetheart," Cady said.

They embraced warmly, feeling safe in each other's arms. Cady Fisher, Cady Fisher, Cady Fisher, she thought: At last! How interesting it would be to be married for the first time at sixty, and how different it would be than any of her preconceptions had been, because now she was a grownup and both of them had changed. Yet in some ways she would have the life she had always dreamed of. She would have financial security. She could have everything she wanted. She couldn't wait to tell her parents, to tell Leigh and Vanessa and Charlie, to tell the world.

Everyone was as happy for her as Cady had expected them to be. Since the wedding wouldn't be large they decided not to wait long and to do it when her summer break began. Then they would go for a long honeymoon to France and Italy. Cady had never been to Europe. In fact, she had never been anywhere. She bought a trousseau and a set of luggage with plenty of room for the things she would buy on their trip.

At the wedding she was wearing an expensive, cream-silk designer suit and carried a bouquet of a variety of cream-colored fragrant flowers. There was a trio playing music, and champagne before the ceremony as well as afterward. Leigh, in peach, which was not her color but Cady had insisted on it because it went with cream, was the matron of honor. Paul was attended by his oldest friend, a man he knew from college. The ceremony was in their newly completed apartment, performed by a judge, and attended by their close friends and some of Paul's business colleagues. His middle-aged children actually came. Although they would never be very fond of Cady, they figured they'd better make peace and make the best of the situation. Their father was an old man. He deserved an absence of stress.

Cady and Paul wore matching gold rings. It was her idea. He had not worn one during his first marriage. Inside they had had inscribed: "Cady and Paul Forever." Cady intended to live happily ever after, or at least as long as ever after lasted.

Vanessa and Charlie held hands during the ceremony. She was separated from Bill and their lawyers were working on the divorce, and now she was spending most of her time in New York. She was living with Charlie, but when she had the settlement from Bill she would buy a small apartment in his building. Or perhaps not, since they were getting along together better than they had expected. Maybe they would just buy a bigger apartment for the two of them. Cady and Leigh had never seen either of them look so content.

Cady's mother beamed through the whole ceremony, and through the cocktail reception in the apartment afterward. Her father looked a little bewildered but pleased. He had sometimes forgotten whether Cady was married to Paul or not, since they'd had so many ups and downs, and since he had become forgetful in these, his later years, but today it was good to see his daughter married at last.

Leigh shed a few tears. So, surprisingly, did Cady. Now she was just as good as either of her two best friends.

chapter
46

It was a crisp fall Saturday afternoon, and Vanessa and Charlie had had lunch in a little French bistro and now were walking home enjoying the city. She remembered the many afternoons she had been by herself, walking through New York, and she thought how much better it was to be doing it here and now with him. He was a good companion.

What was love after all? She had never known it, but this feeling of well-being and warmth certainly came close. Perhaps people overrated love. Was it the pounding heart? Was it fear, hysteria, overwhelming bliss? She didn't want any of those. She wanted exactly what she had: a handsome charming man who adored her, who made her happy, who was skillful and thoughtful in bed and out of it. She thought she had probably mellowed. She was ready to accept whatever good things came her way. She was glad to have them. There was nothing like being deprived to make you appreciate getting your luck back.

Cady and Paul had returned from their European honeymoon and settled into Paul's apartment. After all these years the friends still had the occasional roommates' night together, without spouses. It seemed too late to change. Sometimes, too, they went out as couples. Vanessa was used to having very few good friends, and seeing Leigh and Cady either alone or with husbands was enough. However, Charlie had friends, and she went with him when he wanted to see them. It was pleasant, but it didn't change her life. She would always be the lone wolf. Wolves liked to live together in packs. The lone wolf was the aberration, the one who didn't fit in, and didn't care.

Sometimes she and Charlie looked at apartments together, in a lazy way. "We don't have to decide anything yet," he told her. "It's up to you. Take your time."

She thought she was ready now. His bachelor apartment was getting cramped. They could use another room and more closets, since both had come to the other with a life lived and things acquired. Bill had sold the house in Los Angeles, and suddenly there were a few objects that Vanessa realized she liked, and so she took them. Now Charlie's bachelor apartment boasted framed photographs of her children through the years, and the grandchildren now. She had furniture and paintings in storage, and a few other things; whatever she had thought she would need for her own little pied-à-terre.

Today she and Charlie were looking at Upper East Side neighborhoods to see if any of them appealed enough to want to move there. "Oh, look!" she said to him. "There's the house where we lived when we were all rooming together."

They stopped in front of the town house and memories flooded them. It didn't look very different, even after all these years. He sighed. "So long ago," he said.

"I know. We were different people then. We were children."

"We were, weren't we," Charlie said.

"Well, you were."

"So you made very clear."

She hugged him. "I wonder who's living there."

"Are they starting out? Or are they a couple, established, holding on to the apartment because of the rent?"

"Let's look at the buzzer."

They went over and looked. There were two last names next to the buzzer for their old apartment that told them nothing.

They could be lovers, or a couple where the wife had kept her maiden name. Or roommates.

Vanessa thought then of Susan Brown, of course. She couldn't look at this apartment of the past without thinking of the most significant event that had happened there. If she were still alive Susan would be sixty. They would have completely lost touch with her. Vanessa could hardly remember the other roommates she'd had. But because of the circumstances it was as if there was a ghost hovering over the apartment. It would be nice to believe she was at peace.

"Remember Susan?" Vanessa said.

Charlie almost seemed to shiver, but his voice was calm. "Of course," he said.

"She had such a crush on you," Vanessa said.

He didn't answer.

"Don't you remember?"

"Yes," he said.

"But you always liked me."

"Yes, I did. I loved you."

"Dear Charlie. And now you have me."

"Yes," he said. "Now I do."

"Have you ever been back here?" she asked.

"No. Not after you moved out. Why would I?"

"I guess you're not sentimental," she said, "although there isn't much I miss about it either."

They walked away again, looking at other buildings. He seemed quiet, deep in thought. She wondered what he was thinking. "You don't look happy," she said.

"I'm happy."

"We should move into an apartment with a doorman and an elevator," Vanessa said. "Like what we have now. I've never really understood the charm of a town house. Rich people have them, and there are all those stairs, and then when they get old and arthritic they have to crawl up them."

"Or put in a lift on the stairs."

"I don't see us with one of those." They walked on. "Should we have a terrace?" Vanessa asked.

"I don't really like them."

"I didn't know that."

He shrugged.

"Don't you want a view?"

"We can have a view from the windows."

"All right."

"I think what you want, Charlie, is a cozy little nest."

"That's just what I want," he said.

"Me too."

He didn't say anything else all the way home, still deep in thought and Vanessa didn't know why, but it didn't seem disturbing. When they got back to their apartment he poured a glass of wine for each of them without asking her if she wanted one, and then he stood for a few moments looking out the living room window. "The past never goes away," he said finally.

"Some of it doesn't," she said.

"You want it to, and it won't," he said. He came back to the couch and sat down. "Sit by me," he said, sounding sad and subdued.

She did. "What's the matter?"

"You and I will be together for the rest of our lives if you want to be," he said.

"Of course."

"I want you to know everything about me," he said.

"Don't I?"

"No."

"Oh, is there a deep, dark secret?" she asked lightly.

"Yes," Charlie said seriously. "There is."

She looked at him, surprised. She couldn't imagine what there was she didn't know, or that could be upsetting. "Then tell me."

"I couldn't tell you before," he said. "I

thought I never would, but I couldn't bear not telling you either. We're so close now you have to know. I can't live with it alone anymore. I've thought about telling you but it never seemed to be the right time. I guess there isn't any right time. I have to tell you now and make it go away. I want you to understand."

"I'm sure whatever it is I'll understand," Vanessa said. "Tell me."

"You remember that Labor Day weekend when Susan killed herself?"

"Of course I do," Vanessa said, although his question was rhetorical.

"Well, that hot night when everyone was out of town I went to the apartment because I was lonely, and no one was there but Susan. Even Susan's company seemed better than nothing. You know how deserted the city is on a major holiday like that, everyone who can get out does. Well, she was glad to see me, and we took beers to the roof of the building and talked. I'd never had a real conversation with her before that. It was so hot I remember, so hot, no breeze at all. She wasn't drunk or anything, she was just relaxed. And then she told me she was in love with me and she flung herself on me. She tried to kiss me. I was horrified. I don't know, I was such a kid, and I didn't like her, and I had some silly idea that I was saving myself for you. Not that it was your fault, don't blame yourself, you had nothing to do with it. . . ."

"To do with *what?*" Vanessa demanded.

"I pushed her away. Really hard, harder than I had expected. And she stumbled and fell over the low edge of the roof. It was so low, remember? Really low, and she was so light, and . . . and she fell to her death, only it wasn't a suicide, I pushed her. It was a horrible, pointless, tragic accident."

Vanessa could hardly breathe. She just looked at him, hoping he would go on. Her hands felt icy.

"I was terrified of course," Charlie said. "I took my beer can because it was evidence and ran away. No one saw me come in and no one saw me leave. When the police questioned me I had my mother give me an alibi; she would do anything for me. She and I never spoke about it again. I never spoke about it to anyone. But that one moment darkened my whole life. I think it's why I would never let myself be really happy. Why I couldn't let anyone get close to me. Why sometimes, under all this good nature I display to the world, I think there's something secretive and cold.

"Susan hated you girls but she didn't kill herself over you. She just thought she could take me away from you for revenge. Maybe she thought she loved me, I don't know. It doesn't matter. She was dead."

Not a suicide? Charlie killed her? Vanessa saw that roof again in her mind and shuddered. Poor Charlie, he had been so young, only a twenty-two-year-old kid, gawky and innocent. She imagined him running away, his heart beating so hard he thought he too might die, and she felt his fear. All these years the three of them had blamed themselves for Susan's death, but someone else had been to blame after all. It was almost impossible to believe, but she knew it was true.

"What are you going to do?" Charlie asked quietly.

"Do?"

What could she do? She had no idea what she could do, or would do, or wanted to do, except to try to absorb this shocking information.

She had to tell Leigh and Cady. She had to talk to them. She looked at Charlie's beloved familiar face and felt terribly affected. He was hers. It had happened a lifetime ago. Nobody knew except her and his mother, but soon the other two would know because she would tell them. Leigh and Cady were part of this too. The three of them had lived with Susan's death, albeit in a different way than Charlie had, for almost forty years. They had considered themselves bad people, and suddenly they were not bad after all.

Someone else was the bad person. Or was he? He was, when you looked at it dispassionately, a murderer. But you didn't call it murder when it was an accident, did you? What had he really done?

"Can you forgive me?" Charlie asked.

She nodded.

"Is this going to change us?"

"Us?"

"You and me. Our lives together. Our future. Can you understand what happened?"

"I do," Vanessa said. But she didn't go to him and embrace him. She just looked at him. It was all so new. She had no idea what she felt.

He reached out tentatively and took her hand. "Your hand is so cold," he said. He didn't try to warm it with his and she didn't ask him to.

That night she and Charlie slept side by side without touching, and slept badly.

She wanted to be there for him but he seemed different somehow, a man who had lived for almost as long as she had known him with a terrible tragedy, a secret, a crime. He was a person who had killed another person. It had changed him. It had made him who he was. Who was he anyway? She supposed she was in shock.

In the morning when Charlie was in the shower she called Leigh and Cady and told them she had to see them as soon as possible, that it was urgent, that she couldn't talk about it on the phone. They agreed to meet her for cocktails the next afternoon. Vanessa suggested one of their apartments, if they would be alone. She couldn't tell them in a public place. Leigh volunteered. She would tell David to find something to do for an hour. They were curious of course, but they had no idea how she was going to shake up their world.

When Charlie came out of the shower he looked at her with such sorrow it made her heart break.

"I have to tell the others," she said. "I owe it to them. I'm seeing them tomorrow."

He looked frightened for an instant.

Then he nodded slowly, his face grave.

"You can trust us," Vanessa said. "But they have to know."

Could he trust them? She didn't even know.

chapter
47

The three friends met in Leigh's apartment. She had put out wine and Pellegrino and ice, but that was just a social gesture. They knew they were there for something important and they wanted to get to it. Neither Leigh nor Cady had ever seen Vanessa as rattled as she had seemed on the phone.

"Charlie told me something," Vanessa began. She felt herself choking. She would tell them and then it would be out, and then it would be an event to be dealt with. It wouldn't be a secret anymore. She knew she couldn't handle it by herself.

They looked at her expectantly. "Susan didn't commit suicide," she said. "Charlie pushed her." She told them the whole story, just as he had told it to her.

They were, as she had expected, shocked at this new twist to their old tragedy. They looked at one another for a moment in silence, trying to comprehend.

"All this time when we blamed ourselves

for something that never happened," Leigh said softly. "All the things we did differently because of it. We used to think Susan threw her life away and we had to remember not to throw away ours. We felt so guilty because we thought we had destroyed her. I kept trying to be a better person. I thought she had punished me."

"She never even made a decision," Cady said.

"But no one did," Leigh said. "It was an *accident*."

"Of course," Vanessa said. "He never in a million years meant to hurt her."

"What are we going to do?" Cady asked.

"Do?" Leigh said. "He was just a twenty-two-year-old kid when it happened. A whole lifetime has gone by. He's a part of our lives, of our youth. He's our Charlie. He's *ours*."

"Yes," Cady said, "ours."

"How he's suffered all these years," Leigh said. "Oh God, poor Susan. Our poor sweet Charlie. We care about him. We need him. Vanessa most of all."

"But what are we supposed to do?" Cady asked.

"Do?" Leigh said. "Nothing. We do nothing."

Vanessa's numbness had begun to thaw

and she felt her affection and tenderness for Charlie return, more strongly than ever before. "It would be unimaginable to turn him in," she said, "even if anyone remembered, and no one does. It's long over. I want to protect him."

"As do we," Leigh said.

"Then we can't tell anyone," Cady said.

"What about David and Paul?" Leigh asked.

"No. Not even them. They don't care anymore. It's just an old misfortune of the past. There are secrets wives keep from their husbands. This is our secret."

"I want to tell David," Leigh said. "He'll know something is wrong."

"Will he tell anyone?" Vanessa asked.

"No."

"Then I'll tell Paul," Cady said. "But that's it. Then it has to be forgotten."

"Gone and forgotten forever," Leigh said. "Remember that. It was an accident. We couldn't save Susan, but sacrificing Charlie will serve no purpose."

Vanessa thought of Charlie's stricken face. Now that they all knew, what he had done didn't seem so insurmountable. They could handle it together. Maybe she did love him, or whatever was closest to love. Nothing would change. She would stay with him and they would make a good life together. She would help him heal. Telling her had started the healing process already. Now they had to rally around him and treat him exactly the same as they always had. They would all get through this.

"Swear to silence," Cady said.

"Silence," Leigh said.

"Silence," Vanessa said. "I swear."

"I swear too," Cady said.

The three women looked at each other. He would be safe with them. They would all go on.

epilogue

So now, Leigh thought, they would go on and live their lives knowing something essential that they had never known before. They had had their own mythology about Susan Brown through these decades, and the story had been wrong. Susan had, in a way, been the catalyst that had kept them together. Her death, coming so soon in their lives when they were still so young, had been the most meaningful event they had ever known. Who would ever know whether they would have turned out to be such good friends if they'd had a normal roommate experience: the proximity of necessity and convenience, the drifting away to the next phase of their own destinies, the gradual casting away of the old ties until they were scarcely even memories. But guilt had made them lifelong friends.

For that they could thank Susan, and themselves. They had almost never criticized one another for flaws, for stupid acts, and because of this kindness they had managed to surmount the flaws and stupid acts. Vanessa's promiscuity and the threat to her family had been treated as an amusing adventure. She had been a lost soul, but they had been too involved in their own existences to ponder on that. They had thought of her more as eccentric than sad. Her stories were something they enjoyed secondhand. A woman of such exceptional beauty was expected to make romantic mistakes.

Although they were somewhat sorry for Vanessa, they were also a little jealous of her freedom. But they were safe; they didn't have to live her dangerous adventures. She did.

Cady's friendship was more difficult to deal with, Leigh thought. The two of them had had rocky times. They were basically completely different people with different values, and sometimes she'd had to hold back her criticism of Cady, but whatever it was between them that was warm and good had kept them together through all those years. Their friendship had even survived the bad period when Cady had been living with Leigh and David after her affair with Paul was over, although it had been very strained. Cady had been crazy then.

Their friendship, Leigh thought, had involved an amount of forgiveness. She knew that Cady had thought she was forgiving *her*. She had always known that, besides the love Cady professed for her, Cady was very jealous of her. But there was nothing Leigh could do about it. Now all that tension was over, because Cady had the life she'd always coveted.

The three of them had been friends for almost forty years, and they had grown more than middle-aged. They had lost their youth, their firm flesh, their juiciness, their arrogance, and their ignorant seductiveness. Men no longer looked at them. Heads did not turn; there were no anticipatory smiles when they appeared. They had given up the security of knowing that men thought they were forces to be reckoned with, if only on the level of lust. Now they had become real forces. They were, for better or worse, real people.

They had made it through. Wisdom, she thought, is surviving. They had survived. They would continue to do so, even though she knew there would be bad things ahead of them because this was life.

They had learned the value of friendship with their men as well as with one another. Love had turned into friendship and then into love again for Cady. For Vanessa, friendship had finally turned into love. As for herself, she had grown and matured too. Maturity, even when it was good, wasn't a fair trade for youth and beauty, but it was something you wanted to have so you wouldn't have nothing. Sometimes you felt the loss of youth and all its gifts, and sometimes you were glad it was over. You were smarter. You weren't so accepting anymore. There wasn't enough time. You knew what you liked and what you didn't like.

What we wanted, Leigh thought, is not necessarily what other women would want. Yet we each ended up with what we wanted, which is a miracle, because most people don't.

About the Author

Rona Jaffe is the *New York Times* bestselling author of the internationally acclaimed novels *The Road Taken*, *The Cousins*, *Family Secrets*, and *Five Women*, as well as the classic bestsellers *Class Reunion* and *The Best of Everything*. She is the founder of the Rona Jaffe Foundation, which presents a national literary award to promising female writers. She lives in New York City.